LOVE, DEATH, OTHER AWKWARD SPELLS

By Scott Killian and Ryan Tang

Contents

Chapter 1

Technically, a Necromancer
is Just a Really Good Doctor

Apale-skinned man who was much too thin rode into a dusty town on a creaky old rickshaw that was much too small, pulled by a big patchwork dog who was much too undead.

The wooden sign attached to the side of the rickshaw had once proudly proclaimed–Eld B, the Greatest Pet Doctor in Human History! Now, the paint was faded and the wood had chipped.

It mostly proclaimed the same message, just wearily instead of proudly. However, "Human" had been hastily scratched out, so that only the faintest wisps of the paint still remained.

Eld B's full name was Eldritch B. Blackwood Jr., named after the blast–*not* to be confused with his father, Eldritch P. Blackwood Sr., who was named after the pact.

As for the canine, he was a patchwork creature, with exposed bone peeking through matted fur and mismatched eyes—one a warm brown, the other an eerie, glowing blue. The front left paw was noticeably larger than the others, a makeshift replacement after a ghoul had made off with the original.

Despite his macabre appearance, the dog's tail wagged so vigorously it threatened to fall off with each enthusiastic thump against the wooden frame.

"Now now, Shuck!" Eld exclaimed. "I can fix you up fine when you're injured…but fixing the rickshaw, well, that's a good deal more difficult!"

Shuck—the big zombie dog—barked apologetically.

To an outsider, the apologetic bark would have sounded like a screech from the jaws of hell, but Shuck's pale-skinned owner literally knew him inside and out. Shuck's voice box came from three necromantically amalgamated Cerberus necks, a remnant of the days when he'd served as a watchdog for Eld's father.

"Oh, stop it, Shuck," Eld chuckled. "I'm not mad at you. I just don't want to fail out of carpentry class again. And speaking of things I'm not very good at…let's try and make you a little bit less…juicy."

Reaching into his coat, Eld produced a small, worn grimoire and a pouch of ingredients. He opened the book to a dog-eared page and tossed a pinch of sparkling powder over his dog.

Then he waved his hand in a complex pattern, twisting his fingers to create multiple interlacing stars, before finishing with a harsh whisper. "Cambire canis, minimus apparere!"

A shimmering light enveloped Shuck, and when it faded, a small dachshund stood in place of the patchwork canine. Eld grinned, initially pleased with his handiwork, until he noticed the rickshaw's harness now appeared to be floating in mid-air, connected to nothing.

Then he sighed, rubbing his temple. "Well, I suppose that's good enough. Can't be perfect at everything, can we? I always feel like I'm drawing the stars big enough, but I never quite *feel* the spell."

According to Eld's family friend Professor Grimthorpe, the essence of illusory spells was the will to deceive.

Since Eld never really had a problem with Shuck's appearance, he couldn't quite help the people who *did* have a problem with it.

Still, it was for the best.

Eld never knew how new clients would react to his rather unusual skills. Sometimes, he earned their lifelong gratitude. Other times, well…

The pet doctor shook his head. Best to focus on the cheerful possibility of lifelong gratitude.

The rickshaw creaked to a halt on the outskirts of the town, the late afternoon sun casting long shadows across the dusty road.

Eld's poison-green eyes surveyed the quaint collection of thatched-roof cottages and weathered wooden buildings, a wisp of smoke rising from the local tavern's chimney.

It was a pleasant enough scene, but Eld looked right past the densely inhabited parts of town, straight towards a dilapidated metal shed that looked completely out of place.

"That should do the trick, Shuck. Get you some shade. I always feel like your tendons get a bit melty when it's hot out."

Shuck agreed, happily wagging his tail. The illusion-shrouded Shuck trotted along, his tiny dachshund legs working furiously to pull the much larger vehicle.

When visiting new towns, Eld always enjoyed staying in Old One structures. He felt a certain kinship with them. After all, the night-kin had once ruled the world, and the Old Ones had gone after them, or so the legends said.

Eld's eyes widened as they drew close.

Like the Old One's other abandoned creations, even a basic shed had been built with technology far beyond anything in Eld's time. Nowadays, nobody had any idea how to create an entire structure made of metal, and the best swords of the time were often salvaged from Old One scraps. From what could be gathered by the monuments they'd left behind, the Old Ones had been humans with marvelous technology—marvelous technology that they'd promptly blown themselves up with.

As they passed through the town's stubby cobblestone fence, Eld couldn't help but notice the curious glances and whispers that followed him.

A few children pointed at the seemingly magical floating rickshaw, their eyes wide with wonder. An old man sitting on a porch rocked back so violently in surprise that he nearly toppled over.

Eld offered friendly nods and waves to the onlookers, trying his best to appear harmless and approachable.

Once inside the shed, Eld stretched lazily, his pale, almost porcelain skin sharply contrasting with his jet-black hair and coat, which he determinedly wore despite the sweltering heat.

As he got up from the rickshaw, his coat seemed to move on its own.

Moments later, an undead centipede poked its head out from one of the pockets, its numerous legs twitching curiously. From another fold, a zombie rat peered out with shining red eyes, sniffing the air.

"Franky, Bart, back inside," Eld whispered affectionately. "We need to keep a low profile, remember? I hope these people like us…but many don't." The centipede–Franky–retreated obediently, disappearing into the depths of his coat.

Bart, the zombie rat, chittered irritably.

"Come on," Eld groaned. "Do *you* want to pull the rickshaw?"

Bart chittered again. The noise sounded vaguely like *"not particularly."* Without another squeak, he dove into Eld's coat right behind Franky.

Eld pulled a tattered and worn-out letter from his coat pocket, reading the childlike scrawl.

"Please save Whiskers."

Beneath it was a drawing of a cat, with x's over its eyes to show that it was dead.

The letter had clearly been written by a small child at the end of her wits. There were even little tear stains on the paper.

Back in his days as a child prodigy, Eld had necromantically stopped his heart, but even though his heart no longer beat, it still had more than enough strings for desperate young children to tear at.

Just as Eld was considering how to contact this girl without causing a panic, he noticed a small crowd gathering at a respectful distance. They murmured among themselves, a mix of curiosity and apprehension evident on their faces.

A young girl, no more than ten, approached cautiously. "Are you the pet doctor?"

Eld's lips curled into a gentle smile.

This was probably the person who'd contacted him. "Indeed I am, little one. Eldritch B. Blackwood, at your service." He gestured to the banner tied to his sled. As he spoke, his words became fanciful and grand. Here, before a crowd, Eld was in his element—not just a doctor, but a performer.

The girl's eyes widened. "Can you help my cat? He…" She paused, her words catching in her throat and tears pooling at the edges of her eyes. "He died two weeks ago."

"I read about it," Eld said, briefly waving the letter.

The girl gulped, and the tears began trickling down her cheeks, but Eld smiled.

"It's just a recent departure. Not to worry, not to worry! Dry those eyes, those are effortless for a necromancer like me," Eld said, kneeling to meet the girl's gaze. "In fact…judging by the complete lack of maggots, you've done an excellent job preserving the corpse."

"Yes," Lily stammered back. "I, uh, covered it up. And there was an ice box in one of the Old Ones buildings. I don't know how it worked, but it was cold there."

"An ice box, huh?" Eld replied, raising an eyebrow. He'd seen these strange Old One devices on his travels, usually to store meat. Though, he supposed, corpses *were* meat at the end of the day, after removing sentimental value from the equation.

Eld briefly flashed the letter.

"And you *are* Lily, correct?"

She nodded, twisting her hands nervously.

"And your cat's name is Whiskers, right?" Eld asked.

When she nodded, Eld nodded solemnly.

"A fine name for a cat," he said.

All things considered, this was a very brave child. Not everyone would call one of the nightkin just to save their beloved pet, even if it was a human-like nightkin like Eld. "Well, Lily, why don't you bring your cat to me, and we'll see what we can do?"

As Lily scampered off, a murmur rippled through the growing crowd. Eld caught snatches of conversation.

"Who *is* that man? Lily said he saved Franklin's sheepdog. You know, the man with the big farm a couple of miles from here."

"I heard he can bring any animal back to life!"

"But at what cost? He's not a doctor, he's a necromancer!"

Eld chuckled to himself, partly due to his nerves and partly because he had heard it all before. The pet doctor was used to the awe and fear his *true* profession inspired.

He was having a grand time until a plump, middle-aged shopkeeper pushed her way to the front of the crowd.

"Now see here," she began, shrill with indignation. "We don't want any of your dark magic in our town!"

Eld raised a polite eyebrow. He was used to these criticisms. Fortunately, this woman was still in the talking phase. Eld generally found that far preferable to the torches and pitchforks phase. "Madam, I assure you, my magic is no darker than the ink in your ledger. I simply offer a service – reuniting beloved pets with their owners."

The shopkeeper huffed. "It's unnatural, is what it is!"

Before Eld could respond, Lily returned, cradling a small, lifeless bundle in her arms. The crowd parted, their curiosity momentarily overriding their sharp apprehension.

Eld knelt once more, gently taking the cat from Lily's arms. "Now, let's see what we have here."

He examined the feline carefully, his fingers probing gently. "Hmm, no obvious injuries. Lily, can you tell me how old Whiskers was?"

"He was sixteen," Lily answered. "Is... is that too old?"

Eld shook his head. "Not at all. Age is but a number in my line of work." He dropped his voice to a whisper and tapped the side of his nose. "I'm much older than I look, by a few decades, maybe a century. It's hard to keep track of after a while." Standing, he cradled Whiskers in one arm. "Now, I'll need a few things for the procedure. Would you be so kind as to fetch me a saucer of milk, a pinch of catnip, and…ah, yes, a mouse toy?"

Eld's personal tome was filled with various recipes to reanimate deceased animals, but cats were common enough that he knew his proprietary recipe by heart.

As Lily darted off again, Eld turned to address the crowd. "Ladies and gentlemen, I understand your concerns. But I assure you, what I do is no more unnatural than the potions your local apothecary brews or the spells your town wizard casts."

A tall, thin man with a long beard stepped forward. "I am the town wizard, and I take offense at that comparison!"

Eld bowed slightly.

In his experience, wizards were always taking offense to one thing or another. It could be fun to tweak their noses at times–they were always so uppity about how their spell books were better than necromancer's grimoires when as far as Eld was concerned, they were both just places to write things down.

Unfortunately, those playful taunts sometimes went too far, and violent magical duels against wizards usually led to a lot of dead pets caught in the crossfire. Eld considered himself a man of progress–he wanted fewer dead pets, not more of them.

"My apologies, good sir. I meant no disrespect to your craft. Perhaps you'd like to observe my work? I'm always eager to share knowledge with fellow practitioners."

The wizard harrumphed in typical wizarding fashion but thankfully didn't object.

Lily returned with the requested items and Eld set to work.

He unfolded a small table from his rickshaw, then gently laid Whiskers down on it.

From within his coat, he produced a variety of tools and ingredients. To an outsider, it would have seemed like Eld was producing these items from thin air.

In reality, Bart the skeletal rat was handing Eld the items from his storage pouch. Stitching on those chipmunk cheeks had truly been a stroke of brilliance.

"Now," Eld began, his voice taking on a professorial tone, "the key to successful reanimation lies in understanding the creature's essence. Whiskers here lived a life of comfort and affection. We must recreate those conditions to coax his spirit back."

He sprinkled the catnip over Whiskers' fur, then dipped his finger in the milk and drew symbols on the cat's paws. All the while, he mumbled incantations under his breath, his free hand weaving complex patterns in the air.

Unlike the stars he drew when casting illusion magic, this time, Eld's fingers were swift, sure, and decisive. His fingers painted on thin air, creating a beautiful image of a bridge stretching outward to the heavens.

The crowd watched in fascinated silence as a soft glow began to emanate from Whiskers' body. Eld's movements became faster as his voice rose in volume.

"Come now, Whiskers," he called. "Your time isn't done. Lily needs you. Remember the warmth of her lap, the taste of a fresh kill, the thrill of the hunt!"

With a final flourish, Eld tapped Whiskers on the nose with the mouse toy.

The briefest hint of a groan started through the crowd.

But then, with a sudden twitch, Whiskers' tail began to move. His chest rose and fell with breath, and slowly, his eyes opened.

The crowd gasped collectively. Whiskers sat up, stretched languidly, and let out a plaintive meow.

Lily squealed with delight. "Whiskers! You're back!"

Eld stepped back, allowing Lily to scoop up her newly revived pet. Whiskers purred contentedly, nuzzling against her chest.

The town wizard pushed forward, examining Whiskers with a critical eye. "Remarkable," he muttered. "The cat seems normal. Albeit with a slight glow to its eyes."

Eld nodded. "A common side effect of the reanimation process."

The plump woman who had objected earlier stepped forward hesitantly. "It…it doesn't seem evil or anything."

"Of course not," Eld replied, gently stroking the cat's head in Lily's arms. "Whiskers is the same cat he always was, with the same memories and personality. I simply gave him a second chance at life."

A murmur of approval rippled through the crowd.

Before long, several others stepped forward, asking if Eld could help with their own departed pets. A group of men glanced at each other, and then excitedly dashed off.

Eld raised an eyebrow as they left.

Usually, that level of excitement–and that many men needed to carry a corpse–meant he was about to see something truly exotic.

Still, exotic or not, all pets were beloved by their owners.

And so, Eld smiled and began arranging his schedule.

Just as he'd finished reanimating a pair of geckos, a commotion at the edge of the square caught his attention.

A group of men dragged over a massive carcass with the body of a lion, the wings of an eagle, and the tail of a scorpion.

"Mr. Blackwood!" one of them called. "We heard you can help with any animal. What about this?"

"A manticore? By the Neverending Night…where in the world and all the hells did you find a manticore?"

The man shrugged. "Found him in the mountains. Raised him from a cub. But we ran into a dragon last week while cutting down trees for lumber. He was able to save us, but, he, well…"

Eld pinched the bridge of his nose. "A pet manticore. Of course. Why not?"

He sighed and rolled up his sleeves. "This might take a while, gentlemen and I'll need a lot more than catnip and a mouse toy."

By sunset, Eld had revived cats, dogs, birds, and even a particularly cantankerous goat.

As for the manticore, it'd proved to be a challenge, but with some creative spell-work and a generous application of dragon scales, fortuitously provided by the town wizard, Eld managed to bring it back as well. After all, he had a reputation to uphold. He didn't call himself the Greatest Pet Doctor in History for nothing.

After reviving the manticore, Eld jotted down a few notes in his tome, placing his new recipe just under the instructions for reviving griffons.

As he packed up his rickshaw, preparing to move on, the town mayor approached him. Eld had picked him out as mayor even from a distance—they all seemed to have a fascination with black suits and very tall hats.

"Mr. Blackwood," the mayor began, wringing his hands nervously. "The town council has been discussing your unique abilities. We were wondering if you might consider staying on, at least for a while? We could certainly use someone of your talents."

Eld smiled but shook his head. "I appreciate the offer, truly. But I'm afraid I must decline. My skills are needed in many places, and I've never been one for settling down."

The mayor nodded, disappointment evident on his face. "I understand, but should you ever change your mind, know that you'll always be welcome here."

"Thank you," Eld replied, glad of another successful lifelong gratitude trip.

As Eld prepared to depart, Lily approached once more, Whiskers purring in her arms.

"Mr. Eld," she said shyly. "I just wanted to say thank you again and I was wondering how do you do it? The magic, I mean."

Eld knelt, his voice softening. "Magic, my dear Lily, is the art of bending reality to our will. It's the whispers of the universe that some of us are lucky enough to hear. What I do is like a painter bringing a portrait to life, or a musician making you feel with just a few notes. I simply work with the essence of life itself."

Lily beamed with wonder. "Do you think I could learn to do it someday?"

Eld smiled warmly. "With dedication, study, and a touch of innate talent, it's possible. But remember, Lily, the most important part of what I do isn't just the spells and incantations—it's understanding and caring for the creatures we bring back. That connection, that empathy, is a kind of magic *anyone* can learn."

Lily smiled and ran off, Whiskers purring happily with her.

Eld sighed as she walked off.

Due to his unfortunate childhood, he'd always had a soft spot for kids.

In his experience, empathy was a magic anyone could learn…but certain people were very determined to avoid learning it.

Still, that wasn't his problem anymore.

As the sun dipped in the sky, Eld climbed onto his sled. Shuck barked eagerly, the magic from the illusion spell waning and causing him to flicker back and forth between his original visage and dachshund.

"Farewell," Eld called, waving his hand in a wide and happy arc. "May your pets live long and your spirits remain bright!"

The rickshaw lurched forward and Eld was off, the town's cheers fading behind him.

As the cool night air whipped past him, Eld allowed himself a moment of contentment. Days like this reminded him why he'd chosen this path, despite his family's disapproval. The joy on Lily's face when Whiskers opened his eyes, the wonder in the crowd as they witnessed his work—these were the moments he lived for.

Yet, as the miles stretched on, a familiar restlessness began to creep in.

For all his skill and all the good he did, Eld couldn't shake the feeling that something was missing. He had mastered the art of reanimating recently departed animals, but the truly great necromancers of history had achieved so much more.

There'd been plenty of mythical creatures that'd been driven extinct during times of great suffering, and the Old Ones had written of great beasts called dinosaurs who'd once roamed the Earth. Eld had even seen some of their bones during his travels, but he could never quite imagine what these creatures looked like.

Eld's thoughts turned, as they often did during quiet moments on the road, to the Familial Tome. The greatest treasure of the Blackwood family, passed down through generations, containing the accumulated knowledge of centuries of necromantic study.

Countless talented necromancers had recorded their thoughts in that tome. It was far more expansive than Eld's personal book of spells, and while Eld's father had never been interested in animal reanimation, surely at least a couple of the Blackwoods before him were.

There was that pact animal spell Eld had seen long ago, back when he was a child.

But the book had been snatched away from him before he could learn the spell correctly.

Hopefully, one day, Eld could inherit the Familial Tome and learn of all his ancestor's discoveries. The ability to vastly increase his power and knowledge was an undeniable temptation.

A sudden chill ran down Eld's spine, interrupting his musings. The air around him seemed to thicken, heavy with the weight of powerful magic. Shuck whined, sensing the change.

"Steady, boy," Eld murmured, reaching forward to pat the dog's flank.

Still, Eld had noticed the sudden density of the atmosphere as well. "What do we have here?" he muttered.

The answer came moments later as two figures materialized on the road ahead. Eld's breath caught in his throat as he recognized them—not one, but two liches.

Liches were no ordinary undead. They were exceptionally powerful necromancers who had achieved immortality by binding their souls to phylacteries, allowing them to persist as undying beings of immense magical power. Their very presence seemed to dim the light around them, an aura of death and arcane energy radiating from their ancient bodies.

The first was a welcome sight, a tall and gaunt man with bleached white skin and fraying gray hair. Professor Grimthorpe, an old family friend and one of the few who had encouraged Eld's unconventional path.

The second figure made Eld's heart sink.

Bone-white and regal, with onyx gems for eyes and a twisted crown of black wood adorning his skull.

Eld's father.

Eld brought the rickshaw to a halt, steeling himself for the confrontation to come. As he stepped down, he forced a smile onto his face.

"Professor Grimthorpe, what a pleasant surprise! And Father, I, uh, wasn't expecting to see you." Eld glanced down at the ground, shuffling on his feet. "I thought you were in the southern kingdoms still, doing…whatever…it is you do. Impaling and killing and such…"

Grimthorpe's eyes danced with their usual keen interest. "Eld! I heard rumors of your work in these parts. Fascinating stuff, truly. I'd love to discuss your techniques sometime."

Before Eld could respond, his father's cold voice cut through the night air. "Don't call him that name, Professor. I didn't name him *Eld*. I named him myself. Eldritch Blast Blackwood Junior. Once considered a promising genius in necromancy. Now little more than a traveling *doctor*."

Eld winced at the use of his full name. "Father, I–"

"Silence!" Eldritch Sr. thundered.

The gems in his eye sockets blazed with furious light. "Do you have any idea how you've shamed our family name? Centuries have passed, and you've failed to ascend to lichdom. You haven't even succeeded in creating a phylactery!"

Eld's shoulders slumped. It was an old argument, one he had heard countless times before, but his father wasn't finished.

"Your brother, Cloudehill, has already ascended. Meanwhile, you fritter away your talents on *pets*." He spat the last word as if it tasted foul in his nonexistent mouth.

Grimthorpe cleared his throat awkwardly. "Now, now, Eldritch. The boy's work has merit. His understanding of the soul's connection to the physical form is exceedingly advanced, and his ability to maintain the pet's loyalty to their former owners demonstrates exceptional knowledge of emotions and relationships. Fascinating research for anyone with knowledge of pact magic."

Eldritch Senior rounded on Grimthorpe. *"Pact magic."*

He spoke the words like they were a curse, shaking his head disdainfully. "Don't coddle him, Grimthorpe. He's had more than enough time to prove himself. There is no need for pacts when you have sufficient magical power to *force* people to agree with you!"

Eld winced. His father never did approve of his pursuits, always going on about wasted talent.

Things went sour decades ago when Eld snuck a peek at the forbidden pages of the Familial Tome. Tucked away within was powerful pact magic, including one spell that caught his eye. Perfect Familiar Reanimation.

A spell for reviving familiars and keeping them in a state of undeath forever. Not just restoring life, not just lichdom where you eventually rotted into bone, but true immortality. No stitching, no upkeep, just a perfectly preserved pact animal.

The spell was still incomplete—but just a glance had told Eld that it was painfully close to completion. Just a little bit more research from a talented necromancer, perhaps someone with experience dealing with *all* animals...

But before Eld could commit anything to memory, his father had caught him, sealing the pages and forbidding Eld from touching the Tome until it was time for him to inherit it.

Turning back to Eld, Senior's voice dropped to a dangerous whisper. "I've been patient, son. More patient than you deserve. But my patience has limits. If you don't start taking your heritage seriously, I'll have no choice but to make Cloudehill the family heir."

Eld's head jerked up. "What? But Father, the Familial Tome—"

"Will go to someone worthy of its knowledge," Eldritch Sr. finished. "Someone who understands the true power of necromancy, not this parlor trick you call a career."

Eld's thoughts raced frantically.

The Familial Tome was everything—centuries of necromantic knowledge, spells and techniques lost to time.

Not only that, Eld could scarcely believe his brother Cloudehill had attained lichdom. Cloudehill had always been a lumbering brute with all the magical finesse of a troll attempting wand work. The fact that he hadn't accidentally obliterated himself with a miscast fireball was miraculous enough. His becoming a lich seemed as likely as a ghoul winning a beauty pageant. Yet somehow, the oaf had managed it, leaving Eld to wonder if perhaps he had underestimated his brutish sibling all these years.

Worst of all, Cloudehill's spite ran as deep as the Abyssal Pits of the thirteen Hell Realms.

Eld was genuinely unsure if Cloudehill could read, but even so, Eld knew his brother would sooner reduce the Familial Tome to ashes, scattering its ancient knowledge to the four winds, than allow him a fleeting glance at its coveted pages.

"What would you have me do?" Eld asked weakly.

Grimthorpe stepped forward. "If I may suggest, my academy is always open to talented students. Perhaps a more structured environment would help Eld focus his studies?"

Eldritch Sr. considered this, tapping his bleached bone chin. "Bathurst, Grimthorpe? Hmm. It's not ideal, but it's better than this aimless wandering." He turned back to Eld. "Very well. You will enroll in Grimthorpe's academy. And if you don't show significant progress toward lichdom by the end of the term, the Familial Tome goes to Cloudehill. Is that understood?"

Eld swallowed hard. It wasn't what he wanted, but it was better than losing his inheritance entirely. "Yes, Father. I understand."

"Good," Eldritch Sr. nodded curtly. "Don't disappoint me again, Eldritch. By the Barren Hells, you've done enough of that already." He sighed. "Now come along, your mother will want to see you before we send you off."

His father snapped his bony fingers.

The world around them blurred and twisted, reality itself seeming to fold and unfold. When the disorientation passed, they found themselves standing before the iron-wrought gates of the Blackwood estate.

Unlike most nightkin structures, the Blackwood family manor was located at the boundary between Topside—where humans lived—and the Underworld, where the majority of nightkin dwelled. Eld never understood why that was, seeing his father hated humans more than anyone else.

The mansion loomed before them, a large building of dark stone and twisted ironwork. Spires and turrets clawed at the perpetually overcast sky, while gnarled, ancient trees dotted the expansive grounds, their branches reaching out like grasping fingers.

Ornate crypts adorned the massive yard, some bearing the names of long-dead Blackwood ancestors, others suspiciously new. In the distance, a mausoleum stood, its doors slightly ajar as if inviting—or warning.

Eld's rickshaw and Shuck appeared beside them, the patchwork dog looking out of place in the grim surroundings. Grimthorpe, who had been silent during the teleportation, let out a low whistle.

"I must say, Eldritch," the professor remarked, "Your family's flair for the dramatic never ceases to amaze me."

Eldritch Sr. ignored the comment, marching towards the mansion's towering front doors. "Come," he commanded, not bothering to look back. "Your mother is waiting."

Grimthorpe placed a comforting hand on Eld's shoulder. "Don't look so glum. Bathurst isn't as stuffy as your father might think. I believe you'll find plenty of opportunities to continue your unique studies."

Eld managed a weak smile. "Thank you, Professor. I suppose I'll see you at the start of term?"

Grimthorpe nodded. "Indeed you will. And Eld? Don't let your father's words discourage you. Your work has value, even if he can't see it yet."

As Grimthorpe disappeared, Eld turned back to his rickshaw. Shuck looked up at him, tail wagging uncertainly.

"Well, boy," Eld sighed, scratching behind the dog's ears, "it looks like we're going back to school. Let's hope we can learn some new tricks, eh?"

Chapter 2

Matters of Life and Undeath

"Hurry up," Eldritch Sr. commanded, striding towards the looming front doors.

Even in the presence of the widely respected Professor Grimthorpe, Eld's father spoke brusquely. Considering the undead servants he commanded, Eldritch Sr. had very little practice being disobeyed.

Massive oak panels, carved with writhing, screaming faces, towered before them. As they approached, the faces seemed to twist in agony, their silent howls almost audible in the stillness of the estate.

The doors swung open of their own accord, as if recoiling from Eldritch Sr.'s presence. They revealed a vast foyer, its vaulted ceiling lost in shadows. A grand staircase dominated the room, its railings fashioned from blackened iron twisted into the shapes of skeletal hands.

As Eld and his father crossed the threshold, the soles of their boots clacked against the polished obsidian floor, each step echoing eerily in the entrance. When he was a child–back when his father answered his questions–Eld had asked why footsteps sounded so unusually loudly in the family's hall compared to everywhere else.

Eldritch Sr. had explained that he'd designed the hall's acoustics himself–after all, there was nothing better than unusually loud steps to remind visitors to tread carefully.

Flickering witchlight sconces embedded in the walls cast an otherworldly glow, causing shadows that danced and writhed along the walls adorned with macabre tapestries of his family's conquests.

A hunched man shuffled forward from a darkened alcove.

Shuck took a wary step back, stumbling a little on his overage paw. Beneath his coat, Eld could feel Franky and Bart's anxious writhing.

"Still playing around with animals, are we, Master Eldritch..." the man croaked.

It was more of a statement than a question, and the voice was as dry and irritating as the feeling of drying leaves stuck deeply in one's boots.

Graves, the family butler, was a big pasty sack of a man with hastily tied together patchwork skin, a mosaic of various shades and textures. His makeshift body was loosely held together by stitches that formed eldritch symbols across his body. One milky eye rolled ceaselessly in its socket, while the other, a glassy orb, remained fixed straight ahead.

"I'm not merely playing around, Graves," Eld stiffly replied. "This is all part of my necromantic research."

"Well, I will tolerate their presence, so long as you behave while you're at home…" Graves said. He bowed low, his joints creaking, his skin threatening to come apart at any moment, though Eld could feel the butler's glass eye glowering at his companions.

Eld was willing to admit that rats, centipedes, and giant mutts weren't the cleanliest animals around, but then again, neither were zombie butlers.

"Thank you, Graves," Eldritch Sr. replied, his tone as cold, lifeless, and unappreciative as the mansion itself. "Inform the family we have guests for dinner and get the guest room ready for Professor Grimthorpe."

The butler nodded and shambled away.

Eld couldn't help but notice the stitches holding Graves's limbs together.

In his eyes, the stitch around Graves's right elbow seemed *particularly* loose. The knots themselves were exceptionally shoddy, and if it were Eld, he probably would have used a different material for the thread. He had little experience in human reanimation and even less interest, but he understood the fundamentals of stitching flesh back together.

As much as humans liked to pretend they were different, at the end of the day, they had more in common with animals than they liked to admit.

Meanwhile, Grimthorpe eyed Graves with a mix of admiration and trepidation.

Using reanimated humans as servants was frowned upon among all the nightkin, from lowly ghouls to almighty liches, from arguable humans like vampires and immortal necromancers to undeniable monsters like wendigos and daemons.

Reanimated human servants were the kind of thing that guaranteed torches and pitchforks, and there were a lot more torches and pitchforks than there were nightkin.

Of course, Eldritch Sr. did many things that were frowned upon—all while frowning deeply himself. Normally, liches could no longer frown without their facial muscles, but after ascending to lichdom, Eldritch Sr. had added additional joints to his face, all so he could better indulge in his favorite pastime.

"I see you're still employing reanimated servants, Father," Eld remarked.

Eldritch Sr.'s eye sockets flared, the gems glittering angrily underneath. "They're reliable and don't ask for time off. Perhaps you could learn something from them."

"You could at least have someone else besides Cloudehill do the stitching, the seams are big enough for a small child to fall through—"

Before Eld could finish, a shrill voice echoed through the mansion. "Eldritch! Is that you, darling?" Drizella Blackwood glided down the stairs, her billowing black gown seeming to absorb the surrounding light. She enveloped Eld in a cold embrace. "Oh, how I've missed you, my little grave robber!"

"Mother," Eld mumbled, extricating himself from her rigor mortis-like grasp. "It's good to see you too."

A snide laugh rang out from above. "Well, well. The prodigy son returns. No, that's wrong. Huh. I meant the productive son."

"Prodigal dear," Drizella gently corrected him.

"Oh yeah. That."

Cloudehill descended the stairs, each step punctuated by the clack of bone on marble. Unlike their father, Cloudehill had opted for a more flamboyant lich appearance, adorning his skull with runes and draping himself in ornate robes–black over a field of more black, the Blackwood family colors.

In one hand, Cloudehill held a ceremonial scepter topped by a human skull dipped in gold.

In his other hand, he held another ceremonial scepter, also topped by a human skull dipped in gold.

Creativity had never been Cloudehill's strong suit.

"Hello, brother," Eld said stiffly. "I see lichdom hasn't improved your personality. Still as gaudy as ever."

Cloudehill's jaw clacked in amusement. "At least I have eternity to work on it. How's the pet project going? Still playing doctor with dead squirrels?"

"Boys," Drizella interjected, "Let's not quarrel. Dinner will be ready soon. Eld, dear, why don't you get cleaned up? You smell like…life."

Eld retreated to his old room with Shuck hastily trotting at his heels, the big undead dog's nails clicking against the polished bone-inlaid floor. Shuck might have been the only being who disliked this place more than Eld–Shuck's old home in the Blackwood family kennels had been far worse than any of the Old One buildings Eld had found for them as temporary lodgings during their travels.

With such putrid maintenance, Eld wondered why the family mansion even had kennels to begin with. It must have been some ancestor interested in animal reanimation, but that information was locked deep in the Familial Tome.

Eld clacked his teeth–a habit he always picked up back home, despite his far more human body–and pushed the thought aside for now, stepping into his old room.

His private chambers remained unchanged, a museum to his childhood frozen in time.

Dusty tomes on beginner's necromancy lined the ebony shelves, their spines etched with silver runes that seemed to writhe in the flickering candlelight. Faded diagrams of skeletal structures adorned the walls, meticulously drawn and annotated in Eld's youthful hand.

A four-poster bed was in one corner, its dark curtains embroidered with bloody combat scenes from the underworld—a Cerberus mauling a skeleton or a vampire devouring a zombified leech.

"By the Black Stranger's Twisted Fingers…" Eld cursed, his lip curling. "No wonder I always had nightmares when I was growing up."

In his coat, Bart chittered merrily.

As far as Eld could tell, the zombie rat had the best sense of humor out of all his pets. Though he couldn't speak, Bart *loved* a joke. He was a regular old riff rat.

Eld's old desk stood by the window, its surface scarred with magical burns and stained with long-dried ectoplasm. Half-finished projects littered the desk—a partially reassembled bird skeleton, jars of glowing spectral essence, and a dog-eared journal filled with sketches of revived creatures.

The air hung heavy with the scent of old parchment, grave dirt, and the faint metallic tang of preserved specimens. In one corner, a tall mirror stood, its tarnished surface occasionally rippling as if something moved within its depths.

The mirror was an old family heirloom that Eldritch Sr. had insisted on storing inside Eld's room. As far as Eld could tell, nothing was inside…but he made sure never to stare at the mirror directly.

As Eld freshened up, Franky the centipede and Bart the zombie rat emerged from his coat, peeking expectantly up at him. The two could smell the rot just as well as Eld could. It was a clear-cut sign that they were home, back among the other nightkin.

The nightkin consisted of all creatures bound to the darkness and ill-at-ease in daylight. Though Eld mostly enjoyed traveling as a pet doctor, working Topside in the sun was against his true nature.

But as much as Eld liked the smell of grave dirt, he knew this place was no true home.

"Coast is clear, guys," Eld murmured. "You can go roaming. But make sure not to show up during dinner, alright? I don't trust Cloudehill not to try something nasty."

The two scampered off as Eld readied himself for dinner, checking every fold of his cloak like a general inspecting armor the night before a battle.

As always, dinner was a tense affair, held in a dining room that seemed to exist in a realm between life and death. In a way, the ambiance seemed to reflect the family's mood, which teetered between feeble, stirring attempts at a conversation and deathly silence.

Floating candelabras drifted lazily through the air, their flames an unnatural blue. The long table was crafted from polished ebony and inlaid with bone motifs. The lengthy table could seat twenty, even though it usually seated three.

The five of them occupied one end, with Eldritch Sr. seated at the head. His throne-like chair was adorned with tiny sculpted skulls and vertebrae and loomed over the others.

The rest sat in high-backed seats that pulsed and undulated beneath them. Eld did his best, but the chair oozed uncomfortably beneath him. It felt like his behind was seconds away from falling into a bottomless pit.

In one of his rare fits of whimsy, Eldritch Sr. had tried to create a massage chair by casting necromantic spells on still-living tissue. The project had failed and, in his mind, the only fitting thing to do had been to punish every other diner at the table.

Eld refused to believe his father had even a single altruistic bone in his body. If Eldritch Sr. ever had a speck of altruism, it must have been stored in the flesh that'd sloughed off through his necromantic rituals.

Silent spectral servants glided silently around the table, their translucent silhouettes shimmering as they poured wine the color of congealed blood into goblets fashioned from hollowed-out skulls.

Meanwhile, an unseen orchestra of tormented souls provided a haunting backdrop of whispers and moans.

Graves shuffled in, bearing platters of food that Eld eyed warily. "Is that... still moving?" Eld asked, poking at a quivering mass on his plate.

"Freshly reanimated offal," Drizella beamed. "Your favorite!"

Eld suppressed a grimace. "Ah, yes. Delicious."

Cloudehill smirked. "What's wrong, brother? Can't stomach real necromancer fare anymore? Perhaps you could reanimate the vegetables instead."

"Now, now," Grimthorpe intervened, "Let's not judge. Eld's work with animals is quite fascinating. Just the other day, I was reading about a case where—"

"Enough," Eldritch Sr. cut in, his voice sharp enough to slice through the tension. "We're not here to discuss Eld's hobbies. Cloudehill, tell us about your *real work* in the Eastern Kingdom."

Cloudehill straightened, puffing out his bony chest with a prideful creak. "Ah, the Eastern Kingdom. Glad you asked, Father. My influence there grows by the day. The royal court practically eats from my hand now—sometimes literally." He chuckled, a dry, rattling sound. "I've established a network of necromantic circles throughout the major cities, all operating under the guise of *health clinics*. The fools don't realize they're feeding our power with every visit."

He paused, clearly relishing the attention. "But that's not all. I've made significant strides in our soul-binding research. The latest batch of phylacteries can hold twice the spiritual energy of our previous models. Soon, we'll have an army of bound souls at our command." Cloudehill's eye sockets gleamed with malicious glee. "And of course, all of this is in service of your grand pla—"

Eldritch Sr. silenced him with a sharp look.

Eld's curiosity was undoubtedly piqued, but before he could inquire, Drizella launched into a lengthy and seemingly strategically placed monologue about her latest experiments in flesh-crafting.

As the meal dragged on, Eld found his attention wandering.

His gaze drifted to a painting on the far wall, depicting a black sun hanging ominously over a desolate landscape.

Something about it nagged at him, but he couldn't quite place why.

The painting had hung there since his childhood, but something about it seemed different today.

Eld thought about saying something, but then shrugged and stayed silent.

As far as he knew, neither his father nor Cloudehill knew anything about art. Any comment would only lead to more mocking browbeating.

The rest of dinner passed with Eld's family talking about themselves and Eld staying silent—just how everyone liked it.

When all the food was finished, Eldritch Sr. dismissed the family with the same brusque wave he used to send off the servants, and Eld found himself wandering the mansion's corridors, his mind a whirlwind of conflicting emotions.

The prospect of attending Bathurst Academy of Post-Mortem Studies and Practices should have excited him. Professor Grimthorpe was clearly much more curious about animal reanimation than any of Eld's family ever could be.

But for some strange reason, he felt a gnawing sense of dread.

His fingers trailed absently along the cold stone walls as he walked, barely registering the various decorations that adorned the hallways.

Ancient suits of armor, their visors emanating a green glow, stood at regular intervals and portraits of long-dead Blackwood ancestors watched his progress with hollow, judging eyes.

As he turned a corner, Eld's gaze was drawn to a series of tapestries that lined the corridor. Each one depicted scenes of a world bathed in darkness, illuminated only by a black sun that hung ominously in the sky. In one, legions of undead marched across a barren landscape. Another showed night-kin rulers—vampires, lycanthropes, liches, banshees—all seated on thrones of bone, lording over cowering mortal subjects.

He frowned.

Once again.

It was the black sun, the same as the painting behind the dining table.

That was the difference. Something had changed about it.

The black sun was a common motif in the Blackwood family's decorations. As a child, Eld had often wondered why the family name wasn't "Blacksun" instead of Blackwood. He had never seen a single forest scene through all his time in the family manor.

But there was something off about these black suns...they weren't as Eld had remembered them.

Stepping close, Eld paused before a particularly large tapestry, one he didn't recognize from before.

It portrayed a grand ritual, with robed figures standing in a circle around a black orb. Energy seemed to pulse from the orb, transforming the world around it. The sky above was dominated by the black sun, its corona weaving tendrils of darkness across the heavens.

"This one seems new…" Eld muttered. "Yet very old at the same time…"

Even though the tapestry was new to the house, it was the oldest among all the paintings that Eld had seen thus far.

The worn-out canvas looked like it was about to crumble apart at any moment.

When Eld looked closer, he saw that the whole thing had been stitched together–but not by stitches of thread. Instead, small glittering runes, with gossamer-like magical essence so faint and delicate that it was almost invisible.

Just staring at it made Eld's eyes water.

He knew exactly what this was–time magic.

The ability to rewind time was one of those arcane skills that *technically* counted as necromancy, so long as one's head was tilted properly and their eyes were squinting appropriately.

However, the sheer magical power required to rewind time made it more or less useless in an actual confrontation. All an expert like Grimthorpe could do was use time magic to uncover old secrets, and even then, the results were unclear and imprecise.

The professor—and his academic magic—had to be the source of this repaired tapestry. Perhaps that was what Grimthorpe and Eldritch Sr. had been discussing before they'd gone to pick up Eld.

"But why would he pick this up? I've never known father to care about the arts..."

Lost in thought, Eld almost missed the hushed voices coming from his father's study.

He froze, suddenly alert. Curiosity overcame his melancholy, and he crept closer to the ornate door, its surface carved with scenes of the underworld.

"...the ritual must be completed soon," Eldritch Sr. was saying, uncharacteristically animated. "We cannot afford any delays."

Eld's breath caught in his throat. He pressed his ear closer to the door, his shriveled heart so tense he was afraid it'd start pounding in his chest again.

An unfamiliar voice—cold and calculating, yet supplicant at the same time—responded, "But the risks, Eldritch. If something goes wrong—"

"Nothing will go wrong," Eldritch Sr. snapped. "With this power, we can rewrite reality itself. The age of the living will—"

Eld leaned closer, straining to hear more, but his elbow knocked against a suit of armor. The resulting clang echoed through the hallway.

"What was that?" Eldritch Sr. demanded.

Panic surged through Eld.

He ducked into a nearby alcove, pressing himself against the wall as the study door flew open. His father's gaze swept the corridor, narrowing suspiciously.

After an agonizing moment, Eldritch Sr. retreated, magically sealing the door behind him. Eld exhaled shakily, his mind racing. What was this ritual his father spoke of? And what did he mean by rewriting reality?

"Eavesdropping, brother? How unseemly."

Eld whirled to find Cloudehill lounging against the wall, a smug grin on his skeletal face.

"I was just passing by," Eld lied.

Cloudehill chuckled. "Of course you were. Poor Eld, always left out of the family secrets. But then, what use would you be? You can barely reanimate a coughing baby, let alone contribute to Father's grand design."

Anger flared in Eld's chest. "At least I don't need to hide behind jewels and fancy robes to feel important."

Cloudehill's eyes flashed dangerously. "Careful, brother. You're out of your depth here."

Eld had enough of this taunting. He always felt out of place on the surface world, but his clients respected his skills.

"Prove it," Eld challenged, drawing himself up and moving in close to Cloudehill. "Or are you afraid your *grand power* won't measure up?"

With a snarl, Cloudehill hurled a bolt of necrotic energy at Eld, who saw it coming from a mile away.

Eld dove aside.

The spell sizzled past and left a scorched mark on the wall and Eld retaliated by weaving a complex pattern through the air, his fingers dancing as he painted a sword crossed with a shield.

The nearby suit of armor creaked to life, slowly and clumsily lunging at Cloudehill.

Cloudehill blasted the construct apart with a wave of his hand. "Pathetic," he sneered.

Now it was Cloudehill's turn. His fingers danced through the air, leaving trails of sickly green light. With a flick of his wrist, he sent a barrage of spectral skulls hurtling towards Eld. The skulls gnashed their teeth, filling the air with a shriek.

Eld's eyes widened. He fumbled through a protective spell, his fingers trembling.

A shimmering barrier materialized before him, but it was thin and wavering. The skulls slammed into it, each impact sending cracks spider-webbing across its surface.

"Is that the best you can do, brother?" Cloudehill taunted, his voice echoing unnaturally. Like their father, Cloudehill was a big fan of using voice enhancements in battle as a subtle form of braggadocious psychological warfare.

Sweat beaded on Eld's brow as he struggled to maintain the barrier.

With his free hand, he attempted to conjure a counterspell., but the ceaseless tension of skull attacks got to him. Wisps of dark energy gathered at Eld's fingertips, but they fizzled out before taking shape.

Cloudehill laughed, a sound like bones rattling in a tomb. He raised both arms and the shadows in the corridor coalesced into writhing tentacles. They lashed out, shattering Eld's weakened barrier and wrapping around his limbs.

Eld gasped, feeling the cold touch of the shadow tentacles sapping his strength. He muttered an incantation, his voice shaky and uncertain. A pale light flickered around him, barely strong enough to push the shadows back a few inches.

Cloudehill advanced, each step leaving a trail of frost on the carpet. "You're outmatched, Eld. Always have been." He raised a hand, necromantic energy crackling between his fingerbones.

Eld's spells were failing, his defenses crumbling. He needed something, anything to turn the tide. He needed an edge, something unexpected.

Inspiration struck.

Eld whistled sharply and a second later Shuck came bounding around the corner. Cloudehill paused, momentarily confused by the reanimated dog's appearance.

That momentary distraction was all Eld needed.

He channeled his power into a final spell, one he knew very well.

Despite the tension, the spell came naturally. Eld's skilled fingers danced and twirled, painting padlocks, leashes, chains, and even a cage in the middle of the air. This was a very lengthy spell. It was difficult to use in battle, but consider Cloudehill's bragging and inattentiveness...

Ghostly chains erupted from the floor, wrapping around Cloudehill and binding him in place.

The newly fledged lich let out a cry of shock, but the shell wasn't done yet. Next, a cage rattled around him, followed by a comical leash tying him to the door.

"Not bad for a *pet doctor*, eh?" Eld panted, grinning despite his exhaustion.

The spell was meant to restrain unruly reanimated animals. The last time Eld had used it, it'd been to subdue a zombified grizzly bear, who'd failed to make it through a particularly tough winter. Once reanimated, the mother had been just a little *too* happy to be reunited with her cubs. Her overenthusiasm very well could have hurt them.

Thankfully, Eld's spell had held true then, and he was confident that its strength was more than enough to handle unruly younger brothers, whether they were newly fledged liches or not.

Indeed, Cloudehill struggled ineffectively against the bonds, his eyes blazing with fury. "You miserable little—"

"Enough!"

The combatants froze as Eldritch Sr.'s commanding voice filled the hall. He strode towards them, radiating cold anger.

"What is the meaning of this?" he demanded.

Cloudehill adopted a wounded expression. "Father, Eld attacked me! I was merely defending myself."

"That's not true!" Eld protested. "He started it!"

Even as they came out of his mouth, Eld realized just how childish he sounded.

It was ridiculous, really. Though he looked like he was in his early twenties, Eld was well into his hundreds. And yet, Cloudehill just had that perfect knack for getting under his skin.

"Silence, both of you!" Eldritch Sr. roared. "I expected better from my sons. Cloudehill, you're a lich now. Act like it. And Eld...' He fixed his eldest with a disapproving glare. "This childish behavior ends now. You will go to Bathurst, you will study proper necromancy, and you will not embarrass this family further. Is that clear?"

Eld bit back a retort, knowing it would only make things worse. One stray word and he'd lose the Familial Tome–and all its invaluable knowledge–for good. "Yes, Father," he muttered.

"Good," Eldritch Sr. nodded curtly. "Now, come along. We need to discuss your departure."

Moments later, Eld found himself in the main hall being fussed over by his mother, who'd packed his bags with an assortment of dubious magical items.

"Now, dear, I've included some fresh grave dirt for emergencies," she explained, shoving a jar into his hands. "Oh, and these filed fingerbones make excellent toothpicks!"

Cloudehill lounged nearby, his earlier rage replaced by smug amusement. "Do try not to fail spectacularly, brother. Though I must say, watching you fumble through basic necromancy might be entertaining. Then everyone would consider you the stupid brother."

Eldritch Sr. called for silence, but only to make a threat of his own.

"Eldritch Blackwood Jr., you will depart for the Underworld tomorrow and attend Bathurst Academy of Post-Mortem Studies and Practices. And you had better uphold the family name. Do not disappoint me again or it will be your last. If you are disinherited then we have no use for you in the family." Eld's father spoke the words with the same grimness of a reaper giving a death sentence. Eld had met grim reapers before, but he'd never met a grimmer lich.

With that ominous proclamation, Eldritch Sr. turned on his heel and walked away, his cloak billowing behind him. Cloudehill followed, shooting Eld a smug nod before disappearing around the corner.

As their footsteps faded, Drizella approached Eld, wringing her hands. "Oh, Eldritch," she said, her voice wavering, "You know that just means he loves you, don't you?"

Eld let out a bitter laugh, shaking his head. "Mother, *Father* and *love* don't belong in the same sentence. They're about as compatible as holy water and a vampire."

Drizella's face fell, her already pale complexion somehow becoming even more ashen. She opened her mouth as if to speak, then closed it again, seemingly at a loss for words. After an awkward silence, she stepped forward and enveloped Eld in an embrace.

"Do take care, my little grave robber," she whispered, thick with emotion. Then, just as quickly, she pulled away and hurried off, leaving Eld alone in the vast, empty hallway.

As the last echoes of his family's departure faded, Eld retreated to his room to finish packing. Shuck curled up at the foot of his bed, his mismatched eyes watching Eld's every move. Franky the centipede and Bart the zombie rat emerged from their hiding spots, chittering softly as they began to explore the chamber once more.

A glint from the window caught his eye.

Eld approached, peering out at the night sky.

He could have sworn he saw a strange symbol among the stars—a dark circle ringed with spikes.

But when he blinked, it was gone.

Eld shook his head, chalking it up to exhaustion and nervousness.

As he turned back to his packing, anticipation and dread settled in his stomach. Whatever awaited him at the academy, one thing was certain, his unlife was about to get a lot more interesting.

Chapter 3

When They Go Low,
We Descend Into the Underworld

Eld had only stayed at his family's home for a single night, but the hours had stretched on, feeling like an eternity.

As Eld rose from bed, with Franky and Bart lounging next to him and Shuck crawling out from his comfortable perch underneath the bed, he smirked at his ever-loyal companions.

"A good dawn to you too, fellas. You know, each different species of nightkin has different stories of hell—mostly to argue that their little slice of the Underworld isn't *actually* hell. But after last night, I'm starting my own tradition, where hell looks just like the Blackwood Family Manor...though come to think of it, Father would certainly take that as a drastic compliment."

The one good thing about being back home was the schedule.

Like everyone else in the Blackwood family, Eld had once been human.

It was a bizarre mystery of the Blackwood family.

Normally, the undead couldn't breed. Yet when it came to the Blackwoods, even the most ardent of liches like Eldritch Sr. gave birth to ordinary human children who had to turn themselves undead through necromantic rituals.

But despite his human origins, Eld could never understand why these so-called "ordinary people" loved walking around in the sun so much.

The sun was obviously some kind of great and ceaseless enemy.

It was a giant ball of fire in the sky that scorched Eld's skin and blinded his eyes. Frankly, it was a miracle he'd completed so many successful operations in light of that blasted red orb.

That was the good thing about attending Bathurst. In the Underworld, Eld wouldn't have to worry about the sun.

A knock echoed on his door.

"Mother," Eld muttered to himself. "She's the only person who'd bother bidding me farewell, especially after that debacle last night."

Franky chittered reproachfully at him.

Eld glanced at him.

"Filial piety from a centipede. At this point, I've heard everything, but you *do* have a point, Franky. Mother might be literally smothering, but she's the only person here who ever truly cared about me."

"Coming!" Eld shouted, hurrying to the door.

Drizella Blackwood hadn't quite understood why her talented son—once considered to be a child prodigy—had given up the pursuit of lichdom to become a pet necromancer, but she at least understood the general concept of happiness and life satisfaction.

Indeed, Drizella was waiting for him on the other side.

"You brought your bag and everything, didn't you?" she asked.

"Of course," Eld replied, hefting it.

He still wasn't sure what all those obscure necromantic contraptions were good for, but they were still good luck charms from his mother, and Eld wasn't above either superstition or sentiment. And if worse came to worse...well, he could just throw them at whoever was chasing angrily after him.

"Wonderful dear, wonderful," Drizella said.

Without even the hint of a warning, she'd caught him in yet another strangling embrace. Eld didn't have time to brace himself. He tried his best to return his mother's hug, doing his best when she gave him a sliver of space to shift his arms. In another world, Drizella's ridiculous arm strength would have made her a wonderful strangling serial killer, the stuff of urban legends and campfire stories.

"Now, don't forget the way to Bathurst..." she said, raising a stern finger. "It is through the family crypt, after all."

As was only natural, most entrances to the Underworld were placed in crypts and tombs.

Drizella grinned teasingly at Eld. The smile stretched out her waxy and parched skin, and a small bit fell off. "I remember how the crypt scared you when you were a child."

Eld wanted to reply and say that he wasn't a child anymore, but he held his tongue.

The family crypt contained the remains of all the Blackwood ancestors. In any family, it was wise to acknowledge one's ancestors. For obvious reasons, this was even more important in a family of undead necromancers.

The place was more of a bedroom than a true grave. Quiet was even more important than normal.

Dying didn't mean much for a Blackwood.

Unless they were cremated, or their skulls were damaged too much to hold their soul essence, Eld knew all of these relatives were merely sleeping.

From his mother's stories, Eld knew that the ancestors had once been able to wander the grounds. But when Eldritch Senior came into power, he quickly put a stop to that and banished everyone except for the immediate family to the crypts.

Eldritch Sr. loved demanding filial piety, but giving it wasn't one of his strengths.

"Speaking of which," Drizella said. "Cloudehill drew you a map. He went through the tomb during his ascent to lichdom."

Eld raised an eyebrow. "Cloudehill drew this?"

"He did," Drizella said, beaming proudly. "You know, he wanted to make it up to you for your fight last night. He's grown up quite a bit, you know."

Eld didn't know about that, but he didn't want to argue, so he just nodded. At any rate, the penmanship was certainly Cloudehill's—an inaccurate childish scrawl that made Eld very glad his brother never had a daemon summoning phase.

"One last thing. Take this witchlight lantern dear," Drizella said. "You'll need it to see inside."

She withdrew it from her billowing black cloak, handing the contraption to Eld. The witchlight lantern was shaped in the rough shape of a skull, with a handle fastened to it by the temples. A bright glow poured from the eye sockets.

There were rumors that back in the old days, some particular savage nightkin carved their lanterns from the skulls of witches instead of simply buying them from witches. Nowadays, all the nightkin were technically supposed to be at peace, but Eld never knew for certain, not when it came to his father.

Still, a light was better than nothing.

With the witchlight in hand, Eld bid his mother farewell— yet again—and eagerly left the family manor, but his steps grew less swift and less sure as he slowly approached the ancient Blackwood family crypt, which stood at the far edge of the estate's grounds.

Centuries-old bloodwood trees, their stained red trunks gnarled and twisted, formed a natural barrier around the structure, their branches reaching out like grasping fingers in the pale moonlight. They stretched outwards like hands from the underworld, reading to yank fresh corpses into the crypt at any time.

The crypt itself was carved from black granite, its walls were adorned with bas-reliefs depicting scenes of death and resurrection. Skeletal figures danced along the frieze, their empty eye sockets seeming to follow Eld's every move. The entrance was framed by two massive pillars, each topped with a snarling gargoyle whose wings unfurled towards the starless sky.

A set of worn stone steps led down to the crypt's threshold. The iron-bound oak door stood ajar as if inviting Eld to enter.

Eld descended the steps, then paused before the yawning entrance, its stone maw gaping wide like a hungry beast. The air around the crypt was unnaturally still, heavy with the weight of centuries and the lingering essence of long-departed souls.

Even the whispers of wind through the estate's grounds fell silent here, as if nature itself dared not intrude upon this domain of death.

As if to show just how uninterested nature was in going inside, Shuck nudged Eld and began to whine softly. The reanimated canine's patchy fur stood on end.

Eld had noticed this many times before, but Shuck really was a clever dog—he'd sensed the powerful necromantic energies that permeated the area.

And if Shuck was nervous, well, so was Eld.

During his travels, Eld had encountered plenty of great and terrifying monsters. In fact, he'd even created some himself, having just reanimated a zombie manticore just yesterday.

Idiots like Cloudehill thought that nervousness was equivalent to cowardice.

Eld knew that it usually meant his instincts had sensed some kind of danger that his conscious mind hadn't perceived yet.

He swallowed hard, his grip tightening on the lantern's handle.

"Well, boy," Eld muttered, patting Shuck, "Let's make sure we keep an eye out down here. But I suppose this is fitting. Our grand adventure begins in a musty old tomb heading down to the underworld."

Then he took a deep breath and stepped into the darkness.

The crypt's interior unfolded before him, a labyrinth of narrow corridors and cramped chambers. The walls were lined with niches holding the remains of long-forgotten house servants.

Once upon a time, the nightkin had ruled over normal humans. Back then, the Blackwoods had employed human servants, or so the legends said. Judging by the sheer number of tiny niches, Eld thought that was likely the case—either that or his ancestors were *really* bad at necromancy.

Just as Eld was able to descend the twisting and turning spiral staircase that led to the grand central chamber where the mainline family members were buried, a small urn caught his eye.

The urn was decorated with images of a dog playing out in the field. Eld had seen such urns many times before, and they almost always carried the remains of pets. After all, it would be very weird to put human remains in an urn decorated with images of animals.

Personally, Eld was against cremation—for obvious reasons, it was impossible to reanimate a cremated pet.

For a brief moment, his thoughts lingered back to the Perfect Familiar Reanimation spell within his Familial Tome. Perhaps, with enough work, that spell would be able to overcome even things like fire or decapitation, the bane of all undead.

But for now, all Eld could do was sigh, thinking of the waste of undeath as he stared at the urn. Why would a Blackwood of all people ever do anything so foolish as cremating their dead?

Even stranger, whoever this pet's owner was had a strong enough relationship with their companion that he'd wanted them buried in the crypt, directly before the grand central chamber, which was the greatest place of honor.

"What do you make of that, Shuck?" Eld asked.

Instead of replying, Shuck just nudged his head towards the staircase. He wasn't very interested in the mystery and was still feeling nervous about the crypt.

"Ah, you're right," Eld said. "There's time to worry about that later. Perhaps we can even stay up and discuss it in our dorm room tonight. For now, let's just keep going."

Eld descended the staircase, which creaked discordantly at every step like he was walking on broken piano keys.

At the bottom, he found himself in a grand central chamber. Massive sarcophagi lined the wall, each bearing the likeness of a notable Blackwood ancestor.

He paused before one, its lid carved with the image of a portly man clutching a chicken leg in one hand and a spell book in the other.

"Great-Uncle Magnus," Eld mused, reading the inscription. "*He died as he lived—mid-bite and mid-incantation.* Charming."

Nearby stood another sarcophagus, this one depicting a woman with an exasperated expression. The engraving read, *Here lies Aunt Grizelda, who finally found peace and quiet.*

As Eld moved through the chamber, he noticed a recurring motif carved into the walls and sarcophagi—a black sun, its rays reaching out like grasping tendrils.

It was the same symbol he'd seen in the paintings in the main manor.

And once again, something felt *different* about it.

Though he'd seen the symbol countless times before, something nagged at him, stirring a strange feeling deep in his stilled guts that he couldn't quite grasp.

Occasionally consulting Cloudehill's map, Eld continued moving on, though it felt like the suns were staring at him. Their ominous gaze drove him to walk faster and faster until he reached a bizarre sight that stopped him in his tracks.

"Now what happened here?" Eld muttered.

The tomb itself was grand and impressive, but it had been defaced.

Someone had slashed at the façade with a sword, cleaving great gashes in the edifice as if trying to hide the engraving.

Eld frowned and took a closer look.

The lid showed a skeletal man with an impressive mustache.

And behind him...

Was what looked like an entire clowder of cats.

Eld traced the letters and attempted to decipher the engraving.

"Hieronymus Blackwood," Eld read aloud, squinting to read the words through the gashes, "Pioneer of feline reanimation and mustache maintenance."

Eld's instinct was to smirk—mustache maintenance on a skeleton.

His ancestors were just as eccentric as his current family.

But after thinking about it more, the cuts and slashes bothered him. Evidently, Hieronymus had found his relationships with his cats to be very important. But somebody—and Eld had a very clear feeling of who—had decided to cut out that part of his legacy.

Eld almost wanted to storm back to the manor and give his father a piece of his mind, but if he did that, he had a feeling that Eldritch Sr. would literally just dig out a piece of Eld's mind in response.

For now, all he could do was keep going. He'd get the Blackwood Familial Tome back by hook or by crook, but for now, he was forced to obey his overbearing father.

Eld consulted the map from Cloudehill again, the parchment crackling as he unfolded it. The ink seemed to writhe on the page, forming and reforming into unfamiliar patterns.

"What is this?" Eld muttered, suspicion building in his mind.

But before he could find out more, a sudden skittering sound from behind made him whirl around. The map slipped from his fingers, floating to rest atop yet another sarcophagus. This one bore the likeness of a man with a perpetual sneer, the inscription reading, *Ebeneezer Blackwood—He's still complaining about the accommodations.*

As if on cue, a muffled grumble seemed to emanate from within the sarcophagus. Eld jumped back. He snatched up the map and hurried back to the main corridor, Shuck close at his heels.

"Right, sorry for, uh, interrupting you, Ebeneezer," Eld said, hastily backing away from the sarcophagus.

Shuck nudged Eld pointedly.

The patchwork dog's expression was a mix of fear and irritation.

"Right you are Shuck," Eld said. "Let's figure out where we're *actually* supposed to go."

Eld unfolded the map once more, holding it close to his witchlight lantern. The parchment seemed to crawl beneath his fingers, the crude drawings and instructions shifting and swirling. He squinted, trying to make sense of the ever-changing landmarks and directional arrows.

"That's odd," he muttered, turning the map this way and that. "I could've sworn the Corridor of Whispers was on the left, but now it's…wait a minute…"

Eld's whisper morphed into a groan as the map re-arranged itself.

The *Corridor of Whispers* morphed into the *Hallway of Screams*, before becoming the *Passage of Mild Discomfort*, before finally settling on the *Tunnel of Inconvenient Truths*.

Eld's eyes narrowed as realization dawned.

He flipped the map over and there, scrawled in familiar spidery handwriting, was a short note.

"Dearest brother, I do hope you enjoy your journey. Don't take any wrong turns... or do! It's all the same in the end. Your loving brother, Cloudehill."

Eld's grip on the map tightened, crumpling the edges. "Cloudehill," he growled. "Of course he couldn't resist a parting prank. So much for changing his ways."

With the map rendered useless, Eld knew he had only one option—asking for help from some very grumpy individuals.

He set down his pack and rummaged through it, pulling out a small pouch of grave dirt and a vial of murky liquid.

Eld approached a nearby sarcophagus, its lid carved with the likeness of a stern-faced warrior. *Here rests Thaddeus Blackwood, Ever Vigilant*, the inscription read. With a grunt of effort, Eld pushed the heavy stone lid aside, revealing the desiccated remains within. The corpse still clutched a rusted sword across its chest.

"Sorry about this, Great-Uncle Thaddeus, I need to wake you up. I'd ask Ebeneezer but he seems grumpy." Eld reached into his pack, retrieving a small pouch of grave dirt and a vial of murky liquid. Carefully, he sprinkled the dirt over the body and uncorked the vial, letting three drops fall onto the corpse's forehead.

"I hope you don't mind helping a descendant in need," he added, preparing to recite the incantation. "Family duty and all that."

"Arise, O servant of death," Eld recited, his voice echoing in the cramped space. "Guide me through these shadowed halls."

The corpse shuddered, its jaw creaking open as wisps of spectral energy swirled around it. Slowly, jerkily, Thaddeus sat up, empty eye sockets fixing on Eld.

"Who dares disturb my rest?" Thaddeus demanded.

"Eldritch Blackwood Jr., lich-in-training," Eld replied, trying to keep his voice steady. "I seek the path to Bathurst Academy."

The corpse tilted its head, considering. "Bathurst, you say? Hah! You're going the wrong way, boy. You need to head deeper, always deeper."

Before Eld could respond, another voice chimed in, this one high and reedy. "Nonsense! The way to Bathurst is up, always up!"

Eld turned to see another corpse, this one little more than a skeleton draped in tattered robes, pulling itself from its niche.

"I didn't wake *you*," Eld said, bewildered.

The skeleton shrugged bony shoulders. "I was already awake. It's hard to sleep down here with so much necromantic energies flying around and all. I couldn't let old Thaddeus here mislead you. He was always terrible with directions, even in life."

"Better a poor sense of direction than a hollow head, Ezra," Thaddeus shot back.

As Thaddeus and Ezra bickered, a low rumble echoed through the crypt.

Stone grated against stone as more sarcophagi lids shifted, pushed aside by their awakening occupants. From the wall niches, honored servants stirred, their bones rattling as they oriented themselves to their surroundings.

Even the small urn Eld had seen earlier awoke, with the dog's ashes simply re-arranging themselves into its old form.

Eld's eyes widened.

The necromantic magic binding the dog's body together…

Though the carrier was just a small dog, the power of the spell reverberated in Eld's mind.

The incomplete spell!

Eld hadn't imagined reading that spell as a child. Perfect Familiar Reanimation was real. It wasn't enough to give this dog its body back yet, but it was enough to hold it together in this strange form…

The literally ashy black dog was much smaller than Shuck, but it walked up to the bigger dog, his tail wagging happily as he floated through the air like a carnival performer's smoke cloud.

Soon, the once-quiet crypt was filled with a cacophony of conflicting advice, each resurrected Blackwood certain they knew the correct path to Bathurst.

"Down through the catacombs!" croaked Aunt Hephzibah, her spectral body billowing out of her tomb like mist. "The old ways are always best!"

"Poppycock!" retorted Uncle Balthazar, his bones clattering as he gestured emphatically. "Up to the surface, then three leagues east! I went to Bathurst in my day, and that's how it was done!"

A chorus of rattling laughter erupted from a group of ancient retainers. "The young master must follow the River of Souls," their spokesman insisted, his jaw hanging askew as he spoke. "It's the only sensible route!"

More voices joined the fray, each more insistent than the last.

"Through the Cavern of Echoes!"

"Ride the Nightmare Steed across the Bog of Fear!"

"Take the Ethereal Elevator, thirteenth floor, mind the gap!"

Eld's head spun as he tried to make sense of the contradictory directions.

From the looks of it, the small dog was giving Shuck instructions of its own, but those didn't seem very helpful either. The more Shuck listened, the more confused he got, and soon, his mismatched eyes were spinning in opposite directions.

The crypt, so spacious moments ago, now felt oppressively cramped as more and more undead crowded around, eager to offer their advice. The air grew thick with the dust of ages and the musty odor of long-decayed flesh.

Eld raised his hands, trying to calm the escalating situation. "Please, everyone, if you could just—"

But his words were drowned out as a new argument erupted between Great-Aunt Prudence and her former handmaiden about the best way to pack for the journey. Prudence's insistence on bringing seventeen changes of shrouds was met with exasperated groans from the other undead.

"Enough!" Eld shouted, his patience wearing thin. "Can any of you agree on anything?"

The corpses fell silent, exchanging glances or at least, turning their skulls towards each other in a facsimile of the gesture.

Finally, Thaddeus spoke up. "Well, we might not agree on the specifics, but I think we can all concur that the fastest way down is through the Door of No Return."

A chorus of rattling agreements followed this statement.

"And where," Eld asked, "Might I find this door?"

As one, the assemblage of corpses pointed to a previously unnoticed archway, its stone surface carved with strange symbols.

"Right," Eld sighed. "Of course. Shuck, come on, boy. Let's hope these fellows are more reliable in death than they seem to have been in life."

Eld approached the archway, Shuck padding along beside him. As they crossed the threshold, the stone beneath their feet suddenly gave way. With a yelp of surprise, Eld and Shuck plummeted into darkness.

They fell for what seemed like an eternity, passing through layers of reality like a stone sinking through water. Eld caught glimpses of other worlds as they plunged ever deeper—a realm of endless ice, a sea of liquid fire, a void filled with floating islands of bone.

Just as Eld was certain they would fall forever, they burst through a final barrier and found themselves plummeting through the open sky.

Far below, an island floated in a sea of mist, a grand Gothic structure perched atop it like a brooding gargoyle.

"Bathurst," Eld breathed. "That's Bathurst."

Unfortunately, they weren't landing on the island.

Terror filled him as the water rushed up to meet them.

Suddenly, their descent slowed.

Eld felt as if he were drifting down on a gentle breeze rather than plummeting to his doom. As they neared the ground, he saw someone below, arms raised and crackling with arcane energy.

They touched down softly on a grassy knoll, Shuck shaking himself as if he had just climbed out of water. Eld took a moment to catch his breath, his legs wobbling as he stood.

"Well now, that was quite an entrance," a familiar voice chuckled. Eld looked up to see Professor Grimthorpe approaching, a twinkle in his eye. "I do hope you don't plan to make a habit of dropping in unannounced, Mr. Blackwood. Typically, to reach the Underworld, you take the Ethereal Elevator to the fourth floor."

"Professor," Eld gasped, still trying to process what had just happened. "I…the map…Cloudehill…"

Grimthorpe waved a hand dismissively. "Yes, yes, family pranks and all that. You're here now and that's what matters. Welcome to the Underworld."

The shock was enough that Eld could have sworn his shriveled heart had started beating again.

He shook off the surprise, slowly taking in his surroundings.

They weren't quite on the island. Instead, they were on a dock on the other side of the lake.

He and Grimthorpe stood in and pleasant courtyard decorated with marble stones, ringed by ancient yew trees whose branches seemed to reach for the perpetually twilight sky. Other students milled about, some looking as disoriented as Eld felt, others chatting excitedly or eyeing their fellow pupils with wary curiosity.

A low groan drew Eld's attention.

Nearby, a gaunt figure lay sprawled on the ground, showing no signs of wanting to get up. The being's skeletal face was turned towards the sky, empty hollow eyes staring blankly upwards. Despite his prone position, his attire—a tattered yet formal outfit consisting of a dark tailcoat, waistcoat, bowtie, and striped trousers—gave him an air of faded elegance.

"Come now, Mr. Wilting," Grimthorpe called out. "The ground may be comfortable, but as you very well know, our dormitory beds are far superior."

The prone man let out another pitiful moan, fading slightly into transparency. His jaw moved, revealing a wide grin that seemed at odds with his lethargic state. "But getting up requires effort, Professor. Terrible, terrible effort."

Eld couldn't help but be intrigued.

This Mr. Wilting was a poltergeist if Eld had ever seen one. Poltergeists were a type of ghost that could become corporeal at will. They were a strange mix of skeletons, zombies, and specters.

He approached the lazy student, extending a hand. "Here, let me help you up. I'm Eld, by the way. Eld Blackwood."

Wilting's hollow eyes seemed to focus on Eld, the eternal grin unchanging. One skeletal hand, with long, claw-like fingers, twitched slightly but made no move to accept the offered help. "Charmed," he drawled. "Talbot Wilting, scion of the noble Wilting family. We've been decaying gracefully for generations."

A sharp voice cut through their conversation. "Well, well. If it isn't *Tolbert* Wilting. Still trying to become one with the earth, I see."

A tall, slender man with ash-gray skin and eyes like smoldering coals sauntered over.

Despite his graying skin, he had a very young face—almost boyish. He was just as tall as Eld, but he looked barely older than a teenager. His attire, a perfectly tailored black suit with silver embroidery, gaudily shrieked aristocratic superiority. Every thread seemed meticulously placed, as if dirt and wrinkles feared to approach him. A high-collared cloak draped over his shoulders, its deep purple lining flashing as he moved.

"It's Talbot," the poltergeist murmured from his prone position.

The newcomer sneered. "As if it matters. You're hardly worth remembering, ghost. I'm surprised they even allowed you back into Bathurst. The famous ghost who haunts the freshman year. Did your family have to donate a new wing to secure your place?"

Eld felt a surge of annoyance. "And you are?" he asked, stepping between the baby-faced man and Talbot.

The gray-skinned man drew himself up haughtily. "Mortimer Vex, of the Shadowmere Vexes. You must be…ah, yes. Eldritch Blackwood Jr., I've heard all about you."

"All good things, I hope," Eld replied dryly.

Mortimer's lip curled. "Hardly. The great Blackwood heir, reduced to playing veterinarian with dead pets. It's positively embarrassing."

Eld's fingers twitched, itching to draw a spell in the air, but before he could, Grimthorpe's voice boomed across the courtyard.

"Students! Your attention, please. The ferry to the academy proper will be departing shortly. Please make your way to the docks in an orderly fashion."

Mortimer shot Eld a final disdainful look before turning on his heel and striding away. Eld glanced down at Talbot, who had finally propped himself up on his elbows.

"Need a hand?" Eld asked again.

Talbot sighed dramatically. "I suppose if I must move, assistance would not go amiss."

Eld hauled Talbot to his feet, surprised at how light the poltergeist was. It was as if Talbot's body was only barely more substantial than a piece of parchment.

As they made their way toward the water's edge, Eld strained his eyes to peer through the thick, rolling mist that blanketed the area.

The island where Bathurst rested remained largely hidden, a mysterious realm cloaked in perpetual fog. Only the uppermost spires of the academy were visible, their Gothic pinnacles piercing the veil of mist.

The docks materialized gradually as they approached, emerging from the fog like an apparition.

To Eld's surprise, the docks were *alive.*

They were bake-kujira—great skeletal whales that Eld had only read about in necrotaxidermy textbooks. Their enormous bodies were made of bleached white bone, though a few strands of muscle and sinew still remained.

Every so often, water would pulse from their twisted blowholes. Instead of emitting water upwards, the eruptions launched the boats forward, propelling them rapidly into the shadowy depths.

Grimthorpe stepped up, depositing massive buckets of blood on each of the whale skeletons, which each bellowed hollowed cries of thanks as they imbibed the nutritious red fluid.

The boats themselves were of similar macabre construction. They were large rafts of bone tied together by threads of sinuous flesh. Each of the boats had its own ferryman, a tall humanoid being whose body was covered in robes.

From what Eld could tell, these were the ferrymen's standard uniforms. One of the ferryman looked like just a skeleton. Another had long goat horns, and a third had two long feeler-like antennae sticking out of his head.

Spectral attendants, their translucent bodies flickering in and out of visibility, guided students toward the vessels. Their voices carried on the damp air, mingling with the lapping of dark waves against the shore.

"Line up, line up…"

"Freshmen students here…"

"Sophomores there…"

"Bloodline enrollment students at the far end…"

Briefly, Eld wondered if he was a bloodline enrollment candidate. The Blackwoods were relatively well-known, after all. But considering how irritating Mortimer was, he thought he'd better travel with the rabble.

He and Talbot got into a boat driven by a ferryman who bowed and nodded at them before taking the oars. As he turned, Eld thought he caught a glimpse of cloven hooves.

He muttered at Eld and Talbot when he stepped onto the ferry, his voice sounding like crackling coals.

"A coin please…for the way there…it'll be two coins if you want it to be round trip."

Eld glanced into the fog.

He *did* intend to get back from Bathurst.

"Will my fare be good for the trip after the school year?" he asked.

"Of course, of course," the hooded ferryman said. He grinned, his teeth poking through the darkness of his cowl and revealing a sharp white smile. "Though, if you have some kind of *accident,* you may require my services further. This is a new gig for me, but I predict that academy accidents will be very good for business. Otherwise, we won't have too many passengers outside of the start and end of the year."

A little put off by the ferryman's bluntness, Eld dug into his purse, pulling out a pair of small gold coins with this or that king engraved on it. He'd received it as payment from a mustachioed noble for a particularly difficult reanimation.

"No." the ferryman bluntly replied. "Silver coin. No other currency will be accepted."

Eld frowned.

Silver instead of gold?

He'd never heard of such a thing. He fumbled at his purse for a bit, but then Talbot raised his hand and croaked.

"I can pay for you," he said. "I like silver…second place is better than first, as far I'm concerned. Less attention on me."

Talbot handed the ferryman four coins.

The creature in the cowl grinned again.

"Thank you for your patronage."

Then he headed off without another word.

As Eld gazed out across the misty expanse, he caught fleeting glimpses of the academy's grandeur. Towering spires and flying buttresses loomed in the distance, their details obscured by the swirling fog.

"Quite a sight, isn't it?" Grimthorpe said.

Eld started briefly.

Grimthorpe hadn't boarded the boat with them. He'd appeared beside Eld and Talbot as if he'd teleported. "The boats are a new addition this year. We used to have the students swim across the Lake of Lamentation, but the paperwork for replacing those lost to the depths became rather tiresome."

Eld couldn't tell if the professor was joking.

Shuck pressed against Eld's leg, a cold, solid presence amidst the ethereal surroundings.

The bone-crafted boat was propelled off the dock. For a while, the boat glided silently through the thick mist that blanketed the dark waters. It was a long time before the ferryman needed to row.

"Pretty sweet gig," the ferryman said.

Eld just nodded nervously as he stared at the mist-covered castle in the distance.

Somehow, the obscured view of the school made it more ominous and more exciting at the same time. On the other side of this misty shroud was knowledge, adventure, and no small amount of danger.

As they neared the far shore, Eld noticed something strange in the sky.

The black sun again, but this time, within its eerie light, a face materialized—a hauntingly beautiful woman with pale skin, vibrant purple eyes, and flowing black hair adorned with a delicate gossamer-like crown whose silver strands resembled cobwebs.

Her gaze seemed to pierce right through him, but when Eld blinked, both the vision and the dark sun vanished, leaving only a swirling mist.

"Did you see that?" he asked Talbot, who had managed to find a comfortable slouching position against the side of the boat, seemingly unperturbed by the damp and gloom.

"See what?" Talbot yawned, his skeletal jaw creaking. "I find it's best not to look too closely at anything around here. Ignorance is bliss, and all that."

Eld frowned, certain that something was happening.

The black sun iconography had existed since childhood back at the family manor, but seeing strange symbols in the sky was a very different story.

As the boat bumped gently against the academy's dock, Eld steeled himself. Whatever challenges lay ahead—be they academic, magical, or tied to his family's mysterious plans—he would face them head-on.

"Well, here we are," Eld said, more to himself than anyone else. "Let's hope I can navigate the education better than I navigated the journey here."

Chapter 4

Bathurst Academy of
Post-Mortem Studies and Practices

Eld awkwardly stepped onto the shore, his feet sinking slightly into the damp earth.

He would have preferred a more elegant entry to Bathurst Academy, but moving from a rickety boat of bones into a damp swamp-like morass was nobody's idea of gentle terrain.

Shuck bounded onto shore, then eagerly himself, sending droplets of water flying haphazardly this way and that. As always, Franky and Bart were safe—and most importantly in this case, dry—hiding in their spot in Eld's coat.

Meanwhile, Talbot slouched his way off the boat with an exaggerated groan, only leaving the boat right when it was about to return to shore.

"Ugh…" Talbot groaned. "I hate this route."

Eld thought back to what Vex had said about the "ghost haunting the first year." From the sounds of it, Talbot had been here before.

"You're returning to the school, right?" Eld asked.

"For the umpteenth time…" Talbot groaned back. "The farthest I've made it in my first year is the second midterm…what's the deal with that? A *second* midterm? I've never heard of two middles…but still…while I'd like to graduate, I am more determined not to get kicked out of school entirely…for better or worse, Bathurst is my home! At school, my family isn't around to tell me to study harder!"

Eld smiled.

Talbot was such a breath of fresh air compared to his family. The poltergeist wasn't driven in the slightest.

The winding cobblestone path snaked its way up a steep incline, disappearing yet again into the swirling fog.

"There seems to be a lot of fog here," Eld observed.

"One of Grimthorpe's spells," Talbot replied. "It completely shrouds the area. It's *supposed* to render us undetectable to humans…but it mostly just makes me bump into stuff. I've never been particularly graceful, but in my first year at Bathurst, I set a new record for falling on my face."

As they began their ascent, the mist gradually thinned, revealing glimpses of Eld's new home.

Spires spiraled towards the sky; their peaks lost in low-hanging black storm clouds.

Flying archways twisted like the ribs of some great beast, supporting walls of dark stone veined with luminescent lichen. Menacing gargoyles carved out of oily black stone perched at every corner, their eyes seeming to follow the students as they approached.

At the peak of the hill, the path opened onto a vast courtyard, dominated by a fountain whose central figure was a robed skeleton, water pouring from its empty eye sockets like an endless stream of mournful tears.

Surrounding the courtyard, the academy's various wings stretched out like the tentacles of a deep-sea squid, each one a labyrinth of towers, balconies, and stained-glass windows.

At the top of a grand staircase stood Professor Grimthorpe, framed by the academy's massive double doors. Each door was easily twenty feet tall, carved from ancient oak and inlaid with macabre motifs that danced in the flickering witchlights.

Eld blinked in surprise.

Grimthorpe had been right next to him on the boat. And yet, he was now standing before the school doors like he'd been there all along. In terms of raw magical power, Grimthorpe wasn't quite as powerful as Eldritch Sr., but the wily old lich had a veritable library of handy utility spells.

"Welcome, students, to Bathurst Academy of Post-Mortem Studies and Practices," Grimthorpe's voice boomed across the courtyard. "You stand now at the threshold of a new chapter in your lives…or, in many cases, unlives. Behind these doors lie secrets of the underworld that have been guarded for millennia."

An excited murmur rippled through the crowd of students, but Grimthorpe promptly raised a hand for silence.

"Now, onto practical matters. You'll be choosing your dormitories and roommates shortly. Those of you who have already declared your fields will find your class schedules delivered to your rooms tonight. For the undecided among you, Professor Morticia Hemlock will be available to discuss your options."

At the mention of Professor Hemlock, a woman detached herself from the shadows beside the door. She was tall and elegantly cadaverous, with skin as pale as moonlight and eyes that held a predatory hunger.

As she landed in front of the students, Hemlock smiled widely, revealing a pair of glistening white hooked fangs. A black lace parasol shielded her from the weak light filtering through the clouds.

She was a vampire, but Eld had seen her sort before.

He was much more concerned with the housing situation. He did *not* want to end up with some random asshole.

Eld leaned towards Talbot. "Hey, want to be roommates?" he whispered.

Talbot's eternal grin seemed to widen slightly. "Eh, why not? Saves me the effort of finding someone else."

Grimthorpe continued, "Now, regarding the rules of—"

He was interrupted by the arrival of a hulking man—a man easily seven feet tall, with gray-green skin and mismatched limbs stitched together with thick, black thread.

The stitched zombie lumbered up to the professor and whispered something in his ear.

Grimthorpe's brow furrowed. "I see. My apologies, students, but I'm needed elsewhere. Professor Hemlock will take it from here."

As Grimthorpe hurried off, Professor Hemlock glided forward, her parasol casting deep shadows across her face.

"Listen closely, fledglings, for I'll not repeat myself," she said, her voice as smooth and cold as a tomb slab. "The rules here are simple, yet vital. First, no fighting outside of sanctioned areas. If you feel the need to test your mettle, join the Nocturnal Combat Club."

A few students perked up at this, including a burly troll with pimply green skin who cracked his knuckles eagerly.

"Second, and I can't believe I have to say this every year, no eating other students. You'd be surprised how often it happens."

Eld noticed a few sheepish looks exchanged among some of the more ghoulish students. One of them had been observing Hemlock herself with a dazed drooling expression on his face.

"Third, while you're welcome to explore the academy, certain areas are strictly off-limits. Believe me, you'll *know* them when you see them. The consequences for trespassing are...unpleasant."

Her gaze swept across the crowd, lingering on Eld.

He felt a chill run down his spine.

Had she already singled him out as a troublemaker?

Or was this just his guilty conscious?

"This year, the Splintered Dimension has been added to the list of restricted areas."

A very concerned rumble passed among the students.

Eld turned to Talbot and raised an eyebrow. "Sounds like an unpopular decision."

To his surprise, the typically grinning poltergeist looked just as angry as the rest of them.

"Oh, come on!" Talbot groaned. "Taking away the Splintered Dimension? From *me?* That's like stealing brains off a zombie!"

"What exactly is the Splintered Dimension?" Eld asked.

"It's a crack in reality that drifts through the school's underbelly," Talbot explained. "Leads off to a set of private rooms. According to the other students, they are great for studying, but I mostly used them for mid-day naps. Nothing better than stumbling into the Splintered Dimension when you're too lazy to make it back to your room."

As if on cue, Hemlock picked that moment to cut through the crowd.

"The headmaster's decision on the Splintered Dimension is final. You will find other places to study, I'm sure. Just make sure you attend your classes and do not slack off."

Here, she fixed Talbot with a stare as pointed as her fangs. He somehow managed to slouch even further under her gaze.

"Follow these rules, apply yourselves, and you'll do fine here. "Now, off you go," she said, dismissing them with a wave of her hand. "Your belongings have already been transported to the dormitories."

At Hemlock's words, the massive doors swung open, revealing a cavernous entrance hall that seemed to defy the laws of physics and good taste in equal measure.

The entrance to Bathurst had been crafted to look just like a bat's maw. The unfortunate fangs sticking out of the ground meant that every so often, a student would trip and fall right as they were walking into the halls.

"Let's hope the graduation walkway is a little lower difficulty," Eld remarked.

"I'm just hoping I can *see* the graduation walkway one day," Talbot replied.

As the students filed in, their excited chatter echoed off the impossibly high vaulted ceiling, which displayed an ever-shifting canvas of constellations and nebulae.

Eld and Talbot made their way inside, Shuck trotting at their heels, his paws leaving ectoplasmic pawprints that faded after a few seconds. Chandeliers crafted from bones cast an ever-changing light over the space. The constantly shifting shadows resembled nothing more than a demented puppet show.

Off to one side, a bubbling fountain spewed a strange shimmering liquid that couldn't quite decide if it was water, blood, or liquid starlight. Small, ghostly fish swam through the air around it, occasionally diving into the fountain only to leap out again, trailing sparkles of ectoplasm.

A series of doors and archways led off in different directions, some spiraling up into high towers that seemed to pierce the very fabric of reality, others descending into what looked like catacombs that echoed with distant, ethereal music.

In one corner, a massive grandfather clock tolled the hour, its face showing not just the time but also the phases of the moon, the alignment of the planets, and the current existential mood of the universe. With each chime, small skeleton figurines emerged to perform a macabre dance before retreating into the clockwork.

Eld stood, taking in the overwhelming spectacle. Even Talbot seemed momentarily roused from his perpetual lethargy, his jaw hanging slightly more agape than usual. Shuck, for his part, couldn't decide whether to bark at the moving statues or chase the ghostly fish.

Everything looked wonderful, but there was just one problem…

Eld had no idea where he should go.

It seemed like the other students had the exact same issue.

Eld watched with amusement as another new student—a particularly hairy man who he thought might be a werewolf—unsuccessfully consulted some shimmering runes for directions.

"Do you know how to find the Zombie Zone?" the werewolf asked.

The rune replied with a shriek of high-pitched clicks and whistles. Though Eld couldn't recognize the language, the tone of sarcasm and mockery was universal.

"Don't listen to the runes…" Talbot chuckled. "Rookie mistake."

He pointed at the corner of the room, where faint wisps of colored smoke formed arrows pointing to various parts of the academy.

"Those arrows are the most reliable source of information," Talbot whispered. "If you look close, you'll see that there are signs inscribed in the smoke."

Eld walked to the corner of the hall, glad that he had a veteran with him.

Indeed, when he closely observed the smoke, he realized that each of the arrows portrayed images of various dormitories, each more outlandish than the last.

Cryptkeeper's Corner, accessible only by crawling through a coffin, Banshee's Belfry, where the walls wailed softly, Lich's Lair, surrounded by a moat of liquid shadow, and the aforementioned Zombie Zone, with a sign warning of occasional limb-loss hazards.

"So," Eld said, turning to Talbot, "any preference on where we end up?"

Talbot shrugged, a gesture that involved more rattling than Eld was entirely comfortable with. "Somewhere on the ground floor, preferably. Stairs are such a bother."

That seemed to be Talbot's only real request, so it was up to Eld to make the final decision.

The pair eventually found themselves in a corridor labeled Revenant's Rest. Their room was at the far end, a heavy iron-bound door with their names somehow already inscribed on a tarnished brass plaque.

The room itself was surprisingly spacious, with high ceilings and large, arched windows that looked out over a misty graveyard. Two four-poster beds stood against opposite walls, their curtains a deep, midnight blue. A pair of desks, a bookshelf already stocked with grimoires, and a large wardrobe completed the furnishings.

"Not bad," Eld mused, running a hand along the bedpost. "Bit gloomy, but I suppose that's to be expected."

Talbot had already flopped onto one of the beds, sinking into the mattress. "Wake me when it's time for graduation."

Eld was about to reply when a sharp knock at the door made him jump.

He opened it to find a small creature standing in the hallway. The goblin—for that's what it appeared to be—wore a neat little butler's outfit and bore an expression of utmost seriousness.

"Eldritch Blackwood Jr.?" the goblin inquired, his voice surprisingly deep for his size.

"That's me," Eld confirmed.

"Professor Hemlock requests your presence in her office immediately to discuss your major." The goblin handed Eld two small, black envelopes. "The location is detailed within. Do not be late. When you're done send up Mr. Wilting." With that, he turned on his heel and scurried off down the hallway.

Eld looked at the envelope in his hand, then back at Talbot, who had somehow already fallen asleep. Shuck whined softly, sensing Eld's unease.

He walked over to Talbot's bed, and placed the black envelope on Talbot's nightstand, propping it against a small, grinning skull that served as a paperweight.

"Hey, Talbot," Eld said, knowing full well he probably wouldn't get a response, "I've got to go see Professor Hemlock. There's an envelope here for you too. Might want to check it when you wake up..."

Talbot's only response was a soft rattling snore.

Eld raised an eyebrow.

"*If* you ever wake up…"

He walked off, but out of the corner of his eye, he saw Talbot's mouth twitch upwards.

Eld opened his envelope, read the handwriting within, and set off to meet Professor Hemlock. The path to Professor Hemlock's office led him through a series of increasingly bizarre corridors. He passed a classroom where students were practicing levitating skulls, followed by a classroom where every student *was* a levitating skull.

Next, he passed a great glass laboratory filled with bubbling cauldrons of questionable contents next to a sprawling greenhouse growing plants with far too many teeth.

Finally, he arrived at a door made of polished obsidian. A plaque read, *Professor Morticia Hemlock—Head of Hemocraft and Career Guidance.*

Eld took a deep breath and knocked.

From what he could gather, Hemlock seemed like the prim and proper type. It'd be best to do the same if he wanted to get on her good side.

"Enter," came a silky voice from within.

Eld pushed open the door to find himself in a circular room lined with bookshelves. Arcane instruments cluttered every available surface. Eld saw a glowing compass that seemed to measure the distance to various stars beside a small horn carved out of burnt red copper.

On the center desk was a large crystal ball filled with endlessly swirling mist.

Curious about his fortune, Eld stared directly into it and saw an image of a young man surrounded by three animals, a rat, a centipede, and a dog.

He groaned.

"Franky! Bart! Get back inside the coat!"

The creatures ignored him, chittering happily at Professor Hemlock. She stood by the window, her back turned to them, but upon hearing the animals, she whirled around, her eyes fixed on Eld's companions.

"Young Blackwood," she said, turning to face him. In private company, Professor Hemlock's voice remained just as cold and distant as it sounded in public. "Do sit down. We have much to discuss about your future here at Bathurst."

Eld gingerly took a seat in a high-backed chair. "Professor, I'm not sure why I was called here. I thought I had already chosen my field in Necromancy."

Hemlock's lips curled into a small smile. "Did you now? And yet, your application speaks of a fascination with reanimating small animals. Hardly the focus of a true necromancer, wouldn't you agree?"

As she spoke, she again glanced pointedly at Eld's pets.

Franky and Bart, belatedly realizing they were in the presence of yet another critic, scampered back into Eld's coat.

Shuck simply hid beneath the chair, pressing his body flat against the ground.

Eld felt his face grow hot. "With all due respect, Professor, I believe there's value in—"

"In what?" Hemlock interrupted, her voice sharp. "In creating undead pets? In squandering the noble art of necromancy on tricks?" She leaned forward, her gaze intense. "Tell me, Eldritch Blackwood Jr., what do you truly want to achieve here?"

Eld swallowed hard, his mind racing.

He thought of his father's disapproval, of Cloudehill's sneering skeletal face, of the mysterious black sun he had glimpsed.

But he also thought of Shuck's loyalty, of the joy on that little girl's face when he had revived her cat. He thought of what he'd seen in the Blackwood family crypt and the power he'd glimpsed as a child, tucked away in the Familial Tome.

"I want to understand death," he said slowly, "But not just as an end. I want to explore the boundaries between life and death, to find new ways of preserving the essence of what makes us...us."

Hemlock studied him for a long moment, her expression unreadable.

Then, to Eld's surprise, she laughed. It was a sound like crystal breaking, beautiful yet slightly unnerving.

As the sound of her joyous laughter, the room came alive.

A swarm of mosquitos burst from Hemlock's desk, gently surrounding her. Most people would have been terrified by the swarm of disease-carrying creatures, but Hemlock's confident smile revealed her deep familiarity with them. A veritable colony of bats revealed themselves, all hanging down from the ceiling.

Strangest of all, Eld heard whispering and chittering spirits calling to him from every corner of the room. Unlike his familiars, these spirits weren't reanimated zombies. Instead, it seemed like they were additional friends and companions that Hemlock could temporarily call from the afterlife with some kind of animal séance technique—a level of necromantic mastery that surpassed Eld's own.

Eld's eyes widened. "You…"

"Yes," Hemlock replied, smiling. "There *is* room for familiars in the dark arts, so long as you treat them with proper understanding. Perhaps there's hope for you yet, young Blackwood. Very well, we'll keep you in Necromancy for now. But I'll be watching your progress closely." She handed him a sealed envelope and motioned for the door.

Eld nodded. "Thank you, Professor. I won't let you down."

As he stood to leave, Hemlock spoke again. "One more thing, Mr. Blackwood. Keep your eyes open in this place. Bathurst holds many secrets, and not all of them are found in textbooks. You might find that your…unique perspective…opens doors others cannot see."

With those cryptic words ringing in his ears, Eld left the office. As he made his way back to his room, he couldn't shake the feeling that he had just passed some sort of test—and that many more lay ahead.

When he finally returned to his dorm, he found Talbot exactly where he had left him, still seemingly fast asleep. Shuck bounded up to greet him.

Eld approached Talbot's bed and gently shook his skeletal roommate. "Hey, Talbot, wake up. You need to go see Professor Hemlock to pick your field of study."

Talbot's eye sockets flickered open, a faint glow emanating from within. He yawned, his jaw creaking ominously. "Ugh, must I? What a bother. I've already failed out of half of them…at this point, I feel like I'm learning new words when I pick a new field of study. What did you choose?"

"Necromancy," Eld replied, still not entirely sure if it was the right decision.

Talbot shrugged, his bones rattling softly. "Eh, sounds good enough. I'll do that too, then. Saves me the trouble of thinking about it. Perhaps, with your help, I'll be able to reanimate my academic career! At this point, I suspect that a mere resuscitation won't do it…well, ta-ta now…"

With a lazy wave of his hand, Talbot began to shimmer and fade. He lifted off the bed, hovering a few inches above the mattress.

"See you later," Talbot drawled, and then, to Eld's astonishment, he simply floated upwards and phased through the ceiling, leaving behind only a faint trace of spectral energy.

Eld stared at the spot where Talbot had disappeared, his mouth agape. "Well, I guess that's one way to avoid the stairs."

"It is, I suppose…" Talbot said.

Eld jumped, the voice surprising him.

"I thought you left!" Eld said.

"Yeah, I thought you so too," Talbot said. "But then I saw something interesting."

His head had suddenly popped back out from the wall, lazily staring down at Eld. The rest of Talbot's body was still on the other side, so he simply looked like a disembodied head—judging by his expression, a head that was too lazy to go back to his body.

"Hey, Eld…what did you say your last name was again?"

"Blackwood," Eld replied.

"Huh," Talbot replied. "On the other side of the wall, there's this huge carving…just line after line after line of boasting…sounds like the braggart of the century. The name's Eldritch Blackwood, you know him? Sounds like a relative."

Eld's eyebrow twitched.

"I probably do…" Eld said. "What does the carving say?"

"It's just this huge speech. He starts every sentence with 'I, the soon-to-be-great and soon-to-be mighty Eldritch Blackwood. Says he's going to become the greatest lich in history, and that he'll raise sons who become great liches as well—but only the second greatest in history, after him."

Eld bit back a laugh.

"Yeah. I know the guy."

Talbot shook his head.

"Sounds like a pain in the ass, if you don't mind me saying…I'm feeling the pain even with a translucent ass. Anyway, good luck. Hope we get a lot of classes together…and that Professor Hemlock doesn't just bite my head off."

Talbot's head vanished through the wall, hopefully joining the rest of his body.

After he left, Eld groaned and shook his head.

A diatribe by his father, carved on the other side of the wall.

Talk about a bad omen.

Perhaps his father had chosen to live in Revenant's Rest too.

Having finally arrived, all Eld needed was a long night's sleep to get ready for the next day of school…

But the very thought of sleep irritated him.

Having achieved lichdom, neither Eldritch Sr. nor Cloudehill needed to sleep anymore.

Bart popped out of his coat, giving Eld a concerned look.

"I'm fine Bart…it's just that being haunted by the scepter of your overbearing father…while said overbearing father is still alive…really isn't where you want to be."

Chapter 5

Day One Encounter

The corridors of Bathurst Academy twisted and turned like the intestines of some great, architectural beast…a beast that was suffering from some serious digestive problems.

The hallways rattled with loud mechanical cranks as they rearranged themselves at will. Every so often, Eld and Talbot found themselves back in the corners, consulting the arrows of smoke to intuit their path. Unfortunately, it seemed like the smoky omens sometimes didn't bother keeping up with the corridor's unpredictable moments, forcing the duo to rely on Talbot's shakily remembered past experience.

The passageways teemed with a diverse array of students. Though Grimthorpe himself was a lich, he welcomed every sort of nightkin to the academy.

Vampires glided by, their skin pallid under the academy's mystical illumination, while werewolves loped along, some of the particularly hairy ones already sporting tufts of fur despite the absence of a full moon.

Succubi and incubi sauntered past, leaving trails of shimmering pheromones in their wake, and translucent ghosts drifted through walls and fellow students alike.

"Quite the menagerie," Eld said to Talbot, watching a group of wraiths float by, their hair writhing like pale serpents.

"You're one to talk," Talbot replied.

As if on cue, Franky and Bart stuck their heads out of Eld's coat. Shuck was just around the corner, sniffing around his new surroundings but always ready to return to his friend and owner.

"Still, the sheer diversity of the students has definitely piqued my curiosity," Eld said. An elderly man with long white hair hurried by, and Eld raised an eyebrow. "Wait. Wasn't that a human?"

Talbot nodded lazily. "Nightkin make up a good chunk of the student body. Bathurst is one of the few places that cater to their unique needs. But the rest of them are people who want to rise again after death."

Eld nodded.

The Blackwood family were all initially humans. They'd only achieved unlife through their mastery of necromancy. The same went for other groups of nightkin like ghosts, zombies, vampires, or werewolves.

It made sense that some students attended Bathurst to achieve these powers in the first place. After all, it wasn't like Familial Necromancy Tomes were lying around for random people to pick up.

Every so often, Eld caught faint whispers between the students.

It seemed like most of the buzz was about the Midnight Exhumation—an upcoming campus event that all students in the Necromancy Major were supposed to take part in.

"What's that?" Eld asked.

"Oh, we all go out to the graveyard on the school grounds and start digging…you know, if enrollment ever dwindles, they want somehow to get new students. Bottom lines and all that."

"Seriously?" Eld asked.

"Nah," Talbot chuckled. "It's more just to find body parts that can be used for stitching and reanimation practice. So still the school cheaping out and making us do extra work, but slightly less so, I suppose."

On their way to class, Eld and Talbot passed doors of every conceivable material that whispered to them as they passed.

A strange translucent door made of tightly compressed shadows hissed at them as they passed by.

"Enter the Room of Endless Mystery, and discover secrets about your family that will tear them apart at the seams…"

Eld raised an eyebrow.

"Don't think I need any extra help for that."

A door made of two bleached white trees that were slowly growing into each other—their branches shearing through the other's bark—whispered in two discordant tones, one male and one female.

"Enter the Corridor of Cursed Desires, and find love at the cost of your ambition."

"Oh, that sounds good," Talbot said.

Before Eld could warn him, Talbot swirled towards the trees…only to cry out in surprise as an invisible barrier bounced him back to Eld.

"What was *that?*" Talbot groaned. "I've never seen something I couldn't phase through before."

"You lack ambition," the trees declare. "You have nothing to give us. You shall not pass."

Talbot frowned, then he shrugged.

"Oh, okay, whatever then. I thought it was worth a shot. But I guess it's the bachelor's life for me…"

The next door, which was made of wrought jet black iron with a giant padlock on it, simply said.

"Do *not* bother Professor McGrath."

"Some doors promise great knowledge and others offer simple warnings," Eld remarked. "I've heard those stories before."

The two continued on their way.

A vampire student hissed in discomfort as he passed through a patch of hallway illuminated by a shaft of light from a mischievous enchanted window, his skin smoking slightly before he darted back into the shadows.

The most interesting nightkin Eld found was a pale-skinned female ghost with tangled black hair who seemed to live inside a large wooden box with a transparent screen on it, almost like she was some kind of hermit crab.

Every so often, sparks would fly across the window, and the woman would twist and turn, hissing angrily. Not only that, it seemed like she couldn't move outside of the box.

Her friend, a gorgon with scaly skin, was carrying her through the halls.

"What is she?" Eld asked.

"Oh. She's a ghost who lives in that piece of Old One technology. I think those boxes are called…TBs…no, perhaps…TDs?" Talbot's voice trailed off in confusion, then he shrugged.

"Ah, well, I'm sure you'll find out. I believe that material is covered in the second Human Studies midterm. Never quite made it that far in that class."

Eld eyed the lady in the box.

"She seems unhappy," Eld said.

"Oh, I'm sure she is," Talbot replied. "Not too many people know how to maintain Old One technology anymore…so I think that the box she's stuck in is probably deteriorating. We poltergeists can inhabit objects as well…though luckily, we can pick anything we want."

"Any reason you haven't picked one yet?" Eld asked.

Glancing at that woman on the screen, it seemed like Talbot would love nothing more than having someone to carry him around.

"Oh, just choosing itself can be a chore," Talbot replied.

Eld shook his head, then frowned, staring at the nearby wall.

"Wait a second…I swear we've passed that gargoyle three times now," Eld muttered, eyeing a stone creature that seemed to leer at them as they walked by.

"Nonsense," the gargoyle replied in a gravelly voice, startling both of them. "I'm headed to Advanced Stoneflesh Transmutation and it's somewhere in this blasted wing." The stone creature stretched its wings, shaking off a bit of dust. "Name's Grigori, by the way. Third-year."

Eld blinked in surprise. "You're a student?"

Grigori's granite features shifted into what might have been a grin. "What, you thought gargoyles were just for decoration? We're as keen to learn the dark arts as any nightkin. We can just get paid through the student-work program by standing guard. It can get cold during the winter…but the reduced tuition is sorely appreciated."

He hopped down from his perch, his claws clicking on the stone floor. "You two look lost. First years?"

Talbot yawned. "In a manner of speaking."

Grigori stared at him, then just shrugged. "What class are you looking for?" he asked.

"Fundamentals of Flesh Manipulation," Eld replied.

Grigori nodded. "Ah, with old Cadaver. You're close. Two more lefts, then a right, three more lefts, and then a final right. Watch out for the trick step that likes to swallow first-years whole, you'll end up in the catacombs if you're not careful, and from there…well, you'll be lucky if you make it out by winter quarter."

With that, Grigori left…

And the path grew more complicated before their very eyes.

Just two turns later, Eld felt like they were lost again.

"I'm not sure we're going the right way. I think we should have made a left back there instead of a right."

"Hang on," Talbot said. "Look at the back of the schedule. There should be a map there."

Eld flipped his schedule around, then raised an eyebrow.

"It seems to be drawn out of blood."

"Well, Hemlock is a hemomancer. Of course, she'd used her skills."

Eld raised the map. "The blood is shifting."

Floating lazily beside him, Talbot shrugged. "Does it matter? We'll end up somewhere eventually."

"We're supposed to be in class in five minutes," Eld sighed, trying to make sense of their surroundings. A nearby suit of armor turned its helmet to watch them pass, the empty visor somehow managing to convey judgmental amusement.

Eld took another look at the map.

At this point, the blood looked like it was about to just drip right off.

"I've about had it with these magical maps…" he groaned. "At this point, how about something nice and simple, that doesn't move…"

They reached another turn, and Eld sighed.

"What was it Grigori said again? Left? Right? Then right again? What was…"

The sound of mocking laughter abruptly sliced through Eld's musings.

"What's that?" he wondered, hurrying forward.

Ahead, a group of students had gathered in a room built to look like a yawning cavern. The outer entrance was decorated by a pair of grim reaper statues, who stood there proudly with their hands on wickedly curved scythes.

The cave itself was filled with seemingly innocent stalagmites and stalactites., but every so often, Eld caught brief glimpses of staring red eyes, lurking tendrils, and mouths filled with razor-sharp teeth.

But despite their hideous appearance, the strange disguised cave formations weren't the problem.

At the center of the commotion stood a tall, ash-skinned young man with eyes like smoldering coals—Mortimer Vex.

"Come on, banshee," Mortimer sneered, his voice dripping with contempt. "Let's hear that famous scream of yours. That's all your kind is good for, isn't it? Just screaming all the time?"

The target of Mortimer's torment was a striking young woman with alabaster skin and flowing silver hair that drooped down to the floor, pooling beneath her lacy black dress. Her eyes, a piercing crimson, flashed with anger as she faced down Mortimer.

"Back off, Vex," she hissed, her voice echoing back on itself. "I'm not here for your amusement."

Mortimer's gang laughed crudely.

The arrogant aristocrat had three henchmen in total.

The first was a strange roughly humanoid zombie with countless shades of muscle hastily stitched onto his arms. He had a crude and rather stupid-looking expression on his face, and he was absolutely drenched in stinking salt water. The water dripped from his clothes as he moved, forming a small pool at his feet.

The second was some kind of strange specter made of fizzling ectoplasm. He shimmered and wavered, occasionally fading out of existence before reappearing again. The specter had a bored and aristocratic expression on his face. Even existence itself wasn't good enough for him.

The last gang member was a vampire with a particularly absurd get-up. He wore a black aristocratic uniform with countless accouterments, each of them more absurd than the last.

Blood red thread, designed to look like dripping blood, decorated every inch of his body, and his lengthy blood-red cape was fastened by a pair of pauldrons shaped to look like bats. He even had random medals pinned on his chest.

Eld started reading them but only got to three before he rolled his eyes and gave up.

Fourth Best Bloodsucker.

Third Biggest Castle.

Vampire Games Participant.

Nobody was meant to wear such a heavy uniform. Thanks to the countless medals pulling his body forward, the vampire was almost a hunchback, and every so often, he'd trip over his cape before hastily throwing it back and striking an aristocratic pose.

"These all look like real charmers…" Eld muttered.

"Oh, the school has been tormented by them for a while now. They are all third-years. The waterlogged zombie leaving puddles everywhere is Erik the Drowned. Thinks he's Bathurst's star athlete," Talbot drawled. "The transparent one is Hallo, a particularly annoying specter, and the vampire tripping over his cape is Vlad."

Vlad was a very traditional name for vampires. It seemed like every third one Eld met was called that, though recently, Drake had also been rising in popularity.

"Back off!" the banshee shrieked. "I'm warning you!"

"Oh, looks like we've upset her," Vlad chuckled, his fangs glinting. "Careful, Mort, or she might cry."

Erik grunted in agreement, water gurgling in his throat. "Yeah, wouldn't want to make the little banshee all wet. That's my job." He laughed at his own joke, spraying droplets of murky water.

Eld felt a surge of anger. Growing up with Cloudehill had ingrained in him a lifelong hatred of bullies.

Without thinking, he stepped forward. "Hey! Leave her alone!"

All eyes turned to him. Mortimer's expression shifted from surprise to amusement. "Well, well. If it isn't the pet doctor. Come to defend this banshee reject?"

Talbot groaned. "Eld, what are you doing? We're going to be late for class."

"Oh, now he's concerned with being late," Eld dismissively thought.

"I said back off," Eld replied, standing his ground. "Don't you have anything better to do? Show some maturity! We've all got to be over a hundred here…did you guys suspend your maturity when you suspended your aging?"

"I mean…this is a school…" Erik the Drowned slowly replied.

"Well, *you* don't seem like you've been learning very much," Eld retorted. He jerked his head at Erik's hastily stitched-on muscles. "What are *those* things? Not even the Master of Freaks would come up with something like that. It looks like you took *bodybuilding* a bit too literally."

Mortimer's eyes narrowed. "You've got a big mouth for someone who plays with dead animals. Why don't you run along before you get hurt?"

Eld was outnumbered and outmatched, but he couldn't just walk away.

The problem was that they were badly outnumbered, and looking at Erik, even more badly outmuscled. His pets wouldn't be enough. If they fought with him, they'd just get hurt too.

He needed a different strategy…

Eld's eyes darted between Talbot and the grim reaper statues flanking the wall, and a sudden idea formed.

"Talbot," Eld whispered, "Remember how we were talking about possessing objects? That statue over there. Think you can work your poltergeist magic on it?"

Talbot followed Eld's gaze to the grim reaper statue, its scythe held at the ready. He sighed, flickering slightly. "Ugh, fine. But you owe me a week's worth of homework for this corporeal nonsense."

As Talbot drifted towards the statue, Eld turned back to Mortimer. "Last chance, Vex. Walk away now."

Mortimer was far too arrogant to notice what Talbot was doing. Of course, Eld has expected that—after all, the man had disdainfully referred to the poltergeist as the ghost haunting the first year.

In Mortimer's mind, Talbot could never hurt a big bad third-year like himself…

"What are you going to do?" Mortimer scoffed. "Sic your undead poodle on me? If you do, you'll have to revive that mutt once again!"

Behind Eld, the statue began to move, its stone eyes shining with an eerie light.

Eld allowed himself a small smile. "Something like that."

The reaper flew towards Mortimer's gang, who wheeled back, cursing in terror.

But just as the statue raised its scythe, Talbot's voice echoed from within. "Nope, too much effort. I'm out."

The glow faded, and the statue slowly began flying back to its original position.

Eld's smile faltered. "Uh, Talbot?"

"Sorry, friend," Talbot's disembodied voice yawned. "Possession's more taxing than I remembered. You're on your own."

Mortimer's grin widened. "Looks like your backup plan just went up in smoke. Speaking of which…" He snapped his fingers and suddenly his entire body erupted into flames. The fire danced across his skin, leaving him unharmed but radiating heat. "Let me show you what real power looks like.

Eld raised his hands to fight, but he knew he couldn't beat the pyromancer in a magical duel. For obvious reasons, the flame manipulators were widely feared among the nightkin. Eld's eyes frantically darted from side to side, searching for a way out of this mess.

But before Mortimer could advance, the banshee girl stepped between them.

"That's enough," she announced, slapping her hands onto her hips. "You want a scream, Vex? I'll give you a scream—a real one."

She took a deep breath and Eld had just enough time to clap his hands over his ears before the courtyard was filled with an ear-shattering wail.

The sound was like nothing Eld had ever heard before—a keening cry that pierced through dimensions. The wail seemed to distort the air itself, bending light and warping sound in its wake.

Bits and pieces of stone began crumbling from the ceiling and even the lurking cave monsters gave up on disguising themselves, throwing their tentacles up to clog off their ears.

Mortimer's flames were snuffed out as if doused by an invisible bucket of water. He and his gang of undead brutes staggered back, their hands pressed desperately against their ears.

When the scream finally subsided, leaving a ringing silence in its wake, Mortimer and his friends were already fleeing, their bravado replaced by genuine fear.

Eld lowered his hands, his ears still ringing. "That was impressive," he shouted, barely able to hear his own voice.

The banshee girl turned to him, wincing as she grabbed her throat. "Thanks," she replied, her voice faint and raspy. "I don't like using it very much…it hurts like hell for hours after."

She coughed awkwardly, her whole body jolted and her long silver hair waved chaotically. After a brief fit, the banshee shook her head and flashed a polite and perfunctory smile. "Thanks for stepping in, by the way, even if your backup plan was a *bit* underwhelming."

Talbot materialized beside them, looking as nonchalant as before. "Hey, I showed up. That's more effort than I usually put into anything."

The woman turned to Talbot, her expression remaining disdainfully neutral. "Lilith Nightshade," she said, extending a hand to Eld. Her voice was cool and matter-of-fact. "Banshee-in-training and apparently now the defender of well-meaning idiots."

Eld took her hand, noting how cold her skin felt. "Eld Blackwood. Lich-in-training."

"Talbot Wilting," Talbot drawled. "Perpetually exhausted and wondering why we're still standing around when we could be comfortably seated in class."

Lilith let out an exasperated sigh. "Class. We're going to be late. What do you two have first?"

"Fundamentals of Flesh Manipulation," Eld replied.

"With Professor Cadaver?" Lilith asked. When they nodded, she stated flatly, "Same. I know a more efficient route."

Without waiting for a response, she led them down a series of increasingly narrow corridors, finally stopping in front of a blank wall.

"Open mandrake!" Lilith declared.

With a precise wave of her hand, the stones rearranged themselves, forming an archway that opened into their classroom.

"Woah…" Eld muttered—partially because of Lilith's shortcut, but mostly because of the classroom.

There was more knowledge here than he ever could have imagined.

Unfortunately, almost all of it was related to humanoid reanimation. To get what he was looking for, he still needed the Familial Tome.

But that wasn't too bad.

Based on what had just happened before coming to class, Eld had a feeling that he might have to up his necromantic knowledge, just in case there were any unpleasant accidents on the horizon.

The room beyond was a macabre artist's dream.

Anatomy charts covered the walls, but these were no ordinary diagrams. The ink had been enchanted through magical means so the charts resembled vivisections. The muscles and organs squirmed and pulsed as if still alive.

Jars of preserved specimens lined the shelves, their contents floating in murky liquids and occasionally twitching. A pair of eyes with pitch-black pupils swiveled about, briefly settling to stare right at Eld. At the center of the room stood a large stone slab, currently occupied by what appeared to be the corpse of a giant.

As the trio found seats, the professor emerged from a door at the back of the room. Professor Cadaver lived up to his name—his skin was a patchwork of different tones and textures and one of his eyes was noticeably larger and a different color than the other.

"Welcome, students, to Fundamentals of Flesh Manipulation," he said, his voice a gravelly rasp. "In this class, you will learn the delicate art of molding dead flesh to your will. But first…" He reached into his coat and pulled out a squirming rat. With a quick motion, he twisted its neck. "Who would like to attempt a basic reanimation? Usually, here at Bathurst, we start with small animals first."

Eld's hand shot up.

This was what he had come to Bathurst for, after all. As he approached the front of the class, he noticed Lilith watching him with keen, analytical interest.

Professor Cadaver handed him the rat's corpse. "Remember, it's not about brute spell work. You must coax the spark of unlife back into the flesh."

Eld took a deep breath, focusing on the lifeless body in his hands.

He closed his eyes, centering himself as he had done many times before. He began tracing arcane symbols in the air above the rat's body, his fingers leaving faint trails of energy.

His skilled fingers painted out the story of the rat's life—at least, what little he knew.

Held at Bathurst, likely for experimentation…

Freshly killed just moments ago by a snap to the neck…

If he had to guess, the soul likely hadn't even left the premises.

Eld reached out with his necromantic senses, feeling for the lingering traces of the rat's essence.

Moments later, his suspicions were confirmed. Eld felt a faint flicker of energy, like a guttering candle flame. Eld mentally grasped it, feeding it with his power.

The symbols completed, Eld gently placed his finger, sparking with magical power, at the rat's chest. He stroked the creature once—his touch filled with delicate care.

The rat's fur began to bristle as if caught in an unseen breeze. Eld could feel the energy building, coalescing around the small body in his hands. With a final gesture, he completed the ritual, willing the spark of unlife back into the flesh.

For a moment, nothing happened.

The class eyed him suspiciously, but Eld had already been through countless reanimations. He knew these things took a little bit more time than suspected.

Then with a sudden twitch, the rat's eyes snapped open. It wriggled in Eld's grasp, its movements jerky but unmistakably animated.

"Well done, Mr. Blackwood," Professor Cadaver nodded approvingly. "A promising start. Now, let's see if you can maintain that animation while altering its physical form. Perhaps elongate the tail?"

Eld hesitated. There were no other materials here. Just the rat.

"You mean, without stitching on new parts?" he asked.

"Correct," the Professor clarified, eyeing him curiously.

Eld frowned.

Sometimes, he would use makeshift parts if anything was missing, but he had never altered a reanimated body purely with necromantic energy before and wasn't sure how to proceed. Now that he thought of it, this was a clear hole in his necromantic knowledge.

Noting Eld's uncertainty, Professor Cadaver's expression softened. "Ah, I see this is new territory for you. Well, that's why you're all here, isn't it? Let's take a step back and discuss the principles of altering physical form in reanimated subjects."

As the professor began his lecture, Eld returned to his seat, relieved and eager to learn.

He listened intently, taking detailed notes as Cadaver explained the process of reshaping dead flesh. Despite the implications of creating a bigger and stronger reanimated zombie, the process was actually extremely delicate, especially compared to the more immediate power granted by stitching. Necromantic reshaping involved slowly coaxing the organs to grow and change with necromantic magic.

Professor Cadaver finished lecturing about reshaping and then asked, "Now, would anyone like to try applying what we've just learned?"

"I do!" Lilith's voice rang out, startlingly loud. There was a faint hint of the scream from before in her voice. For a second, it felt like the world had briefly fizzled in and out of existence.

Professor Cadaver raised a furry eyebrow at her outburst. Lilith straightened in her seat, composing herself, and raised her hand properly.

"Very well, Miss Nightshade. Come up to the front."

As Lilith passed Eld's desk, she shot him a look—part challenge, part determination.

Eld, even focused on his notes, realized that for Lilith, this was more than just learning. It was a competition.

Chapter 6

Daemonic Disruptions
and Tentacled Troubles

Though all students at Bathurst were allowed to choose their specific major, they were still required to gain a generalized understanding of all the dark arts. According to Headmaster Grimthorpe, all magic was intertwined—therefore, a better understanding of imbuing curses could very well grant improved performance in a seemingly unrelated field like familiar summoning.

That was how Eld found himself in the cramped Daemonology classroom, a small room made of redwood that seemed to be in a constant state of controlled chaos.

Dim light from ensconced candlesticks flickered from the walls.

The shelves were laden with ancient tombs that seemed to be bound in human skin and bizarre hooked artifacts that looked like their purpose was caught between prayer and torture.

Arcane symbols and illustrations of mythical creatures adorned the walls.

Even in all his years caring for animals, Eld had never seen these creatures before. They had all too many eyes, horns, and fangs for his liking. The air was thick with the scent of incense and old parchment, creating an atmosphere that was simultaneously musty and scholarly.

Professor Albright stood at the front of the room, his appearance jarringly normal amidst the occult surroundings.

With neatly combed salt-and-pepper hair and a pressed tweed jacket, he looked more like a village scribe than a master of daemonic lore. His wire-rimmed glasses perched precariously on the end of his nose as he surveyed the incoming students.

Eld and Talbot found seats near the middle of the room.

Just as they'd settled in, Eld noticed Mortimer and Erik entering side by side.

"Great…" Eld muttered. "Did the Professor summon them as some kind of demonstration? How are some third years even in our class?"

Talbot lazily glanced over before slouching even more than normal.

"Oh, these general education classes are full of upper-year students…everyone tries getting out of them until they realize that Grimthorpe and Hemlock are serious about not letting them graduate."

As soon as they walked in, Mortimer and Erik's eyes locked onto Eld's.

Mortimer's lips curled into a sneer, while Erik flexed his biceps, water dripping onto the floor with each movement.

"I don't think they're happy to see us," Eld noted.

Slouching in his seat, Talbot barely opened one eye socket. "Wake me if they start anything interesting. If not, well…mind if I copy your notes later?"

"You'll be lucky if I let you," Eld shot back. "I'm still pissed about the reaper."

"Ah, come on," Talbot groaned. "I was able to stall them for a while, wasn't I? It's the general's fault if he misuses his soldier. And trust me. I'm your most useless soldier."

Eld chuckled, shaking his head in disbelief.

Talbot was lazier than a cauldron of bats during the daytime, but his honesty made it hard to stay *too* mad at him.

"Good evening, class," Albright said, politely coughing to gather everyone's attention before pushing his glasses back up the bridge of his nose. "Today we delve into the history of summoning. Please open your textbooks to page 15."

Eld turned the textbook to the appropriate page, his eyes widening. The Old Ones had their warlocks too, including a man named Michael Scot.

As the rustle of pages filled the air, Professor Albright waved his hand, muttering something under his breath. Whatever it was, it took a great deal of time, and the Professor stopped at several points for a fresh intake of breath. He spoke in a rapid-fire and harsh tongue, filled with almost entirely consonants.

With a dramatic wave of Albright's hand, a clawed hand appeared, tearing a rift in reality itself. A deep voice boomed through the classroom, setting Eld's hair on end.

"What is your command…"

"The usual," the professor curtly replied.

He waved his hand, and then the clawed hand began to write on the board, repeating exactly what Albright was saying.

Eld briefly glanced at Talbot, wondering if the ability to summon extradimensional beings to do basic tasks would interest him, but true to form, the poltergeist had dozed off, a very satisfied grin plastered on his snoozing face.

"In the 13th century during the time of the Old Ones, Michael Scot gained notoriety for his supposed ability to command daemons. Legend has it he forced these daemons to join him as workplace companions. His work *Liber Introductorius* detailed—"

The black hand suddenly jerked violently to the side, scratching out everything it had previously written. It scribbled a new message across the chalkboard, written in jagged and spiky white letters.

YOU MADE A MISTAKE

Albright's eyes widened, and his face twisted into an expression of sheer terror.

He turned to the class, but before he could react, the black hand dissolved into a cloud of wispy smoke that poured into his body, seeping in through his eyes, nostrils, and mouth.

Albright's body began to twitch and convulse, his movements becoming haphazard and erratic. When he turned to face the class, his eyes had rolled back, showing only whites.

When Albright spoke again, his words were deep and distorted—the same deep voice that had boomed through the classroom was now overlaid onto his once polite voice.

"Don't listen to that stiff..." the possessed professor growled. "As you just saw, he knows nothing about daemonology. Turn to page 56. We're going to start by talking about *my* favorite warlock, Aleister Crowley."

The students exchanged nervous glances before complying. Even Talbot perked up.

As the class turned their notebooks, the possessed professor launched into a colorful description of Crowley's exploits, peppered with personal anecdotes that no textbook could possibly contain. As he spoke, his body continued twitching and jerking, as if the professor was fighting to regain control.

"Crowley wasn't just dabbling in the occult, kiddies," the daemon-professor cackled. "He was revolutionizing it! Did you know he once summoned a lesser daemon just to win a game of chess? Now *that's* style! Daemon was a good friend of mine too…always said that any contract with ol' Crowley was worth taking."

That just went on and on.

For the next twenty minutes, the class was treated to an exuberant, if somewhat disturbing, account of Crowley's life and works. The daemon seemed to revel in the more scandalous details, much to the horror and fascination of the students.

Eld finally caught Talbot's attention.

"Should we take notes about this?" he asked.

"Oh, I wouldn't worry about it," Talbot murmured back out of the corner of his mouth. "Albright gets taken over every so often…I mean, do a summoning every single day for centuries, you're bound to slip up every so often. The daemons just like talking about the good old days, this won't be on the test."

But it seemed like this daemon was a *bit* more pedogeological than the rest.

"Things were *so much fun* when good ol' Crowley was around. He used daemonology to do whatever he wanted! That's the kind of chaos we thrive on!"

His face still convulsing and twitching, the daemon-professor cast his eyes across the room.

"The current generation of summoners don't have his stuff…imagine calling a daemon like me to write on a blackboard. Before this, I specialized in eating ex-lovers! I'm looking for someone who *really* can use my talents, and hopefully, one of you snots can become the next Crowley…I smell the sweet scent of hedonism on some of you."

"Now." the daemon-professor demanded, clapping his hands together with a sound like thunder. "Let's practice some real summoning. Pair up and create your circles. We're bringing some lesser imps from the abyssal pits. It's all detailed on page 66."

Eld glanced around nervously. Taking orders to summon a daemon from another daemon didn't seem like a very smart idea.

But it seemed like he was the only student hesitating.

Everybody else just rushed into action—everyone else but Talbot, that was.

"Looks like you're catching onto my kind of thinking," Talbot muttered. "It's not worth risking our lives to get better grades…that's why I don't want to rush to class. What if an accident happens?"

"Yeah, I don't know about all that," Eld snorted. "But let's take this one easy."

Eld turned to the appropriate page.

Everything *seemed* to be in order.

The summoning circle was clearly labeled, but Eld still didn't trust it.

He knelt over, *very slowly* and *very carefully* drawing his summoning circle on the floor. In fact, Eld spent much more time reading up on the banishing incantations than the summoning ones. Those seemed particularly useful, just in case someone else made a mistake.

Nearby, Mortimer and Erik were huddled closely over their design, snickering and chuckling. Every so often, the two would glance over in Eld's direction, mischievous grins on their faces.

"What the hell are those two up to?" Eld wondered, whispering to Talbot.

"Um…Eld?" Talbot replied. His voice sounded high-pitched and strained. "I feel…strange…"

"What?"

Before Eld could even ask for more information, Talbot shimmered and vanished, reappearing across the room in Mortimer and Erik's circle.

Talbot glanced beneath his feet, then simply phased away, returning to Eld with a dazed and annoyed expression on his face.

Right when he made it back to Eld, he was suddenly yanked back across the room again, prompting another crude chuckle from Mortimer. Eld glanced over briefly at the daemon-professor, but naturally, the possessed professor wasn't doing anything. He just watched the whole thing with a look of keen interest.

"Cut it out, you two," Eld hissed at Mortimer and Erik. "We're supposed to be summoning imps, not poltergeists."

Mortimer feigned innocence, his eyes wide. "We can't help it if your friend is drawn to superior circle work. Maybe you should practice more."

Erik grunted dimly in agreement, water gurgling in his throat as he chuckled.

After Talbot got yanked back another time, Eld had enough.

He marched over to Mortimer and Erik, his patience worn thin. "Knock it off," he demanded. "We just want to get through class without any incidents."

Around the classroom, other people had set aside their summoning circles to watch the encounter. Mortimer and Erik were known throughout the school as bullies, and it seemed like Eld was one of the first to stand up to them.

A stitched zombie's eye fell right out of a ghoul's eye socket, but he hastily stuck it back in with a resonant squelch so he could continue watching.

The air was filled with tension.

But then, Mortimer raised his hands in mock surrender. "Fine, fine. We'll leave your floaty friend alone. No need to get your grave dirt in a bunch."

The red-eyed aristocrat spoke in an utterly irritating manner as if Eld was the problem for telling him to stop.

To make matters worse, the daemon-professor's eyes were now on them.

"Let me see your circle…" the possessed Albright growled at Eld. "Come on now…"

Eld gulped.

It seemed like he didn't have much of a choice with those rolled-back eyes somehow still staring at him, so he knelt and began diligently copying the runes from the textbook.

He copied the patterns of the summoning circle with the same care he used when whittling artificial wooden bones for pets with broken or removed body limbs.

Within moments, he'd completed the circle.

Perhaps Grimthorpe had a point. Though it was an entirely different field, Eld already had a great deal of practice working swiftly and with great care.

The daemonic professor nodded in approval.

"Speak the incantation…" he said, grinning from ear to ear.

Eld smiled back. Even though this wasn't actually his professor, it was nice to know he'd done a good job.

But then he realized who the Professor was nodding at.

Mortimer dashed over, his face twisted in an expression of malicious glee as he wildly altered the runes in Eld's design.

"What are you—" Eld started, but it was too late. The final syllable of his incantation hung in the air as the changes took effect.

The air around the circle began to shimmer and distort, a tell-tale sign that something was manifesting—something far different from the lesser imp he had intended to summon.

"No, wait—" Eld cried, but his words were drowned out by the sound of the floor cracking like an egg.

But what came out was no adorable chick.

A blinding flash filled the room, accompanied by maddening wails of pain. The screaming came not from any of the students, but seemingly from the air itself, like reality was being wrung apart before their very eyes.

When the light faded, a nightmarish creature stood within the circle.

Writhing tentacles sprouted from a bulbous body, covered in dozens of unblinking eyes. A maw lined with razor-sharp teeth opened and closed rhythmically, drooling some sort of acidic slime that hissed and bubbled as it hit the floor.

"What *is* this thing?" Eld muttered.

"Beats me," Mortimer snickered. "But it's your problem buddy."

As if to highlight just how stupid Mortimer's decision had been, the abomination went for him first.

Black oozy tentacles streaked towards him.

Mortimer let out a cry of fright, hastily backing off. With a hurried curse, he summoned a massive pillar of flame, cackling as he launched it at the bulbous monster.

The attack promptly dissipated.

"Oh," Mortimer said.

That was when chaos erupted in the classroom.

Students scrambled for cover as the abomination lurched forward, its tentacles lashing out. Desks were overturned, books went flying, and panicked screams filled the air.

Talbot, in a rare burst of energy, dove into a desk, possessing it and using its legs to hurry out of the room.

The possessed Professor Albright cackled with glee. "Now *this* is entertainment! A Great Old One—one who hasn't settled down like those old coots in Necropolis. Haven't seen one of these bad boys since the Innsmouth incident of 1998! I long for the great old days…hah! Get it?"

Eld's dodged a swinging tentacle, scampering aside.

Seeing as even Mortimer's flames had been useless, there was no way to defeat the creature head-on. Their only hope was to banish it from where it'd come from, but the summoning circle had gotten damaged when it erupted outwards.

He needed to find a way to redraw it, but how? The monster wasn't just going to stand still like some model.

Eld's hand brushed against his pocket, where Bart, his undead rat, nestled.

"Bart," Eld whispered urgently, "I need your help, buddy."

The zombie rat poked its head out, whiskers twitching. Its red eyes fixed on Eld, awaiting instructions.

Eld set Bart on the ground, directing him with quick gestures. "Distract that thing. Lead it around the room, but don't let it catch you!"

The rat seemed to nod in understanding before scurrying across the floor, weaving between desks and chair legs with significantly improved agility—after he was confident in his abilities to strengthen a revived creature, Eld had made sure to apply that knowledge to his three closest companions.

The abomination's many eyes swiveled, tracking Bart's erratic movements. Its massive body turned, momentarily ignoring Eld and the other students.

Eld began redrawing his summoning circle, carefully correcting the altered runes. His chalk flew across the floor as he worked, sweat beading on his brow.

Come on, Bart, Eld thought. *Just a little longer.*

The rat led the creature on a chase around the classroom, avoiding whipping tentacles and acidic drool.

Students huddled under desks, watching the bizarre spectacle unfold.

Mortimer and Erik, the instigators of this chaos, found themselves cornered by the creature. Erik's waterlogged body made him slow to react, while Mortimer's usual bravado seemed to have deserted him in the face of the tentacled terror.

"Somebody do something!" Mortimer shouted, his voice cracking with fear.

Eld ignored him, focusing on completing the circle.

Every line, every symbol had to be perfect or they would all be in even more danger. Whatever this thing was…Eld had no intention of bringing him a friend.

Finally, Eld completed the circle. "Bart! Bring it here!"

The undead rat made a beeline for the circle, the abomination hot on his tiny heels. As Bart crossed the chalk line, Eld began the banishing incantation, his voice strong and clear despite the chaos around him.

It worked.

The circle's runes began glowing bright white, and then the creature roared in fury as the pull of the circle grew stronger and stronger, like the full moon's influence on the rising tide. The abomination thrashed and fought, its tentacles flailing wildly…

But Eld's will was stronger.

With a final word of power, he completed the spell.

A vortex of energy swirled around the abomination, dragging it back to whichever hell it had come from. The creature's roar of defiance was cut short as it was sucked into the portal, leaving behind only a faint smell of brimstone and a room full of stunned students.

Eld turned to the daemonic Professor, unsure of what would happen.

Perhaps a rebuke?

But his banishing spell had caught the daemon inside Albright as well, or so it seemed on the surface.

Eld wasn't so sure. There seemed to be a strange shimmering around Albright's shadow, and Eld could have sworn he heard a faint whispered cackle.

The dazed professor shook his head, blinking rapidly as if waking from a deep sleep. He looked around the devastated classroom, confusion evident on his face. "Well," he said, his voice back to its normal, mild-mannered tone, "that was quite the practical demonstration, Mr. Blackwood. Or should I say *daemonstration?* Well done indeed."

Eld's entire body sagged with relief, scooping up Bart and giving the rat an appreciative scratch. "Thanks, little guy, I owe you one."

Talbot emerged from his hiding spot in the desk, looking both impressed and slightly nauseous. "Remind me to sit farther away from you in future classes." he raised a bony finger. "Or better yet, to skip them entirely."

Across the room, Erik stared at Eld with a mixture of grudging respect and lingering animosity. Mortimer, for his part, looked both frustrated and intrigued by the unexpected outcome of his prank.

Somehow, Mortimer's infinite arrogance won over his confusion.

As the chaos subsided, he sauntered over to Eld, a smirk on his lips despite his disheveled appearance. "Well, well, Blackwood. Looks like you can do more than just play with dead animals after all. Though you were still playing with that dead rodent, weren't you?"

Still catching his breath, Eld fixed Mortimer with a hard stare. "Maybe if you spent more time studying and less time sabotaging others, you wouldn't need me to clean up your messes."

Mortimer's smirk flattened. "Oh, come now. Don't act so high and mighty. We both know you enjoyed the little thrill.

Face it, Blackwood, you're not as squeaky clean as you pretend to be. You're a Blackwood and we both know what that means."

Eld blinked.

Since he hadn't seen the Familial Tome in many years, he didn't know exactly what it meant. He had a strange feeling this was more than just a haphazard shot at his father.

But he wasn't going to ask *Mortimer* for details.

The pale-skinned pyromancer leaned in, his eyes smoldering red with fury as his voice dropped to a low whisper. "I'll be watching you. This isn't over."

With that, Mortimer turned on his heel and sauntered away, leaving Eld to ponder the warning.

Professor Albright, still looking somewhat dazed, cleared his throat. "Right, well, I think that's quite enough excitement for one day. Class dismissed."

He glanced at the board. "And, uh, yeah, I guess we moved from Scot to Crowley. Well, please, do read up on Aleister Crowley for the next class. Preferably without any practical demonstrations."

Eld and Talbot packed their things, waiting for the other students to file out and simply processing what had transpired.

"You know," Talbot mused, "I'm starting to think I should have picked a less exciting school to attend...is there any place that offers vocational training? Perhaps as a...I don't know? Sleep study subject? With you as my roommate, this year has been quite a bit more exciting than I bargained for, and by exciting, I mean terrifying and potentially fatal."

Eld chuckled, but there was something in Talbot's typically lazy proclamation that caught his attention.

"Speaking of fatal, Talbot, you're a poltergeist. How exactly does one...well, die again? It's not like decapitation would work on you, and you could phase through flames if you reacted fast enough."

Talbot pinched what was left of his lips together and raised an eyebrow. "Curious about offing me already, roomie?"

"No, no," Eld hastily replied. "Just wondering. I mean, I guess you could be banished from a place? But actually die?"

Talbot flickered slightly as he considered the question. "Oh, there are a myriad of ways, my necromantically inclined friend. Exorcism is the classic, of course. Then there's soul dispersion, where our essence is scattered to the ethereal winds. Some particularly nasty curses can unravel our very being."

He paused dramatically before continuing, "And let's not forget the more exotic methods. Chronological reversal, where we're forced to experience our death in reverse until we cease to exist. Or my personal favorite, the Void Gulp—imagine a tear in reality that swallows you whole."

Eld listened, fascinated and slightly horrified.

Since he had a human body, he technically couldn't be exorcised, but the rest of it sounded like it'd kill a good old undead like himself as well.

"And certain enchanted items can kill undead too, right? Causing them to cross over immediately?"

"Ah, yes," Talbot nodded. "*Blessed* weapons." He made lazy quotes with his fingers when he said *blessed*. "Items imbued with positive energy, that sort of thing. Nasty business. Stab a poltergeist with one, and then we're crossing right over."

"Cross over to what, though?" Eld asked, his brow furrowing. "I mean, we're already in the underworld, aren't we? At least, that's what the brochure Grimthorpe gave me said."

Talbot's expression became uncharacteristically serious. "That, my friend, is the million-soul question. Nobody knows for sure because no one dead twice over has ever come back to tell the tale."

"You mean, there's something beyond this?" Eld gestured vaguely at their surroundings.

"Maybe," Talbot shrugged, his usual nonchalance returning. "Could be an even deeper underworld. Could be oblivion. Could be we all turn into singing furniture for all I know. The uncertainty is part of the charm of unlife, don't you think?"

Eld shook his head, chuckling despite the weighty topic. "You have a strange definition of charm, Talbot."

Talbot chuckled. "Well, the sad thing is…it doesn't seem to work on the ladies either."

Chapter 7

Furry Friend

Eld and Talbot emerged from Professor Albright's Daemonology class last, still processing the chaos. Talbot slouched with exhaustion, his eternal plastered grin somehow managing to look weary. It seemed like just the force of raising his cheeks was making his forehead wrinkle.

"Should be time for lunch," Talbot said. "Hopefully, they are serving some good Old One cuisine today…it was a revolutionary day when Grimthorpe excavated the recipe for hot pockets. Have you ever had them before?"

"Hot…pockets?" Eld hesitantly replied.

He was, of course, thinking of clothing, and that didn't sound appealing at all. Of course, due to the sheer diversity of nightkin at Bathurst, they were always serving weird food of one kind or the other. Perhaps the stitches in clothing helped reinvigorate the stitches that held certain zombies together…

But before Talbot could reply, his jaw suddenly unhinged to a seemingly impossible degree, dropping straight through the floor in a tremendous yawn.

"On second thought, I think I've had enough excitement for now," he said. "I'm off for a nap. I'll see you later."

With that, the poltergeist followed his jaw through the floor, phasing downwards as he retreated to their room.

Eld chuckled, shaking his head. "Sure thing, Talbot. See you later. Now, to find the path to the refectory by myself…"

He pulled his map out of his pocket, turning it this way and that as he tried to find a path to the refectory. Unfortunately, much of Hemlock's blood had dripped off at this point, and the battle with the tentacled abomination had damaged the rest of the map beyond repair. Half the thing was covered in an oily black substance that looked more like pus than ink.

"Well, I guess I *could* ask for another one," Eld muttered. He crumpled up the now foul-smelling map and tossed it into a nearby trashcan.

Franky slithered out of Eld's coat, staring at him with beady black eyes. Though the centipede was silent, Eld already knew what it was suggesting.

Eld snorted. "Look. I'd *like* a nice normal map, but it seems like Professor Hemlock is the only option. Something tells me that the elevator passes Mortimer is selling aren't any good either."

His stomach growled loudly.

Banishing otherworldly abominations was hungry work.

"Well, the one good thing is that this was my last class for the day," Eld thought to himself. *"I guess if worst comes to worst, I could wander around aimlessly until someone comes to help me out…it's honestly worked better than expected so far."*

As soon as those words had crossed his mind, Eld was sent sprawling to the floor as he crashed straight into what felt like a very furry brick.

"What in the Neverending Night?" Eld cursed. "There are all sorts of nightkin these days!"

The man who'd bumped into Eld turned, a concerned expression on his face.

"Oh. Sorry about that," the man growled apologetically.

He offered a massive shovel-like paw to help Eld back to his feet.

The man's teeth were a bizarre mixture of friendly and feral—just a bit too sharp, a bit too long to be entirely human. When the student grinned, it was a gesture caught between a warm smile and a canine's snarl.

His voice was just like his teeth.

One word would sound enthusiastic and jovial, a perfect fit for the gym bro stereotype. The next would echo menacingly through the air. Eld had never met anyone who spoke that way before, but as he took a closer look, he realized that he recognized this student.

Eld had seen him around campus before, but the two had never spoken. If Eld wasn't mistaken, the two had a few classes together. He must have just left the Daemonology classroom too.

And the man wasn't a furry brick—he was a werewolf. But considering his build, Eld could have been forgiven for mistaking him as some kind of hirsute gargoyle.

The young man was deeply imposing, with shoulders as broad as the horizon and thickly coiled muscles that reminded Eld disturbingly of the abomination he'd just banished.

His rugged features were framed by haphazard dark hair that reminded Eld of a haunted forest. As Eld watched, a few of the strands shifted, revealing what looked suspiciously like fur.

Recognition suddenly flashed in the burly werewolf's eyes.

Just like his voice, the stranger's eyes were mismatched. One was amber, the other was blue and it looked excited and curious, shining with an almost childlike wonder.

Eld looked back at him suspiciously.

He didn't have anything against werewolves. They were just nightkin, the same as Eld. There was just one problem.

Sometimes, with the furrier nightkin, after they heard that Eld was a pet doctor, they would try and shake him down for some discount healthcare, including one particularly foul-smelling gentleman who had demanded a prostate exam.

"How can I help you?" Eld asked.

"Aren't you the guy from the Daemonology class?" the werewolf asked, both eyes narrowing. "The one who banished that abomination?"

"I am," Eld nodded. "And though you might think I was also the one who summoned it…"

"Oh, it was that pile of coyote dung Mortimer, I saw that part, trust me. The student's hand clapped Eld on the shoulder and he noticed that the nails were more like claws, leaving small indents in his coat. "That was some impressive work. Quick thinking!"

"Thank you," Eld replied, grinning.

Whether as a student or a pet doctor, a slight touch of vanity was still one of his weaknesses.

The werewolf's friendly grip tightened painfully around Eld's shoulder.

"What's your name, by the way?" Eld asked. "I've seen you around campus before, but I don't believe we've ever been properly introduced."

"Sorry, where are my manners?" The student scratched his chin and puffed out his chest. "Wolfgang, Wolfgang Salzburg. Great to meet you!"

At this point, the two had been talking for a while, and Eld couldn't help but notice the attention Wolfgang was attracting.

Students passing by waved and called out greetings, many addressing him by name. A group of vampire girls giggled and batted their eyelashes as they walked past, causing Wolfgang to flash them a roguish grin.

"Quite popular, aren't you?" Eld observed, raising an eyebrow.

Wolfgang shrugged, but there was a hint of pride Eld detected. "Being one of the stars of the Nocturnal Combat Club has its perks. Speaking of which," his grin widened, revealing even more of those unnervingly sharp teeth, "have you thought about joining?"

The question caught Eld off guard.

He had heard about the club—mostly warnings to stay far away from it. According to the rumors, the only members were real gluttons for pain. "Me? I'm not very good at combat magic. I'm more of a theoretical necromancer. When it comes to a battle, my pets usually do the fighting for me. I've got a few handy restraining spells, but that's about it."

Wolfgang waved off his concern with a clawed hand. "That's okay. You can learn easily enough. The important thing is that you can think on your feet. So, what do you say?"

Eld hesitated. "I'm not sure. What exactly does this club do?"

Wolfgang's eyes lit up with enthusiasm. "Oh, it's great! We have eight different teams, each consisting of three people. My team has one more spot open, and I think you'd be perfect. We've been winning everything 2-0 so far, but, well, some backup would be appreciated."

A ghostly cheerleader floated by as Wolfgang spoke, winking at him. "Great match last week, Wolfie!" she called out. Wolfgang acknowledged her with a nod before turning back to Eld.

Eld's thoughts flashed back to the chaos of the Daemonology class.

While being the big hero had its perks…there were some definite downsides to combat.

Like not being the hero and just getting killed pointlessly.

"I don't know, Wolfgang. What if I get hurt? I'm not exactly built for combat."

Wolfgang laughed, a sound that was halfway between a chuckle and a bark. "Don't worry about that. The academy has all sorts of protective wards in place. No one's ever been seriously injured. Well, not permanently, anyway."

That last part did little to assuage Eld's concerns.

Sensing Eld's hesitance, Wolfgang gave him a friendly punch on the shoulder that sent the smaller man staggering back.

Eld raised an eyebrow. "You see what I mean?"

Wolfgang just shook his head, letting out another barking laugh. "Come on, Eld. We need someone with your quick thinking. Our last fighter graduated last year and you'd be a great addition to our team. Plus, it's a lot of fun. Where else can you legally blast your classmates with magic?"

As if to emphasize his point, a small explosion echoed from a nearby classroom, followed by maniacal laughter.

"See?" Wolfgang grinned. "Just another day at Bathurst. And you know…rumor has it that some of our lovely classmates have a *bit* of a grudge against you. Are you sure you want to pass up the opportunity to get some self-defense training? Besides, you'll get to use your familiars too. The Nocturnal Combat Club rules allow them."

That did it.

Eld needed all the practice he could get if Mortimer and Erik were going to continue their idiot pranks, and some extra training with his friends certainly wouldn't hurt.

"Alright then," Eld said. "I'll give it a try. Though you might be overestimating my quick thinking. Outthinking Mortimer sounds like outrunning a mummy trapped in its sarcophagus."

Brushing off Eld's concerns, Wolfgang's face split into a triumphant grin.

He threw an arm around Eld's shoulders, nearly knocking him over with the force of the friendly gesture. "Perfect! Let me show you where we meet. I'll introduce you to your other teammate, Orlando."

Orlando…

The name sounded vaguely familiar to Eld, but he couldn't quite place exactly where.

As they walked down the hallway together, Wolfgang excitedly explained more about the club. "So, we meet three times a week for practice, but there are always people down in the club chambers ready to practice so don't be shy. It's a mix of physical training, spell work, and strategy sessions."

Eld's stomach grumbled again, reminding him that his original intention had been to find someone to show him to the refectory for lunch. His current situation seemed like an extremely severe case of mission creep.

Wolfgang noticed and laughed.

"Oh, we'll have food there too," he said, flexing his muscles. "These didn't grow out of nothing.

On their way to the meeting hall, they passed a bulletin board covered in posters advertising various school events. One particularly large poster caught Eld's eye—it showed Wolfgang in mid-transformation, his face half-human, half-wolf, with the words *Nocturnal Combat Club Championship* emblazoned across the top.

"That's from last year's tournament," Wolfgang said, noticing Eld's gaze. "We came in second, but this year, with a Blackwood on the team, I'm sure we'll secure the title!"

"So you've heard of my family too, huh?" Eld asked.

"Oh yeah, for sure!" Wolfgang said, waving his paw eagerly back and forth. "You know, when I first joined up, some of the older members were *still* talking about how much potential your brother Cloudehill had."

After hearing Cloudehill's name, Eld sneered in irritation—he hadn't even meant to, it was purely by instinct. He stood up a little straighter and genuinely felt more confident.

Outwitting Mortimer was one thing.

Outwitting *Cloudehill*?

And apparently, Cloudehill had been some kind of hotshot in this club.

Well, then, that reminded Eld of an old zombie saying. In the land of the lobotomized, the half-brained man was king.

It seemed like Wolfgang noticed Eld's consternation, as the hairy man raised an eyebrow.

"To be clear," Wolfgang said. "They were only talking about your brother's magical potential…if I remembered the stories correctly, it sounded like he wasn't very good at strategy."

Eld just shrugged noncommittally. It seemed like Wolfgang wanted to ask more, but he shook his head and continued leading the way.

Perhaps it was out of politeness, or perhaps he merely wanted Eld to join his club faster.

As they continued down the corridor, more and more students called out to Wolfgang. A group of ghouls gave him a rotting thumbs-up, while a pair of banshees whispered and giggled as they passed.

The man had enough fans for two clubs.

"So," Eld said, curiosity getting the better of him, "What's it like being the big wolf on campus?"

Wolfgang ran a hand through his hair, looking slightly embarrassed. "It's not all it's cracked up to be, honestly. Sure, the attention is nice, but sometimes I feel like people only see the *Combat Club Star* and not... well, me."

Eld nodded, pleasantly surprised by Wolfgang's candor and humility. He had a feeling that the two of them would get along. "I can imagine that would get old pretty fast."

"Yeah," Wolfgang sighed. "Don't get me wrong, I love the club and the competition. But it's nice to talk to someone who doesn't just see me as *Wolfie the Wonder Wolf* or whatever ridiculous nickname they've come up with this week."

Wolfgang's pace slowed.

The well-lit corridors of the academy gave way to dimmer passages, where the walls were lined with flickering witchlights.

"We're heading into the catacombs," Wolfgang explained. "The club chamber is deep within the school's foundations."

The air grew cooler and damper as they descended a winding stone staircase, every step carrying the faint scent of earth and decay. Eld was reminded of his family crypt he had fallen through that had brought him to this place.

"Why so far down?" Eld asked.

"Privacy, mostly. Plus, it's a great place to practice without disturbing the rest of the school. You'd be surprised how much noise a duel can make."

Before long, they came to a fork in the passage.

Wolfgang paused, turning to Eld with a serious expression.

"Pay attention now, Eld," he said, his amber eyes reflecting the dim light. "It's easy to get lost down here. If you decide the club is for you, you'll have to find it on your own next time. Consider it a bit of a pre-test to see if you're as smart as I think you are."

Chapter 8

Duels and Disclosure in the Deep

The descent into Bathurst Academy's catacombs might as well have been a journey into a different world. If Bathurst was in the Underworld, this must have been some kind of Basement World.

Wolfgang eagerly led Eld down a series of winding staircases, each step taking them further from the familiar halls above.

The light from floating witchlights glinted off the slick stone walls, moisture seeping through cracks and crevices that had existed for centuries. The sound of their footsteps echoed in the narrow passages, accompanied by the occasional drip of water and the distant, unidentifiable noises that always seem to inhabit such ancient places.

As they continued descending, the staircases grew increasingly steep and increasingly shoddy, to the point that they stopped resembling staircases at all.

"Watch your step," Wolfgang cautioned as they navigated a particularly treacherous stretch of worn stairs. "These old stones can be slippery. Wouldn't want to start your Combat Club career with a broken neck."

Eld raised an eyebrow.

"I wouldn't call this a staircase so much as a mudslide…"

Wolfgang just chuckled, dropping down to all fours to ensure a smooth descent.

Inside Eld's jacket, Bart chittered, letting out an excited cry of familiarity.

"Yeah. I don't know where Shuck is right now," Eld said, turning his head this way and that. The passageway was very dark, but he would recognize his old friend's distinctive outline anywhere. "Still, that dog has a nose for trouble. So if I slip and break my neck, I'm sure he'll call a healer."

Bart chittered again, this time reproachfully.

Eld rolled his eyes, shaking his head as he mockingly pretended to take offense at the rat's words.

"Come on now Bart…did I accidentally shorten your brain when I lengthened your tail? If you get injured, we won't need to call a healer. I'll be there to heal you! I'm the greatest pet doctor in history!"

Hearing the old slogan echo through the darkness seemed to bolster both Bart and Franky's spirits, and the monstrous rat-centipede duo chittered happily.

With that, Eld carefully planted his feet, inching his way down the muddy slope.

The deeper the two went, the more the atmosphere seemed to press in on them and the darker the corridors got, as if the air and darkness were being compressed by the sheer weight of the world above.

Then again…

It might have just been Eld's sorely lacking fitness. Life was a lot easier when he had Shuck pulling him around in the good old rickshaw.

After a point, one of the corridors seemed to go on forever, stretching out into eternal inky darkness that made Eld feel like stepping into it would send him drifting off into space.

But then, Wolfgang raised a hand.

"Careful…" he muttered.

The way the werewolf spoke set Eld's hair on edge.

What in the Thirteen Torturous Hells would make a man like *this* careful?

A faint toll bell chimed in the back of Eld's mind, and then a pair of massive cooper doors seemed to materialize out of the gloom. One moment, all Eld saw was perfect darkness, but the blinding copper light was so bright that it seemed to sizzle his eyeballs.

The grand doors stood at least ten feet tall, their surface covered in runes that pulsed faintly in the dim light.

At the center, joining the two doors was a heavy lock that seemed to be made of some dark metal. It pulsed with an energy that Eld could feel even from several feet away.

Unlike the runes Eld had seen earlier, which served to insulate the catacombs and create an environment of perfection, the magic in these runes was endlessly ominous.

They were written in an old language that Eld didn't understand in a flowing rusty red script that might have been blood.

But even though Eld couldn't understand the message, he got the intent—stay away.

In fact...

Right when Eld stepped towards the imposing entrance, a voice echoed in his mind, repeating the message over and over again with monotonous insistence.

"Splintered Dimension, no students allowed. Splintered Dimension, no students allowed."

The sudden intrusion into his thoughts made Eld flinch.

The thought had appeared so violently it was like someone had driven a stake into his brain.

He shook his head, trying to clear the voice from his mind, but it was no good.

The voice only vanished when he backed off entirely, and even then he felt a faint reverberation in the very back of his mind.

"What's behind there?" he asked, gesturing towards the forbidding entrance.

Wolfgang glanced at the doors, his expression a mix of curiosity and wariness. "Your guess is as good as mine," he said with a shrug, his clawed hands spread wide. "No idea why it's blocked off this year…but places at Bathurst are usually restricted for a reason, you know? So I mind my own business, got enough problems as it is."

Eld thought for a second, then nodded.

There was wisdom in the werewolf's words.

"I think you're right," Eld said. "If we're already fighting each other…there's probably no need to fight the professors too."

"That's the spirit," Wolfgang chuckled.

As they continued past the doors, Wolfgang's face clouded over, his mismatched eyes growing distant. The torchlight caught the edges of his features, highlighting the tension in his jaw and the furrow of his brow.

Eld had only known the man for a short amount of time, but he'd already noticed a pattern in his behavior.

Normally, Wolfgang seemed to perfectly split the duality between man and wolf. But every so often, when something excited or irritated him, he'd swing all the way to one side.

"Something on your mind?" Eld asked.

Wolfgang turned to him, chuckling. Unlike his usual amused laugh, this one was angry and sarcastic. "Is it really that obvious?"

"Not really," Eld lied. "But I figure that if we're going to be teammates, we might as well get to know each other better, you know?"

Wolfgang hesitated, but then he cocked his head.

"Sure, why not? You seem like a good sort of fellow. My biggest problem is my pa—never approved of me coming to Bathurst. Says it's *taming* my wild nature. He preferred my old school, Blood Moon Academy. He was furious when I transferred here."

"Your father wanted you to maintain wild nature as a werewolf?" Eld asked, surprised.

Most of the time, werewolves actively *tried* to tame themselves. Turning into a massive bloodthirsty wolf and savaging everybody in a mile-wide vicinity was one of the premier ways to attract torches and pitchforks.

Wolfgang snorted, a sound halfway between derision and pain. His claws flexed unconsciously, leaving small scratches on the stone wall he was leaning against. "He was the one who made me a werewolf in the first place. As if I asked to be turned. As if I wanted to spend every full moon locked in the basement, terrified I might hurt someone. But to my pa, it was…"

Wolfgang broke off, gulping loudly.

The raw emotion in Wolfgang's words hung in the air between them, almost palpable in the confined space of the corridor.

But then, Wolfgang suddenly seemed to catch himself, his eyes refocusing on Eld.

A look of embarrassment crossed his face, softening his fierce features. "Sorry," he said, looking sheepish. "Mum tells me that I tend to overshare. Don't mean to dump all my furry problems on you."

Eld shook his head, offering a sympathetic smile.

"It doesn't bother me," Eld said, reassuring Wolfgang. "My father is a little like yours, actually. He's always demanding more and never satisfied with anything I do. It's all *uphold the family name* and *when are you going to become a proper necromancer* with him. Actually, he's the reason why I'm at Bathurst to begin with."

As Eld spoke, he found himself revealing more than he had intended.

There was something about the dark, enclosed space of the catacombs that seemed to encourage openness. It felt like he was safe speaking his secrets out into the abyss. "He thinks my interest in reanimating animals is a waste of time. Wants me to focus on raising human corpses and creating phylacteries. He thinks life is just about raw power and nothing else…"

Wolfgang nodded, a toothy grin spreading across his face.

The expression transformed his face, making him look younger and more carefree. "Your pa making you come here, mine trying to drag me away…I'd offer to trade, but seems like *both* our pas are real boneheads, eh?"

They shared a chuckle, the tension of the moment dissipating like mist in sunlight.

As their laughter faded, replaced once more by the ambient sounds of the catacombs, Eld felt a sudden sense of camaraderie with Wolfgang that he hadn't expected.

On the surface, the two of them couldn't have been more different. One of them was a thin necromancer and the other was a giant werewolf, but they had much more in common than he ever could have expected.

Weirdly, the similarity was comforting.

Even among different species of nightkin, there were still bum fathers.

The two newfound friends continued their journey through the winding passages, Wolfgang occasionally pointing out landmarks to help Eld navigate in the future. "Remember this statue of the three-headed dog," he said, gesturing to a particularly grotesque sculpture. "Turn left there and you're halfway to the club chambers."

Finally, after what felt like hours of walking but was likely only twenty minutes, they arrived at a large chamber that had seemingly been carved straight into the pitch-black rock with engraved runes that glistened with magic.

Despite the frightening surroundings, Eld felt a strange sense of relaxation and peace emanating from the walls.

"Those help us prevent injury," Wolfgang said. "Or, erm, well. *Mostly* prevent injury. The Department of Contracts has been very clear about this. We can't say that our wards fully prevent injury."

On that promising note, the two stepped inside.

The space was vast, easily the size of the Great Hall above, with a ceiling so high that it seemed to fade into the shadows.

Torches and magical lights illuminated the area, revealing an impressive array of training equipment and weapon racks.

The chamber was already buzzing with activity. A handful of students were already there, engaged in various forms of combat practice.

The clang of metal on metal rang out, punctuated by shouts and the occasional burst of magical energy. Excited shouts echoed through the cavern and the air crackled with power and excitement.

In one corner, Eld spotted a familiar face.

Lilith and her team, all sporting matching blue and silver uniforms, were practicing parrying maneuvers with rapiers, their blades flashing in the torchlight.

"I didn't know *she* was a fighter…" Eld muttered to himself.

But Lilith wasn't just a fighter. She was a good one.

As Eld watched, Lilith executed a particularly complex series of feints and strikes that left her opponent disarmed and off-balance.

Seeming to sense Eld's gaze, Lilith looked up and caught sight of him.

She gave a brief, businesslike nod of acknowledgment before returning to her practice. Eld waved back awkwardly, feeling out of place in this realm of martial prowess.

Fighting Cloudehill back home or wrangling reanimated squirrels was one thing. Here, everyone seemed to know what they were doing.

A tall, aristocratic-looking young man approached Eld and Wolfgang, a quizzical expression on his face.

His features were sharp and angular, with high cheekbones and a nose that looked like it had been chiseled from marble. He moved with a grace that spoke of eons of training and his posture radiated an air of bone-deep superiority.

"Already fraternizing with the enemy, I see," the young man said, eyeing Eld with thinly veiled disdain. His voice was cultured and refined, each word precisely enunciated. He spoke every word so perfectly that it sounded almost artificial like he was some kind of golem that had learned language artificially.

When he smiled, he revealed perfectly white teeth—though two of them were razor-sharp fangs.

Wolfgang clapped a hand on Eld's shoulder, the gesture both reassuring and slightly painful given his considerable strength. "Orlando, this is Eld Blackwood, our new teammate," he said. "Eld, meet Orlando von Ravenscroft."

Orlando inclined his head slightly, the barest minimum of courtesy. His eyes, a piercing blue that seemed to look right through Eld, were cold and evaluating. "Charmed, I'm sure," he replied, in a tone that suggested he was anything but.

As Orlando turned away to retrieve some protective gear from a nearby rack, Eld leaned close to Wolfgang. "I don't think he likes me," he whispered.

Wolfgang laughed, a warm, rumbling sound that seemed to vibrate through Eld's bones. "I don't think Orlando likes anyone," he said, pitching his voice low enough that Orlando wouldn't overhear. "But he's a great fighter. You'll get used to him. Maybe. Eventually."

Eld raised an eyebrow. "Have you gotten used to him?"

"Not really," Wolfgang replied. "But the two of us *have* gotten used to winning…so make sure you're up to snuff."

"That's not reassuring at all," Eld groaned.

With that, the three of them began donning their protective gear, a process that involved strapping on various padded pieces and adjusting amulets that glowed with protective enchantments. Orlando moved with ease, his fingers quickly securing buckles and adjusting straps. Wolfgang's movements were less refined but equally efficient, his enhanced strength allowing him to manhandle the heavier pieces into place.

Eld fumbled with unfamiliar buckles and clasps, feeling like a child playing at being a warrior. He struggled to figure out which piece went where. Even worse, he was acutely aware of Orlando's impatient sighs and Wolfgang's poorly concealed amusement.

Once armored, Orlando strode to the weapon rack and selected an impressive claymore. The blade was easily as long as Eld was tall, gleaming wickedly in the torchlight. Yet despite his slender build, Orlando hefted it like it weighed nothing, giving it a few practice swings that whistled through the air.

Wolfgang opted for a pair of short swords, their curved blades reminiscent of fangs. He tested their balance with a few experimental swings, the weapons becoming natural extensions of his arms.

They both turned to Eld expectantly. "What are you using?" Wolfgang asked, gesturing to the weaponry on display.

Eld glanced at the weapons, feeling overwhelmed by the choices. There were swords of every description, axes, maces, spears, and even a few exotic weapons he couldn't name.

"Any chance at a long-range item?" Eld asked, raising his eyebrows hopefully. "I'm not too skilled up close."

"You're supposed to use spells from far away," Wolfgang replied.

Eld glanced around the room, taking in the seasoned fighters again. He had a feeling this wasn't the sort of club that would find his leash and chain spells amusing.

After some more deliberation, he reached for a small stiletto dagger. It was embarrassing to admit it, but that seemed like the only item he could easily carry.

Orlando cringed visibly, his perfect features contorting in a grimace of disbelief. He turned to Wolfgang with an exasperated expression. "Why did you invite him to the team?" he asked, not bothering to lower his voice or hide his disdain.

"Because he's resourceful," Wolfgang replied firmly, his eyes flashing with a hint of annoyance. "You didn't see him in Daemonology. Trust me, he's got potential."

Orlando rolled his eyes but said nothing further as they moved to an open area of the chamber. Eld couldn't help but notice other students glancing their way, curiosity and skepticism plain on their faces.

He felt exposed, acutely aware of his inexperience and the ridiculousness of his tiny dagger compared to the impressive weapons wielded by those around him.

"Alright," Wolfgang said, raising his swords into a ready position. "Let's see what you can do, Eld. Don't hold back—the gear will protect us."

Eld nodded, gripping his dagger tightly as Orlando and Wolfgang began circling him.

The stone floor was cool beneath his feet, the air charged with anticipation.

When Orlando lunged forward with his claymore, Eld barely managed to dodge, the massive blade whistling past his ear close enough that he felt the displaced air.

Wolfgang followed up with a flurry of strikes and Eld clumsily fell back, his dagger woefully inadequate against the onslaught of two blades at once. Every so often, he managed to raise his dagger and parry, but he failed to land a single attack of his own.

The clang of metal on metal echoed through the chamber, drawing the attention of nearby students who paused their practice to watch.

As the sparring continued, Eld found himself constantly on the defensive, as always, unable to find an opening against his more experienced opponents.

Frustration mounted as he realized how out of his depth he truly was. This was his fight with Cloudehill all over again. The only difference was that his opponents were far savvier than his brother could ever be.

Every time Eld raised his hand to try and draw the symbols he needed to cast a spell, Wolfgang would interrupt him, swinging his blades in a wide arc.

The message was obvious: "Try to draw something, and I'll cut off your fingers."

Before long, Eld felt as tattered and exhausted as a crumbling ghoul. His breaths came in ragged gasps, sweat beading on his forehead despite the cool air of the catacombs.

"Is that all you got?" Wolfgang growled dismissively. "I'm disappointed."

Eld feinted like he was going to cast a spell, but then he opened up his coat.

Bart and Franky already knew what to do.

Orlando let out a startled yelp as Franky crawled up his leg, the unexpected sensation momentarily throwing off his perfect poise. Seizing the opportunity, Eld darted in, tapping Orlando's side with his dagger. Despite Wolfgang's reassurances, Eld was afraid of actually hurting his new teammates.

Meanwhile, Bart weaved between Wolfgang's feet, causing the werewolf to stumble and lose his balance. Right as Wolfgang lunged at Bart, Eld tripped him, sending him staggering across the floor.

For a few glorious moments, Eld managed to hold his own, using his undead familiars to create openings for quick jabs and feints.

But due to his reluctance to land a solid blow, the fight continued dragging on.

Suddenly, Wolfgang called a halt to the match, lowering his swords.

Eld did the same…

But then the werewolf lunged forward, driving one of his blades straight into Eld's gut.

"What are you—"

Eld gasped, more from shock than pain. He looked down, expecting to see blood blossoming across his chest, but there was nothing—not even a tear in the fabric of his protective gear. The blade seemed to have simply phased through him, leaving no mark of its passage.

"See?" Wolfgang said, grinning as he withdrew the blade.

His amber eyes danced with amusement at Eld's stunned expression. "Told you the gear was enchanted. It only works in the training room, but so long as the magic is maintained, it's impossible to do any real harm to anyone wearing it."

Eld let out a relieved chuckle, his heart still racing from the unexpected demonstration. "Neat," he said, then paused, a new concern occurring to him. "But, uh, what if you'd stabbed me in the head? Does it protect against that too?"

Orlando, who had been watching the demonstration with poorly concealed impatience, let out a long-suffering sigh. He pinched the bridge of his nose making a face so bitter that it seemed like Eld's questions were physically painful to him. "No, it doesn't…I would suggest wearing a helmet," he said. "I only keep my face uncovered so everyone can see how handsome I am."

"Really?" Eld asked.

That seemed particularly foolish.

"No," Orlando replied, his voice dripping with sarcasm. "Of course not. I'm not an idiot."

He waved his hand through the air.

"The catacombs themselves are enchanted for additional safety. You probably noticed when you came in. Now, this runeplate builds on that safety—when used inside the catacombs, we become impervious to lethal blows. Of course, that only works when *both* kinds of magic are operating. On top of that, anyone *wearing* the runeplate is unable to deliver a lethal blow either. Otherwise, people would just wear these things everywhere."

Eld nodded.

Orlando's explanation was rude but logical. At the combat club, he really could go all out, doing everything in his power to train his skills.

"Now that we've got that out of the way, can we begin again?" Orlando asked.

Eld nodded, raising his dagger again as his pets skittered between his feet.

Chapter 9

Sutures and Secrets

Eld burst through the door of the Corpse Stitching classroom, his chest heaving as he gasped for breath. His hair stuck up at odd angles and a thin sheen of sweat glistened on his forehead.

Shuck closely followed behind him.

The reanimated dog's incessant barking was the only reason why Eld had woken up in time to make it to class in the first place.

His whole body felt battered and bruised after all his training and the run to class hadn't helped matters at all. The armor at the Nocturnal Combat Club prevented lethal wounds, but they only diluted the pain rather than erasing it. When Eld began getting ready for class, he felt like he'd gotten out of a rack instead of getting out of bed.

Considering how hard Wolfgang and Orlando worked, Eld's brain even felt a few grooves smoother.

He wanted nothing more than to be sleeping and recovering…

But Bathurst's rules were clear. What students did on their own time was their responsibility. No professor would allow him to skip class on account of the Nocturnal Combat Club.

The bell had rung long ago, but there was still a seat for Eld in the back. He practically fell into it, his knees and back aching miserably.

As he caught his breath, Eld took in his surroundings.

The Corpse Stitching classroom was meticulously organized.

Every surface glistened with an unnatural sheen, obviously polished by an utterly obsessive hand. Shelves lined the walls, filled with jars of preserved body parts floating in murky fluids, each labeled in neat, cursive handwriting. Tools of various shapes and sizes hung on the pegboard, ranging from tiny needles to a bloodstained wrench which Eld found discomfiting just to look at.

The smell of formaldehyde permeated the air, but there was something else too—something distinctly magical that made the room feel almost comically sterile despite its grisly contents. Even the floorboards seemed to have been scrubbed within an inch of their existence, not a speck of dust to be seen anywhere.

Eld wrinkled his nose.

Shuck made an irritated noise, and then walked back out to the hall, shaking his head instead of his tail.

"Can't blame him for hating it here...this room smells 'blank.' There's no other word for it," Eld thought to himself.

At the front of the room stood Professor McGrath, an Underworld-renowned expert on corpse stitching and technological modifications.

Standing barely three feet tall, the leprechaun's appearance was jarring, to say the least. His tuft of bright red hair juxtaposed against his pallid, pastel green skin. A meticulously trimmed beard framed a mouth filled with teeth that were far too sharp for comfort. It was almost like McGrath had replaced his teeth with his beloved needles.

Eld hadn't seen many leprechauns before.

Though humans usually associated them with playful mischief, there were others, like McGrath, who had a much darker side.

Professor McGrath's strangest feature was the contraption he was riding on. It was built with Old One technology. Their complex technology was so advanced that most people could barely begin to understand it, but McGrath was an expert.

A pair of mechanical legs, crafted from brass and steel, whirred and clicked as they carried the professor around the room. Steam occasionally hissed from vents in the joints, as McGrath used a control panel to adjust the length of the legs.

Though the Professor himself was short, the legs allowed McGrath to tower over his students one moment and scuttle between desks the next.

McGrath's eyes, magnified to an unsettling degree by a pair of brass goggles, fixed on Eld. The goggles whirred and clicked, focusing with unnerving precision. "Tardiness is the thief of knowledge, Mr. Blackwood," he said. "See that it doesn't happen again."

Talbot drifted over, flickering with curiosity. "Why are you all sweaty?" he whispered, eyeing Eld's appearance with amusement. "Looks like you've been wrestling with a reanimated bear."

When they'd woken up that morning, Talbot had already left for class.

That was how tired Eld was.

"I joined the Nocturnal Combat Club," Eld muttered back, still slightly winded. "I'll tell you about it later."

Professor McGrath snapped his fingers.

The sound echoed through the room, causing several students to jump in their seats. In response, a swarm of tiny fairies materialized, each no larger than a human hand. They zipped around the room, their wings a blur of iridescent colors, depositing various body parts on the tables with surprising efficiency.

"I've always believed in learning by doing," McGrath announced, his mechanical legs carrying him to the center of the class. "So, I'll demonstrate, and then we'll see what you can do."

The professor snatched up a disembodied shoulder joint from the nearest table. His fingers, unnaturally long, deftly manipulated the flesh and bone, wriggling through the meat like maggots. "Observe closely," he instructed. "The key to proper reanimation lies in the initial joining."

The class watched in as McGrath jammed the shoulder joint into place with a sickening pop. Several students winced at the sound, while others leaned in closer, eager to catch every detail.

After securing the joint, McGrath produced a needle seemingly out of thin air. His hands were almost unerringly swift. Moments later, the skin was all sewn up with small black stitches.

Eld had never seen such a quick and efficient technique before.

"This, my eager pupils, is the Weave and Bind method." McGrath's needle flashed in and out of the pale flesh with a hypnotic rhythm. "Developed by yours truly, it ensures a seamless connection between flesh."

The professor's stitches formed a complex pattern, almost like a spiderweb.

The black thread moved of its own accord at times, weaving through layers of skin and muscle as if alive. The longer Eld stared at it, the less it seemed like thread and the more it seemed like some kind of artificial vein. "The thread is infused with necromantic energy," McGrath proudly continued. "It not only holds the flesh together but also acts as a conduit for the animating force."

As McGrath finished his demonstration, he held up the newly stitched shoulder for all to see. The joint moved with uncanny smoothness that surpassed even natural movement. Fingers flexed and the arm rotated, all without being attached to a torso.

"Now," the professor said, his grin revealing those unnervingly sharp teeth, "It's your turn."

There was just something about Professor McGrath that ensured nobody wanted to disappoint him.

The students hurriedly began their macabre work, the room soon filled with the sounds of squelching flesh and muttered incantations. Some approached the task with enthusiasm, while others looked slightly green around the gills.

Eld was in the latter group.

He stared at the pile of body parts before him, feeling a knot of unease in his stomach.

Talbot, noticing Eld's hesitation, drifted closer. "Why are you hesitating?" he asked. "Don't tell me the mighty necromancer is squeamish."

Eld sighed, picking up a severed hand with obvious reluctance.

The fingers twitched slightly as he held it, causing him to nearly drop it in surprise. "Working with dead animals is one thing, but working with dead people…I don't know. It's always bothered me. There's something more personal about it."

"Well, better get used to it." Talbot floated lazily around Eld's head. "Can't be a proper necromancer if you're squeamish about corpses. Besides, think of it as arts and crafts. Very morbid arts and crafts."

"It's a long story," Eld said.

Talbot stared at him for a long moment, then nodded.

"You can tell me when you want," Talbot said. "Even wake me up for it, if you need to."

"Thanks," Eld smiled. Despite his laziness, Talbot was a good friend, but this was a very long story.

A big part of Eld's squeamishness around reanimating humans came from his father. When Eld brought back a pet, he made sure to bring back their soul as well, giving them a second chance at life. Aside from Graves—who was already a consummate suck-up—the servants at Blackwood Manor were husks—soulless beings whose flesh was being used against their will.

And since the use of husks was so thoroughly frowned upon, Eld didn't want to bring it up in class. There was a world of difference between working on a shoulder for practice and creating an undead zombie slave.

Eld's father always said that his squeamishness made him an inferior necromancer, but after speaking with Wolfgang, Eld was more and more determined to chart his own path. Still, he needed actual skill to do that, and it all started with learning Professor McGrath's method.

Taking a deep breath, Eld steeled himself and began the stitching process, doing his best to imitate McGrath's technique.

Eld had stitched body parts together before, but that was just, well, stitching—attaching everything so that he could reanimate it with necromantic magic.

McGrath's technique was different.

From what Eld had observed earlier, it wasn't just simple needlework.

McGrath also pulsed magic into his sewing. The stitches he made were essentially a transliteration of the symbols that most spellcasters drew in the air. Essentially, he was combining both steps of the reanimation process into one, mending physical wounds and bringing the target back to life in one fell swoop.

To his surprise, he found the work oddly soothing once he got past his initial revulsion. His fingers moved with increasing confidence as he replicated McGrath's Weave and Bind technique.

The thread shined faintly as he worked, responding to his innate necromantic abilities.

Talbot raised a lazy eyebrow.

"Damn. You're good at this…" he muttered.

But Eld wasn't the only one.

Across the room, he noticed Lilith working with intense focus, her silver hair floating around her as if stirred by an unseen wind. Her pale fingers moved fast, stitching flesh together with an almost artistic flair.

Suddenly, she threw her hands up in triumph.

"I'm done!" she cried, her voice rising to an excited piercing shriek that made several nearby jars crack and a few students clap their hands over their ears.

Professor McGrath winced, his mechanical legs emitting a distressed whine. "No need to shout, Miss Nightshade." He rubbed his ears. "I'd rather not add deafness to my list of afflictions. Though I suppose it might be a blessing in this particular class."

He scuttled over to examine Lilith's work, his goggles whirring as they adjusted their focus. Lilith stood proudly by her creation, a fully reassembled arm that twitched and moved as if trying to crawl off the table. "Hmm, pretty good, Miss Nightshade," he nodded approvingly. "Your binding shows promise, though your knots could use some work. Remember, we're aiming for reanimation, not strangulation."

Despite his jab, Lilith beamed with pride, casting a smug glance around the room. Her red eyes seemed to glow with satisfaction as she basked in the professor's praise.

Eld took another look at his stitched arm.

Lilith's looked good…

But he felt like his was better.

Lilith's arm had tried to crawl off the table, but Eld's was actually doing it.

Wait.

"Everlasting Night…" Eld cursed as the arm began scampering off.

He dove and caught it, but now he was holding hands with a reanimated hand that squirmed in his grip. That was just awkward.

Still, he wanted to get his work evaluated.

To his surprise, his stomach quivered with nervousness, almost like he was a kid again showing his dad one of his reanimated projects. Back then, when Eld was young, Eldritch Sr. had greatly approved of Eld's experiments, claiming it proved the genius of his bloodline. It was only when Eld began specializing in pet reanimation rather than pursuing power that Eldritch Sr.'s praise had morphed into disdain and eventually hatred.

Eld raised his hand, trying to keep his voice level. "Professor, could you take a look to make sure I did it correctly?"

McGrath's mechanical legs skittered him over to Eld's table almost before Eld had lowered his hand, leaving a trail of steam in his wake. The Professor leaned in close, his magnified eyes examining every stitch with intense scrutiny. The brass goggles clicked, various lenses sliding into place as he inspected Eld's work from every angle. After what felt like forever, he straightened up, a perplexed look on his face.

He glanced at Eld, then back to the arm, coughing slightly before finally speaking.

"Well, Mr. Blackwood," he said, genuine surprise lingering on his words, "I couldn't have done it better myself. Bravo! Your stitching is precise, your knots are secure, and the necromantic flow is remarkably smooth. You seem to have a natural affinity for this work."

Eld felt a surge of pride at the praise, a warm glow of accomplishment spreading through him.

"Take that, father," he thought. *"Turns out there's more in common between pet reanimation and human reanimation than you thought."*

However, it was quickly tempered by the frustrated look that flashed across Lilith's face. Eld could have sworn he heard a faint, high-pitched keening sound emanating from her direction.

He hadn't meant to one-up her, but she'd taken it that way.

Eld turned to Talbot.

"Hopefully she doesn't haunt me," Eld muttered.

"For what?" Talbot asked drearily. He hadn't even noticed Eld's demonstration.

From the looks of it, he'd dozed off.

Talbot had yet to even begin his project. The pile of body parts on his table remained untouched.

"Oh, gravemold," Talbot cursed. "Look at the time."

With deceptive casualness, he reached over and swapped his pile of unassembled parts with the completed project of the student next to him.

Unfortunately for Talbot, his neighbor was more observant than he had anticipated.

The student, a beautiful witch with pale skin and raven black hair that sparked with magical energy, noticed the switch immediately. With a wicked grin and a flick of her wrist, she cast a spell.

Talbot let out a yelp as his body suddenly shrank to the size of a doll, while his head remained its normal size. The effect was comically absurd, like a spectral bobblehead floating in midair.

His tiny arms flailed comically as he tried to maintain his balance and he eventually thudded to the floor.

"I deserved that," Talbot admitted, his tiny body struggling to support his oversized head as he waddled over to return the stolen project. "Though I must say, this is a new perspective on the class. Everything looks so much bigger."

The witch smirked, clearly pleased with her handiwork. Despite her youthful appearance, her voice was old and scratchy. Eld supposed it was different to tell ages when it came to witches—though the best strategy was just not to ask them.

"Next time, do your own work or I'll shrink something you'll miss even more," the witch chuckled.

Talbot groaned. "I don't know about doing my own work, but after that threat, I *can* promise not to take yours."

As the class wrapped up, Eld felt a sense of accomplishment despite his initial hesitation.

He had not only completed the assignment but had excelled at it. The triumphant necromancer carefully packed away his tools, stealing glances at his successfully stitched and reanimated limb, which was now flexing its fingers as if waving goodbye.

Just as the students were packing up their things, the classroom door burst open with such force that it nearly came off its hinges.

Professor Grimthorpe strode in, his usual calm and almost magisterial composure noticeably absent. His robes were askew, his hair disheveled and there was a wild, frantic look in his eyes that Eld had never seen before.

Grimthorpe barely spared a glance for the departing students, making a beeline for McGrath. The leprechaun professor looked up in surprise, his mechanical legs whirring as they adjusted to keep him at eye level with the agitated Grimthorpe.

Eld, curious about Grimthorpe's unusual behavior, lingered by the door, pretending to adjust his bag. He angled himself to better overhear the conversation, all while trying to appear nonchalant.

"I looked where you said it would be," Grimthorpe hissed, his voice low. There was an edge of desperation to his tone. "Nothing. Not a trace. Are you sure it still resides on academy grounds?"

McGrath's mechanical legs shuffled anxiously, steam hissing from the joints as he shifted his weight. "I don't know where else it would be." He tugged nervously at his beard. "When it was bound, it was buried in the crypts in the catacombs beneath the school. At least, that's what my sources say."

Grimthorpe's eyes narrowed and McGrath took a step back. "Your *sources* had better be reliable, McGrath," he growled, looming over the smaller professor. "If this turns out to be a wild goose chase, you'll find yourself teaching Remedial Reanimation in the sewers."

By then, the other students had left—and Eld's eavesdropping would be far too obvious. With no other choice, he slipped out of the classroom, his mind whirling with questions.

"What could they possibly be looking for?" Eld wondered. *"And what's got Grimthorpe so worried?"*

In all his time knowing Grimthorpe, he had never seen the usually unflappable professor so disturbed. Whatever this mysterious entity was, it posed a significant threat.

His musings were interrupted by Talbot, who had managed to return to his normal size. The poltergeist drifted alongside Eld as they made their way down the corridor, oblivious to the weighty thoughts occupying his friend's mind.

"Hey Eld," Talbot called. "You know the Midnight Exhumation is coming up, right?"

Eld blinked, momentarily confused by the change of subject.

His brain struggled to shift gears from ominous mysteries to ordinary school events. "Midnight Exhumation?" he echoed.

Then he blinked.

"Oh, right. You were talking about it earlier, right? Digging up parts?"

"Free labor for the school, more like," Talbot muttered. "We're supposed to go digging in the graveyard at midnight. Sounds like a real blast, doesn't it? Nothing says *quality education* like grave robbing in the wee hours. Anyways, it's after the first month of school, so it's coming up quick."

As Talbot continued to ramble about the upcoming event, describing the various tools they needed and speculating on what they might unearth, Eld's thoughts drifted back to the conversation he had overheard. Something was going on at Bathurst, something that had even the unflappable Professor Grimthorpe on edge.

Chapter 10

Arise and Grind!

The first month at Bathurst Academy had flown by for Eld in a bewildering blur of peculiar classes, magical mistakes, and increasingly strange encounters. Despite his original reluctance to go to the school, it had been the best thing that had ever happened to him. It felt like his skills as a necromancer grew every single day, and his familiars were more than willing to help him test his newfound skills.

It was the night of the Midnight Exhumation, but there were still a few minutes until midnight proper.

Eld sat cross-legged on his bed, bent over Bart, his undead rodent friend. A lone enchanted candle dimly lit the chamber.

"Hold still, Bart," Eld murmured, his brow furrowed.

With a delicate hand, he attached a lizard's tail where Bart's fleshy rat had once been. The new appendage twitched and curled, its shining scales glimmering eerily in the candle's pale flame.

Across the room, Talbot snored softly. At Eld's feet, Shuck dozed peacefully, his mismatched patchwork body rising and falling with each breath.

"There," Eld said, setting down his tools and admiring his handiwork. Bart scampered up his arm, the lizard tail leaving a cool trail on Eld's skin. "What do you think? A bit flashier than your old tail, eh? The good thing about this is that if it gets scary, you can shed it to make a quick getaway."

Bart let out an interested squeak.

"Try it," Eld said.

The tail separated itself from Bart's body, writhing furiously as Bart scampered off. Moments later, the nub—empowered by Eld's significantly increased necromantic energy—glowed brightly, and a new tail sprouted.

Bart glanced at the new tail, then at the shed decoy, which was quickly rotting away to a pile of grave dirt.

The rat squeaked in what Eld chose to interpret as approval.

Grinning, Eld stood and stretched, his joints popping after hours of hunched work. He glanced at the clock on the wall.

"Almost time for the Midnight Exhumation," Eld thought. *"I better get moving."*

Once, he'd looked upon the event with trepidation, but now that he was excelling in more and more of his necromantic classes, he was outright excited.

For a necromancer such as himself, no pursuit uncovered more elusive secrets than a hands-on examination of Death's canvas. And he had become far more accustomed to dealing with all kinds of remains.

He had prepared his tools earlier in a small leather satchel, carefully choosing each instrument. A tingling sensation rose in his limbs as he grasped the bag. It was like even the sparks of magic in his body were eager to get started.

He reached over and gave Shuck a gentle pat on the head.

The dog snored once, but then his eyes flickered open.

Tail wagging and tongue hanging, he quickly lopped after Eld, hurrying forward on his mismatched paws.

Now that Eld had improved his necromantic techniques, he'd experimented with shrinking Shuck's oversized paw, but the dog had already adjusted to the mismatch, so that had just caused him to start tripping again.

Eld had quickly returned the paw to its prior state, realizing that he should have known better than to teach an old dog a new way to walk.

As Eld made his way through the winding corridors of Bathurst, the excitement in his chest mingled with nervousness.

"What's going on?" Eld wondered. *"Shouldn't there be a ton of people getting ready to go outside right now?"*

He supposed that the students in the other fields were either still sleeping or holed up in the library cramming for upcoming exams, but where were the Necromancy majors?

They couldn't have *all* started slacking off like Talbot, right?

Was some illness going around? It took a *lot* to take down the nightkin, especially because many of them were already specialized carriers of pestilence to begin with.

But the halls remained empty until he reached the main entrance, where a familiar figure caught his eye. Lilith stood by a window, her silver hair shining softly in the moonlight.

She turned as Eld approached, her red eyes widening slightly in surprise.

"Eld? Where are you going at this hour?"

"The Midnight Exhumation," Eld quizzically replied, hefting his bag of tools. "I was just heading out to the graveyard."

He tilted his head to the side. "Aren't you a Necromancy major too?"

Eld figured that was why the two of them had so many of the same classes, but considering Lilith's boundless ambition, it was possible to know for sure. She could have somehow stitched up her own proprietary quadruple major.

"Didn't you hear? It's been canceled this year. Professor Grimthorpe announced it in my last class."

Eld's excitement deflated like a punctured balloon. "Canceled? But why?"

Lilith shrugged, her shoulders rising and falling gracefully. "He didn't say. Just that it wouldn't be happening and to stay in our dorms tonight."

"Oh," Eld said, trying to mask his disappointment. "I must have missed the announcement. I've been a bit preoccupied with studies, I guess."

Lilith raised a brow. "Studies, hm? Or perhaps you've been too busy preparing for the Combat Club qualifiers?"

She'd been at the practices, of course, same as Eld.

Which, of course, only made Eld wonder where she got her supernatural stamina from.

"Well, that's part of it," Eld admitted.

"I hope you're ready for some real competition," Lilith replied. Her words were as sharp as her team's rapiers.

Eld chuckled nervously. "Speaking of which, the next round of matches is coming up in a couple of weeks, aren't they?"

"Indeed they are," Lilith said. "I do hope you're prepared, Eld. If we compete, I'd hate to wipe the floor with you too quickly. The winners of each bout will qualify for the Tournament of Shadows, just before the end of the term."

"We'll see about that," Eld retorted, though his voice lacked conviction. He was all too aware of how much catching up he had to do.

Everyone in the Nocturnal Combat Club knew to stay on the aggressive and keep their opponents from casting spells. And while Eld was improving under Orlando and Wolfgang's tutelage, he was still more of a master pincushion than a master swordsman.

"Well, now that I've come out here for nothing," Eld said. "Do you have any plans?"

Lilith yawned. "Well. I was going to go to sleep. Just got out of a last-second cram session. But if you wouldn't mind, I *suppose* you could walk back to my dorm with me. I live in the Banshee's Belfry."

Eld chuckled. "A little on point to pick that as your dorm, don't you think?"

"Come on," Lilith protested. "I know it's a stereotype, but for good reason. The stones of the building are etched with sound-dampening runes. Makes sure none of us cause mass damage with ill-timed snoring or sleep talking."

Eld's chuckle deepened, but he nodded. "I'll walk you back," he said.

Lilith smiled, but there was a faint hint of nervousness there that confirmed Eld's suspicions. Earlier, the banshee had seemed a little harried.

Something was bothering her, and while Lilith could be a handful, Eld respected her intelligence. He'd already noticed a few strange coincidences. If Lilith noticed them too, he definitely wasn't imagining things.

The two chatted aimlessly, just going through simple small talk about the weather or the food at the refectory.

It was only around halfway there that Lilith changed the subject.

"So, how are you finding Professor McGrath's class?" Lilith asked, a hint of genuine curiosity beneath her usual competitive tone.

Eld shrugged and tugged at the collar of his jacket. "It's fascinating, but I'll admit, some of the more invasive procedures make me a bit queasy. That whole business the other day, moving all the arm muscles to the legs and the leg muscles to the arms. I have no idea what was the point of all that."

Lilith laughed. "The great necromancer, squeamish about a little flesh manipulation? Don't tell me a *Blackwood* is going soft?"

"Hey, there's a difference between reanimation and full-on body modification," Eld protested, but he was smiling.

Despite their growing academic rivalry, he found himself enjoying these moments with Lilith. She was more than just ardently competitive. She also had a keen wit and a kind personality at heart.

As they approached the entrance to Banshee's Belfry, they noticed another student coming out, a shovel tucked behind their back.

"Hey!" Lilith called out. "Where are you going?"

The ghostly pale girl with translucent skin, jumped, startled. "I…uh…Midnight Exhumation?"

Eld and Lilith exchanged a look. "It's been canceled," Eld explained gently. "Grimthorpe's orders."

The girl's shoulders slumped. "Oh. I was really looking forward to it."

"Tell you what," Lilith said. "Why don't you join me for a study session tomorrow? We can go over some advanced banshee techniques. Teach you how to control those vocal cords."

The girl's face lit up. "Really? That would be amazing!"

As the younger student hurried back inside, Eld gave Lilith an impressed look. "That was nice of you."

Lilith shrugged, a faint blush coloring her pale cheeks. "Well, we banshees have to stick together. Besides, I remember how it felt to be a freshman last year."

They reached Lilith's door, and she turned to face Eld, her expression suddenly serious. "Be careful, Eld," she said softly. "There's something…off about the school lately. The professors too. I can feel it in the air."

Eld nodded. "I've noticed something too. The other day, after stitching class. Grimthorpe seemed seriously disturbed by something."

Lilith's forehead wrinkled. "I heard the same thing—but after my Hemomancy class. He was furious with Professor Hemlock."

So Hemlock was tied up in this too…

"Do you have any idea what it might be?" Eld asked.

"I don't know…" Lilith replied. Her words were hesitant and her face was set in a mixture of irritation and apprehension.

Eld got the distinct feeling that Lilith *hadn't* been cramming for a test. She'd been doing extra research to try and figure out what was going on, but neither of them had enough pieces.

"I'll let you know if I find anything else," Eld said.

Lilith hesitated, then nodded.

"Okay. Then I will too then."

With that, Eld smiled and bade her farewell.

"Farewell, Lilith. I hope you get a lot of sleep."

"You too Eld," she replied.

As he watched her disappear into her room, Eld felt a strange mix of emotions. Camaraderie, rivalry, and a growing sense of unease about what lay ahead. He started back towards his dorm, but halfway there, he stopped.

If Grimthorpe had suddenly canceled the Midnight Excavation, then…

"You know what?" he muttered to himself. "I'm going anyway."

Eld turned on his heels and made his way towards the back door which led to the graveyard. Shuck nudged him pointedly. The patchwork dog's head jerked back towards the dorms, his tail wagging.

"Are you sleepy?" Eld asked.

But the dog shook his head, nudging Eld again.

Eld raised an eyebrow.

"You think we should get Talbot for backup?"

The dog nodded his head eagerly.

"I don't know about that Shuck," Eld replied. "Remember that whole debacle with the grim reaper statue?"

Shuck just looked confused.

"Oh, right," Eld noted. "You weren't there for that. Well, try to wake him up if you can, but be prepared to be disappointed."

Shuck trotted off, his faith in Talbot seemingly far greater than Eld's. Eld just shook his head and hurried on. Since the halls were totally empty, he left the school without any issues and soon found himself approaching the iron-wrought graveyard gates.

In the distance, shadowy figures were slowly shambling back and forth, their movements somehow both erratic and monotonous as they dug holes with repeated herky-jerky movements.

Eld frowned, recognizing the telltale movements.

"Husks…" he whispered to himself. "But what are they doing here in Bathurst?"

If Eld remembered correctly, Grimthorpe had vocally disapproved of Eldritch Sr.'s use of husks.

So why were they here?

Bart squeaked softly, popping out of Eld's coat, his new lizard tail curling around Eld's wrist. The rodent stared fearfully at the husks, trembling in place.

"Yeah, yeah, I don't like them either," Eld admitted. "I mean, nobody does…they're the reason why most people fear necromancy."

As Eld continued observing the husks, goosebumps rippled across his skin, and not just because of the cold.

"This many husks in one place are dangerous," he thought to himself. *"Not even father would risk something like this."*

The husk's herky-jerky movements *seemed* reliable for now, but he knew better than to count on them. Since husks didn't have a soul, all that was left were feral instincts. Normally, those feral instincts were submerged—kept tame by the will of whoever reanimated them.

But they were also deeply unstable.

If one went crazy, the whole lot of them would—that was where the zombie apocalypse cliché came from.

But there was a good side to Grimthorpe using husks. Eld had long experience with them, and he knew how they thought—or rather, he knew how they didn't think. He snuck past them easily, avoiding them when he could. When he was forced to move inside a husk's field of vision, he waited for the precise moment when they began digging to dart past.

When in doubt, husks always stuck to their primary assigned task to the detriment of everything else.

As Eld snuck past the husks, he felt a sudden vehement writhing, and then Franky reared out, poking almost his whole body out of Eld's coat.

"Steady there Franky," Eld said reproachfully. "You're going to get caught."

But for once, the typically timid centipede didn't care.

He kept pointing his head forward and chittering excitedly.

The centipede had noticed something…

But all Eld saw was grave after grave.

He shrugged.

"Alright, I'll go with your gut then," he said. "Point the way…but make sure you do it subtly."

Franky slunk back into the coat, directing Eld with a series of nudges.

The graveyard was massive, arguably bigger than the academy itself. Every so often, Eld saw areas with plenty of holes and discarded shovels—presumably the remains of previous Midnight Excavations.

But Franky didn't want to stop anywhere near there. The centipede kept diligently nudging Eld onwards. Before long, Eld's already-tired legs were aching, but he kept going. Out of all his pets, he trusted Franky's necromantic senses the most.

If he said there was something, there probably was something.

After what felt like an eternity of walking, they arrived at an older section of the graveyard, where the headstones were worn and weathered and their inscriptions long since faded.

Under the branches of an old oak tree, Eld noticed something odd.

An empty patch of earth with no grave markers at all. He approached and a familiar voice made him jump.

"You needed back-up for this? But I guess there's nobody around to attack you…which makes me the perfect backup."

Eld whirled around to see Talbot floating nearby, Shuck padding silently at his side. The ghost seemed especially smug in the moonlight.

"Talbot! I didn't think you'd want to come." Eld said, glancing nervously at the distant husks. The husks were currently moving in a rhythmic pattern, slowly and steadily clearing the graves. But they'd make it here sooner or later. Eld wanted to be long gone by then.

Talbot shrugged. "I didn't. But Shuck wouldn't let me sleep. Kept whining and pawing at me until I got up."

Eld raised an eyebrow. "Really? And here I thought you were worried about me."

"Please," Talbot scoffed. "I just want to wrap this all up and get back to slumbering."

As they talked, neither noticed that Shuck, Bart, and Franky had all started digging furiously at the base of the oak tree. The two smaller pets had catapulted themselves from Eld's coat, and Shuck joined them.

It wasn't until Shuck let out a soft bark that Eld and Talbot turned to look.

"Shuck!" Eld whispered urgently, moving to quiet the dog. "The husks will—"

But he froze when he saw the animals' eyes. All of them glowed with a faint purple light. Somehow, the pets seemed more powerful than before…

"This isn't normal." Eld's brow furrowed as he watched his pets dig with unnatural fervor. "Whatever's down there it's affecting all of them. Honestly, it's making me feel a little jealous. They aren't even this excited to see *me* most of the time."

Shuck continued pawing at the ground and Franky continued scrabbling.

Even Bart had gotten into the excitement, using a loose bone he'd found as a shovel.

Eld decided to join them, taking the shovel from his pack.

After a moment, he struck something solid.

There was a dull thunk and he felt the tip of his shovel sink into something.

Shuck's tail began wagging so hard it actually fell off, the mismatched patch of fur and bone clattering to the ground. Separated from his body, the tail rapidly rotted into grave dirt. Shuck turned and stared at the remains of his tail, before shrugging and moving right on to wagging the nub.

Despite the tension, Eld couldn't help but laugh.

"Maybe I should have given *you* the lizard tail," he said.

But even though Eld had hit something solid, when he gazed at the hole, he couldn't see anything. The only thing that stared back at him was pitch-black darkness—the same darkness he'd seen in the school's catacombs.

Eld glanced up at the sky, where the full moon was shining brightly.

The darkness seemed to swallow the moon's light hole.

Frowning, Eld dug a bit more, trying to clear away the surrounding earth to get a better look at what was going on. There was a sickening squelch, and Eld dropped the shovel with a yelp.

"What? What is it?" Talbot peered into the hole.

Eld's face had gone pale. "I think I just put my shovel through someone's head. It felt so…pulpy."

The earth began to shift and crumble.

Eld and Talbot scrambled back as a being slowly emerged from the ground.

It was a woman or at least…

Something in the shape of a woman.

Her skin was as pale as moonlight, and long black hair fell around her face in thick tendrils that seemed to move of their own accord. A small tiara rested on her brow, a large black gem set into its center. There was a nasty cut in her cheek—the result of Eld's misplaced shovel.

Her eyes were deep pools of purple, filled with swirling patterns of light that resembled distant stars and galaxies. As Eld stared closely, he thought he recognized specific constellations. It was as if the entire universe had been boiled down into her gaze.

Eld felt both infinitesimally small and inexplicably connected to something greater than himself as he stared into those eyes.

His feet moved of their own accord, bringing him towards the woman. He was drawn to her just as falling fruits were drawn to the earth.

The gash across the woman's cheek made by his shovel began to knit itself back together. Black blood oozed from the wound before it sealed completely, leaving unblemished skin behind.

The woman's eyes focused on Eld.

"Eldritch B. Blackwood," she said. Eld blinked in surprise. Her voice was a rigid statement. She knew exactly who she was.

"Help me," she whispered.

Then she collapsed right back into the freshly undug grave.

Chapter 11

Three May Keep a
Secret If All of Them Are Undead

The sudden thump seemed to echo through the dreary silence.

Eld hastily glanced back at the husks, fearing that they'd heard him, but nothing.

"What was that?" Talbot asked. "Did she say your name?"

"She did…" Eld stammered.

He could hardly believe this was real. It all felt like a dream. Perhaps he'd fallen and hit his head after running into Lilith.

Eld glanced over to make sure Talbot wasn't looking then pinched himself, feeling his cold and clammy flesh between his fingers. It was a stereotype, but it was a stereotype for a reason. Based on past experiences, a good old pinching usually worked.

The other well-known option to wake up from a dream was to kill himself, but Eld always found that to generally be a bit too all-in.

Eld walked over, standing over the strange woman's unconscious body.

Her skin shined with a strange pale light that reminded him of the moon. Though she was unmoving, long shadows danced around her body, twirling and dancing as if they had a mind of their own.

The shadows seemed endlessly deep, but then Eld noticed something lurking inside of them.

A spiky black shape, one he recognized from home.

The black sun.

He'd first seen the symbol in the sky, then again on his way to Bathurst. And now, it was endlessly repeating itself, flashing back and forth inside the dancing shadows that surrounded this unconscious woman.

"Do you see that?" Eld asked, pointing at the shadows.

"See the woman who'd just passed out?" Talbot asked. "Um, yeah. I'm tired, not blind."

"No, the black sun," Eld said.

Talbot stared at Eld like he'd grown a third head. Considering the student body, the second head wasn't altogether unheard of at Bathurst, but the third was still considered bizarre.

"The black sun? What are you talking about?"

Before Eld could reply, Talbot shook his head.

"You know what? Never mind. That's another adventure for the day," the poltergeist yawned. "Time to head back to bed, Eld. We have class tomorrow, and I expect I'm going to need some help."

"What is wrong with you?" Eld groaned. Despite his irritation, he kept his voice to a bare whisper for fear of attracting the husks. "We can't just leave her here…"

Without waiting for a response, he knelt beside the mysterious woman, her long dark hair spilling across the damp earth like ink.

Shuck whined softly, nudging Eld's hand with his cold nose. The patchwork dog's mismatched eyes darted between his master and the unconscious woman and he let out a low whine.

"No, I don't know what that was either, Shuck," Eld replied. "I have no idea how she knew my name, but she was right that she needed my help."

Talbot flickered with agitation. "Are you out of your mind? This isn't some stray reanimated cat you can take home, Eld. This is a person you reanimated! A person, Eld! We should just leave her here! We don't know who—or what—she is!"

"I reanimated?" Eld asked. "I mean, I think she was already alive."

"Already alive? Already alive and just napping in a grave? By the Grasping Vines of Rot, of *course* you reanimated her!" Talbot replied, throwing his hands up. At this point, the poltergeist's voice was quickly rising, so Eld hastily shushed him.

Talbot flickered irritably, but to his credit, he lowered his voice.

"Listen Eld…I'm not sure where you come from, but usually, things stay in graves after you put them there. You must have…I don't know, cast a spell without thinking. Or maybe some reanimating potion slipped out of your pack."

Eld frowned.

Talbot had a point there.

Though his necromantic skills had improved, he'd never heard of anyone capable of reanimating someone just by splitting their face with a shovel.

If anything, that usually had the opposite effect.

But here, the woman had seemed like she was already alive. Eld was sure of it. It wasn't just the fact that he hadn't cast any spells—it was his pets' behavior beforehand.

Eld opened his mouth to reply to Cloudehill, but he suddenly paused as a strange unshakeable familiarity interrupted his train of thought.

He took a closer look at the woman, carefully studying her face.

There was something about her, something that tugged at the edges of his consciousness. It was *almost* like he was seeing a long-lost childhood friend.

But that feeling didn't make any sense.

The Blackwood Manor was isolated from any outsiders, so the only other child Eld had played with had been Cloudehill.

"Look, we can't just abandon her here," Eld said.

"Why not?" Talbot countered, drifting closer to peer at the woman's face. "Let's go get the professors. They're better equipped to handle…whatever this is." He gestured vaguely at her.

The professors.

For some reason, that suggestion filled Eld's heart with unease.

Grimthorpe's words suddenly echoed ominously through Eld's mind.

"Are you sure it still resides on academy grounds?"

It sounded like Grimthorpe had been talking about something alive, something like this woman.

He gulped, then shook his head firmly as he turned back to Talbot. Though he didn't mean to, Eld found his voice rising louder and louder.

"No, we can't risk it. Something strange is going on and I have a feeling she is connected to it." He motioned to the unconscious woman. "We need to figure this out ourselves first."

Talbot launched his hands into the air in exasperation. "And how exactly do you propose we do that? In case you've forgotten, we're students, not detectives!"

As Talbot finished his sentence, his words seemed to echo through the graveyard.

Eld whirled around just as Shuck let out a low growl, his hackles rising.

By the Corpse Father's Twisted Entrails…

The air grew thick with an unseen energy, causing the hairs on the back of Eld's neck to stand on end.

Eld and Talbot turned to see the husks in the distance, their vacant eyes now fixed squarely on their location. The mindless undead began to shamble towards them with single-minded purpose.

"We're out of time," Eld muttered. He was so anxious his shrunken heart felt like it was going to start beating again. "We're out of time. We have to move. Now."

Without waiting for Talbot's response, Eld scooped the unconscious woman into his arms. Her weight was surprising. Some parts of her body seemed oddly heavy. Her head and legs felt like they were loaded with bricks. But other parts of her seemed oddly ethereal.

As bizarre as it sounded, Eld got the distinct feeling that she somehow existed in multiple planes at once. It was like she was a ghost and a real person all at the same time.

He groaned as her body almost plopped out of his hands.

Talbot let out a long-suffering sigh that sounded like wind whistling through an empty room. "Fine! I'll help. But you owe me so much homework for this, Blackwood. I'm talking a semester's worth, at least."

The poltergeist floated over. Instead of carrying the woman's body, he possessed her boots, floating them upwards to hold her aloft.

As they continued their desperate trek back to the main building, a strange feeling of destiny seemed to weigh down each and every one of Eld's steps. He couldn't shake the feeling that this night would change everything, not just his time at Bathurst, but the course of his entire life.

It was like the air itself was screaming to him that he was meant to be here this night, meant to rescue this girl.

They navigated the winding paths of Bathurst Academy with the desperation of vampires fleeing the sunlight. Eld's arms ached from carrying the unconscious woman, but he dared not slow their pace.

They skirted the edge of the graveyard, but there was no easy path.

The gnarled trees surrounding the wrought-iron gates reached out with skeletal branches as if trying to ensnare them.

The husks' shuffling footsteps echoed behind them.

As they continued chasing them, Eld could feel the necromantic energy gradually rising. For now, the husks were just following their orders to detain visitors.

But Eld turned back and saw that every so often, one of the husks would stumble. A few of them were drooling, and their mouths were getting a little bit too wide.

If this went on for much longer…

"Behind here!" Talbot's voice echoed and the boots glowed white before pointing towards a crumbling stone wall that seemed like it'd been part of the academy's original structure before expansion.

Eld quickly followed him.

The two huddled in its shadow as a group of husks shambled past.

Eld did not need to breathe and neither did Talbot, but he was acutely aware of the woman's slow, steady breathing against his chest. He hastily put a sleeve over her mouth and nose—careful not to snuff out her breath but doing what he could to muffle it.

For one horrible moment, Eld saw a rotting head staring at him from across the wall, but it was nothing more than his overactive imagination. In reality, the husks had shambled right on past them, staring menacingly but ineffectively into the distance.

Once the immediate danger had passed, Eld let out a sigh of relief.

When things were tense enough, even necromancers like him started seeing things.

The two friends pressed on and before long, they were back on campus.

The looming silhouette of the Hemocraft Tower rose before them, its windows glowing with an eerie red light. They gave it a wide berth, knowing that Professor Hemlock often worked late into the night on her mysterious blood magic experiments.

As they approached the main courtyard, Shuck suddenly froze, his hackles rising. A patrol of husks was making its rounds, their vacant eyes sweeping the area.

"Here too?" Talbot whispered. "They've never been on campus before."

Eld grimaced.

Talbot had been around the school for years. The fact that Grimthorpe was suddenly using husks as guards had to mean something awful.

But there was no time to sit and think about that now.

"The fountain," Eld whispered, nodding towards the ornate structure in the center of the courtyard. Its waters ran black in the moonlight, fed by some underground spring that students gossiped was connected directly to the River Styx.

They crept forward, using the fountain's shadow as cover.

The woman in Eld's arms stirred slightly, her bizarre mismatched weight causing him to nearly lose his balance. He tightened his grip, silently pleading that she remain unconscious for just a little longer.

Once again, they remained silent until the patrol passed by.

As they did, Eld got a good whiff of them.

The rotting smell of the husk's body had been covered up by a ridiculous cocktail of perfumes.

And as Eld took a closer look, he realized that the husks were wearing the tattered remains of what looked like fine silks.

Perhaps they'd once been nobles in their past life.

"You know," Talbot whispered, "I agreed to be your roommate because you seemed calm, collected, and reserved. You seemed unimpressive, passive, and unmotivated to be anything more than you already were. *Not* a troublemaker. *Not* someone who would go off half-cocked when he sees a pretty face!"

Eld managed a weak chuckle, adjusting his grip on the woman. "You thought I reanimated her, right? Well then, consider it extra credit in practical necromancy."

Eld couldn't help but wonder about the identity of the mysterious woman in his arms.

Who was she?

And why was she buried in Bathurst's graveyard?

Talbot hoisted her up, emerging from their hiding spot as the husks disappeared out of sight. "You know, when this inevitably blows up in our faces, remember that I told you so."

As they approached the main hall, Eld suddenly stopped.

Shuck let out a low whine, sensing his master's tension. The patchwork dog's mismatched eyes darted back and forth, scanning for danger. In the hallway ahead, a group of husks shambled aimlessly, their vacant eyes staring into nothing.

"Corpse Father's Bleached Bones," Eld cursed, ducking behind a large ornamental urn. "There's so many of them."

"Wait a second," Talbot muttered. "Something's weird about them.

Talbot left the woman's boots, shimmering and disappearing into thin air.

Though he couldn't see Talbot, Eld knew that he was drifting close. His translucent form allowed him to get near without detection.

He floated back to Eld, his standard grin replaced by a frown. "Eld, your magical sense is better than mine. Look at their eyes. Is that what I think it is?"

Eld squinted, focusing on the husks' glassy stares.

A faint, pulsing glow emanated from their pupils. Eld recognized the feeling from the Blackwood Family Manor.

"An oculus spell. One of my father's favorite techniques. Someone's using them as remote viewers."

"Great." Talbot groaned, throwing his spectral hands up in exasperation. "So not only do we have to avoid the husks, but whoever's controlling them too. Any brilliant ideas?"

Eld nodded, inspiration striking him faster than even he anticipated. After his last month at Bathurst, he was getting good at wiggling out of sticky situations.

He set the woman down gently, propping her against the urn, and reached into his pocket.

"Bart," he called softly. The zombie rat poked its head out, whiskers twitching. Its beady eyes sparkled with intelligence as it looked up at Eld. "I need your help, little guy."

Bart gazed back at him, opening his mouth to show that he expected some treats later. It seemed like the rat was acutely aware that he was currently the catch-all solution to Eld's problems.

Eld traced arcane symbols through the air, painting runes that resembled eyes and telescopes as he murmured the familiar incantation under his breath.

For a brief moment, the words of power hung in the air, shimmering with ethereal energy despite how softly Eld had spoken them.

Before long, Bart's eyes began to glow with the pulsing light of an oculus spell. "Alright," Eld said, setting the rat down. "Go on ahead and scout the way for us."

As Bart scurried off into the darkness, his tiny claws clicking softly on the stone floor, Eld turned to Talbot. "I'll use him as our eyes."

A hint of admiration danced in Talbot's spectral eyes. "Not bad, Blackwood."

The clandestine journey through Bathurst's labyrinthine halls was an exercise in stealth and paranoia. Eld's consciousness flitted between his own body and Bart's, the zombie rat's enhanced senses providing a crucial advantage. The corridors, finally familiar after a month of class, had transformed into a treacherous maze with the introduction of the husks.

It seemed like every part of the school had suddenly turned hostile.

Ancient tapestries depicting long-dead necromancers seemed to ripple with unseen currents, their woven eyes following the group's every move. Every time they turned a corner, Eld automatically checked to see if someone else had cast an oculus spell on him.

It was never there, but the paranoia only mounted.

Suits of armor creaked ominously, as if on the verge of animation.

The very stones beneath their feet seemed to whisper of past campus disasters, the weight of centuries of magical practice pressing down upon them.

Bart scurried ahead, his tiny claws barely making a sound on the polished floors. Through the rat's eyes, Eld saw the world in shades of gray and ultraviolet, picking up traces of magical residue invisible to the human eye. It was both disorienting and fascinating, a perspective he had never experienced before.

"Hold up," Eld whispered, his voice barely audible even in the hushed corridor.

He blinked rapidly, readjusting to his own vision. "There's a group of husks around the next corner. We'll have to find another way."

Talbot, floating nervously beside him, nodded. "What about that classroom?" he suggested, pointing to a door slightly ajar. "We could cut through and come out on the other side of the East Wing."

Eld nodded.

That seemed as good a plan as any.

They slipped inside, Eld carefully maneuvering the unconscious woman through the narrow opening.

Just like every other classroom at Bathurst, the place was a study in organized chaos – beakers bubbled with unknown concoctions, star charts covered the walls, and a partially dissected creature that might have once been a griffin lay sprawled across the teacher's desk.

Normally, Eld would have been fascinated.

Now, he had no time.

As they crept between the rows of desks, a sudden noise from the corridor froze them in their tracks. Shuffling footsteps approached, accompanied by the telltale moan of a husk patrol.

Eld's mind raced, searching for a solution.

His eyes fell on a large wardrobe in the corner, likely used to store dangerous magical artifacts. "In here," he hissed, already moving towards it.

They piled in, Shuck squeezing in last and pulling the door shut with his teeth.

The wardrobe was cramped and smelled strongly of mothballs and brimstone. Eld could feel the woman's slow, steady breathing against his chest.

Through a crack in the wardrobe door, they watched as two husks shambled into the room. The undead creatures moved with jerky, uncoordinated motions, their glassy eyes sweeping back and forth.

One bumped into a desk, sending a cascade of quills clattering to the floor.

The creature turned towards the sound, and Eld's breath caught in his throat.

If that was enough to drive it feral…

Beside him, Talbot had gone completely still, barely visible in the darkness.

After what felt like an eternity, the husks finally shuffled out of the room. The group waited several more agonizing minutes before daring to emerge from their hiding spot.

"That," Talbot said, his voice shaky despite his usual blasé attitude, "Was too close."

Eld nodded grimly, readjusting his grip on the woman. Her weight seemed to have increased tenfold during their impromptu game of hide-and-seek. Normally, he would have just blamed his physical weakness, but that wasn't the case.

He'd grown much stronger thanks to his training at the Nocturnal Combat Club.

This woman…

Eld knew it was rude to say it outright, but there was just something inexplicable about her weight. It seemed to fluctuate in his hands. Sometimes, she wasn't there at all—less than a specter like Talbot. Other times, she was even denser than iron.

"We need to keep moving. We're not safe until we reach the dormitories."

Talbot nodded and they pressed on, their progress slowed by the need for constant vigilance. Bart scouted ahead once more, while Shuck brought up the rear, his keen senses alert for any sign of pursuit.

Before long, they were near the dormitory wing, but the echoing footsteps of the husks filled the air with tension.

They were close to their goal, but the final stretch would be the most dangerous.

Eld thought back to what Lilith told him: that *all* students were forbidden from leaving the dorms that day. Grimthorpe— or whoever was working with him to control these husks— intended to police that to its fullest.

The hallways here were swarming with husks.

Eld took a deep breath, steeling himself for the final push.

The woman in his arms shifted slightly, a small furrow appearing between her brows.

It seemed like she was awakening.

Briefly, Eld found himself wondering, not for the first time that night, just who – or what – she was, and what consequences their actions might bring.

But there was no turning back now. They had come too far and risked too much.

According to Talbot, the Midnight Exhumation was to find more body parts for experimentation. Eld already knew that this was a real living woman, not just some experiment subject.

And between Grimthorpe's words and the fact that this woman had recognized him on sight, he suspected a much deeper secret here.

With a nod to his companions, Eld stepped forward, the weight of destiny heavy on his shoulders. His consciousness flitted rapidly between his own body and Bart's enhanced senses, divining a path.

"Eld!" Talbot's whisper sounded like it came from inside Eld's head. His shared consciousness with Bart made everything feel surreal. "There's a bunch of those brain-dead husks up ahead. We gotta find another way around."

"I know." Eld nodded, he had already seen them through Bart's eyes, though Talbot hadn't. He pointed.

"This way."

They kept going, jumping at every shadow and creaky floorboard.

As they neared the dorms, Eld felt like he was carrying the weight of the world, not just one mysteriously undead woman. The mysteries from tonight swirled endlessly in his mind, and it was all he could do to push them aside and focus on the path Bart had discovered for them.

As they neared the central atrium, voices echoed from around the corner.

Sentient beings—not husks.

Eld gestured frantically to Talbot, who quickly possessed a nearby suit of armor. The metal creaked and groaned as the ghost settled into it, bringing it to life.

With inhuman strength, Talbot, in the animated armor, helped Eld hoist the woman up and behind a large tapestry depicting the founding of Bathurst—thirteen nightkin of all different species standing around a large stone chalice that contained a spiky orb of pure darkness—the seemingly ever-present black sun.

There was something different about the sun this time though, and Eld noticed despite the circumstances. It seemed to be sinking into the chalice, almost like it was setting.

They had barely concealed themselves when Professors Grimthorpe and McGrath rounded the corner.

"…telling you, the readings are off the charts," McGrath was saying, his mechanical legs clicking rapidly as he struggled to keep up with Grimthorpe's longer strides. The leprechaun professor's face was flushed with excitement, his eyes wild behind his brass goggles. "A burst of arcane energy that powerful…it has to be what we're looking for."

Grimthorpe's face was set in grim lines, his usual composure replaced by the same ardent intensity Eld had seen at the end of his Stitching class. "And you're certain about the location? The old oak in the far corner of the graveyard?"

"Positive," McGrath confirmed, waving a contraption that looked like a cross between a pocket watch and a crystal ball. It emitted a soft, pulsing glow that matched the precise rhythm of the woman's breathing. "If we hurry, we might still…"

Their voices faded as they passed, but Eld's mind was reeling. They were looking for something—or someone—by the old oak…the exact spot where they had found the unconscious girl!

The coincidence was just too deep to ignore.

But why?

What made her so important that it had two of Bathurst's most prominent professors sneaking around in the dead of night?

Once the coast was clear, they emerged from their hiding spot and pressed on.

They were nearly to the dormitory wing when disaster struck.

As they rounded a corner, they came face to face with a zombie, but not a husk.

It was Professor Cadaver.

The patchwork professor's mismatched eyes widened in surprise, one bulging comically while the other narrowed suspiciously.

"Mr. Blackwood? Mr. Wilting? What are you doing out of bed at this hour?" Professor Cadaver's voice was a rasp, like dry leaves scraping against stone.

Eld's thoughts grasped at the void, searching for an excuse. He could feel the woman stirring in his arms, threatening to wake at any moment. "We were just…um…"

"Sleepwalking!" Talbot interjected, his voice echoing metallically from within the suit of armor. "Poor Eld here has a terrible case of it. I was just guiding him back to our room."

Cadaver's eyes narrowed further, threatening to disappear entirely into the patchwork of his face. "Sleepwalking? Then what's that you're carrying, Mr. Blackwood?"

Eld blurted out, "It's a project! For your class, Professor. I was so excited about what we learned today that I couldn't sleep. So I thought I'd get a head start on…on…"

"On combining multiple reanimated parts into a single, cohesive form," Talbot finished smoothly. "Isn't that right, Eld?"

Eld nodded vigorously, silently thanking Talbot for his quick thinking.

To further his argument, he revealed Bart from his coat pocket, showing off his new lizard tail. "Exactly! I know it's after hours, but I just couldn't wait to try it out. You know how it is when inspiration strikes. It was your work on modification that allowed me to do this."

Cadaver studied them for a long moment, his stitched brow wrinkled in thought.

The silence stretched on, broken only by the soft creaking of Talbot's armor and Eld's pounding heart. Then, to Eld's immense relief, Cadaver broke into a wide grin that threatened to split his patchwork face in two.

"Well, I must say, I'm impressed by your enthusiasm, Mr. Blackwood!" Cadaver exclaimed, clapping his hands together with a sound like dry twigs snapping. "It's not often I see students so dedicated to their studies. Carry on, but do try to get some rest. We can discuss your project in class tomorrow."

As Cadaver shambled off, his uneven gait stomping down the corridor, Eld let out a breath he hadn't realized he had been holding. "That was too close."

They made it back to their room without any other incident, though every shadow seemed to hide a potential threat.

As Eld gently laid the woman on his bed, Talbot exited the armor with a sigh of relief.

Talbot drifted over, radiating concern. "Eld, what are we going to do now? We can't keep her here forever. Someone's bound to notice eventually."

Eld sank into his desk chair, running a hand through his onyx hair.

The events of the night were catching up to him, exhaustion settling into his bones. "I know, I know. But we can't turn her in either. Not until we know more about who she is and why the professors are looking for her."

"Well, we don't know for sure if the professors are looking for her," Talbot commented, hovering over the woman. "They might have been looking for…"

He trailed off.

The web of coincidences was such that even Talbot was out of excuses.

But as if on cue, the woman's eyes fluttered open.

The room seemed to darken, the shadows deepening as her gaze swept across the space. It was as if they were suddenly suspended in the void between stars, the mundane details of the dormitory fading away in the face of something vast and incomprehensible.

Then her eyes locked onto Eld and a small smile graced her lips.

The room snapped back into focus.

"Hello, who are you?" she asked, her words slow and hesitant.

Chapter 12

Sneaky, Sneaky Subterfuge

Eld gaped back at her.

"Who, who…" he stammered.

This woman had stared right at him and said his name! How could she…

"Who am I?" he finished rather lamely.

Right then, the old clock tower struck three, its mournful chimes echoing across the Bathurst grounds.

When the clock finished chiming, the woman stared up at Eld quizzically.

"Oh. So you don't know who you are either? Is that common around these parts?"

As she spoke, her words seemed to thrum with meaning, like they were being projected directly into Eld's mind. It reminded him of the hidden bronze doors in Bathurst's catacombs, the ones that blocked off the Splintered Dimension.

Eld blinked and stammered some more.

"Um, no, I…um…"

Talbot materialized beside him.

"Eld, I think she doesn't remember what happened in the graveyard."

"The graveyard?" the woman said, frowning. "I was in the graveyard? Was I dead?"

"That's what I thought. Apparently…not exactly, but who knows," Talbot chimed in. "Maybe it was more like taking a really long nap. Underground. In a place that definitely wasn't a standard-issue coffin."

Eld shot Talbot a look that clearly said *not helping* before focusing on the woman again. "Look, we don't know exactly what's going on, but we're going to work it out."

The woman turned her head from side to side. As she did, her black hair twisted and turned, writhing as if they were tentacles.

She stared back at Eld, her face set in a delicate expression of confusion.

"I don't even know where I am," she mumbled.

Eld leaned forward, keeping his voice gentle. "You're safe. We're in my dorm room at Bathurst Academy.

"I don't know what that is," she said.

Eld frowned pensively.

Not remembering Bathurst?

That was *very* strange.

As far as he knew, Bathurst had been around forever. Grimthorpe was the twentieth or so headmaster, and not even the Old Ones knew how old he was. But if this woman was somehow older than Bathurst, if such a thing was even possible, how was she speaking the same language as them?

"What do you remember?" he asked.

As the woman replied, Eld paid close attention.

To his surprise, she didn't seem to be speaking the words she was saying. She spoke in quick and harsh syllables that were somehow automatically translated in his mind…

"I…I'm not sure. There are flashes, but they don't make sense. A black sun, hanging in a sky that shouldn't exist. And…tentacles? So many tentacles, writhing in a void."

She wrapped her arms around herself and shuddered like she was not only fearful but also freezing inside.

Eld winced sympathetically.

The black sun in the sky. It was a terrible omen, but it probably also meant no warmth.

"Hey, it's okay." Eld reached out to pat her shoulder awkwardly. "We'll, uh…figure this out together."

She looked up at him, her gaze piercing. "Who are you? Have we met before?"

Eld's heart sank.

Whatever had happened to this woman seemed to have wiped away her memory of their encounter in the graveyard. Back then, she'd spoken his name clearly, but now…

He exchanged a worried glance with Talbot before turning back to her.

"I'm Eld," he said.

When he didn't see any recognition, he decided to go for his full name, even though he hated it.

"Eldritch B. Blackwood, actually. Eld is a nickname."

He finished the sentence hopefully, but nothing.

Biting back his disappointment, Eld nodded his head at Talbot. "That's Talbot. We're the ones who found you."

"I'm…" The woman hesitated, her head turned up as if thinking, then she responded, "I'm Azalea. At least…I think I am?"

She held her head, her black hair swaying behind her.

"There's just a lot I don't remember. And I feel…well, I'm not feeling my finest, though I don't quite remember what my finest is."

Eld smiled, hoping he looked more confident than he felt. "Well, don't worry. For now, you're safe here."

A commotion outside drew Eld's attention.

He moved to the window, peering out at the grounds below.

As he'd suspected, most of the action was taking place in the graveyard.

Husks shambled furiously back and forth, with multiple professors joining them. Eld saw Grimthorpe at the center of it all. The headmaster's robes were unmistakable. He was furiously gesticulating in the distance, evidently ordering a search.

"They're still looking for something." Eld sighed. "And I assume that something is you, Azalea. We need a plan."

Talbot floated lazily over. "Well, we can't keep her here forever. Someone's bound to notice eventually. And I, for one, am not keen on becoming an accessory to whatever this is. If I get kicked out of school, father and mother will make me…work." His face transformed into a grimace at the idea.

"Well, I don't think we can sneak her out," Eld said, thinking back to his trip here. "The ferrymen will stop her. They all work for Grimthorpe, and I'm sure he'll alert them. We need to make it look like she belongs here."

"And how would you do that?" Talbot replied.

Eld suddenly snapped his fingers. "A transfer student! Wolfgang told me he transferred here from a different school—surely people come to Bathurst all the time."

"They do…but *how* exactly do you plan to pull that off?" Talbot asked, raising an eyebrow. "In case you've forgotten, we're not exactly in the school's administrative loop."

Eld's expression turned grim. "We're going to have to forge some documents. Which means…" He took a deep breath. "We need to break into the administration's office."

Talbot's jaw dropped, which was quite a sight given his skeletal nature. "Have you lost your mind? That's suicide! Or, well, uh, whatever the undead equivalent is…double suicide?"

"Do you have a better idea?" Eld countered.

He pointed to the activity in the courtyard.

"Do you really think we can hand her over?"

Talbot floated over to the window.

Genuine guilt flickered across his face as he watched the chaotic scene.

"I suppose we can't…I admit it Eld…something is rotten here, and it's not just your pets."

"Well, then let's do something about it," Eld insisted. "Here's the plan."

Eld took a deep breath, then began outlining his scheme. "I'll sneak into the administration's office and forge a transfer letter. We'll say Azalea is a new student from…I don't know, somewhere far away."

Talbot raised another eyebrow. "Somewhere far away," he drolly replied. "That won't get anyone's attention."

Eld thought longer.

"Hel. Hel Academy. Cloudehill went there at first after his scores weren't good enough for Bathurst. I'm guessing people transfer from there all the time."

Talbot didn't say anything, so Eld assumed that was a better option.

"Great. And as I sneak in, Talbot, you'll just keep watch and warn me if anyone's coming." Maneuvering through the unknown admission's office would be too dangerous if he had to keep flickering back and forth with Franky using the oculus spell. The constant change of perspective—and change in vision quality—could be extremely disorienting.

"And if we get caught?" Talbot asked.

"We won't. Once we have the letter, we'll *introduce* Azalea to the administration. She'll be an official student, but hidden in plain sight."

Azalea had spent the whole time listening intently. Though Eld had no idea where she was from, it was obvious she understood everything they were saying.

When Eld finished, she spoke hesitantly. "What about me? What should I do while you're gone?"

Eld turned to her. "Stay here. Keep the door locked. Don't let anyone in, no matter what. We'll be back as soon as we can." He whistled softly and Shuck padded over from his corner. "This is Shuck, he'll stay with you and keep you safe. Won't you, boy?"

Shuck's stub where his tail had been wagged in response, thumping against the floor.

Eld added, "And try to think about any other memories that might come back. Anything could be helpful."

Talbot snorted. "Just don't go wandering off anywhere. Especially not into any unmarked graves."

Eld shot him another irritated look.

Talbot had been invaluable during the time of crisis…but he'd gone right back to being himself again.

"Are you going to be okay with everything?" he asked, turning back to Azalea. "I know it's a lot to take in."

Azalea hesitated, but then Shuck snuggled his head into her lap and she smiled. Eld couldn't help but notice that she'd taken to the undead dog right away without any problems. Normally, it took a while before people realized that Shuck's frightening appearance belied his consummately dog-like personality.

"I think I'll be alright," she said, petting Shuck with both her hands. "It's not like I have many other options, do I?"

"We'll figure this out," Eld promised again—though he still didn't know what *this* was. It wasn't just the woman's missing memories. It was the strange ominous shadows that clung to her, the obvious power that radiated from her body that even she didn't seem fully aware of.

Azalea smiled again.

Her hand shot out and touched Eld's.

"I trust you," she said.

Her eyes met his and the whole world fell away.

Azalea's eyes, with their endless darkness and swirling silver specks, seemed to suck Eld's soul away. The more he stared into them, the more lost he became. It felt like he was drifting right off into space.

He thought that he'd left his body, but a sudden burst of heat brought him right back to reality.

"What is this?" Eld wondered to himself.

His mind felt like it'd been lit aflame and the blood in his body began to burn, almost like it'd been boiled.

A dim and sudden thumping echoed through his body.

It took a second before Eld realized that he could actually feel his heart pounding in his chest. It wasn't just his random imagination. His shriveled heart had somehow restarted.

His cheeks flushed bright red as his blood began pumping into his face again.

Unsure of what to do, Eld hastily recoiled his hand.

His body slowly began to cool again and his heart stilled its thumping.

"Um…" Eld stammered. "Uh, you know, just…remember to keep the door locked and don't let anyone in."

Azalea stared back at him and nodded.

"Yeah. I'll…I'll do that. I…"

She looked just as confused as Eld. He couldn't help but wonder if she'd felt something strange too.

"Um, by the way," she said. "My friends call me Lea. Hearing that name makes me feel…warmer, somehow."

She smiled. "And maybe I was thinking we could be friends too."

For a while, the two just stared awkwardly at each other.

Then Eld nodded.

"Yeah. Okay. Um, well, I'll be off then. Or, I mean, I'll be off then, *Lea.*"

She smiled at that, but there was still another awkward pause before he actually left, closing the door behind him.

To Eld and Talbot's dismay, the husks were still out in full force when he left their room.

The two friends took cover behind a statue of a warlock holding a rapier. A female daemon, carved of marble, had latched herself onto his back. While it was an artistically impressive accomplishment, it did mean that Eld had to squeeze in tightly. Talbot even had to phase out and go translucent.

"What did I say, Eld…" Talbot moaned. "You will doom us with your weakness for pretty faces."

Despite the circumstances, he snickered.

"I saw how you two were looking at each other. Love at first sight doesn't even begin to describe it."

"I don't know what if that's what it was…" Eld replied hesitantly. Lea *was* attractive, he wasn't going to deny it. But he'd never heard of someone's heart restarting before. That went beyond love. It had to be a supernatural ability of some kind.

But what could it be?

"You know what," Eld said, shaking his head. "Let's just get to the office."

Talbot snickered again. "A man after my own heart…ignore your problems and hope they resolve themselves. I just wish you'd ignored this woman entirely."

Still, though, Eld could tell that the poltergeist's heart wasn't quite in the rebuke. He wanted to help Lea too.

And having navigated the halls once, Eld and Talbot had an easier time with it the second time. Eld ducked behind countless statues and alcoves slowly but steadily making his way towards their location. Talbot had an easier time of it, his incorporeal nature allowing him to scout ahead undetected.

Unlike last time, Talbot was a much more active participant. The poltergeist had a good heart beneath his layers and layers of laziness.

Their path took them deeper into the academy's depths, where the administration's office was. To sneak Azalea into the school, they would have to break into Grimthorpe's office.

But as they descended into the catacombs, the air grew thick with the musty scent of ancient stone and something older and far more arcane.

Something strange was happening.

"What is that feeling? This wasn't there when I visited Hemlock," Eld said.

"Hold up." Talbot came to an abrupt stop. "Look over there."

Eld peered around the corner and grew excited.

The familiar bronze doors to the Splintered Dimension.

But unlike before, there was no buzzing warning.

The entrance, normally sealed tighter than a pharaoh's tomb, stood open, but any thought of seizing this opportunity vanished when Eld saw the guards pouring out of the bronze doors.

They were unlike any husks Eld had ever encountered, far stronger and larger than even the ones that guarded the Blackwood Family Manor.

Towering monstrosities of stitched-together flesh, easily twice the size of a normal man, goosestepped out of the passageway. Unlike the normal husks, their movement was unerringly precise, without a hint of shambling. Their lifeless eyes scanned the corridor ceaselessly, massive fists clenching and unclenching with sickening squelches.

"Flesh golems," Eld whispered, his voice a mix of awe and revulsion. "I've read about them, but I never thought I'd see one up close. It takes *serious* magical skill to create one of these things."

"Let's keep it that way, shall we?" Talbot suggested, eyeing the monstrosities nervously.

Eld's curiosity had already been piqued, but as the flesh golem walked by, he felt a faint hint of painful familiarity in the golem's reanimating magic.

"No way…" he muttered to himself.

Despite the danger, he *had* to know.

He reached into his pocket, pulling out Franky the zombie centipede.

"What are you doing?" Talbot demanded as Eld began tracing arcane symbols in the air.

"Getting a closer look," Eld replied, finishing the incantation.

His vision swam before snapping into focus through Franky's compound eyes. Bart had better earthly senses than Franky, but the centipede's magical detection was unmatched. "Keep watch. I'll be quick."

Before Talbot could protest, Eld sent Franky scurrying towards the open doorway.

The centipede's slender body allowed him to slip past the golems unnoticed, venturing into the forbidden depths of the Splintered Dimension.

The narrow corridor opened into a vast, circular chamber.

At its center stood a massive stone altar, surrounded by patterns carved into the floor. Every available surface on the walls was covered in depictions of the black sun.

But this time, the sun's typically spiky rays writhed like tentacles. On one particularly haunting mural, the sun had become some kind of hideous monster, wrenching farmers off their lands. Instead of a mouth, the sun seemed to absorb the farmers whole by stuffing them straight into the inky darkness.

As Franky scuttled along the chamber's edge, Eld's borrowed vision caught sight of a familiar figure.

After getting that faint whiff of magic, Eld had known, deep in his shriveled heart, who it must have been.

But still…

Seeing him was a different story.

There, by the altar, stood his father, Eldritch Sr.

The lich was meticulously arranging various arcane objects on the stone surface—crystals that seemed to absorb light, vials of swirling, oily liquid, and what looked like human bones.

Eldritch Sr. muttered endlessly under his breath, speaking discordant and jarring syllables from a tongue that Eld did not recognize. He was conducting some kind of ritual.

At the far end of the dais was a large tome glowing with necromantic energy.

Eld had only seen that tome twice in his life before, but he would recognize the familiar strands of Blackwood energy anywhere—it was the Familial Tome.

Eldritch Sr. always claimed the tome was the family's greatest treasure, something that could never leave the family manor, and yet, he'd brought it to Bathurst.

His bony fingers carefully traced the lines of text. His muttering and scowling suggested that he wasn't merely copying a spell—he was creating a new one of his own.

Eld watched with rapt attention, but the ritual was taking a very long time. Every so often, Eldritch Sr. would stop entirely to reread the spell.

Whatever it was, it *had* to be something powerful. Eld had never once seen his father hesitate before, yet here, he looked almost like a student again.

Unfortunately, Eld's investigation was cut short when a movement caught Franky's attention. Another flesh golem, even larger than the ones guarding the entrance, lumbered into view, breaking off of the pack.

"No! Franky!" Eld cried.

Franky skittered backward, sensing the looming threat.

For one moment, Eld dared to hope...

The centipede managed to flee from the Splintered Dimension, but the golem's dead eyes were fixed on the tiny centipede. The massive creature's speed rapidly built, and with surprising speed for something so massive, it lunged.

Franky was snatched up in a meaty fist and a second later, the ocular connection was severed with a bright flash. Eld's vision snapped back to his own eyes, a cry of anguish caught in his throat.

The oculus spell didn't share pain, but he knew what this meant.

His friend was gone.

Franky had been crushed in an instant by the golem.

"Eld? What happened?" Talbot asked, but his voice seemed like it was a million miles away.

"Franky," Eld choked out, struggling to focus. "He's gone. He was..."

Eld gulped back tears.

He *could* bring Franky back.

He was a necromancer, after all.

But this was on another level. The centipede's parts were strewn throughout the catacombs. His head had been shattered and his soul would have to be gently coaxed back into his body.

But then Eld realized that there was no time to properly mourn, no moment to honor his tiny friend's sacrifice.

The thundering footsteps of the pursuing golem forced them onward, grief giving way to survival instinct.

They ran blindly through the twisting catacombs, Eld's heart pounding a frantic rhythm of sorrow and fear. But while the flesh golem was more fluid and coordinated than the husks, it wasn't much smarter.

The same pattern of ducking in and out of statues and classrooms threw it off, and before long, Eld and Talbot collapsed in front of Grimthorpe's office.

His legs felt like jelly and not just from the mad dash.

Franky's loss pressed down on him like the dirt above a coffin.

He gasped, fighting back tears.

Sensing Eld's distress, Talbot floated closer. "I'm sorry about Franky. He was a good centipede."

Eld nodded, unable to speak.

He knew he had to get his friend back, somehow.

But right now, he had another job to do.

Seeing his father had just made the situation all the more real. Whatever it was Eldritch Sr. wanted, it couldn't be anything good, and based on Grimthorpe's sheer desperation, it was probably connected to Azalea too.

They had to keep her hidden.

Otherwise, Franky would have sacrificed himself for nothing.

Eld gulped. "Let's get what we came for and get out before anything else goes wrong."

First, Eld set his ear against the door, listening carefully.

There was nothing there, and he couldn't detect any necromantic energy either.

Next, his fingers danced through the air, drawing images of keys and lockpicks.

Moments later, the door swung open, revealing an empty room.

He rifled through the administration's files until he found a blank transfer form. With shaking hands, he began to forge a letter of acceptance for Azalea, or rather, for *Lea*, the exchange student from Hel Academy they had decided to invent.

Considering all Eld was doing for her here, it felt safe to consider her a friend at this point.

Just as he was putting the finishing touches on the document and adding the school's stamp of approval, voices in the hallway made him freeze. He quickly sealed the letter, using a hastily whispered spell to copy a wax seal before diving for cover behind a large bookcase.

The door burst open, admitting a very agitated Professor McGrath and a concerned-looking Professor Cadaver.

"This is a disaster!" McGrath said, his mechanical legs whirred as he paced. "Eldritch Sr. assured me his information was accurate. If we don't find the Black Sun soon, Grimthorpe will have both our heads!"

Cadaver's patchwork face creased with worry. "Surely he wouldn't go that far. We're tenured, after all."

McGrath let out a bark of humorless laughter. "You don't know Grimthorpe like I do."

Eld froze at the bitter fear in McGrath's voice. He'd always thought of the old academic lich as a friendly uncle, but apparently, he didn't know Grimthorpe at all.

But it was what McGrath said next that really sent a shiver down Eld's spine.

"He's been searching for that Black Sun of his for generations. Won't take no for an answer. Every little rumor *must* be investigated. I can't even count the number of wild geese I've chased…and that's literal wild geese. For a while, he thought they'd swallowed some valuable gem. But even I have to admit, this latest lead seems the closest."

The Black Sun.

There it was, plainly spoken.

So far, Eld had merely *seen* images of the black sun.

The vision he'd seen outside the family manor…

The way that the portraits at his home had somehow transformed…

The shadows dancing around Azalea…

But now, McGrath's words confirmed the conspiracy. His mind was still reeling when McGrath and Cadaver continued on their way.

Eld waited a few more agonizing minutes before emerging from his hiding spot, the forged transfer letter clutched tightly in his hand.

"Let's get out of here," he whispered to Talbot as he walked out of the office.

The poltergeist nodded emphatically and they began the nerve-wracking journey back to the dorm.

But to their relief, the husks had finally left.

The school halls looked almost normal.

After having seen his father, however, Eld didn't feel particularly happy imagining where the husks had been sent off to.

By the time they made it back, Eld felt like he had aged a decade. Azalea jumped at their entrance, her eyes wide with relief.

"Well?" she asked. "How did it go? Am I a student?"

Eld collapsed onto his bed, holding up the forged letter triumphantly. "We did it. As far as Bathurst is concerned, you're now Lea Helsdottir, an exchange student from Hel specializing in Necromancy."

"Hel Academy…" Lea repeated, testing out the words. "Lea Helsdottir."

Sitting up, Eld ran a hand through his hair. "You wouldn't believe what we saw down there. Flesh golems the size of trolls, a creepy ritual chamber, and…"

Eld broke off, thinking of Franky. As creepy as the catacombs were, he knew he had to return there.

But he brushed the thought aside for now.

He had something he wanted to ask Lea.

"Get this, my father was there."

"Your father?" Lea asked, looking confused.

It was clear that she had no idea who Eldritch Sr. was…

Which, in Eld's mind, made her exquisitely lucky.

"Yeah, he's…well, he's a real pile of manticore dung, to be frank. Combines the ambition of a vampire with the crude extortive mindset of a troll. But anyway, he was arranging stuff for some ritual. And then I overheard McGrath and Cadaver talking about the Black Sun…"

He eyed her inquisitively.

"You mentioned that earlier, didn't you?"

By then, Lea's face had already turned white as a ghost's sheet.

Lea's face went white. "Did you say Black Sun?"

"Yeah, why? Does that mean something to you?"

Lea hesitated, then held out her hands. "It might be easier if I show you. My visions, I mean."

"Visions?" Eld asked.

But all Lea did was hold her hands out as if that explained everything, so he took them.

Eld took Lea's hands.

The moment their fingers touched, his mind went haywire. It was like falling from a ship and landing in frigid arctic water.

He could feel his heart pounding again, almost threatening to burst out of his chest, but the vision made that seem like a meaningless afterthought.

The cold rapidly permeated his entire body, and he soon saw a world plunged into eternal darkness, a massive black sun looming in the sky like a cancerous growth.

The earth was overrun with shambling husks. The living ran screaming, only to be overwhelmed by the endless hordes of undead.

Vampires stalked out in the open, no longer hiding their true nature.

Werewolves howled triumphantly from rooftops, able to change forms at will.

Reapers soared through the air, their scythes flashing as they claimed lives with enthusiastic abandon.

All manner of night creatures reveled in their newfound dominion.

Cities crumbled, nature withered, and humanity cowered in the ruins of their once-great civilization. The world had become a playground for the dead and the damned.

When the vision faded, Eld found himself gasping for air, his hands shaking.

"I…um…"

He didn't even know where to begin.

Even after returning to ordinary life, it felt like the visions of violence were still flashing ruthlessly before his eyes.

"That was intense," he said.

Lea nodded, her face pale. "I saw that stuff all the time…when I was…dreaming? Sleeping? I don't know…before I met you…whatever that was. Back then, that was all I could see. And I don't know what it means."

Eld ran a hand through his hair, his mind reeling.

He thought about seeing his father—who had always claimed that the nightkin should rule the world again.

He thought about what McGrath said about Grimthorpe's hidden ruthlessness.

"I don't know what's going on," he said. "But it sounds like they are trying to summon this Black Sun somehow."

He shook his head. "We can't let it happen. No way."

It sounded almost naïve, but in that vision, Eld hadn't seen any pets.

That sheer amount of power was utterly against nature.

"What can we do?" Lea asked, her voice frightened. "I…back when…all I can remember is a time when the Black Sun was still high in the sky."

She glanced around the room.

"I don't quite know where this is. But it feels so much more peaceful and right."

Eld grit his teeth. "Lea. I believe that the school is looking for *you*."

"Me?" Lea stammered. "But…why?"

"Because they want to bring back the Black Sun—and you are the only person who remembers it. Until now, I just thought the Black Sun was something people put in pictures. Like it was a stylistic choice or something. But after tonight, I realize that it's all too real."

Eld cursed under his breath, shaking his head.

Based on Lea's vision, the new Black Sun would cover the entire world, and fleeing would be useless. According to Eld's father, this ritual would even give them the power to rewrite reality.

It wasn't just about Lea either.

Who knew if anyone else was buried in the graveyard?

Grimthorpe could very well find another source of information. It wasn't enough to play defense.

They had to actively stop him somehow.

"Alright. So here's the plan," he said. "The professors are up to something, but we don't know just what yet. We'll have to keep an eye out and do our best to research the Black Sun.

Use your memories, find out what's going on, and do our best to stop it."

Lea nodded shakily.

It wasn't a perfect plan, but it was the best they had. At any rate, Eld's experience hiding things from Cloudehill had taught him that plain sight was often an underrated alternative.

They spent the next hour going over Lea's fabricated backstory, making sure she had every detail memorized.

As the plan came together, Eld found himself growing increasingly aware of Lea's presence. There was something about her that drew him in, like a moth to a flame. Every so often, their hands would brush together.

When they did, Eld would once again feel that strange twisting feeling from before. His soul would feel like it was being dragged off into space and his congealed blood would begin pumping again.

At the end, Lea nodded.

"Okay. I think…I think I get everything."

She picked up the letter.

"So I'll just deliver it to the office?" she asked.

Eld nodded.

"Yeah."

"Well, that's great then," Lea said. "Though I suppose they'll probably make me get a different room…"

Her voice sounded *just* reluctant enough for Eld to dare to hope.

"Yeah, I guess so," Eld said. "But hey, you can always come visit. And we'll see each other in class."

Lea smiled, and the room seemed to brighten.

It was almost like light was being emanated from her skin.

Then, without warning, she threw her arms around Eld in a tight hug. "Thank you," she whispered. "For everything."

Talbot cleared his throat. "You know, I'm here too. Should I give you two some privacy?"

Eld's face burned as he awkwardly recoiled the embrace, very aware of Talbot's gaze boring into him. "Right, well, we should probably get you to the administration office first thing in the morning. The sooner we get you officially enrolled, the better."

Chapter 13

Love Bites & Sometimes Reanimates

To Eld's relief, Lea was able to transfer to the school without any problems.

Before long, it felt like she'd been there the whole time.

The weeks flew by and Eld's life soon fell into a predictable schedule, balancing his classes and Combat Club training while investigating futilely with Azalea whenever the two got the chance.

But their investigation went nowhere.

Other than occasional grumbling from various Necromancy students about the canceled Midnight Exhumation, it seemed like things were back to normal again, at least, as back to normal as things could be at a place like Bathurst.

"Hey! Hey!" Talbot scowled.

Eld abruptly glanced upwards.

"My lunch meat!" Talbot shouted. "It's running away! Look! It's getting farther and farther away from me!"

Eld scoffed.

"Um…Talbot…you're just drifting backward…"

"Oh," Talbot replied. "Whoops."

The poltergeist went translucent, reappearing right in front of the table.

"Stupid wind…" he grumbled. "Making me work hard just to stay in place…who ever heard of something so ridiculous?"

With Talbot's dilemma resolved, Eld eyed the strange lump of bleached white meat on his plate. He hated to admit it, but Talbot had a point.

Lunch at Bathurst was always an adventure and the special of the day looked like it might crawl off the plate if he didn't keep an eye on it. Eld gingerly poked at the mystery meat and wondered if it was genuinely dead or just playing possum.

For all he knew, it might have just *been* a possum—one that was so albino even its meat was white.

Talbot hovered on the seat next to Eld, food plopping through him as he ate. "What are you eyeing that thing for? Planning a dissection?"

Eld sighed, pushing the plate away. "Not hungry. Got a letter from home. Parents are coming to the Nocturnal Combat Club qualifying matches. If your team wins their bout, they will move onto the playoff round, the Tournament of Shadows!"

"Ouch," Talbot winced, setting down his fork. "That's rough. Is your dad still on the *proper necromancer* kick?"

"When isn't he?" Eld said. "I swear, if I have to hear one more lecture about the *noble art of lichdom*, I might just let myself get eaten by a ghoul. But that's…you know, that's not the *real* problem."

Eld snuck a piece of chitin out of his pocket, carefully examining it. Based on the way the joint bent, he thought it was probably a leg. Just statistically speaking, most pieces were probably legs…

"Still thinking about Franky?" Talbot asked.

"Not just thinking of him," Eld replied.

He'd been sneaking into the catacombs after class, slowly and steadily trying to find what was left of his centipede friend.

The process was painstaking.

After getting crushed, most of Franky's body had simply dissolved into grave dirt without Eld's necromantic energy holding it all together. And if there was anything the catacombs had in abundance, it was grave dirt. It was only Eld's familiarity with Franky that allowed him to sift through all the detritus.

The only positive was that Franky had escaped the Splintered Dimension before getting crushed. If he'd been caught there, Eld didn't even know where he'd begin with the reanimation process.

As it was, Eld was already spending every waking moment outside of class and club practice sifting through it, carefully tracking down what was left of his ever-loyal friend.

"I think I have enough to bring him back," Eld said. "That was just his seventieth leg. And I have a fair amount of his body and head too. It'll be an incomplete reanimation, but…"

"You sure that's wise?" Talbot replied. "I've heard the horror stories about pets coming back wrong."

Eld had heard them too, but in all his years of work, he'd never once caused them.

"I'm always careful," he said. "And besides…I owe him, Talbot."

Lea slid into the seat across from them, her cosmic eyes bright. "What are we whispering about?"

"Eld's playing archaeologist in the catacombs," Talbot said before Eld could shush him.

Lea frowned. "Is this about Franky? I'm sorry Eld."

She reached over the table and clasped his hand in both of hers, gently rubbing it. As soon as their hands touched, Eld's blood began pumping again.

Eld gulped, gently pushing her hands back as his cheeks abruptly blushed thanks to his now pumping blood. He still hadn't figured out what Lea felt when they touched, but it seemed like she liked it. Recently, she'd been taking almost every opportunity to hold his hands.

Not that he quite minded, of course…

But at the moment, he was just a *little* too focused on Franky to enjoy anything. He didn't want Lea to feel guilty though. Even from the brief moment they'd met, Franky had liked Lea—all his pets had.

"I'm okay, I promise."

Lea didn't look convinced, but before she could say or do anything else, Lilith joined them, slamming her tray down with her typical enthusiastic force.

"You ready for the qualifiers, Eld? I heard Mortimer's team has some nasty tricks up their sleeves."

"Is that so?" Eld replied.

The conversation shifted to combat strategies and team formations, but Eld's thoughts kept drifting back to the dark tunnels beneath the school.

He would find the rest of Franky, no matter what.

Lea switched sides to sit by Eld and leaned in, dropping her voice. "It'll be okay. You'll find the rest of Franky. And I couldn't help but overhear that your parents are coming to the matches tomorrow. Talbot and I have got your back. And who knows? Maybe seeing you in action will change your dad's mind."

With her sitting so close to him, Eld felt butterflies flying haphazardly in his stomach. They were so excited it felt like they were bumping into his organs.

Now *that* was just natural excitement.

Eld didn't know where the blood pumping came from, but he had enough common sense to tell that he also had a good old-fashioned crush.

Weird, considering how they met.

It wasn't every man who got to dig up their crush in the school graveyard.

"I appreciate the confidence," Eld said, turning away to hide the redness in his face. "Though I'm pretty sure the only thing that'd impress my father is if I raised an entire army of the dead. Even then, he'd probably just complain about their posture."

Lea chuckled, easing the tension between them a bit.

"Yeah, from what you told me, he sounds like a real piece of work."

Across the table, Lilith raised an eyebrow.

"You don't know who Eldritch Blackwood Sr. is?" she asked.

"Um, no," Lea admitted.

She tilted her head to the side.

"Come to think of it, I'm not entirely sure I know you. I think I've seen you in class before, but…"

"Lilith Nightshade," Lilith said, briskly introducing herself. "As I'm sure you can tell, I'm a banshee."

"I'm Lea Helsdottir," Lea replied. Eld was happy to hear how smoothly she introduced herself. So far, the disguise had been working perfectly.

Eld glanced at Lea again.

As excited as he always was to see her, he wanted to bring Franky back first.

Once he did, he could…well, he didn't exactly know what he'd do.

Despite his age, Eld had embarrassingly little experience with women.

His usual work, while rewarding, hadn't brought him into contact with many nightkin, and his love of the dark had meant that most human relationships would have naturally failed.

And before that, bringing a girl back to the Blackwood Family Manor…

Well, that was something he'd only do to a girl he despised, not anyone he liked.

"I'll, um…I'll be right back for a bit," he said. "I've got something I need to do."

"Okay!" Lea replied, cheerfully smiling. Whenever she was happy, light seemed to radiate from her pale skin. "But, wait, I had something I wanted to ask you."

She leaned in, her voice dropping to a whisper. "Have you found out anything more about, you know, what you saw? Your father in that chamber?"

Eld shook his head, his expression darkening. "No, and it's driving me crazy. The black sun motifs, they're everywhere at home too and that book he was reading from was our family's grimoire. But I can't make sense of it all."

"We'll figure it out," Lea assured him, giving his hand another squeeze. "Together, like you said, remember?"

Eld nodded. "Yeah, together. Thanks, Lea."

He patted her hand and slowly withdrew it from her grasp, his heart thumping so hard in his chest that he thought it might burst right through.

"Smooth. Really Smooth, Eld," he told himself.

As he walked away, he couldn't help but notice Lilith and Talbot's snickering.

Normally, he'd try and come up with a comeback, but he had more urgent matters to attend to, or at least, that was what Eld told himself.

Eld walked out of the refectory, heading over to an empty corner surrounded by brightly crackling motes of light.

The motes began shouting out advice as soon as he came close.

"Go downstairs to head to Stitching Class. The school recently opened up a shortcut for well-behaved students."

"I heard there's free bottles of gnome blood on floor seventeen today. Should be a delicious treat for any vampire!"

"Head to floor fourteen…they are hosting a scholarship competition for the most handsome werewolf."

Eld rolled his eyes.

At this point in the school year, everyone knew that the motes were full of batshit. Nobody paid attention to them anymore.

Fortunately, that also gave Eld some privacy.

It would have probably been smarter to do this in his room, but after getting that final leg, Eld was too excited to wait.

Despite Lea's ever-charming presence, the last few weeks had been agonizing. He wanted to bring his friend back right away.

Reaching into his pocket, Eld pulled out Franky, or what was left of him.

The zombie centipede was a patchwork of stitched-together parts, many segments still missing. Eld had carefully reconstructed as much as he could and stolen what he needed from school grounds to recover the rest, but he suspected that much of Franky's original was just lost to the ether.

He would have to find or make new parts to fully reconstruct his body, but for now…

Eld traced symbols through the air, whispering incantations under his breath. He traced out Franky's body, painting a shimmering centipede in the sky before moving on to detail their many adventures together.

He painted an image of them fleeing from an angry husk at the Blackwood Family Manor…

He remembered them laughing together in some far-flung town after reanimating a particularly grumpy cat…

And he re-painted how Franky had died, caught off-guard by the flesh-golem hidden beneath Bathurst…

Lastly, he threw his coat above Franky's body. Inside the black coat, Bart—Franky's ever-loyal companion—chittered loudly, undoubtedly pleading for him to wake up.

And he did.

Franky's movement was jerky and uneven, but his now mismatched eyes still looked up at Eld with loyalty.

"Hey buddy…" Eld whispered.

Franky chittered weakly.

The new threads holding his body together twisted and turned, writhing smoothly in tune with the centipede's movements. Professor Cadaver's lessons had been invaluable in putting Franky's body back together.

Eld thought back to the cremated dog in the Blackwood Family Crypt.

He still had no idea how that creature had come back to life, but with Franky, he'd accomplished something somewhat close. The Weave and Bind method had allowed him to create a new set of lifelike threads that held all the crumbled parts together.

"I know you're not fully back yet," Eld said. "That was…well, that was a tough one."

Franky's remaining antennae twitched, a few legs scrabbling against Eld's palm.

Eld smiled. "Seems like enough of you is here to help me put the rest of you back together."

He concentrated, placing his hands on Franky's body.

Now that the centipede's soul had returned, Franky could help Eld redirect the necromantic energy. Slowly and carefully, Eld poured his magical energy into Franky, this time using Professor Cadaver's growth techniques.

The shattered flesh mended…but only partially.

Franky was still missing several pieces of chitin on his body. Most of his middle was held together entirely by the network of threads. Several of his legs were still missing too, and when he returned to Eld's coat, his movements were an awkward zigzag.

"I'm sorry, buddy," Eld whispered. "I thought that would work."

Franky stuck his head out and chittered. "I know *you* think it's alright…but really, Franky, you should hold me to a higher standard. You're a great friend and well, I should be a better doctor for you."

Still, it was better than nothing. Eld knew he needed to improve his skills and find more compatible parts, but this was the best he could do for now. At least he had his friend back with him.

Inside his coat, Franky and Bart were chattering furiously. It sounded like Bart wanted to know what it was like to visit the afterlife a second time.

With that, Eld returned to the dining table.

His friends were still there, and Lea suddenly perked up, waving at someone across the cafeteria. "Oh, there's my roommate! I've been wanting to introduce you all. Especially you, Talbot. She's a poltergeist!"

Eld turned to look, spotting a translucent being weaving through the crowd.

As she got closer, he could make out long, silvery hair, along with a permanent rictus grin similar to Talbot's.

The poltergeist glided up to their table, offering a spectral smile. "Hi there! I'm Wysper. Lea's told me so much about you guys."

Talbot, usually Mr. Lazy-and-Aloof, suddenly looked like he had seen a well, ghost. "Uh, hi," he stammered, his usual lazy drawl replaced by an almost squeaky tone.

Lilith smirked, raising an eyebrow. "Well, well. Looks like someone's got a soft spot."

"Shut it, banshee," Talbot grumbled, but he couldn't take his eyes off Wysper.

Eld had to bite back a laugh. He had never seen his ghostly friend so flustered.

He couldn't help but wonder what it was.

The fact they both had empty eyes?

The glowing translucent skin?

Maybe it was just the silver hair, perhaps it was a rarity among poltergeists.

The two had similar clothes too—brightly colored, with a vague hint of jester-ness to them, though Wysper's outfit was much better taken care of.

"So." Wysper floated closer, passing right through the table, much to the annoyance of a nearby student whose drink suddenly frosted over. "I was thinking maybe we could all grab dinner sometime? There's this new place in the Underworld I've been dying to try. Pun totally intended."

"Oh, that would be delightful!" Lea exclaimed, her translucent skin sparkling like the moon. "Eld, we should go too? You, me, Talbot, and Wysper. What do you say?"

"Like a date?" Eld blurted out.

Everyone looked at him.

Eld groaned. He had shouted that out like an overexcited animal.

Which, he supposed, the nightkin were, at the end of the night. Especially during moments like these…

Still, Eld wished he could rewind time. Or maybe just dissolve into a puddle on the floor. Whichever was less embarrassing.

Lilith groaned so loudly, a few nearby students looked over in alarm.

A pair of arm-wrestling werewolves actually yelped and fell out of their chair.

"For the love of all that's unholy, Blackwood. How thick can you get? I've met zombies with better social awareness than you."

Eld felt his face burning hotter than a phoenix's feather. "I didn't mean—"

"Save it," Lilith hissed, standing up with an exasperated huff. "I'm out before I lose any more brain cells to your obliviousness. Try not to mess this up, okay? Though why Lea likes you is beyond me. Maybe she has a thing for hopeless cases."

With that, she stalked off, her hair almost seeming to bristle with irritation. An awkward silence fell over the table, broken only by Talbot's nervous cough.

Lea cleared her throat, a faint blush coloring her pale cheeks. "So dinner? What do you guys think?"

"Uh, yeah," Eld managed to blurt out, his brain finally catching up to the situation. "Sounds great. Talbot?"

Talbot, still staring at Wysper like she was the ghostly equivalent of the sun, jerked back to reality. "Huh? Oh, yeah. Sure. Whatever. I mean, I'm not doing anything. Not that I'm desperate or anything. I just, yeah. Dinner. Cool. Which, you know, I am. Cool, that is. I'm cool."

"Great!" Wysper beamed, either oblivious to or politely ignoring Talbot's fumbling. "It's a date! Or not...You know what I mean. How about tonight? The Bone Appetit. Don't worry, the name's worse than the food or so I've heard."

As they hammered out the details, Eld was jittery with the prospect of a date with Lea.

Okay, Talbot and Wysper too, but still. Progress, right?

Maybe he wasn't as hopeless as Lilith thought.

Chapter 14

Bone Appetit

A hollow knocking echoed through Eld's room—two slow knocks and then a fast one. The sound was followed by a loud series of whirls and thumps.

"Got it," Eld said, walking over to the door.

As he grew closer, he heard a distinctive sparking noise on the other side.

He opened it up, revealing a floating white machine surrounded by blue energy. The machine was buzzing and beeping loudly, and at the top was a smiling face made out of glowing lights that crackled with electricity.

"Hello," the machine—or rather, the poltergeist possessing the machine—said. Its voice was deep, echoing, and filled with menace. "Is this the residence of Eld Blackwood?"

"Um, yes, that's me," Eld replied, raising an eyebrow. "And you're—"

Before he could speak another word, the machine let out a loud ding.

The hatch at the front opened up, revealing Eld's black cloak.

"Your clothes are done," the poltergeist said. "That will be two silver coins."

"Of course," Eld said.

He pulled out the two coins from his bag.

"Um…do I just toss them in?" Eld asked.

"No. There is a slot," the machine replied, its voice echoing through the room.

Eld took a closer look and realized that the machine had a silver lock-like device at the top with slots for coins. He placed his silver in there and the machine buzzed.

With that, Eld took his freshly washed black cloak. He raised it up to his face and smelled it. Eld cleaned his robe regularly, but he'd never smelled it *this* clean before. It was like he'd freshly bought it from a merchant.

Old One technology was truly impressive…

"Good day sir," the poltergeist said, flying off. "I appreciate the business."

As the machine flew off the hallway, his voice continued echoing ominously down the hall.

Eld watched him leave, unsure of what to say.

Lilith had told him about the poltergeist who'd haunted a pair of Old One cleaning and drying machines, but he hadn't expected the man's voice to be quite so grim sounding. That poltergeist sounded like he should be haunting a scythe instead.

Then again, Eld supposed that money was money. If Talbot was a bit more industrious, he might try and inherit those machines. Word around the halls was that the cleaning poltergeist was graduating soon.

From inside Eld's room, Franky let out a small and squeaky chitter, cutting through Eld's whimsical thoughts. Now that the centipede had been put back together again, he was slowly and steadily adjusting to his new body.

The centipede's movements were still jerky and uneven, but at least he could get across the room without too many problems.

Bart followed closely behind Franky, and the two eagerly sniffed Eld's coat, which he threw in front of them.

The two looked at him, looks of shock and confusion in their face.

"Yeah, yeah, I know," Eld said. "Maybe a little too clean. I know you guys like it stinky."

Bart let out a particularly indignant squeak.

"Look guys," Eld said. "I'm not sure if Lea goes for…you know. Grave dirt, chitin pieces, bone shards…things like that."

Bart chittered irritably. The reproachful glare in his eyes clearly said "her or us."

Eld rolled his eyes.

"Alright, don't get ahead of yourself. I'm not kicking you guys to the graveyard, I'm just trying to make a good first impression. In fact, the two of you are still welcome to go inside."

As Eld threw his familiar cloak back around his shoulders, the two miniature zombie companions hopped back to their usual positions.

Across the room, Shuck padded over, sniffing the robe before staring quizzically at Eld.

"So you noticed the cleaning too, huh?" Eld asked, a wry smile on his face. "If you like it, maybe you should hop in with the rest of them?"

Shuck made a noise that was halfway between a bark and a scoff before padding off.

Eld thought that he was going back to sleep, but he came back moments later with a wilted rose under his mouth.

"Oh, this one is nice," Eld said, his eyes widening.

Shuck dropped it in front of Eld, then barked happily as Eld gave him a few friendly head scratches.

"Where did you find this?" Eld asked. "It's very fashionably wilted."

Shuck shrugged as best as a dog could. Eld had a distinct feeling that this rose might have been acquired illegally, but he had enough plausible deniability.

He carefully fastened the rose in his breast pocket, grinning in the mirror.

Humans usually liked fresh flowers, but nightkin preferred ones that were just out of bloom. They symbolized dedication and a willingness to work through imperfections.

Then again, Eld wasn't sure if Lea was even a nightkin or not.

He frowned, turning to Franky.

"I mean, she *has* to be, right? Skin that pale…plus she has lived longer than any human could…and I mean, the shadows dancing around her…"

Franky just stared back at Eld with his mismatched eyes and uneven head, obviously telling Eld there was no way he, a recently reanimated centipede, would possibly know the answer to Eld's ramblings.

Eld chuckled.

"Yeah, yeah…I guess there's no way you would know. Still. At the very least, she seems to have adjusted to the darkness."

Franky just continued staring and Eld rolled his eyes.

"You might be a smartass, but I'm glad you're back too buddy."

Just as Eld finished tucking Franky and Bart back into his coat, a brightly glowing being suddenly phased through the wall. The illumination was utterly blinding—far worse than the light that occasionally peeked through the excessively playful curtains.

Spots of light flashed around Eld's eyes.

He cried out in shock, covering up his face and hastily squeezing his eyes shut in fear of permanent damage.

"By the Neverending Night…what *is* that?" he asked.

But to his surprise, Shuck let out a friendly bark.

"It's me, Eld! How do you like my new date outfit?"

"Ta—Talbot?" Eld stammered. He recognized the voice, though Talbot sounded strangely strained…almost like he was trying at something for the first time in his life.

He opened his eyes again.

Slowly, steadily, and painfully, his eyes adjusted to the light.

Talbot floated in front of him, his permanent rictus grin even more excited than usual.

"What did you do?" Eld asked, still utterly bewildered. "Is that…a new outfit?"

Talbot was wearing a huge hat that was so fanciful and grand it looked almost like a chandelier. His clothes were no longer patchwork and shabby. Instead, they were practically gleaming, shining so brightly it seemed like he was wearing gilded ectoplasm.

"How…how did you…"

"How'd I change clothes?" Talbot asked, his voice still with a hint of strain to it.

Eld nodded.

Talbot's clothes were translucent, just like him. Technically, they should have been part of his body…or so Eld thought. He didn't really know much about poltergeist physiology.

"Well, it's interesting…" Talbot said.

A vein at his forehead popped out, throbbing dangerously.

"I *can* wear clothes…you know, just sling them over my body…but we poltergeists…"

Talbot broke off.

He cursed under his breath, panting.

The lights around him began flashing wildly.

"I…it…"

"Are you alright?" Eld asked.

"As I was saying…"

Sparks flew from Talbot, and the lights abruptly dimmed.

"Oh, bullocks," Talbot cursed.

With a final gasp, the lights died.

Moments later, Talbot reappeared, wearing the same scruffy patchwork clothes from before.

"By the Great Twisted One…" Talbot gasped. "I thought I might die…"

He slumped to the ground.

Talbot was so tired that he didn't even phase through. He just hit the floor with a dull splat.

"Um, a hand please…" Talbot said.

Eld reached out, pulling him back to his feet. The poltergeist's arm seemed like it was charged with static electricity, and Eld winced as he felt a brief painful shock.

"Anyways…" Talbot said. "A poltergeist can manifest clothes in addition to wearing them. Impressive poltergeists try to wear exceedingly fanciful clothes…but I think that I bit off a bit more than I could chew…"

Eld glanced at Talbot again.

His eyes were still flashing from the excessive brightness. In his mind, Talbot had bit off a *lot* more than he could chew, like a zombie trying to gulp down an elephant in a single bite. But he was too polite to say anything.

"So, how do we leave campus?" Eld asked, electing to just change the subject. "I haven't been around this part of the underworld for quite a while."

"Oh, there's a ferry," Talbot said, shaky his head woozily. "Same way we get here. It'll take us to Necropolis, the, well, I guess it's like the college town."

"I see," Eld replied, making a mental note for later.

For now, Lea seemed to be really enjoying her time at Bathurst, and despite her and Eld's failings, she was eager to unravel Grimthorpe's plot.

But if worst came to worst, perhaps Eld could smuggle her out somewhere in the underworld. Now that she was a registered student, that would make things a lot easier.

"Well, let's meet by the dock?" Eld said.

"Yeah…" Talbot creakily replied. "Say, do you think I should try and manifest a better outfit again? Make a good first impression?"

Eld raised an eyebrow.

"If I run out of energy and fall asleep in your soup, that won't be a very good first impression."

"Erm, I suppose you're right," Talbot said.

With that, the two drifted down the hall, with Shuck padding close behind them. Based on Lea's interest in animals, Eld felt like Shuck would probably be a much better wingman than Talbot, who wasn't even floating in a straight line right now.

The two left the school, walking through the grounds and towards the docks.

Tonight, the path to the docks was almost suspiciously pleasant.

Ravens flitted through the twisted yew trees, cawing proudly as they flew from branch to branch. Black cats frolicked through the grass and the sky was decorated with swarms of death's head moths.

There was not a single husk to be found…

Franky stuck his head out of Eld's coat, nudging him pointedly.

It was clear that the recently reanimated centipede was thinking the same thing.

"Yeah, it's almost like that night was a bad dream," Eld admitted. "It's…honestly, it's a little scary, knowing the school can just suddenly go on lockdown like that."

He thought back to Professor McGrath's words.

"It makes you wonder what Grimthorpe's true colors are…and I still have no idea what my father was doing down there."

Even with Eldritch Sr. coming to watch the Nocturnal Combat Club qualifiers, it wasn't like Eld could actually interrogate him. Being honest to himself, Eld's best bet was probably hoping for Cloudehill to idiotically slip up.

The two made it to the dock early, about ten minutes before Lea and her roommate arrived.

Eld noticed that Wysper had updated her attire, switching to a flowing dress that trailed behind her like stars. However, this outfit seemed far more sustainable than what Talbot had attempted to manifest.

As the two drew closer, Eld nudged Talbot.

"What was her name again? Lea's roommate."

"Wysper," Talbot replied, his voice uncharacteristically irritated.

"What?" Eld asked, lowering his voice. "Are you worried I'll make her look bad forgetting her name?"

Talbot turned to Eld. For a brief moment, it seemed like he was going to yell or throw something, but then he saw Eld's face.

"Alright, I'll admit it," Talbot chuckled. "You got me pretty good with that one."

Right as the two ladies drew close, the ferry arrived.

The ferryman at the helm wore a roughshod cloak that covered his body—the same uniform the ones who brought them to school had worn. Through the cloak, Eld saw what seemed to be an endless array of tentacles. He couldn't get a clear glimpse of the man's face, but he thought it must have looked like a squid.

"Perfect," Lea beamed.

"Perhaps this was a good omen," Eld said, smiling hopefully.

Lea chuckled, which he took to be another good omen.

Beneath their feet, the rickety ferry creaked and groaned as it navigated the murky waters around Bathurst.

Eld gripped the railing, watching spectral ghostfish dart beneath the surface. Every so often, the fish would draw dangerously close to the boat, but instead of being run over, they'd simply phase through, appearing on the other side.

Beside him, Lea gazed at the water with equally eager wonder.

"Fascinating…" she whispered. "Those creatures weren't around before."

Eld turned to her, frowning.

"Hm? What did you say?"

"These fish weren't here before…back when…"

Lea's voice turned weak and uncertain.

"Back when…"

She shrugged confusedly.

"Back when I was awake, I guess."

She watched the fish phase through the boat again, shaking her head. Shuck padded next to her, nudging her gently with his big paw. She smiled and patted him on the head.

Keeping his hand mostly hidden in his cloak, Eld gave the big black dog a thumbs up.

"It's fascinating, really," she said. "The fish have adapted. To stay away from the boat."

Eld thought back to the bake-kujira by the docks on the way to Bathurst. He had a feeling these fish were probably trying to avoid those monstrosities more than anything else.

"Yeah. I guess they have," he said.

Though Lea's statement had been innocuous, it got Eld thinking.

The ghostfish had been around for a very long time…in fact, he'd even encountered some scattered Old One writings describing them. If Lea hadn't seen ghostfish before, she had to be even older than the Old Ones!

The whole thing just made him even more curious about Lea's true past.

"First time going to Necropolis?" the ferryman asked gruffly.

His question jerked Eld right out of his musings.

"Um, yeah," Eld stammered, shaking his head.

Lea glanced up from the peaceful waters, smiling. "Is it always this atmospheric?"

The ferryman snorted, a strange squishing sound coming from his slick and oily face. "Used to be. Now it's all witchlights and noise. Young souls these days, no appreciation for the classics."

He scowled. "Sooner or later, they'll be calling this place *New* Necropolis…by the Neverending Night, what has the world come too?"

From the sounds of it, the ferryman must have been pretty old, but Eld politely refrained from commenting.

It was only when they got off the docks that the thoughts clicked together. The ferryman had black oozing tentacles, just like the monster that Mortimer had accidentally summoned in class. And the possessed professor had called the creature a Great Old One. Not only that, he'd said that there were plenty of old coots living in Necropolis…

Eld turned around, his mouth half-opened to ask a question, but the ferry had vanished into the fog, disappearing after they'd disembarked.

"Weird…" Eld muttered.

"Oh, they're always doing that," a snooty voice echoed behind them.

Eld turned around, expecting to see Mortimer. Instead, he found Talbot, his chest puffed out so far that Eld though the poltergeist would tip right over.

"The ferrymen think that these oh-so sudden vanishings make them seem more valuable. Well, the discerning eye of a Wilting family member could see right through *that.*"

Eld glanced at Wysper, trying to see if she was impressed.

The poltergeist seemed like she was caught halfway between amazement and disbelief. Eld had felt that way himself many times before, though usually at Talbot's laziness rather than his worldliness.

Though the boat was gone, the city sprawled before them in all its macabre glory.

Gothic buildings built out of black bricks floated in the skies, held aloft by brightly glowing levitation rings. Eld's eyes widened as he scanned the towering buildings, which looked like a mix of apartment buildings and stores.

Some of the shops seemed to cater entirely to students, with places to buy textbooks and potion-making supplies. Others were for the general population, like a shop that bought and sold families—Cats, Bats, Rats, and More!

Eld smiled at the sign, which showed the three animals smiling together with a large witch's hat in the background. Perhaps they would also sell insects there, but he found it unethical to kill a living creature just to strengthen his own companion. It was much better to salvage for parts…though he wasn't sure if there was a store that just sold body parts in the middle of the street.

Even at a place like Necropolis, some things were a bit too unsavory to do in broad moonlight.

Cobblestone streets wound gently between the floating buildings, and the light of the moon was complimented by ghostly lampposts.

"This is beautiful," Lea said, blinking.

Shuck let out a happy bark, then ran off into the distance. Eld's cloak trembled, then moments later, Franky and Bart skittered out as well.

"It's so nice," Lea said. "It's like this place was meant for us."

"Yeah," Eld replied, his voice trailing off.

After so long in the world of humans, he'd forgotten just how beautiful the Underworld could be. This was his place, where he could enjoy his life with the other nightkin, especially with such a lovely woman.

"Oh, this is nothing," Talbot said. "You should see the Wilting family estate. Now *that* is impressive."

Wysper raised a twitching eyebrow. "That's fascinating Talbot. Really."

Her voice was tinged with irritation.

Based on how she was reacting, Talbot must have spent the entire ferry ride bombarding her with tales of his family's exploits. It seemed like she wasn't sure what was real and what was fake at this point.

Under normal circumstances, Eld would have probably told him to rein it in, but he hadn't even noticed the two of them at all. He'd been focused entirely on Lea.

As they made their way through the winding streets, Talbot's boasting grew more outlandish. "Of course, being a Wilting, I've got connections all over the Underworld. See that cafe? The one with the big M on it? My great-aunt Grizelda haunts the ice cream machine."

That got Wysper genuinely interested again.

"Is that so? Your family is familiar with Old One technology? I've always considered that one of the most interesting fields of study. I was trying to refurbish a television the other day. I'm hoping to get it into hauntable condition."

"Hauntable condition? The Wilting family doesn't bother with any of that repair stuff," Talbot replied. "We don't need to! A broken machine is a perfectly suitable home…sometimes, it can even be a source of great humor! Great-Aunt Grizelda is always telling me how funny it is when people complain about the ice cream machine not working."

Eld glanced at Lea, who giggled.

Talbot was digging such a deep hole for himself that not even a tomb robber would be able to get him out.

Indeed, Wysper's brief excitement rapidly vanished.

"I see. Well, I wish your aunt the best. Hope she doesn't…get electrocuted or anything like that."

"Oh, she won't be!" Talbot merrily replied. "That's the advantage of a broken machine. You know, if we find a machine that's big enough, maybe the two of us could—"

"I think that might be a bit too early for a first date," Wysper icily replied.

"You know, let's hurry to the restaurant," Eld hurriedly interjected.

They passed a plaza where skeleton musicians in brightly colored attire played surprisingly joyous melodies on instruments painted bright white with inlaid gold.

In a nearby park, ghostly children chased each other through tombstones, all while carefully supervised by a matronly skeleton with a bright pink bonnet.

Finally, the four of them stood before The Bone Appetit, a restaurant that looked like it had been designed by someone with a very questionable sense of humor and an unlimited budget of skulls.

Eld eyed the entrance which was, predictably, a giant, grinning skull, "Well at least they committed to the theme."

Shuck nudged Eld's elbow and whined.

There was a sign at the edge of the door, which displayed a skeletal dog with a big red X over its body.

"No dogs."

Eld's shoulders sagged and he frowned.

"Well, I guess there's no dogs," he said. "Go play outside for a bit, Shuck. I saw you wagging your tail at those kids earlier."

Shuck wagged his tail at the kids again, then was off.

Eld scooped up Bart and Franky. Technically a rat and a centipede were a good deal likelier to carry disease than a dog, but what the proprietors didn't know couldn't hurt them.

The Bone Appetit's interior was exactly as tacky as its name suggested. Finger bone chandeliers hung from the ceiling, lighting obsidian tables below that were polished to a mirror sheen.

"Oh, don't worry," Lea said. "An owner with bad taste doesn't always mean the food tastes bad too. I've heard great things about this place."

"I'm sure it'll be wonderful," Eld replied, hoping his voice wasn't too eager. Lea undeniably had that effect on him, making everything else fade into the background.

On the other side of the table, Talbot was regaling Wysper with tales from his previous years exploits at Bathurst.

From the looks of it, it seemed like he'd recaptured her interest again.

"My, my Talbot," Wysper grinned. "You seem like quite the trickster!"

"Oh, this isn't even the beginning of it," Talbot replied, his eternal grin widening alongside hers. "Well, there was this time with Professor Cadaver's prized skeleton. Let's just say it ended up where no bones should ever go…"

Unfortunately for Talbot, it seemed like his propensity for exaggeration was unavoidable. Eld seriously doubted the Headless Horseman had given Talbot his head to hang on the Wilting family mantle, and from the disdainful look on Wysper's face, she didn't believe it either.

Shaking off a laugh, Eld turned to Lea. The candlelight made her cosmic eyes sparkle like twin galaxies.

"How're you settling in?" he asked, fumbling for small talk. "Crazy few weeks, huh?"

Lea nodded, absently tracing the table.

Despite her beauty, Eld couldn't help but notice that wherever her finger passed, pitch black symbols briefly glowed before fading, almost like she was temporarily burning holes in the table.

"It's been interesting. Still get odd looks in Advanced Necromancy. It's weird. I can't even control it, but sometimes, when I touch things...they just spring back to life. Pretty sure Professor Hemlock thinks I'm either a prodigy or an elaborate hoax."

"They're just jealous," Eld blurted out. "I mean, you're top of the class already. Took me a whole week to figure out which end of a femur to hold."

Lea blushed, her pale cheeks briefly flashing red.

Eld hadn't even known she could do that. It made her even more stunning, if possible.

Her fingers brushed against his.

Eld's blood heated and his heart began beating again.

Soon, he was blushing too.

"I, um...I..."

He was just stammering and she was just looking at him, but for some reason, it all felt so incredibly meaningful.

Their moment was cut short by the arrival of menus.

Judging by the haunting décor, Eld had half-expected the menus to be bound in human skin.

When he opened his, a small note said that they were.

This menu is bound in 100% organically sourced ethically generated human skin.

Eld blinked and read the note again.

He briefly wondered what it could possibly mean, but every possibility he imagined threatened to eviscerate his appetite if he delved into it further. He shook his head and decided not to stop dwelling on the binding.

"Ooh, Cerberus Surprise!" Wysper exclaimed, her eyes literally lighting up. "Heard its killer. Like, actually tries to eat you if you're too slow."

"I'll stick with Stygian Stew." Talbot grimaced, closing his menu and placing it in front of him. "Don't need three-headed indigestion."

They ordered—Eld chose the safer-sounding Elysian Fields Salad.

As they waited for food, the group began laughing at Talbot's over-the-top impression of Professor McGrath.

For what already seemed like the umpteenth time, Wysper's interest dramatically increased again, after having fallen just moments before.

Eld smiled to himself. He had to give Wysper credit. She was giving Talbot plenty of chances...

Perhaps Talbot's work as a caricaturist was what would finally win Wysper's heart. From what he could tell, his roommate was cycling through every single one of his talents today. Unfortunately, he had a feeling Talbot would find a way to blow this too, maybe some exceedingly fanciful story about how he out-acted a doppelganger.

But despite the joy on the other end of the table, Lea grew quiet.

Her gaze turned distant, as if seeing beyond the restaurant walls.

Eld turned to her, his eyes bright with concern.

"Is something wrong?" he murmured.

"Eld," she said softly over the clinking silverware, "I've been having more flashes. Memories, I think. But they're odd. Scary, sometimes."

Eld leaned in, forgetting everything else. "What kind of memories?"

Lea bit her lip. Slowly, she reached under the table. "Can I show you? Like I did before? If that's okay?"

Eld nodded, taking her hand without hesitation.

He didn't see anything. It felt almost like before, with his heart pumping again and a faint blush reappearing on his cheeks.

He was very aware of how soft her skin felt, how perfectly their fingers intertwined. In that moment, he forgot about visions and mysteries, just enjoying holding her hand.

Then the world fell away.

Eld stood in a barren wasteland, cracked earth beneath his feet.

The sky churned with bruise-colored clouds, split by sickly green lightning. The air felt thick with decay and something older, more primal.

All around, the dead marched. Not mindless husks, but aware undead. Their eyes glowed with inner fire as they moved in perfect formation, an army stretching to the horizon.

"How could this be?" Eld muttered to himself.

Even among the undead, there was a great deal of variety, ranging from necromancers like Eld who'd suspended their bodily functions to ghouls, zombies, ghosts, skeletons, and, of course, liches.

Like all nightkin, the undead had their differences with each other. Getting them to work together and ignore their disparate personal goals was just like herding black cats.

But here, they all moved with perfect unison.

Which said that they were being *commanded* by someone.

Atop a hill of fused bone stood a being radiating power.

"No way…" Eld stammered. "How…what?"

He half-expected a response, but there was nothing.

Lea was just sharing this vision with him, after all.

But Lea was *inside* this vision too.

She…

Eld watched, frozen, as Lea, or someone who looked identical to her, approached, slowly and steadily walking towards the figure at the top of the hill.

She moved with manic reverence, her face twisted in a look of utter zealous determination. Power radiated from her body, her hair twisting and twirling like tentacles. Her shadow seemed to drag on endlessly behind her, carving a black scar in the ground she crossed.

The being began chanting.

Though Eld couldn't make out the words, he felt their weight.

Every word echoed endlessly, like a stone dropped into a bottomless well.

His teeth ached. His bones vibrated. As the chanting peaked, the being's robes billowed, revealing an embroidered emblem.

The Blackwood family seal.

Eld jerked back, nearly knocking over his water. The restaurant rushed back into focus. Lea stared at him, her hand still outstretched.

"Eld? You okay?" she asked. "What did you see?"

He opened his mouth, but no words came.

Lea looked so innocent, nothing like the manic look on her face in his dream.

How could he explain?

How could he reconcile the ancient, dark Lea with the one across from him? And what did his family have to do with it?

And…

How could this even be a vision from her perspective if she was in it?

There was so much that didn't make sense. Eld's brain filled with static, just like a haunted television.

"I'm not sure," he croaked. "It was even more intense than the last time. I'll say that."

Lea pulled back, hurt flashing in her eyes. "I'm sorry. I shouldn't have—"

"No, it's okay," Eld cut in, regretting his reaction. "I just need to process. It was a lot."

The rest of dinner passed in a haze.

Eld ate mechanically, barely noticing his salad's occasional escape attempts.

He vaguely registered Talbot's endless boasting and Wysper's frequently chilly responses, but his mind whirled with questions.

As they left, heading back to Bathurst, Eld felt like a lobotomy patient.

He walked the girls to their dorm on pure instinct, barely speaking.

At Lea's door, she paused. "Eld, I'm sorry if the vision upset you. I didn't mean to ruin the night."

"You didn't ruin anything," he said quickly.

But it seemed like his tone wasn't quite convincing enough.

"Really," Eld insisted. "I just need time to process. It was a lot."

Lea nodded, hurt and understanding warring in her eyes.

Then, catching Eld off guard, she kissed his cheek.

"Goodnight, Eld," she whispered, he could feel her breath on his neck.

She broke away, her face moving close to his and they locked eyes.

She squeezed his hand and then slipped inside her dorm.

Eld stood frozen, his cheek tingling. Despite his turmoil, butterflies swarmed his stomach.

The lovely woman he'd just dined with looked *nothing* like the one in the vision.

As he and Talbot headed back, Eld barely registered his friend's excited babbling about Wysper. Any other time, he would have teased Talbot mercilessly, but now, his mind was a battlefield—fear and suspicion of Lea versus his undeniably growing feelings for her.

One thing was clear—tomorrow's matches at the Nocturnal Combat Club were the least of his worries. He'd hardly thought about them the entire night, even with his parents coming to watch.

Sleep came late, filled with dreams of marching dead and a devouring black sun.

Chapter 15

Trial by Combat

Eld peeked out from behind the heavy velvet curtains, his heart pounding in his chest.

"Wow. This whole combat thing looks a lot more impressive when it's out in the open."

Shuck peeked out of the curtains, then hastily ducked back inside again. Apparently, stage fright was a cross-species experience.

"It's always like this," Orlando replied. The vampire's lips were curled in a well-practiced expression of arrogance. "Though the Nocturnal Combat Club typically battles underground, the school brings us out to the central ballroom for our arena bouts."

His sneer deepened.

"You've spent far too much time Topside, Eld. You've forgotten the nightkin's penchant for pageantry."

Eld snorted.

Penchant for pageantry.

That was the exact kind of absurd phrase Orlando loved.

Eld knew that the humans had a perfectly healthy penchant for pageantry, arguably just as healthy as the nightkin's. And even more than that, he saw that Orlando's eyes were glimmering equal measures of excitement and tension.

Whether or not Orlando wanted to admit it, he was feeling nervous—just like Eld was.

Eld breathed the scene in, excitement gradually building in his stomach.

The tournament hall buzzed with excitement, a cauldron of anticipation ready to boil over. Like Orlando said, the battlefield had moved from the catacombs to the school's central ballroom. A newly erected circular arena dominated the center of the room, surrounded by tiered seating that stretched up into the shadows.

Eld's eyes scanned the crowd, searching for familiar faces.

Every fourth fan in the audience seemed to be there for Orlando.

The vampiric swordsman had attracted the most delusional fanbase Eld had ever seen. Countless female nightkin held up posters asking Orlando to turn them into his vampire spawn.

Eld was so busy rolling his eyes he almost missed her, but there, in the third row, sat his mother. She caught his gaze and waved enthusiastically, her smile beaming with pride. Eld returned the wave, feeling a surprisingly familiar mixture of gratitude and embarrassment.

His father was nowhere to be seen.

Eld frowned.

So Eldritch Sr. couldn't attend his son's bouts, but he was willing to sneak into campus on a random night just to cast spells in the Splintered Dimension?

Just what *had* his father been doing that night?

Despite he and Lea's best efforts, they hadn't even found a single hint of the ritual. Although there were many paintings of the black sun all throughout campus, there was surprisingly little information in the school library.

"Eld! Eld! Eld!"

The shout was faint at first, but even just a faint hint of her voice drove all thoughts of his father out of his mind.

He turned and a few seats away from his mother, Eld spotted Talbot and Lea. Seeing them there, supporting him, brought a smile to Eld's face. Whatever happened today, he wasn't alone.

A heavy and very furry hand clapped down on Eld's shoulder. The barbed claws digging into his flesh nearly made Eld jump out of his skin.

He turned to find Wolfgang grinning at him, the werewolf's fur bristling with pre-match adrenaline.

"Did you really have to do that?" Eld groaned.

"Ah, just preparing you for an ambush," Wolfgang chuckled. But then his mischievous glean entered his eye. "Ready to show those no-account fathers what we're really made of?"

Eld nodded, trying to match his teammate's confidence. "As ready as I'll ever be."

"Good." Wolfgang gave Eld's shoulder a tight squeeze. He was clearly trying to be reassuring, but it really just felt like Wolfgang was warming up his dislocations.

"If you two are done with your little lovefest, we're on after the Banshee Bunch," Orlando snootily interjected. "Should be a good warm-up act."

Eld turned to the arena, his eyes widening.

The Banshee Bunch. That was Lilith's team. Though it wasn't proper form, he definitely wanted her to do well.

The tournament master stepped into the center of the arena.

He was a tall man with a very pale face. To Eld's surprise, he seemed like an ordinary human, though his extreme comfort among the nightkin suggested at least some experience with the supernatural.

His striped robes were adorned with embroidered scenes of magical combat that seemed to shift in the light. When he spoke, his voice boomed through the hall.

He didn't need any magical amplification—he was just very loud and very confident.

"Welcome, one and all, to the Nocturnal Combat Club Qualifying Matches! Today, we'll see which teams have what it takes to advance to the Tournament of Shadows. Remember, only four of our eight competing teams will move forward. May the best necromancers, shapeshifters, and assorted creatures of the night prevail!"

A cheer went up from the crowd, the sound reverberating off the stone walls. Eld felt a shiver run down his spine.

"First up," the announcer continued. "We have the Banshee Bunch facing off against the Oni Onslaught!"

Eld watched as Lilith and her team took their places in the arena.

They looked confident, their matching uniforms a swirl of midnight blue and silver. Across from them stood three hulking figures that could only be the oni team. They had red skin and wickedly curved horns that shined like jet-black scimitars. Unlike Lilith's team, their outfits were plain and simple, little more than brown rags.

"Wait a second," Eld muttered. "The runeplate isn't as effective here, is it? Without the extra runes from the catacombs?"

"Yeah, it's not," Orlando said. His eyes narrowed as he noticed Eld's discomfort. "Don't disgrace yourself. This is the real fight now—going back downstairs would be like using training wheels on a bicycle."

Eld shuddered, abruptly realizing that these fights would be more dangerous than he anticipated.

The matches were a series of one-on-one bouts, with the announcer picking contestants from each side.

Lilith was selected first, facing off against a burly red oni clutching a massive spiked club.

Despite the tremendous difference in size, the battle ended in moments.

Lilith moved like a dancer, her steps light, graceful, and sure.

When she opened her mouth to scream, the sound was focused into a pinpoint beam that sent her opponents staggering back.

Next, the banshee beside her created a wall of sound so shrill that Eld could briefly see it. It was like simply using his ears wouldn't be enough to process the noise. The deafened and disoriented oni fell to the ground, and Lilith darted.

She was swift and supple as a bloodthirsty leech, effortlessly evading her opponent's blows while landing a series of strikes that would have been fatal if not for the protective gear.

Her rapier screeched and scratched against her opponent's armor and the oni fell to the ground, faintly twitching.

"That was vicious…" Eld muttered.

"Well, in the Catacombs, there are additional layers of protective spells," Wolfgang reminded him. "You could gut a man and he'd still survive. Here, well, nobody has died. Yet."

Before Eld knew it, the match was over.

The Banshee Bunch stood victorious, not a hair out of place. The single member of the Oni team who hadn't outright fallen unconscious looked shell-shocked, as if he weren't quite sure what had just happened to him.

"And the winners are…the Banshee Bunch!" the announcer declared, to raucous applause. "Next up, we have the Grave Robbers facing off against the Primordial Punchers!"

Eld's stomach did a backflip.

That was them.

The Grave Robbers. He still wasn't sure about the name. In fact, Orlando wasn't either—it was one of the few things the two agreed on.

But Wolfgang had insisted it was "totally badass."

Based on the confused and somewhat disturbed whispers from the crowd, it seemed safe to say that the name was more along the lines of "totally bad."

As they made their way to the arena, Eld got his first good look at their opponents.

The Primordial Punchers were a strange team, to say the least. Like the Grave Robbers themselves, there wasn't a set theme.

Their first fighter was a skeletal Viking, complete with horned helmet and a beard made of what looked like moss.

Next to him stood a blob monster that seemed to be constantly shifting and reforming, transforming so rapidly that Eld couldn't even begin to speculate what his true form was.

But it was the troll that really caught Eld's attention.

He was easily eight feet tall, with tusks protruding from its lower jaw and muscles that looked like they could bend steel.

The announcer's voice rang out, "Ladies, gentlemen, and assorted entities, let the match begin! First will be Orlando von Ravenscroft against Ragnar Tibula!"

Orlando stepped forward first, facing off against the Viking skeleton, who hefted a large ax above his head.

They just circled each other, each sizing each other up. Then, in a blur of motion too fast for Eld to follow, they clashed.

Ragnar's ax smashed into Orlando's claymore.

For a brief moment, the vampire's knees buckled.

A gasp went out among the crowd, with plenty of women promising to nurse Orlando back to health.

But there was no need.

After three more exchanges, it became clear that Orlando was clearly toying with Ragnar, dodging attacks and retaliating with strikes that were more show than substance.

After a few minutes of this, Wolfgang growled in frustration.

"Hurry up and finish it, Orlando! We don't have all night!"

Orlando sighed, as if deeply put upon. "Very well. If you insist on rushing art."

In three swift moves, he literally disarmed the Viking, sending both his skeletal limbs tumbling to the ground. With a smooth kick, he swept his opponent's legs off the ground before pinning him to the ground with the flat of his claymore.

The referee counted upwards, and at thirteen, the match was over.

"It's either a thirteen-count knockout, or four accumulated points," Wolfgang explained. "Though worst comes to worst, you can just chuck your opponent out of the ring. That works too."

Eld raised an eyebrow as medics helped Ragnar re-attach his arms.

"Shouldn't you have explained that before bringing me here? Back in the Catacombs, we were just fighting until the bell rang for class. I wasn't even aware that the fight could stop."

"Ah, well, I mean, there's nothing wrong with excessive passion," Wolfgang retorted.

"Next, we have Wolfgang Fangson against…"

The announcer paused, turning to the blob.

"How, exactly, do I pronounce this?"

The blob created a mouth on his body with a loud squelching noise.

"Blarghleblargum!" the blob replied. "Don't worry about it. People get confused all the time. The three z's are all silent."

Eld wasn't even aware of the zs to begin with. He couldn't even begin to fathom where they might have been.

As Wolfgang and the blob entered the arena, Eld worriedly eyed the troll. That left them as the final match.

But things would be alright if Wolfgang won…

"Begin!" the announcer cried.

Wolfgang roared like a haunted vehicle.

And he hit like one too.

Unfortunately, his brute strength seemed to have little effect on the amorphous creature. His swords passed right through the blob.

Wolfgang's face wrinkled in discomfort and confusion as his blades got stuck Leaving his swords stuck in his foe's body, he followed that up with a vicious kick. His opponent went flying into the sky before promptly bouncing off the ceiling.

When he landed, Blarghleblargum threatened to utterly envelope Wolfgang.

For a while, the two viciously struggled.

Wolfgang's claws slashed his foe's body to ribbons, but they would simply reform.

"Idiot…idiot…" Orlando groaned. "You need to throw him out of the ring. Brute strength won't work!"

But in his battle frenzy, Wolfgang didn't hear Orlando's advice.

The two foes traded blows back and forth, neither gaining a clear advantage. Wolfgang's failed hits didn't score any points, and the blob didn't seem to have any offensive moves to begin with…

At least at the start.

After twenty minutes of battle, Wolfgang found himself completely engulfed by Blarghleblargum.

Wolfgang struggled within the gelatinous mass. Seconds ticked by, feeling like hours. The crowd held its breath, waiting for the werewolf to burst free yet again, but the familiar roar didn't come.

There was no explosive escape, not this time.

The blob simply held on, its body rippling with Wolfgang's weakening struggles. Finally, the referee called it after Wolfgang fell still for thirteen seconds.

"Point and match to the Primordial Punchers!"

As the blob released him, Wolfgang emerged, gasping and covered in slime.

He looked stunned, as if he couldn't quite believe what had happened. Eld felt a pang of sympathy for his teammate, who stalked silently back to their side of the auditorium.

Wolfgang hated losing more than anything, and judging by how he was staring into the audience, he was undoubtedly thinking of his father.

But Eld didn't have time to worry about Wolfgang. It was all up to him now. Well, him and a few helpful friends.

The pressure settled on Eld's shoulders as he stepped into the arena—if he couldn't win this match, he and his team would be eliminated. The troll slowly stepped into the arena. The beast loomed over him, a veritable tower of muscle and bone.

But as Eld watched him move, he quickly realized he had one major advantage—speed. The troll was incredibly strong, but it moved like a yoked glacier.

Eld darted around it, peppering it with small strikes with his dagger that seemed to only annoy the behemoth.

He would have to add spells to the mix. In the middle of a tight fight, he had no time to draw his usual symbols, but here, Orlando's tutelage was invaluable. Eld concentrated on his glinting dagger, then ducked low, stabbing forward.

"Point to Grave Robbers!" the referee called as Eld landed a solid hit with a necrotic blast of energy. Instead of drawing out the spell, he'd used his weapon as a magical focus—weaker, but much faster.

But by the next exchange, the troll had wised up.

He started predicting Eld's movements and it nearly caught him with a massive fist. Eld barely dodged, but the troll's other hand came out of nowhere, sending him sprawling out of the ring.

"Point to Primordial Punchers!"

Eld got to his feet.

Time for a different approach.

He reached into his pocket, pulling out Bart. The zombie rat looked up at him, his lizard tail twitching expectantly. As Eld channeled necromantic energy, the rat began to grow, shifting and expanding until it was the size of a large dog.

The crowd gasped in surprise. The troll just looked confused. His eyes slowly went from Bart to Eld again, as if were unsure who was his opponent.

Bart darted forward.

The troll lunged at Bart, but the zombified rat darted forward, exposing only his tail.

The troll viciously grabbed it. Moments later, the very confused troll was holding just a tail—with no rat to be found.

Chittering, Bart slammed his newly generated tail into the troll's legs, tripping it.

As the troll stumbled, Eld saw his opening.

His fingers darted through the sky, swift but sure. Moments later, he charged forward, a wreath of necromantic energy in his hands.

The troll turned, but it was too late.

Thanks to his classes at Bathurst, Eld had learned far swifter ways of incapacitating his enemies. Eld shouted and released his magic, sending a wave of cold that momentarily slowed the troll's movements.

In that instant of reduced mobility, Eld struck with his dagger. One, two, three rapid hits in succession, each blow further empowered by necromantic energy.

His opponent staggered, then fell to his knees with a loud groan. He was still conscious, still fighting to get back to his feet.

Eld darted forward, but the referee stepped between them.

"That was four points," the referee declared. "The match goes to the Grave Robbers!"

The announcer raised Eld's hand in the air and shouted, "The Grave Robbers advance to the Tournament of Shadows!"

The crowd cheered. Eld stood there, breathing hard, barely able to believe it. They had done it. They were moving on to the Tournament of Shadows.

Eld looked up at the crowd. His mother was beaming and so were Talbot and Lea. His father *still* wasn't there, but then he felt a faint flare of familiar necromantic energy.

Immediately, Eld turned towards the exit. His father was there, locked in what looked like a heated argument with Grimthorpe.

Both lichs' eyes burned with literal flames as their hands gesticulated wildly. Clearly, the two liches were in some kind of argument.

What could they possibly be arguing about? Eld didn't even know where to start investigating. He and Lea still needed more information, though perhaps this argument would somehow create an opportunity.

His thoughts were interrupted as Wolfgang grabbed him in a bear hug, lifting him off his feet. "We did it, runt! We're going to the Tournament of Shadows!"

Orlando, meanwhile, had vanished behind a ceaseless swarm of female fans.

As they made their way back to the preparation area to change out of their gear, Eld caught sight of Lea and Talbot hurrying towards them.

"Congratulations!" Lea exclaimed, her eyes shining with pride and admiration. "That was amazing, Eld!"

Talbot held up a bottle filled with swirling, iridescent liquid. "I think this calls for a celebration. What do you say we take this back to the dorm and have ourselves a little victory party?"

Eld grinned, happy to see that Lea's hesitation after their date had vanished almost entirely. He was still eager to investigate Grimthorpe, but a night of celebration was just what the two of them needed.

"Sounds perfect," he replied.

Eld walked over to briefly greet his mother, but as always, his brief greeting turned into an hour-long fussing.

When Eld was finally able to leave, the walk back to the dorm was a blur of excited chatter and playful jostling.

Wolfgang had insisted on joining their little celebration, much to Talbot's chagrin. The poltergeist kept shooting worried glances at the bottle he was carrying, as if afraid the werewolf might accidentally smash it in his enthusiasm.

"I still can't believe that move you pulled with Bart," Lea said, falling into step beside Eld. "I've never seen anyone use a familiar quite like that before. Though come to think of it, I don't think I've ever seen anyone using a familiar before." she tapped her chin, then shrugged.

When they two briefly touched hands, Eld felt his cheeks warm at the compliment. "Thanks. I'm just glad it worked. For a minute there, I thought that troll was going to squash him flat."

Talbot scoffed. "Bart's way too wily for that. Aren't you, little buddy?" He reached out to pat the zombie rat, who was perched on Eld's shoulder, only for his hand to pass right through. "Oh, right. Forgot to solidify."

They reached Eld and Talbot's room, piling in with a chorus of laughter and shushing noises.

Wolfgang claimed the desk chair, sprawling in it like a king on his throne.

"Alright, ghostie." Wolfgang started prying at the cork. "Let's see what you've got in here."

Talbot produced a set of glasses from seemingly nowhere, a neat trick, considering he didn't have pockets. With smiling aplomb, the poltergeist began pouring. The liquid inside the bottle seemed to pour strangely, swirling up the sides of the glasses instead of down.

"A toast." Wolfgang raised his glass. "To the Grave Robbers, future champions of Bathurst!"

They clinked glasses. Eld took an optimistically large sip and nearly choked. It tasted like liquid starlight, fizzy and bright and just a little bit dangerous.

As the night wore on, the conversation flowed as freely as Talbot's mystery brew. They relived every moment of the matches, with Wolfgang providing colorful commentary.

"And then that blob tried to suffocate me! Can you believe it? As if a little slime could take down Wolfgang the Wondrous!"

Lea rolled her eyes, but she was smiling. "Is that what we're calling you now?"

"Why not? It's got a nice ring to it, don't you think?"

The others debated the merits of Wolfgang's new title, with Talbot astutely pointing out that the slime indeed *would* have suffocated him.

But as the argument went on, Eld found his mind wandering back to what he had seen after the match. His father and Grimthorpe, arguing in the shadows. He must have been frowning, because suddenly Lea was there, her hand on his arm.

"Hey," she said softly. "Everything okay?"

Eld hesitated, but looking into Lea's cosmic eyes, he felt the words bubbling up, as if she had commanded him to speak.

"I saw my dad after the match. He was arguing with Grimthorpe."

Lea's brow furrowed.

"Arguing with your dad, huh? Didn't you also say that Grimthorpe disapproved of your dad's servants?"

"He did," Eld replied.

"Maybe he's the good guy in all this…" Lea mused.

"It's a hopeful thought," Eld said. "Grimthorpe was always kind to me. But based on what I've seen, it just doesn't seem likely. If he's a good guy, why all the secrecy? Why not just come out and say what's going on? And he was still using husks too. It feels like we don't have the full picture."

Lea squeezed his arm but didn't say anything else, just leaned her head on his shoulder and teased his arm with her finger.

A warm feeling spread through Eld's chest that had nothing to do with Talbot's magical brew. He started to say something, he wasn't sure what, when Wolfgang's booming voice cut through their moment.

"Oi, lovebirds! Stop whispering in the corner and join the party!"

Eld felt his face burn as if enflamed just before Lea quickly withdrew her hand. They rejoined the others, but the moment lingered in Eld's mind, a bright spot amidst all the uncertainty.

Eld knew how dangerous opposing his father would be.

But with Lea by his side, perhaps even something that harrowing could be fun somehow.

The night wore on and the bottle emptied.

Eld found himself feeling more relaxed than he had in weeks. The weight of cosmic mysteries and family secrets seemed lighter somehow, balanced out by the warmth of friendship and the glow of victory.

Wolfgang was the first to call it a night, citing the need for his *beauty sleep*. As he lumbered out the door, he paused to ruffle Eld's hair affectionately. "You did good today, pup. Keep it up, and we might just make a *proper necromancer* out of you yet."

Coming from Wolfgang, it was high praise indeed. Eld grinned, ducking away from the werewolf's massive paw. "Thanks. See you at practice."

Lea left soon after, but not before giving Eld a quick hug that left him feeling like he might float right off the ground. "Get some rest. You've earned it."

And then it was just Eld and Talbot, cleaning up the aftermath of their impromptu celebration.

Well, Eld was cleaning.

Talbot was mostly just floating around, offering unhelpful commentary.

"You know," Talbot said, watching Eld struggle with a particularly stubborn stain on the desk, "I think Lea might have a thing for you."

Eld nearly dropped the rag he was holding. "What? No, we're just really good friends."

Talbot's eternal grin seemed to widen. "Uh-huh. Sure. And I'm the Ghost of Christmas Past."

"Shut up," Eld grumbled, but he couldn't quite keep the smile off his face.

Chapter 16

Blood Ties and Missing Links

The mid-year slump had hit Bathurst Academy as hard as a troll's headbutt.

Even the ever-present mist seemed more sluggish, clinging to the windows of the Hemomancy classroom like a drowsy black cat. Eld stared out at the gloomy landscape, his mind a million miles away from Professor Hemlock's lecture.

He and Lea's investigations were still as fruitless as ever.

Every so often, the two entered the catacombs, hoping for just the merest hint of a hint.

But they never found anything. Even when they poked around the doors to the Splintered Dimension, the blaring golden doors remained sealed shut, without a hint of Eldritch Sr. to be found.

But now, Lea's seat was empty, and Eld didn't know why. She had never missed a class before. The sight of the empty chair burrowed into his mind like a parasite.

Did she get lost?

Was she sick?

What if someone found out what she *really* was?

The possibilities swirled in his mind, each more worrying than the last.

"...and so, the blood oath passes through generations, binding not just the individual, but their entire lineage," Professor Hemlock droned on, a distant hum in Eld's consciousness.

The words drifted past him, failing to catch in the web of his distracted thoughts.

Eld had no doubt that during the test, he'd be kicking himself for missing so much crucial information. But he just didn't care.

He was so worried about Lea that his heart almost started pumping on its own again, even without her.

What could have happened? It was probably something innocuous, but what if it wasn't? What if it was related to the Black Sun conspiracy?

A sharp crack, like a shattered tree, snapped Eld back to reality.

"Huh?" Eld gasped. "What just? Oh…um, sorry Professor."

Professor Hemlock stood before him.

"Mr. Blackwood," she said with icy disapproval, "perhaps you'd care to demonstrate the practical application of today's lesson?"

Before Eld could stammer out an excuse, Hemlock raised her hands.

The air around her shimmered, and suddenly the classroom was filled with a swarm of bats and mosquitos.

"Wait," Eld gasped. "*What* were we learning?"

Hemlock just smirked as the creatures descended on Eld in a flurry of flapping wings and needle-sharp proboscises.

Eld yelped, throwing his arms up to protect his face.

But to his surprise, the creatures didn't attack. Instead, they swirled around him in a dizzying vortex, their tiny minds brushing against his necromantic senses.

Despite the initial shock, Eld found himself fascinated.

These weren't mindless undead, but living familiars, each with its own spark of personality.

Almost instinctively, Eld reached out to them, touching their mind with his. As soon as he did, any hint of hostility faded away and the creatures perched gently on him.

A bat nuzzled his cheek, its leathery wings surprisingly soft. A mosquito landed on his finger, its compound eyes regarding him with what seemed like friendly curiosity.

"Um, I think I did it," Eld said.

Around him, the class gasped in surprise.

"Lucky bastard," Talbot grumbled. "When that happened to me, they stung and bit me until I phased out…and then followed me around waiting for me to phase back in."

"It was truly a horrible performance, Mr. Wilting," Professor Hemlock said. "You poltergeists don't even have blood for them to take…they were following you out of sheer hatred."

The whole class—even Talbot—laughed.

At the end, Professor Hemlock turned back to Eld, sighing and shaking her head.

"To your credit, Mr. Blackwood…you do have a way with animals. But still…just pay attention next time."

She waved her hands and her familiars returned.

"Class dismissed."

His shoulders sagging in relief, Eld sat back down. He'd escaped Hemlock's test, though he was lucky it was related to animals. A more complex test and he undoubtedly would have failed…

"Um, Eld?" Talbot asked.

"Yeah?" Eld asked.

"She just said class dismissed…that usually means we go to the next class?"

"Right, right," Eld said, hurriedly getting up and scooping his things into his bag.

Talbot just shook his head.

The walk to Alchemy class was a blur of worried thoughts and half-formed theories. Normally, Eld excelled in this subject, but lately, all of his grades had been slipping. The longer he and Lea failed to find anything about the Black Sun, the more time they'd spent looking.

Logically, there was less and less time for school.

Eld knew he should be concerned about his grades, but he couldn't muster the energy to care.

And with Lea missing, he was even more worried than before.

He was so lost in thought that he almost walked right into Professor Medusa. The gorgon's snake-hair hissed in surprise, a few of the serpents rearing back defensively.

"Oh! Mr. Blackwood," she said, adjusting the protective black shades she wore over her eyes. "Do watch where you're going. I'd hate to add another statue to my collection."

Professor Medusa gestured to the frighteningly lifelike stone figures scattered around the classroom, their faces frozen in eternal terror.

Eld had never been sure if those statues were really former students or just very convincing sculptures. Either way, they certainly kept the class on their toes.

"Um, yeah. Sorry Professor. Will do…or, I mean, won't do. I mean, well, you get what I mean."

An eyebrow arched over Professor Medusa's shades.

"I'm not even sure a daemonology expert like Professor Albright would know what you mean. It seems like you've taken to speaking in tongues, Mr. Blackwood."

Without even trying to mutter another word, Eld slunk to his seat.

"Now then," Professor Medusa began, her snakes settling into a relaxed coif. "Today we'll be discussing the influence of celestial bodies on alchemical transformations. Mercury is in retrograde, which means it's the perfect time for transmuting lead into gold! Or maybe silver. I always get those two mixed up when Jupiter is ascendant."

Normally, Eld would be scribbling notes furiously.

Professor Medusa was one of the most eccentric professors at Bathurst.

A natural genius at alchemy, she frequently messed up her descriptions, sometimes even confusing planets for phases of the moon. Talbot still snickered at the class where she'd spent the entire time calling "Waning" the fourth planet from the sun.

Stellar notetaking was the only way to untangle her chaotic web of contradictory explanations. Only by carefully comparing things said across different classes was Eld able to divine the correct path.

But today, he could barely focus on the messy sigils Professor Medusa was scrawling on the blackboard.

His mind kept drifting to Lea, wondering how she was doing. He remembered how this class always seemed to stump her, despite her overwhelming brilliance in other subjects.

It was as if anything related to astrology just slid off her brain. Helping Lea succeed was a big reason why he'd taken notes so carefully to begin with.

Without her, he didn't see the point.

It wasn't like Eld was in need of gold.

In fact, he'd heard rumors that due to alchemists' excessive transmutation of gold, certain towns were considering using paper currency covered in eldritch runes. The complex web of curses would make them almost impossible to forge.

That made him wonder what kind of currency they'd used in Lea's time.

Based on her vision—and based on the cult-like version of her he'd seen in her vision—they might not have used currency at all.

"Mr. Blackwood!" Professor Medusa's sharp voice cut through his thoughts. "Perhaps you'd like to tell the class which phase of the moon is best for creating a Seeing Stone of Clarity?"

Eld blinked, his mind blank. A Seeing Stone of Clarity undoubtedly would have been useful right now…but he had no idea how to make one.

"Uh, full moon?"

The gorgon sighed. "New moon, Mr. Blackwood. Or perhaps a waxing moon…full moon is the *last* answer I would have suggested."

Her snakes drooped in disappointment, hissing sadly.

"Honestly, it's like you're not even trying today. One more slip-up and you'll be having a very close conversation with my petrifying gaze, protective glasses or not."

Eld blinked groggily.

With such an obvious threat, he didn't want to slip up, but his heart just wasn't in it. The rest of the class passed in a haze of celestial charts and alchemical formulae.

When the bell finally rang, Eld felt like he had been put through a mental wringer.

As he packed up his things, a familiar voice called out, "Mr. Blackwood, a moment please."

Eld turned to find Professor Grimthorpe standing in the doorway. Unlike Eldritch Sr., Professor Grimthorpe's skull had not been adjusted for scowling. He simply stared at Eld, his expression unreadable as his eyes flickered with internal fire.

Eld's stomach did a nervous flip.

What could Grimthorpe want?

Did he suspect something about Eld and Lea's investigations into the Black Sun?

Without any helpful explanation, Grimthorpe gestured towards the wall and a study seemed to materialize out of thin air.

Inside the study, books teetered in precarious stacks that threatened to tumble apart at any moment. Strange chittering artifacts that looked half alive skittered across the room, poking and probing at the walls. The air smelled faintly of burnt incense and something else…

Eld frowned.

Leftover lasagna perhaps?

He followed the professor into the study, trying to keep his face neutral.

"Have a seat, Mr. Blackwood." Grimthorpe gestured, pointing casually at a chair that was made of human bones.

Eld eyed the chair suspiciously.

There *were* human students at Bathurst, mostly elderly humans trying to obtain immortality. A chair made out of human bones seemed to send a very ominous message.

Grimthorpe chuckled, his jaw clacking dryly.

"Ah. Old décor. A gift from your father, in fact, to commend me for becoming headmaster, all those years ago. No worries. I can change it if it bothers you."

"It will be fine," Eld said, sitting in the chair. Just like the chairs in the Blackwood family home, the advantage of sending a message was outweighed by the disadvantage of irritation and discomfort.

It seemed like Eld had passed some kind of invisible test, because the flames in Grimthorpe's eyes flickered a little more brightly.

"How are your studies progressing?" Grimthorpe asked.

Eld perched on the edge of the chair, trying not to think about whose femur he might be sitting on. "Fine, sir. Just a bit…tired lately."

Grimthorpe's eyebrow arched. "Oh? Anything in particular on your mind?"

There was something in the professor's tone, a hint of fishing, that made Eld choose his words carefully. "Just typical student stress, sir. Exams coming up and all that."

"I see." Grimthorpe leaned back in his chair, his fingers steepled. "And how are things with your father? I understand he attended the Combat Club qualifiers."

Eld paused briefly.

He'd seen Grimthorpe and his father arguing. There had to be a reason why Grimthorpe was asking about his father.

There was some kind of game here, he just didn't see it. And since he still wasn't sure if Grimthorpe was on his side or not, he decided to play it close to the chest.

"He did, yes. Briefly. I didn't get a chance to speak with him much. As you've noticed, my father and I have never really seen eye to eye."

Grimthorpe's eyes narrowed slightly, a calculating look crossing his face. "Tell me, Eld, have you ever had the chance to peruse your family's grimoire? The Blackwood Familial Tome is quite renowned in certain circles."

Eld's pulse quickened.

For a brief moment, he considered lying—but there was no real reason to.

"Only briefly, sir," he admitted. "I saw a few pages on pet reanimation. There was a spell there that I've been interested in perfecting. It captured my curiosity and I've been interested in the field ever since. But my father disapproved. I believe that Cloudehill has seen much more than me."

"Ah, yes. Eldritch Sr. was always rather *protective* of family heirlooms," Grimthorpe mused. "And even more protective of what he considers the family legacy. But surely you must know something of your ancestors? The Blackwoods have a long and interesting history."

Eld shook his head, trying to keep his expression neutral. "Not much, I'm afraid. Father isn't one for family stories. In fact, he banished our predecessors to the family crypt long before I was born."

Grimthorpe chuckled for a moment. Clearly, he knew something Eld didn't. But instead of explaining, he leaned forward. "Nothing at all? No tales of great rituals or powerful artifacts? No mention of, say, a certain celestial phenomenon?"

Eld blinked.

There it was. An indirect question about the Black Sun.

He shrugged.

"Ah, you know, my father and I just aren't really on speaking terms. My mother talks quite a great deal, but rarely about the Blackwood family's history. Seeing as she married into the family, she doesn't know much about it."

"I see." Grimthorpe's gaze was penetrating, as if he could see right through Eld's evasions. "Well, if there's anything you need to discuss, about your studies or anything else, I am always available. We *are* old family friends, after all."

The tension in the room could be cut with a knife. Eld felt like he was walking a tightrope, each word a potential misstep.

"Thank you, sir. I appreciate that."

Grimthorpe nodded, a small smile growing at the corners of his mouth. "Of course, my boy. After all, knowledge is power. And in our line of work, power can be everything."

"Yes," Eld replied.

He met Grimthorpe's eyes, but then, he saw something unmistakable.

There, half-hidden under a stack of papers, was a letter. The handwriting on the envelope was his father's.

Making a split-second decision, Eld leaned forward, *accidentally* knocking over a precariously balanced pile of books. As Grimthorpe hastily moved to catch them, Bart's lizard tail lashed out, snagging the letter with unearthly speed and stuffing it inside Eld's robes.

"I'm so sorry, Professor!" Eld exclaimed, helping to gather the fallen tomes. His heart was pounding, but he forced his voice to remain steady. "How clumsy of me."

Grimthorpe waved off his apologies. "No harm done, Mr. Blackwood. Now, unless there's anything else...?"

Eld shook his head, perhaps a bit too quickly. "No, sir. Thank you for this."

He left Grimthorpe's study.

Behind him, the lich headmaster casually stood, waving his hands to dismiss the room. In just the blink of an eye, the study was gone, replaced by solid rock.

Eld wanted nothing more than to tear the letter apart and see what was inside.

Guilt warred with curiosity—the letter could very well reveal Grimthorpe's allegiances. Though Grimthorpe had always treated Eld well, he couldn't trust the man.

But now wasn't the time.

Shaking his head, Eld hurried down the hall.

Soon the sounds of the other students faded away, vanishing completely as he focused on his new task. The walk to Lea's dorm seemed to take an eternity, and when he finally arrived, he found the door locked.

He knocked on the door hard.

"Lea? Lea? Are you there?"

He heard nothing. But then he felt a strange pulse.

It was Lea, directly inside Eld's mind. Her voice reverberated, almost like she was speaking directly to his soul.

"Eldritch B. Blackwood," she whispered. "Help me."

It was the same thing she'd said when they first met. But just as soon as her voice echoed in Eld's mind, it was gone again, and he was standing in front of a locked door.

He hesitated.

Was this crossing a line?

But worry for Lea overrode his doubts. He didn't know what that strange cry in his soul was, but he knew it was real.

Reaching into his pocket, Eld pulled out Franky.

The reanimated centipede was looking stronger and stronger with each day, but he was still a far cry from his full self. Despite his best efforts, Eld had never found the remaining parts, nor had he been able to acquire suitable replacements, even in Necropolis.

"Hey buddy," Eld said. "I know you're not fully back yet, but I need your help. Can you get in there and unlock the door for me?"

Franky's remaining antennae twitched, a few legs scrabbling against Eld's palm.

He chittered, the sound was weak, but he remained as loyal as ever.

The partially reanimated centipede awkwardly made its way under the door, its uneven gait causing it to zigzag slightly. After a moment that felt much longer than it should have, Eld heard the lock click open.

"Good job, little guy," he murmured, scooping Franky back into his cloak.

Taking a deep breath, Eld pushed the door open and stepped inside.

The room was dark, and there, on the bed, was Lea.

She was fast asleep, her cosmic eyes closed, her chest rising and falling in a slow, steady rhythm.

Eld approached cautiously. "Lea?" he called softly.

Nothing.

He walked closer, calling her name again. Still no response.

When she didn't stir, he reached out to gently shake her shoulder.

The moment his hand made contact, a jolt ran through him. This was a far deeper level than just his heart pumping again. It was like someone had stabbed an electrified wire straight into his heart.

No, it was even deeper than that. Something older, more primal. Some force that was beyond even lightning.

For a split second, Eld felt a connection, a sense of recognition so strong it made his head spin. And then it was gone, leaving him gasping and disoriented.

"What in the name of all that was unholy was that?" he gasped, coughing for air.

Lea's eyes fluttered open, confusion clouding their cosmic depths. "Eld?" she mumbled, her voice thick with sleep. "What are you doing here?"

Eld struggled to find his voice, still reeling from the strange sensation. "You missed class," he managed. "I was worried. Are you okay?"

Lea sat up slowly, rubbing her eyes. "I…I'm not sure. I've been so tired lately. And my dreams…" She shuddered. "They're getting worse."

Eld perched on the edge of the bed, concern overriding his lingering unease. "What kind of dreams?"

Lea's gaze went distant. "Darkness. More of that sun that devours light instead of giving it. And voices, so many voices, all calling my name. But it's not my name, not really. I mean it is, but it isn't. I don't know *what* they are saying." She trailed off, shaking her head as if to clear it. "I'm sorry. I'm not making any sense, am I?"

Eld took her hand, ignoring the faint tingle that ran up his arm at the contact. "More sense that I'd like to admit."

Lea smiled weakly. "Thanks for checking on me, Eld. I don't know what I'd do without you."

Eld grinned. "Probably would have missed tomorrow's class too, is what I'm guessing."

But beneath his cavalier surface, Eld was worried.

A sudden unbreakable sleep, just like when he'd found her buried beneath the ground. It sounded like something out of a fairy tale, but whatever conspiracy they were caught up in was definitely no fairy tale.

Chapter 17

Dust and Discord

The stolen letter and its contents…

Lea's abrupt sleep, so similar to when Eld had found her in that graveyard…

And above all, the mysterious Black Sun ritual, the only thing that possibly tied everything together.

There were no obvious explanations, but Eld knew where he could go to find them.

No matter how many times Eld visited the Grand Library of Bathurst Academy he was always amazed. The library was carved into the oily black stone beneath the school, embedded into the very foundation through a combination of spellcraft and good old fashioned digging.

Though if the husks Eld had seen the other day were anything to go by, the digging might not have been entirely voluntary.

"What *is* this?" Talbot asked, picking up a small pink booklet.

The poltergeist squinted, tilting the pages to the side.

"Modern Gardening Tools."

He opened the leaflet, flipping it around.

"This is crazy," he said, tilting the page to Eld. "Look at these machines! I bet I could make a real ruckus haunting one of those. And they claim the fertilizer they are selling is some kind of super dung. What kind of super animal do you think the Old Ones bred for it?"

Eld snorted.

Super dung from some kind of super animal sounded ridiculous, though knowing the Old Ones, they probably *could* have come up with something like that.

Talbot finished leafing through the brochure, then sighed. "Don't think this is going to help Lea any though. Nothing about magical sleeps."

"Yeah, I guess that's another failure," Eld replied, sighing.

The two friends had claimed a small stony alcove on the third floor of the library as their research base.

Stalactites hung from the ceiling like petrified icicles, glowing softly with preservative enchantments to prevent them from falling on students. The air smelled of old parchment and the faint scent of guano.

They had been there since breakfast, surrounded by piles of books, scrolls, and stone tablets—information from all ages. Considering the poltergeist's utter lack of classroom attention, Eld had never actually seen Talbot read a book before. At the very least, this experience had confirmed that Talbot was indeed literate.

For a brief moment, Eld snickered to himself, but then he shook his head and brushed the rather uncharitable thought aside. In truth, Talbot's help was greatly appreciated.

It was often said around campus that five hundred lifetimes wouldn't be enough to read every single book in the Bathurst Grand Library. After the afternoon's work, Eld wasn't even sure that an immortal lich like his father could do it.

There was simply so much content that a tiny little brochure could easily get lost under a deluge of leather bound tomes.

The Bathurst Grand Library had a simple policy. If anyone found a book, it would be accepted and organized to the best of the librarian's abilities.

One would think that an immortal librarian bound to the school itself was perfect for such a task, but with nothing better to do, she was constantly devising new and increasingly confusing reorganization systems.

And from Professor Hemlock's constant griping, Eld understood the librarian's tenure contract had been signed in blood, so there was no easy way to get rid of her.

"This is garbage," Eld sighed, throwing his own brochure aside. "All the Old Ones liked to do was brag about how great their machines were…"

The pages of the brochure were stiff and cold, almost icy.

The black ink of the words glowed faintly. Preservation spells had been cast on all of the library's materials to make sure that they wouldn't fade away. Eld recognized the faint strands of Grimthorpe's time manipulation magic. The time magic seemed powerful on the surface, but the sheer amount of magical energy required meant that it could only be used to restore old academic materials. Something with actual combat implications, like stopping time, was beyond even Grimthorpe's bony grasp.

Talbot nodded, holding up a brochure that described some kind of mechanical carriage, which the Old Ones called 'cars.' From what Eld could gather, the Old Ones liked their cars a great deal, going so far as to write stories where they were sentient.

"Look at this nonsense. This company claims their cars are the most durable in human history. Well, if they are so durable, then how come there aren't any around for me to haunt? Instead, it's Great Uncle Ebenezer driving around in one, not good old Talbot."

Eld picked up another brochure, then sighed and shook his head.

"More nonsense. This brochure claims their car is the fastest…how can all of these cars all be the fastest?"

He shook his head, tossing it aside.

"A technologist like Professor McGrath would find this fascinating. Me…"

From beneath Eld's chair Shuck let out a long whine.

From the sounds of it, he didn't think much of cars either.

"We should probably just skip anything the Old Ones had," Talbot said. "Half of these brochures talk about websites and online resources. Nobody can look that stuff up anymore anyways, except for the ghosts who haunt computers…"

"And I'm guessing you don't know any?" Eld asked. Despite his many boasts to Wysper, Talbot wasn't actually that well connected.

"Who do you think I am?" Talbot replied, lazily shaking his head. "Besides, the ghosts that haunt computers are rich. Apparently, there's loads of good stuff in there…if I found one, I'd probably haunt it myself. Now that sounds like the life, just being carried around everywhere I went. It'd be like a tiny little palanquin."

"Well, let's just move onto these then," Eld said, pointing at a thick stack of books. "They look promising."

Like the menus at Bone Appetit, these seemed to be bound in skin, though Eld had a feeling that this skin hadn't been *ethically sourced*. Just touching it suggested highly dubious origins. Still, that seemed like the exact kind of thing someone writing down a vile dark ritual would want to bind their books in.

But it was no good.

The first book was a cookbook, with recipes on how To Serve Man and the second was a *truly* terrible novel. After just a few sentences, Eld felt plain terrible for the person who'd been flayed to bind the book.

"Talk about dying in vain…" Eld muttered, closing the book on a sentence that was particularly pointlessly flowery.

The third book was an instruction manual on how to bind books in human skin.

"This is useless," Talbot groaned, flickering with frustration and lifting a skinbound book of his own. "This is a book on how the nightkin can live peacefully with humans. Step one is to not bind books in their skin anymore. Truly inspiring work by Dracula the Diplomat over here."

Rolling his eyes, Talbot slammed shut his particularly dusty tome, sending a small cloud of particles into the air.

Eld sneezed, earning a glare from his ghostly friend.

"Shut it," Talbot groaned. "Don't you remember what I told you about the librarian?"

Eld nodded.

"Yeah, you *don't* want to mess with her," Talbot said. "I know you've only come here before during classroom trips…truth be told, that's the only reason I've ever been here before either…but she gets real nasty when the professors aren't around."

"Got it, got it," Eld said. "Well, what about these then?"

He groaned, and hefted a large stone tablet between himself and Talbot.

The tablet was inscribed with brightly glowing green runes and almost as tall as Eld himself. If it weren't for the strange rock, which was so lightweight that it felt hollow, he wouldn't have been able to carry it.

"This looks really promising. The magic coming from it almost feels like Lea. There's just something familiar about it."

"Sure," Talbot replied. "But I didn't know you could read Urquruan hieroglyphics."

"Uh, I can't," Eld replied, staring into the tablet. "In fact…"

The hieroglyphics were all twisted together in endlessly spiraling patterns. Just staring them made Eld dizzy.

Talbot shoved the tablet away.

It fell off the ledge, but instead of cracking on the ground, it hovered in the air, the lightweight stone floating like it was in the water.

"Yeah, nobody can read Urquruan hieroglyphics," Talbot said. "Nobody alive at least. Anyone who looks at them for longer than a minute goes mad. No wonder their society fell apart. Just imagine your wife handing you a grocery list…you can't tell if she wants you to get milk or if she wants to kill you!"

Eld eyed the floating tablet for a few seconds, then thought better of staring at it for any longer.

As he shifted uncomfortably, the stolen letter crinkled in his pocket.

Despite asking for his help, Eld hadn't told Talbot about *that* just yet. Talbot had already been reluctant enough to research Lea's origins. Finding out that Eld had stolen property from two liches would probably be a bit too much.

Besides, it wasn't like Talbot could actually *do* anything.

Eld fiddled with the letter in his pocket, tracing the magical seal that kept it closed. He had tried everything he could think of to open it, but so far, nothing had worked.

Shaking his head and clearing the thought away for now, Eld gestured back at the pile of books. "Well, maybe we can find another tablet. One that doesn't drive the reader crazy."

Talbot groaned. "I don't know about that…we've been through every book on dark rituals and cosmic events in this section. There's nothing about any Black Sun!"

Eld hated to admit it, but Talbot had a point. His eyes felt gritty from hours and hours of reading, and his back ached from hunching over texts. But he couldn't stop now. "There has to be something. We just haven't found it yet."

Talbot rolled his eyes. "Yeah, and maybe if we keep looking, we'll find the meaning of life tucked away in a fortune cookie. Face it, Eld. We're wasting our time! I can't believe you talked me into this!"

The longer Talbot spoke, the more animated he got.

The poltergeist waved his arm at the nest of books around them in a gesture of utter fury.

"Studying on the weekend! That's my personal hell! I can hardly believe we're doing this! I thought you were going to help me with my studies, not find more studies for me to participate in! I—"

"Shh!" Eld hushed him, glancing around nervously. "I thought you said shouting would summon the—"

As if on cue, a chilly wind swept through their small alcove.

Though Eld couldn't see any change, he felt it. His spine tingled with fear and he had the distinct feeling of being walled in. Immediately afterwards, the library's guardian materialized between the stacks.

Wispy tendrils of ectoplasm curled around book spines and scroll cases.

The librarian wore a plain and simple black robe that covered her entire body, revealing only a gray face that was a constantly shifting mass of features, never settling on one appearance for more than a second.

But all the appearances were irritated.

"*Silence*," she hissed. "This is a place of learning, not petty squabbles."

Eld and Talbot froze, unable to move or speak.

Eld thought it was just mere terror, but when he tried to apologize, he realized it was something more. Some kind of spell had been cast on him. The air refused to leave his mouth.

Neither dared to move until the spectral librarian faded back into the ether. Only when the last wisps had disappeared were they able to speak again.

"Nice going, loudmouth," Eld muttered.

Talbot pulsed with indignation, flickering in and out. "Me? You're the one who's dragged us down here on this wild goose chase! Some of us have actual studying to do, you know."

He pointed angrily at Eld. "And by someone, I mean you. What happened to all the help you offered when we brought Lea back to the school?"

"This is important, Talbot." Eld turned back to his scroll. The characters seemed to swim before his eyes, and he blinked hard to refocus. "I can feel it. We're close to something big."

Talbot grumbled angrily. "Look. I can't afford to fail my next test."

Eld raised an eyebrow.

"Aren't you the ghost that haunts the first year? You can just repeat it!"

"Not this time," Talbot said. "I've got a big fat Gravestone in every single one of my classes."

"A what?" Eld asked.

"A Gravestone," Talbot replied. "It means your academic career is so abysmal, it's beyond saving. It's like being buried in a tome of your own failure. And I've got straight G's in all my subjects! So come on! How about learning some actual necromancy—and even better, letting me tag along and copy all your work!"

Eld winced.

From the sounds of it, this Gravestone was no joke, and he *had* promised Talbot academic help in exchange for his, well, actual help.

But this was too big. He felt it in his bones.

"I'm sorry about your grades," Eld said, trying to keep his voice low. He ran a hand through his hair, realizing too late that his fingers were covered in dust.

"You look like you've aged fifty years," Talbot observed.

"I might as well have," Eld shot back. "This whole thing. It's bigger than school. I'm just sure of it. I'm going to stay here as long as it takes."

"As long as—"

Eld cut off Talbot before he could get worked up again.

"Look, Talbot. The Black Sun, Lea's mysterious past, my family's involvement, it all has to be connected somehow."

Talbot's expression drooped. "What exactly are you hoping to find, Eld? Some ancient prophecy that explains everything? A step-by-step guide to unraveling cosmic mysteries? And what happens if you do? What exactly are you going to do, huh? Take on the professors? Take on your dad?" He let out a breathy laugh. "Yeah right. They are liches and you're…you're just a glorified pet doctor!"

"Trust me, Talbot," Eld said. "I've been thinking the same thing for the last few weeks. But it doesn't matter. I need to do something. Some—""

As Eld threw up his hands in excitement, he accidentally sent a nearby stack of scrolls tumbling. He scrambled to catch them before they hit the ground, earning another glare from Talbot.

"Something. Anything. I can't just sit back and do nothing while Lea suffers from those nightmares. While my father and maybe even Grimthorpe plot who knows what."

Talbot was quiet for a long moment. When he spoke again, his voice was uncharacteristically serious. "And what about you, Eld? What about your future? Your dreams? Are you really willing to throw it all away for this obsession? For Lea? A girl you barely know? A girl you literally dug up?"

Eld opened his mouth to retort, but the words died in his throat.

Talbot had a point here.

He thought back to his first day at Bathurst, how excited he had been to learn real necromancy. How he'd been encouraged by Professor Hemlock herself to pursue his preferred field of familiar reanimation.

Now he was spending more time sneaking around than in class, chasing shadows and conspiracies.

Eld's shoulders slumped and he sat back in his chair.

But as if on cue, the letter suddenly fluttered out of his pocket.

"What's that?" Talbot asked.

Eld hastily grabbed it, but that only increased Talbot's suspicions.

"What's that?" the poltergeist repeated.

Eld hesitated for a split second before going ahead. "It's a letter. From my father to Grimthorpe. I took it from his office. I'm going to look at this first. Then maybe we can give up."

Talbot's response was exactly what Eld had expected. The poltergeist recoiled and slammed his hands on the table. "You did what? You stole from *Eldritch Blackwood?* And *Headmaster Grimthorpe?* Are you insane?"

"I had to, Talbot. It could have answers. Look. Maybe we can take a break for a bit and study together. But first, we should—"

"First we should what?" Talbot shouted. "You think there's answers in that letter? What it has is a one-way ticket to expulsion if you get caught! Have you completely lost your mind?"

The temperature in their alcove dropped suddenly, becoming far colder than last time. It was like icy restraints had suddenly materialized around Eld's body.

Books rattled on their shelves as the librarian coalesced once more, its endlessly morphing features twisting in various kinds of silent fury.

"Last warning," she growled, her voice like nails on a chalkboard. "One more disruption, and you'll be joining my *special collection.*"

As she faded away, Eld could have sworn he saw faces pressed against the inside covers of nearby books, their expressions frozen in eternal terror.

He shuddered.

Though the librarian's silencing aura had vanished, the two friends remained quiet.

Talbot's face shifted uncomfortably as Eld stared back at him, waiting for him to speak.

Finally, Talbot spoke. "I can't do this anymore, Eld. I won't tell Grimthorpe about the letter, but I'm done. This whole thing it's too much. You're too far gone."

Eld felt a flash of anger. "Too far gone? I'm trying to uncover the truth!"

"At what cost?" Talbot shot back. "Your grades? Your future? Our friendship? Ever since we dug up Lea, you've been different. Obsessed. You two are practically joined at the hip, and now you're stealing from professors?"

"It's not like that," Eld protested weakly, but even as he said it, he knew Talbot had a point.

When was the last time he had done anything that didn't involve Lea or the Black Sun mystery?

Maybe the Nocturnal Combat Club Qualifier?

And even then, he didn't even know when the next stage in the Tournament of Shadows was anymore. Wolfgang had been cursing him out every day in class for missing practice.

"Isn't it? Face it, Eld. You're in over your head. I'm not going to watch you drown yourself in this madness anymore."

"Talbot, wait—"

But his friend was already floating away, passing through shelves and stone as if they weren't there.

Just before he disappeared entirely, Talbot turned back.

"You know, since you're willing to go so far, why don't you just break into the Splintered Dimension? Maybe there will be more books there! You've already stolen from a professor. While you're at it, why don't you burn down the school?"

The sarcasm in Talbot's voice was sharp enough to cut like a knife.

And then he was gone, leaving Eld alone among the shelves and books.

Eld just sat there, Talbot's words pressing down on him.

Had he really gone too far?

Was he throwing everything away for what?

A mystery he might never solve?

But then he thought of Lea, of the terror in her eyes when she woke from her nightmares, of the strange connection he felt every time they touched. And of the Black Sun, looming over it all like a dark promise of things to come.

No. I can't give up now.

He was close to something. He could feel it.

Eld's eyes drifted downwards and he imagined himself in the catacombs.

The Splintered Dimension. Off-limits to students, guarded by wards and enchantments.

Talbot's words echoed in his mind. *Why don't you just break into the Splintered Dimension? Maybe there will be more books there?*

It was meant as a biting piece of sarcasm, but as Eld stared at that forbidding door, he thought that his friend may be correct. If Grimthorpe were trying to hide evidence of a magical conspiracy, nowhere would be better.

Why else would the Splintered Dimension have been closed off?

In fact, hadn't Eld seen books, off in the background on that night he'd seen his father? The Familial Tome had certainly been there, at the very least.

Eld grit his teeth.

He knew it was crazy. Dangerous. Possibly the stupidest thing he had ever considered doing. But as he clutched the stolen letter in his pocket, Eld made his decision.

Chapter 18

The Midnight Gaunt

Bart led the way through the catacombs later that night. The zombified rat's eyes glowed with the familiar oculus spell that allowed Eld to see through his eyes.

Slowly and steadily, Bart crept forward, peering across every corner before proceeding.

Eld followed two turns behind him, so tense that he thought a single errant footstep might jolt his heart into starting again. He technically wasn't breaking any rules by being out, but he didn't want to be seen going in and out of the catacombs this late. It wouldn't take a conspiracy theorist to figure out he was headed for the Splintered Dimension.

Of course, the ambiance didn't make things much better.

The catacombs were creepy enough during the day, when they were filled with talking students.

At night, every shadow seemed to hide potential threats.

Through Bart's eyes, Eld scanned each intersection carefully before moving forward.

There!

"Careful Bart…" Eld instinctively muttered under his breath even though he knew the rat couldn't hear him.

Thankfully, the rat froze, slowly and steadily backing off. Neither of them wanted a repeat of what had happened to poor Franky.

Through the rat's vision, Eld had noticed a group of husks shambling aimlessly in a nearby corridor. Normally, just seeing a husk was cause enough for concern, but there was something different about them.

Their movements were erratic, almost feral. They pumped into each other, growling viciously before abruptly turning away from each other, looks of angry frustration etched on their faces.

They want blood.

The disturbing thought crossed Eld's mind, and moments later, he realized what these were.

"By the Corpse Father's Leaking Brains," Eld muttered. "What has gotten into Grimthorpe? Letting wild husks wander through the catacombs? Even father would have hired someone to eliminate them by now."

Wild husks were dangerous and unpredictable. They had probably broken off from the rest of the pack and were now wandering down here searching for fresh prey.

The fact that the school hadn't culled them yet meant he would have to be extra careful now.

Eld felt a familiar nudge at his shoe and he leaned over, carefully scooping up Bart.

"You were right to come back," Eld muttered. "Here. We'll creep past them together. But let me distract them a little bit."

Bart briefly nodded, and then Eld reached out, grabbing his friend's lizard tail.

He yanked it clean off, then tossed it down the hall, in the opposite direction of them.

The wild husks turned, shoving and biting each other as they surged towards the seemingly living meat. The demented creatures had no loyalty to each other—Eld saw one husk shove another's twitching fingers straight down its gullet. Instead of eating the dead flesh, it chomped it to pieces before spitting it back out again, acting solely to hinder its rival.

Carefully, Eld and Bart maneuvered past the squabbling zombies, sticking to the side of the wall. Just as he thought he was in the clear, he rounded a corner and collided with something solid.

"Oof!" A voice exclaimed.

Eld's heart nearly jumped out of his body until he realized that the voice was shockingly familiar. "Wait. Lilith?"

The banshee turned, looking as startled as he felt. "Eld? What are you doing down here?"

"I could ask you the same thing," Eld said.

Lilith's eyes narrowed. "I asked first."

Eld laughed nervously. "Oh, you know, just out for a late-night stroll. Stretching the old legs."

"With an oculus spell active on your undead rat?" Lilith asked skeptically, pointing at Bart's glowing eyes.

"I, uh…" Eld fumbled for an excuse, but before he could come up with anything better than "just practicing", a low moan echoed through the corridor.

Both of them turned to see a husk shambling towards them, its dead eyes fixed on their living flesh. Lilith tensed, preparing to unleash her banshee scream, but before she could, another husk appeared behind the first.

This one's hands glowed with magical power.

A mage husk!

Before Eld could even shout out a warning, the mage husk croaked.

"Silence!"

The air itself rippled, and Eld felt a faint whiff of the librarian's magic.

Lilith's voice abruptly died in her throat and her eyes widened in panic.

Eld's mind raced. Wild husks were known for their unpredictable mutations. For some reason, losing their minds also meant that they didn't need to follow the standard laws of magic. They would continue to gain random powers over time, and the silence spell was one of the worst things Eld could have imagined.

Unable to speak, he let his actions do the talking.

Keeping Bart tightly clutched in his right hand, he grabbed Lilith's arm with his left and began pulling her down the corridor.

The husks gave chase, their shuffling gait belying a surprising speed. Eld's heart pounded as he tried to think of a plan.

Against wild husks, his necromantic magic might just make things worse. There was no telling how the feral abominations would react to one of his spells. It might end up empowering them.

Lilith, despite being silenced, was far from helpless.

As they ran, she grabbed a loose femur from a nearby skeleton display and wielded it like a club. When the first husk got too close, she swung, sending its head flying.

Without its head, the creature slumped lifelessly to the floor as its head rolled to a stop in the distance.

Eld couldn't help but be impressed. He shot her a look that said "nice!"

She shot him a look back that clearly said, "less looking, more running!"

The mage husk proved to be a bigger problem.

Its hands glowed with evil red magic as it lobbed fireballs at them, forcing them to dodge and weave as they ran. One came so close that Eld felt the heat singe his eyebrows.

After that close call, Lilith pointed urgently at her throat, then at the mage husk.

Eld understood. If they could break the silence spell, Lilith could use her scream.

Eld pointed at the mage husk, then at his other hand, then at the edge of the corridor.

Lilith nodded, readying her makeshift bone club.

The two allies made a mad dash across the corridor, sprinting for all their might. Just as they made it to the other side, Eld skidded to a stop, turning to face their pursuers.

Quickly, he sketched patterns in the air, composing a new spell based on what he'd learned at Bathurst. He worked quickly, hastily sketching out the patterns before the husk got too close to draw on his necromantic energy.

And instead of targeting the husk itself…

When Eld finished, he pointed at the archway.

The air itself froze around the archway, creating a chilling zone between the mage husk and themselves.

The husk stared at the wall of cold, then shook its hard savagely, charging right through.

The wall of cold slowed its movements, turning its greying flesh blue.

But once it made it to the other side, the mage husk raised its hands, preparing another spell. But before it could cast anything, Lilith was there.

She swung her club again, catching the husk square in the jaw.

There was a sickening crunch, and suddenly, the silence spell shattered. Lilith wasted no time. She took a deep breath and unleashed her banshee scream.

The sound was deafening in the confined space of the catacombs.

Eld clapped his hands over his ears, watching in awe as the mage husk's body was torn apart by the deadly sonic blasts.

When the echoes finally faded, the corridor was silent save for their heavy breathing.

Not only had the mage husk been destroyed, the corpse of the other one had been blown apart too. Judging by the hideous squelching and thudding noises echoing through the hall, Lilith's scream had even shattered the remaining wild husks off in the distance.

"I'll trade you my necromancy for your voice?" Eld said.

"Not a chance." Lilith managed a weak smile. "Now, want to tell me what's really going on?"

Eld's eyes darted down the hall.

They were getting closer and closer to the Splintered Dimension, where he'd seen his father. He was so close to potential answers, to finding if these books surrounding his father had been removed from the library.

"Look, Lilith, I appreciate the help, but I really need to—"

"Oh no, you don't," Lilith cut him off, her eyes narrowing. "You're not running off until you explain why you're skulking around the catacombs in the middle of the night."

Eld took a step back, raising his hands. "It's complicated, okay? I promise I'll explain everything later, but right now—"

Lilith's patience snapped.

She traced a glowing sigil in the air, a complex pattern that looked like a mixture between a noose and a cocoon.

Eld felt magical energy wrap around him like invisible ropes, pinning his arms to his sides. He struggled against the binding, but it was useless.

The spell—seemingly a cousin of the leash spell he'd used on Cloudehill—had caught him completely off guard.

He reached out, concentrating to try and summon his necromantic magic, but as soon as he tried to draw a sigil, she just slapped his hand.

That was the problem with symbolic magic. It was much more powerful than ordinary spells, but it had a much higher set-up period. But without tracing symbols, Eld had no hope of breaking past Lilith's trap.

He was good and stuck.

"Lilith! What are you doing?" Eld protested.

Even his voice sounded weak.

"What I should have done weeks ago," She crossed her arms across her chest. "You're going to tell me what's going on right now, Eldritch Blackwood. I've noticed your grades slipping, I'm the teacher's aide in two of your classes. Your tests have been horrible lately. You're distracted in class and now I find you sneaking around the catacombs at night with an oculus spell. Start talking."

Eld sighed and slumped against the wall, the binding spell allowing him just enough movement to sit down. "Fine. But you have to promise to keep this a secret. I mean it, Lilith. This is bigger than just me. It's about…well, remember the night of the Midnight Exhumation? When we ran into each other and talked about how weird everything was?"

Lilith's expression softened slightly.

She sat down across from him, her earnest eyes never leaving his face. "Alright, I promise. Now spill."

He began to explain everything—the Black Sun, Lea's mysterious past, his suspicions about his father and Grimthorpe. As he spoke, Lilith's expression shifted from skepticism to shock to intense curiosity.

When he finally finished, Lilith was quiet, processing everything she had just heard. "So, you're planning to break into the Splintered Dimension? To see if the books from the library are there?"

Eld nodded. He braced himself for a lecture or worse—a threat to report him to Grimthorpe.

Instead, Lilith placed a gentle hand on Eld's knee. "Count me in."

"Wait, what?" Eld blinked rapidly. He was positive that he had misheard. "You're not going to try to stop me?"

Lilith rolled her eyes. "Please. If there's a mystery this big to solve, I want in. Besides," she chuckled, "Someone needs to keep you from getting yourself killed or expelled."

Eld felt a wave of relief wash over him. "Thanks, Lilith. I mean it. But, uh, do you think you could maybe undo this binding spell now?"

Lilith pretended to consider it. "I don't know."

"Lilith!"

She laughed. "Alright, alright."

She made a series of gestures and the magical bindings dissolved.

Eld flexed his arms gratefully. He climbed to his feet and offered Lilith a hand up. "Ready to break into the Splintered Dimension?"

Lilith took his hand, pulling herself up. "Lead the way, Blackwood. This ought to be interesting."

Eld put Bart back on the floor. The zombie rat's eyes were still glowing brightly.

"Well, technically, he should be the one leading the way."

The two closely followed Bart as he scurried back along the catacombs, towards the door that Eld had seen that fateful night he found Lea.

"Do you know where we're going?" Lilith muttered.

"Yeah. We found this door…well, the night I found Lea."

"*Found* Lea?" Lilith sharply asked.

"I, um…"

Eld's breath caught in his throat.

In his haste, he'd forgotten that Lilith didn't know about Lea's origins.

"Um…alright. I'll tell you."

As they crept through the pitch black corridors, Eld kept his voice hushed. "It all started when we found Lea in the graveyard. On the night of the Midnight Exhumation."

Lilith just listened silently, her eyes wide.

Eld went on.

"At first, I thought she was just another reanimation gone wrong, but then…"

Lilith ducked under a low-hanging cobweb. "Then what?"

"She knew my name, Lilith."

Lilith raised an eyebrow. "Okay, that is weird."

"Yeah. She asked me to help her."

"Help her do *what?*"

Eld paused at a corner, letting Bart go first and peering through his eyes before continuing. "I'm not entirely sure yet. Ever since then, she's been having these visions. Terrible ones."

With that, Eld told Lilith everything—Lea's visions, the Black Sun floating in the sky, even the mysterious things that had happened to him before he found her.

He expected her to laugh.

She didn't.

"This sounds like some deep magic," Lilith said. "Old stuff."

Eld frowned.

"Old stuff? You mean like…Old One technology? I don't know about that, Lilith. This definitely seems magical."

"No, no," Lilith said. "Older than that. Way older. From a civilization before even the Old Ones."

"What do you mean?" Eld asked.

"Magic not of this world or the underworld. Void magic." She cocked her head. "You know. The Great Old Ones."

Eld thought back to the possessed professor and then to the grumbling ferryman, the one who'd treated Lea with a strange amount of respect. "You know, some of them were complaining about how things were run these days. Back in Necropolis."

Lilith snorted. "Yeah. I've heard about them. Mostly just has-beens complaining about the good old days. Though truth be told, nobody is sure if those even *are* Great Old Ones…"

"Well, if the void magic is this old, that at least explains why it's been so hard to find anything on the Black Sun," Eld said. "But I *know* this is important. The more I dig, the more questions I have, and now, with my father and Grimthorpe involved…"

Bart let out a chitter of fear.

Lilith grabbed Eld's arm, pulling him into a shadowy alcove as a spectral cat prowled past.

Eld had feared the worst, but it was just one of the wild animals that had snuck into Bathurst. Due to the forever darkness around the academy, plenty of animals, nocturnal, magical, or in this case both, found it a more suitable home.

Once it was gone, Lilith turned to him. "Listen, whatever it is, if you're going to keep investigating this, you need to be smarter about it. Your grades are slipping, and the professors are starting to notice."

"I know," Eld sighed. "But how am I supposed to focus on classes when all of this is happening?"

Lilith rolled her eyes. "Simple. You compartmentalize. During the day, you're the perfect student. Pay attention in class, do your homework, participate in discussions. Save all the mystery-solving for after hours."

"Could I really—"

"You have to," Lilith replied. "Otherwise, we won't even come close to figuring this out. Keep blundering around like you have been and the professors will be on us in no time."

"I can't help but notice you said us," Eld replied.

"Oh, I can't believe I'm helping you do this," Lilith whispered. "It could cost me everything…but I'm not just helping you. I'm helping Lea too. That girl is too good for this world and far too good for you."

Eld nodded. He couldn't disagree with that.

"But don't forget. Time management, Blackwood, and maybe cut back on sleep a little. We are necromancers, after all. A little death won't kill us."

The entrance to the Splintered Dimension was just were Eld had remembered—a pair of bronze doors covered with ominous runes. It materialized out of thin air as they drew close, followed by the blaring mental pressure and shrieking alarms.

"KEEP OUT. KEEP OUT. KEEP OUT."

Lilith's face was twisted in pain. "Hurry," she muttered. "We need to find a way in there, otherwise this will drive us mad."

Suddenly, an eerily familiar cold snap swept through the corridor.

"Silence…" a voice hissed.

Everything fell silent—even the blaring warning.

Eld and Lilith froze as the librarian materialized nearby, her wispy tendrils from the very bricks by the wall.

What?

Now?

The strange creature carried a large stack of books, holding them aloft with tendrils of black shadow as its cloak flapped behind it.

The librarian drifted past their hiding spot, but just when they thought they were in the clear, Lilith let out a choked gasp of surprise and dropped her makeshift club.

The stolen piece of bone hit the floor and rolled out into the open. The librarian's head snapped around, its ever-changing features settling into suspicion. It glided over to the club, turning its head this way and that.

Eld held his breath, feeling Lilith tense beside him. The librarian twisted and writhed, searching for the cause of the disturbance. Eld was sure they were done for. But then, with a dissatisfied hiss, the librarian moved on and it faded back into the shadows.

"That was too close," Lilith whispered once it had returned to the bronze door. "The chilling field…I thought I'd lost my voice again."

This time, it was Eld's turn to shush her.

"Open…" the librarian whispered in its creaky voice.

Eld watched with bated breath as the doors creaked open and the librarian flew inside.

Lilith made to follow her, but Eld held her back, shaking his head.

"We can't risk it," he insisted. "If the librarian is delivering books to the Splintered Dimension, it's probably in on the conspiracy. We have to wait for it to leave."

Thankfully, it was easy to tell when the librarian was nearby.

Eventually, the cold dissipated and the screeching alarms returned.

"Let's go," he said.

"What plan did you have to open the door?" Lilith whispered back.

Eld had been thinking about it all day—before realizing that nothing was better than the good old fashioned way.

Master magicians like Grimthorpe always defended themselves against magical attacks, but often overlooked simplistic solutions.

Eld pulled out the set of fingerbones his mother had packed for him, then hurried to the door. They might have had perfect toothpicks, but they were also perfect lockpicks.

Using the same deft fingers he'd gained through years of pet surgeries, Eld picked the locks, carefully manipulating the fingerbones. As he did, he couldn't help but wonder just why his mother had packed them.

Was this her way of giving him some hint? Some attempt to counteract Eldritch Sr.? Or was it just her usual whimsy?

A smooth and very welcome click cut through Eld's thoughts.

"Got it!"

The bronze doors opened and the sirens faded away. The two entered and then the doors clanked shut behind them.

"Stay hidden," Eld said.

Lilith nodded and joined him, fading into the deepest shadows. The Splintered Dimension was unlike anything Eld had imagined. Before, he had only seen his father illuminated by the black torches, surrounded by books.

Now, he realized why the Splintered Dimension had once been such a popular location for studying.

It was as if they had stepped into another world entirely—a far more peaceful one.

A grove of ancient oak trees stretched out before them, their gnarled branches heavy with books and scrolls on hanging shelves. The space seemed to defy the laws of physics, far larger than should have been possible.

Lilith smiled happily at the room.

"I used to love studying here," she said. But then her noise abruptly wrinkled.

"What's that smell?"

"Brimstone," Eld replied, wincing. "More evidence that my father was here…"

He gazed through the large catalogue of books.

Somewhere…

The secret had to be somewhere here.

"Let's split up," Eld suggested. "We'll cover more ground that way."

They separated, each taking a different path through the impossible forest of knowledge. Eld's eyes scanned the spines of books, searching for anything related to the Black Sun.

To his relief, everything seemed to be in alphabetical order. For once, his father's obsessive organizational habits were in his favor. But as he slowly went through the list of As, his heart abruptly sank.

Every word with a B in the cover had been removed. Whoever removed them had been excessively thorough, as certainly there must have been books on 'bats' or other things of a far more innocent nature.

The sight only deepened Eld's suspicions.

His father—and whoever his father was working with— were indeed conducting a ritual, and they did *not* want to be found out…

"Eld!" Lilith's excited whisper cut through his disappointment. "I found something!"

He hurried over to where she stood, clutching a heavy tome. "Is it about the Black Sun?"

Lilith shook her head. "No, but it might be even better. I think this could help us break the seal on that letter from your dad."

"Are you serious?"

"Dead serious," Lilith grinned. "Pardon the pun. Now let's get out of here before the librarian realizes we're in here."

Eld dithered, then nodded.

If they stayed too long, the librarian might return.

Settling for what he had, Eld carefully tucked the book into his bag. As they made their way back to the entrance, he couldn't shake the feeling that they were on the cusp of something big.

Whatever secrets that letter held, they were one step closer to uncovering them.

Chapter 19

Lucky Guess, Unlucky Encounter

With their clandestine mission complete, the corridors of the catacombs seemed a little less daunting, a little less creepy.

The tome Lilith had found was safely tucked into Eld's pack and they had gotten in and out without the librarian binding their souls into book covers.

Now all they had to do was get back to their rooms and no one would be the wiser.

"So why were *you* out so late Lilith?" Eld asked as he ran. "I spilled all my secrets to you. I think it's just fair you do the same."

"You would love to know that wouldn't you?" Lilith teased, her cheeks turning slightly pink.

"I would." Eld chuckled, adjusting his backpack. "That's why I asked."

"Maybe one day I'll tell you, Blackwood, when you're older."

"That's not fair," Eld protested.

Lilith stopped in her tracks, silver hair whipping around her face as it settled. "Fair? Okay, let's go put the tome back then."

Recoiling to put more distance between her and the backpack, he laughed nervously. "Okay. Okay. I get it." Eld shrugged and tilted his head. "You don't want anyone to know that you were having a hot make-out session with Erik the Drowned."

Lilith's jaw went slack and her eyes went wide. Eld didn't understand why she had shock painted on her face, but then he realized.

"Wait." He stepped back, a smirk tugging at the sides of his lips. "You *were* making out with Erik the Drowned? *Erik the Drowned*!"

"How did you—"

"I didn't, I was just joking!" Both Eld's hands went up to his head. "Oh wow. That is…wow. How does that even work? He's so…soggy."

Lilith's face was beet red. "He's not that bad."

"Lilith, his maker definitely forgot to give him a brain. His muscles aren't even his! I heard he checks new graves every night for better parts."

The way Lilith recoiled told Eld that the rumor was right.

"He's a good kisser," she defensively shot back.

"I guess if you like being submerged," Eld shrugged.

She raised a brow, tilting her head and puffing out her bottom lip. "Well, maybe I do! I've got needs too, you know. We all can't be Perfect, Miss Lea with the most handsome boy at the school fawning—"

Lilith caught herself and cupped both hands over her mouth.

"Oh," Eld thought.

A long awkward silence followed and they continued to walk, both of them looking straight forward. Eld finally broke the silence.

"I, uh, I won't tell anyone. You know, Erik has nice, uh, hair. Very, uh…water swept."

Lilith turned and shot him a glare. "Shut up, Eld."

They made it to the main hall and parted ways without saying another word.

Eld made his way towards the dormitories, very confused as to how he had gotten so lucky with his guess.

He couldn't get the image of Lilith and Erik out of his mind. It'd wormed into his brain just like the shrieking of the Splintered Dimension sirens, even though he didn't want to imagine it at all.

And for that other thing, she'd said…

Eld shook his head. He didn't even have time to think about that right now.

As he approached the landing leading to the dorms, he heard voices and laughter. He smiled, but the closer he got, the crueler the sounds seemed to him.

A pit grew in his stomach as he recognized Mortimer's sneering tones.

Peering around the corner, Eld saw Mortimer and his cronies, including Erik the Drowned, huddled in a circle and giggling.

The gang of thugs were clearly tormenting something small on the ground.

Eld's stomach twisted even more as he realized it was a large spider, its legs twitching helplessly as they hit it with stinging hexes.

Mortimer's voice was a mixture of arrogant cackling and twisted spells. Judging by the sparks of embers, the spider's legs were slowly and steadily burning from within.

Eld considered just sneaking past. He was tired, sore, and in no shape for a confrontation. But as he watched the spider's attempts to escape, he knew he couldn't walk away. After all, helping animals was why he'd come to Bathurst in the first place.

Taking a deep breath, Eld stepped into view. "Hey! Leave it alone!"

Mortimer's head snapped up, his eyes narrowing as he spotted Eld. "Well, well. If it isn't the pet doctor. Come to rescue a fellow pathetic creature?"

Eld stood his ground, even though his instincts screamed at him that he was making a mistake. Just the way Mortimer's thugs instinctively fanned out told him that he was in for a fight. Even worse, Shuck was back at the dorm, resting with Talbot, and Franky was in no state to fight. He was badly outnumbered and judging by the fresh stitches on Erik's arms, even more badly outmuscled.

"Just let it go, Mortimer. What's a spider ever done to you?"

Erik guffawed, water dribbling from his mouth as he laughed. "It exists. That's enough."

Eld's eyes narrowed. "What if someone did that to you?"

Clearly, understanding hypotheticals wasn't one of Erik's strengths. "Why would I do this to myself?" the zombie stupidly replied.

Mortimer raised his hand, preparing another hex. "Run along, Blackwood. Unless you want to join our little friend here."

Despite the situation, something in Eld refused to give in. He was sick of this bullying nonsense. The whole lot of them were well over a hundred—yet given a second chance to go back to school, Mortimer and his thugs were acting just like elementary age bullies.

Before he could think better of it, Eld's fingers danced through the air, sketching out a new pattern. The winds chilled, obeying the command of his necromantic magic.

For a brief second, Eld dared to hope that he could just whisk the spider away.

But Mortimer was faster. His fingers danced in a simple circular pattern.

Then with a flick of his wrist, he conjured a magic fist and sent Eld flying backwards. The back of Eld's head cracked against the stone wall, stars exploding behind his eyes.

Eld staggered to his feet.

The metallic tang of blood mingled with the bitter taste of humiliation, but he had bigger concerns. Before he could recover, Mortimer and Erik were on him, their boots crashing crudely down into his body. The kicks rained down like a violent storm, driving the air from his lungs, each blow like a hammer striking an anvil.

Eld tried to fight back, swinging his arms back and forth, but he couldn't ward them away. Any attempt to conjure a spell was promptly canceled by a vicious kick.

After a few more blows, Eld had no choice but to curl into a ball, trying to protect himself. Mortimer's foot connected with his head and his vision blurred, darkness licking at the edges.

Mortimer's voice sliced through the haze. "One less challenger in the Combat Club finals."

Fighting through the pain, Eld cracked open an eye.

Mortimer's hand was wreathed in flames, the fire danced around his fingers, ready to unleash destruction. "Let's see how well you can reanimate *yourself*."

Erik leaned in close, his waterlogged features twisted with cruel delight. "Say goodbye, Eld. Not that anyone will miss you," he growled, the stench of decay and brine overwhelming.

The flames in Mortimer's hand flared brighter, casting flickering shadows on the walls. Panic surged through Eld, adrenaline cutting through the pain.

In a desperate attempt to get them to stop, he blurted out the first thing that came to mind. "Erik's seeing Lilith! They've been meeting in the catacombs to make out!"

To his disbelief, it worked.

The words hung in the air. Mortimer's flames snuffed out, his concentration broken. "What?"

Erik's waterlogged face went pale. "I…uh…"

Mortimer turned to his friend, momentarily forgetting about Eld. "Is that true? You're seeing the banshee freak?"

Erik stammered, clearly caught off guard. "Well, she's got a nice…"

Eld didn't wait to hear the end of that sentence.

With every ounce of strength he had left, he surged upward, driving his fist into Mortimer's groin. Mortimer doubled over, howling in pain. As Erik turned in disbelief, Eld turned and delivered a solid punch to the drowned zombie's soggy jaw.

Both of them staggered back, giving Eld the space he needed.

Frantically, he concentrated, extending his necromantic sense towards the writhing spider on the ground. He felt the familiar tingle of energy, then carefully directed it, using all the lessons he'd learned from his classes.

Even though he hadn't been paying much attention recently, his previous months of study—plus his natural talent—won out.

With a victorious chitter, the arachnid began to grow.

Its legs lengthened and thickened until it was the ten times the size it had been before. As Eld continued pouring energy into the creature, he felt the spider's righteous fury and desire for revenge.

Mortimer, Erik, and the other thugs hastily backpedaled, cursing and beating a hasty retreat.

A thin gang member Eld hadn't seen before, who looked like some kind of drow, tried kicking the spider, only to regret it instantly as he fell on the floor, screeching and writhing as venom coursed through his body.

The rest of the gang grabbed him before streaking off.

Mortimer and Erik were the only ones who dared to remain, but as they turned towards the spider, Eld pulled Bart out of his pocket.

Before long, the zombified rat had swelled to match the spider's size.

Mortimer and Erik's eyes widened in shock as they found themselves facing two oversized, very angry creatures.

The spider clicked its mandibles while Bart's whipped his reptilian tail back and forth.

"Get them!" Eld commanded.

The spider and Bart leapt forward. Erik yelped as eight hairy legs wrapped around him, while Bart sank his unnaturally large teeth into Mortimer's leg.

"Get them off! Get them off me!" Erik yelped.

His struggles only tangled him further in the spider's web-like grip. He thrashed wildly, but the spider held firm.

Mortimer gritted his teeth against the pain and tried to shake Bart off. The rat clung on, his bony jaws locked onto Mortimer's calf. Blood seeped through Mortimer's fine pants, staining the ground below.

Mortimer snarled and conjured a burst of flame across his body. Bart squealed, releasing his grip as the smell of burning fur filled the air.

But the battle was at best, a draw. The spider's venom had already knocked Erik unconscious and Bart still had plenty of fight left in him.

"This isn't over, Blackwood!" Mortimer bellowed.

He grabbed Erik by the collar, hauling him upright. With a final glare at Eld, he dragged Erik away.

Eld slumped against the wall, every part of him aching. He would probably regret telling Mortimer about Lilith and Erik later, but right now, he was just glad to be alive.

He shook his head and cursed.

If it wasn't for the Black Sun conspiracy, Mortimer alone would be enough of a problem for anyone. He combined the petty cruelty of a childhood bully with the boundless entitlement of a noble scion.

After a few minutes, Bart returned, shrinking back to his normal size as he scurried up Eld's leg.

The spider followed closely.

Unlike Bart, the spider had only shrunk slightly. It wasn't used to being empowered with necromantic energy.

"Hey there," Eld said softly to the spider. "Sorry about all that. Let's get you back to normal, huh?"

He reached out with his power again, whispering an incantation and shrinking the spider back to its original size. To his surprise, instead of scurrying away, the spider moved closer to him.

Eld chuckled weakly. "Don't tell me you want to come along too?"

The spider chittered its multiple eyes fixed on Eld.

Eld sighed, a smile on his split lips despite the pain. "Alright, come on then. I guess there's room for one more."

He chuckled, eyeing the creature carefully. Despite the internal damage that'd been inflicted by Mortimer's torment, the spider was still alive.

"Well, I suppose it's about time I get a living pet," Eld chuckled.

He opened his coat, and the spider happily climbed inside, nestling next to Bart. As Eld made his way to his dorm, he pondered names for his new eight-legged friend. The spider was female—also a first for his pets.

"How about Webster?" The spider remained silent. "No, too obvious. Arachne?" A disapproving chitter came from inside of his coat. "Okay, okay. What about Spinderella?"

The spider gave a little wiggle that Eld chose to interpret as approval.

"Spinderella it is then," Eld said, patting his pocket gently. "Welcome to the family."

As he finally reached his dorm room.

He collapsed onto his bed and Bart, Franky, and Spinderella settled onto his pillow.

Shuck had slept through all the commotion, resting beneath the bed.

Tomorrow would bring new challenges—explaining his bruises, keeping Mortimer from spilling Lilith's secret, and decoding the stolen tome. But for now, surrounded by his peculiar little family, Eld felt oddly at peace.

Chapter 20

The Literal Headmaster

As hard it was for Eld to believe, the next day was Sunday—still part of the weekend.

When he'd first arrived at Bathurst, he'd found it unusual for the nightkin to enjoy a day of rest, especially on a day named after the Sun. After actually attending the school for a while, he realized it was simply a requirement to keep their brains from bursting. With a subjects as delicate as necromancy and daemonology, a well-rested brain was of utmost importance.

Eld spent the morning catching up on the seemingly endless assignments he had been putting off, occasionally taking breaks to mend the wounds Mortimer and Erik had inflicted with some good old fashioned necromantic healing.

The room was filled with the scratching of his quill and the soft rustle of paper as he moved from one task to the next. Every so often, Eld's thoughts drifted to his father's sealed letter, but he shook that worry aside for now.

It was just like Lilith said—he had to compartmentalize.

If he didn't finish all his work, he'd give the professors, especially Grimthorpe, some hint that he knew something was wrong. And not only that, the entire reason Eld had gone to Bathurst to begin with was to inherit the Familial Tome.

As ridiculous as it might have seemed, his grades were of paramount importance right now.

Talbot lay on his bed, back turned to Eld.

Since their argument they hadn't spoken more than two words to each other. Eld badly wanted to apologize, but simply saying sorry just seemed like a shallow gesture, especially because he had no intention of giving up his quest to help Lea.

At the end, he did the only thing he could think of to apologize—he finished Talbot's homework. By afternoon, he had not only completed his own work but also Talbot's.

Eld stood up, stretching his stiff muscles, and walked over to Talbot's bed, where the ghost was lounging in his usual state of perpetual relaxation.

"Hey," Eld approached, setting the stack of parchments onto the bedside table. "I, uh…" He rubbed the back of his neck.

Why was this so hard?

Elf took a deep breath.

He would almost rather be fighting Mortimer again than have to be in this awkward tension with his best friend. Despite his perpetual laziness, Talbot always had Eld's back when it really mattered. If it weren't for him, they never would have saved Lea.

"I went ahead and did your homework for the week too and don't worry, I switched up some of the answers so it doesn't look like you copied off me or anything."

Talbot remained silent, still staring at the wall.

"The premium service," Eld joked.

Nothing.

"Look. I'm sorry about everything," Eld sighed. "I know I haven't been a great friend recently. I know I, well, basically lied to you about helping in exchange for getting Lea out of there.

But I want you to know that everything is going to improve from today, right this instant."

Spinning his head around without moving his body, Talbot raised a desiccated brow. "Oh really? So no more risking your life investigating the Black Sun?"

"Um, well…" Eld stammered.

Talbot looked at him judgmentally.

"Look, I'm still going to investigate. I'm just not going to let it get in the way of—"

Talbot groaned. "Eld. I told you. This is dangerous. You need to stay out of it. For your own good. We might be arguing, but I'm still trying to be your friend here!"

Eld tried to stammer out a response, but without saying anything else, Talbot floated right through Eld and out of the room.

Eld slumped back into his chair, feeling a wave of frustration wash over him. "I don't know what I'm supposed to do here!"

His voice echoed in the empty room.

Talbot hated taking risks. All he wanted was to live his life peacefully and slowly drift through Bathurst.

Honestly, Eld didn't entirely disagree. Before being brought here, he'd also lived his life peacefully as a pet doctor.

But his very heart was telling him that something terrible was afoot.

He couldn't just ignore it.

Letting out a long sigh, he pulled out the letter from his father to Grimthorpe and began examining the seal again. The seal's embedded magic seemed to mock him personally, pulsating with a faint, defiant glow.

Whenever he tried removing it, his fingers were automatically repelled, almost like there was an invisible oily barrier just above the letter.

Eld carefully removed the tome he'd stolen from the Splintered Dimension from his backpack and set it on his desk.

The musty scent of old parchment filled his nostrils as he pored over the arcane text, eyes darting from one diagram to the next.

Eld poured through the forbidden tome.

"Lilith was right," he muttered. "This tome is filled with information on disenchant spells."

He thought back to the blaring bronze doors and the consternation over the locked Splintered Dimension. No wonder this book had been locked away alongside everything else.

After he was confident that he'd found the right spell, Eld nodded and cracked his knuckles.

"Alright. Let's try this again."

He cleared his throat and began to chant. "Sigillum revelare, mysteria aperire."

The words felt heavy in his throat. As he cast it, he realized something very peculiar. His mouth seemed to go dry and his fingers went cold.

This wasn't necromantic magic.

It was…something else, something that cut off magic at its very source.

Void magic.

The magic of the Old Gods. That had to be it. No wonder it'd been brought into the Splintered Dimension.

As if on cue, Eld's coat suddenly shook. Bart hastily sprinted out, carrying the still-recovering Franky with him. Only Spinderella—who was, after all, actually alive—stayed there without other concerns.

"Seems dangerous, Bart?" Eld asked.

From his new hiding spot under Eld's bed, the rat nodded.

Simultaneously emboldened yet also more fearful, Eld moved his fingers exactly as the book instructed, leaving faint trails of silvery light in their wake. He tapped the sealed letter three times with his index finger, then drew a complex sigil in the air above it.

A faint glow emanated from the envelope, beating like a pulse.

Eld leaned forward—only to deflate as the glow faded, leaving the seal intact.

"Damn." He slumped back in his chair, running a hand through his disheveled hair. "How could that have happened? I could have sworn…"

The seal seemed to taunt him.

He could feel his father's necromantic energy emanating from it. The magic was tied together in a complex array, meant to repel any attack.

"That's it," Eld muttered. "Father must have studied this book too. So he knows how to circumvent some of the basic techniques…but surely, he hasn't protected himself against *everything*."

He exhaled and straightened, then flipped to the next page of the book.

There were loads of different disenchants here. He'd get there eventually.

After another twenty minutes of studying, his eyes lit up at a particularly promising incantation. This one required a pinch of powdered moonstone, which he withdrew from his pack of school supplies before sprinkling it around the letter in a carefully measured circle.

"Claustra solvere, vincula frangere."

The air around him seemed to thicken as he spoke and repeated the gesture—a simple tracing of the circle followed by a grandiose point at the seal.

A soft hiss filled the room as the moonstone began to glow and tiny sparks danced across the envelope's surface.

Once again, the air was rife with the strange void magic of earlier.

Shuck let out a strangely high-pitched bark. The reanimated dog wasn't frightened exactly, but he *was* cautious. Eld had a feeling that he wouldn't be venturing closer.

"Sorry about that Shuck," Eld said. If even the big dog was feeling it, this void magic had to be something truly powerful. "But this is the only way I can imagine cutting through my father's protection."

Eld thought he saw the seal begin to waver—but then the sparks of void magic were abruptly deflected. When the magic sank into his desk, it faded away, as if it'd never been there at all.

Eld sighed.

"Foiled again, it seems."

He went back to the book.

Hours ticked by, marked only by the steady drip of melting candle wax and the occasional frustrated groan from Eld. He tried spells in languages long forgotten and traced runes with his own blood. After failing to unlock the book after a three hour ritual, Eld threw the book aside and temporarily turned to daemonology, calling forth a spirit of unlocking...

But again to no avail.

When he had finally gone through every spell in the book, his floor had a huge hole in it and a faint mist faintly smelling of peppermint hung in the air. Countless bags of depleted reagents were scattered across the room.

Eld slid down into his chair, magically and financially spent. Not only had Eld been defeated by his father's protective magics, he'd probably have to make a costly trip to Necropolis to replenish his school supplies.

The sealed letter sat before him, still pristine despite his best efforts.

"What are you hiding?" he whispered, glaring at the envelope as if he could intimidate it into revealing its secrets. "And why are you so damned difficult to open?"

Subterfuge and trickery had never been Eldritch Sr.'s strong point.

The fact that it was his father foiling him only infuriated Eld even more. Maybe Talbot was right—Eldritch Sr. was an almighty lich, and Eld was nothing more than a skilled pet doctor.

The thought spurred Eld back into action and he reached for the tome once more.

There just *had* to be something he had missed, some obscure spell or technique that would finally crack this mystical lock. If only he knew where to look.

But before he could even get started, Talbot floated back in and lazily laid on his bed.

"I guess I should tell you this. This doesn't mean we're speaking. Consider it a courtesy for the homework. Word of warning." The poltergeist stretched out, his bones cracking. "Lilith is on a warpath, and she's looking for you."

Eld's face went pale. "What did she say?"

Talbot shrugged, his bones rattling softly. "I don't know. I got out of her way and came back here to hide."

Just then, a sharp knock echoed through the room.

Talbot smirked, floating through the wall. "That's probably for you. I hope she smacks you."

The knocking grew louder and more insistent.

Eld took a deep breath and expected to see Lilith, but when he opened the door, it was a goblin wearing gray robes with a glowing green insignia on them—a bat holding a specter, the Bathurst Academy logo.

"Eldritch Blackwood Jr.?" the goblin asked.

His voice was very formal and official. From the looks of it, he was one of the school's teaching or administrative assistants.

"That's me," Eld replied hesitantly.

"This is for you."

The goblin quickly handed Eld a letter and dashed away, muttering under his breath about uppity first years getting summoned so early.

When Eld stared at the letter, his heart dropped into his stomach. In hindsight, he would have rather been slapped by Lilith or even faced one of her screams.

The note was plain and simple—a summons to Professor Grimthorpe's office.

"Um. I'll be back," Eld said.

"You alright?" Talbot asked.

Even the genuine concern in his friend's voice wasn't enough to shake off Eld's fear.

"I hope I'll be," Eld said.

Without another word, he left his room, hurrying down the hall. There was something in Grimthorpe's note—a particular rigid strictness in the handwriting—that told Eld that he did not want to be late.

Without his blood pumping, Eld's hands were cold at the best of times, but as he approached Grimthorpe's office, his palms grew downright frigid with nervousness.

The frightening possibilities whirled through his mind.

Had Grimthorpe found out about his late-night excursion into the Splintered Dimension? He'd *thought* he'd scouted out the area thoroughly, but maybe there was something he'd missed.

Or worse...

Had he somehow discovered the stolen letter?

The path to the Professor's offices was just like Eld had remembered, though this time, he strode past Hemlock's office to reach the very end.

The wooden door to Grimthorpe's office stood at the very end, the black wood looking even more menacing than it would have otherwise. A simple silver plaque hung at the front—Headmaster.

Eld took a deep breath, steeling himself before knocking on the door.

"Enter," Grimthorpe called from within.

The door swung open of its own accord, revealing a space shockingly similar to Grimthorpe's study. There was even the same messy pile of books and letters—though of course, one letter was missing.

Eld blinked in surprise.

"Professor, I..."

Grimthorpe sat behind his massive desk, a goblet of deep red liquid in his hand. The headmaster's gaze fixed on Eld, a strange, disconcerting smile growing on his face as he waved his hand.

"Oh, this room looks like this no matter where I call it," Grimthorpe replied. "A perk of tenure. It's rather like the Splintered Dimension."

His words seemed to hang in the air and Eld could have sworn that the Headmaster had placed a particular emphasis on those last few words.

But before he could wonder further, Grimthorpe rose from his seat.

"Anyways, young Blackwood. Thank you for coming. I wanted to see how you were doing since our last chat."

Without further explanation, Grimthorpe strode to a large cabinet in the corner of the room. He tapped it with his finger on it and muttered an incantation under his breath. The cabinet swung open, revealing not shelves or hanging clothes, but a hidden passageway.

"After you." Grimthorpe gestured Eld forward, his eyes twinkling with amusement at Eld's obvious surprise. "The real office is through here."

Eld hesitated before stepping through the hidden doorway.

He'd expected something like a long and twining staircase, but instead, the door seemed to shimmer as he stepped through and he found himself in a vast circular chamber.

The austere white walls of carved yew tree planks staring back at him made Eld feel like he was on trial. Like most places in the school, the dimensions were illogical, far bigger than he'd thought from the outside.

The room was dimly lit by floating orbs of misty white that made the room seem to exist in a perpetual twilight. The walls were curved in odd angles that didn't intersect properly, and if Eld studied them too hard, he found his head started to hurt because of the incomprehensible geometry.

But it wasn't the odd architecture that caught Eld's attention—it was the rows upon rows of glass jars lining the walls, each containing a disembodied head.

They were arranged on ornate shelves of wrought iron and bone, spiraling from floor to ceiling.

The heads ranged from the seemingly human to the monstrous, all perfectly preserved as if freshly severed. Their eyes blinked and rolled, mouths working silently in the viscous liquid. Some wore expressions of serene contemplation, while others seemed frozen in eternal shock or outrage.

The jars themselves were of varying sizes and shapes, some tall and cylindrical, others squat and round all customized to fit their inhabitant's shape.

Each was filled with a softly bubbling, transparent liquid that shimmered with inner light. Eld had never seen such a substance before, not even among his father's things, but it radiated with pure necromantic magic.

Grimthorpe followed close behind. "Welcome to the Chamber of Eternal Counsel."

Eld's jaw dropped. "The Chamber of…what?"

The heads bobbed gently in the preservatives as they all turned at once to gaze at Eld.

"The Chamber of Eternal Counsel," Grimthorpe replied. He spread out his arms, sweeping them around the chamber. "These are all the previous headmasters. Or, well, most of them anyways. A few suffered irreparable injuries. This is a tradition unique to Bathurst, I might add. Other schools may have their talking portraits, but we prefer a more, ah, *direct* approach."

For a vague moment, the lich's face seemed to darken, his grandfatherly disposition temporarily fading away.

"Um, I see…" Eld shakily replied.

It was similar to his family's tomb, but these headmasters seemed *far* livelier than any of Eld's relatives.

As if on cue, one of the heads—belonging to a wizened old woman with hair like tangled seaweed—spoke up. "Direct indeed! Though I must say, the fluid does wonders for my complexion."

Some of the nervousness dissipated from Eld in the face of such cheery absurdity. If this lady was still worried about her complexion, it couldn't be that bad, could it?

He moved closer to examine the jars.

The biggest jar belonged to a dracolich, its bony dragon visage somehow managing to look both regal and annoyed. Next to it floated the spectral head of a ghost.

Eld turned back to Grimthorpe. "A ghost? How did you decapitate a ghost?"

"Just here for tradition, lad." The ghost cheerily replied, his eyes darting towards a tangled nest of ectoplasm on the back of the jar. "Got the rest of me tucked away for safekeeping."

Perhaps strangest of all was a framed portrait hanging between two jars. The portrait itself had been painted in immaculate detail, almost like it was one of the Old One's photograph machines.

However, a hasty jar had been scrawled onto the portrait, the crude and unskilled black lines looking painfully out of place.

Within the jar, a painted head moved and spoke just like the others. "Ah, to be young and corporeal again." The portrait sighed wistfully. "Though I suppose I can't complain. At least I don't have to worry about algae buildup."

Grimthorpe leaned in and whispered in Eld's ear. "A possession gone awry. He tried to push his soul into a new, younger body and ended up in a painting instead."

As Eld made his way around the room, his attention was drawn to a large, shadowy corner that seemed to materialize out of nowhere. At first, he'd thought that the room was an octagon, but new angles continually emerged upon closer examination.

There, lounging on what appeared to be a massive, scaled cushion, was a reanimated dragon. Its bones gleamed in the dim light, wisps of necrotic energy curling around it.

Beside it, a hydra's skeleton coiled, its multiple heads swaying gently.

"S-sir." Eld couldn't help but stammer in awe. "Are those...?"

Grimthorpe chuckled. "Ah yes, my little pets. Magnificent, aren't they? Took years to perfect the reanimation process for creatures of that size."

Sensing they were being discussed, both creatures turned their attention to Eld. The dragon's jaw creaked open, a low growl rumbling from its empty ribcage. One of the hydra's heads snapped forward, bony teeth clacking together mere inches from Eld's face.

Eld leaped back with a yelp.

Grimthorpe's laughter filled the chamber. "Now, now," he chided the creatures, though there was no real reproach in his tone. "Play nice with our guest."

Turning back to Eld, Grimthorpe's expression grew more serious. "You may be wondering why I've brought you here, Mr. Blackwood. The truth is, I value your potential. I believe you have a unique perspective that could be beneficial to the school."

So far so good. Nothing about the letter or the library, Eld thought to himself.

Eld swallowed hard, unsure how to respond. "Thank you, sir. That's very kind of you to say."

Grimthorpe waved a hand dismissively. "Not kindness, my boy. Practicality. Now, would you care for a drink? I have a rather excellent vintage of blood wine—fermented from the finest grapes grown in the killing fields of Vlad the Impaler, of course."

Before Eld could answer, Grimthorpe had conjured two glasses and was pouring a deep crimson liquid into each. He handed one to Eld, who accepted it with only slight hesitation.

As far as he could tell, Grimthorpe hadn't snuck anything inside of it…though he very well could have prepared something beforehand.

"To the future of Bathurst." Grimthorpe raised his glass in a toast.

With no obvious choice, Eld mimicked the gesture, taking a small sip.

The wine was surprisingly pleasant, with a rich, earthy flavor. There was just the slightest hint of something metallic.

Grimthorpe swirled the blood-red wine in his glass. "You know, Eld. Bathurst has so much more to offer beyond your years as a student." He gestured heartily, nearly spilling his drink. "Take Professor McGrath, for instance. Started as a rather unremarkable student, if I'm being honest."

He paused, pointing a long bony finger at Eld. "Don't tell him I said anything, mind you."

Eld allowed himself a brief smile. The thought of the highly technical McGrath being a middling student was rather hard to believe.

"But he stayed on," Grimthorpe said, his tone turning ever more passionate. "He delved into our advanced research programs, and now look at him! Revolutionizing the field of biomechanical necromancy."

"Those legs are definitely something," Eld said, trying to suppress a shudder. He had no problem with insect legs, but there was just something about McGrath's machinery that gave him pause.

"And then there's the networking opportunities," Grimthorpe continued. "Our alumni gatherings are legendary. Why, just last year, we had a moonlit seance atop the Haunted Hills. Made contact with some fascinatingly ancient spirits, I tell you." He leaned in conspiratorially. "But that's nothing compared to the Necropromicon coming up. Now there's an event you simply can't miss!"

Eld finished the sip from his glass and wiped his mouth with the back of his hand, curiosity piqued. "The Necropromicon, sir?"

"Oh yes!" Grimthorpe exclaimed, setting down his drink and clapping his hands together with childlike glee. "It's positively delightful. A grand celebration of all things undead, celebrated in accordance with the tenets set for in the Necronomicon. We have a corpse reanimation contest—extra points for style and longevity. And the spirit summoning circles! Last year, we managed to conjure the ghost of Merlin himself. Bit grumpy about being disturbed, but full of fascinating insights."

As Grimthorpe rambled on about spectral parades and zombie dance-offs, Eld found himself oddly captivated. Despite the many goings-on, it would be nice to take a step back and just enjoy his school life.

The Necropromicon sounded like the exact kind of thing he and Lea could enjoy together.

"And don't get me started on the Bone Banquet," Grimthorpe chuckled, taking another sip of his wine. "Chef Ghoulash outdoes himself every year. His Rigor Mortis Risotto is to die for—figuratively speaking, of course. Though last year a student did choke to death on a severed finger."

Grimthorpe sighed contemplatively.

Then with a casualness that seemed almost practiced, Grimthorpe changed the subject. "Tell me, how are you finding your studies? And your extracurricular activities?"

Eld had only just started relaxing—thinking that this really was an old family friend checking in him on him—but Grimthorpe's next words caught him completely off guard and put him right back on edge.

"That exchange student, Lea—you two seem to have grown quite close."

Eld nearly choked on his wine. "Oh, uh, yes. Lea's, she's great. A good friend."

"Just a friend? Come now, Mr. Blackwood. I may be old, but I'm not blind. I've seen the way you look at her."

Grimthorpe leaned forward and stared at Eld with an intensity that made his skin crawl. "Tell me more about Lea. Where did you say she was from again?"

Eld shifted in his seat, acutely aware of the dragon's low growl from the corner.

"Uh, I don't think I said she's from anywhere," he said. "At least, I mean, I wouldn't dare to…"

Grimthorpe waved his hand irritably, cutting through Eld's stammering.

"No, no, I simply meant if *you* knew where she's from."

"I think she's from the Eastern Kingdoms," Eld replied. "She doesn't like to talk about her past too much."

That part was true, at the very least.

Grimthorpe raised an eyebrow. "Not Hel? As her transfer papers stated?"

Having written the transfer papers himself, Eld was very aware of that.

He shrugged. "Ah, you know. She doesn't like talking about her past much, like I said."

Eld laughed—and hoped he didn't sound *too* nervous. "Speaking of which, didn't Cloudehill come here from Hel Academy too? I imagine the rigor of Bathurst was quite something to him."

Grimthorpe chuckled. "Oh, I'm very well aware of the academic difference between you and Cloudehill," he said. "But back to Lea."

Grimthorpe tapped his chin thoughtfully. "Fascinating place, the Eastern Kingdoms. So many unique magical traditions. Has she ever mentioned any particular customs or practices from her homeland?"

Even during the brief interlude where they'd bantered about Cloudehill, the headmaster's gaze had never left Eld, and

Eld felt as if those piercing eyes were trying to bore into his mind. He took a sip of wine to buy himself some time.

The liquid suddenly tasted far more metallic than before.

"Not really, sir." Eld swallowed hard. "Like I said, she doesn't talk much about her past."

Grimthorpe hummed, a sound that somehow managed to convey both disappointment and disbelief. "I see. And what about her studies? Any subjects she seems particularly gifted in?"

Eld tried to recall any details about Lea's academic performance that wouldn't raise suspicion. The truth was that she was brilliant at every class, almost bizarrely so. If Eld had to guess, it probably had something to do with the void magic Lilith had mentioned. Even his brief dabbling into it had taught him that it was far more powerful than mere necromancy.

It was far more than just canceling spells. While Lea struggled to control her powers, it was like she could will things into existence, pulling magical strength from a source beyond this world.

"She's quite good at Necromancy, sir. And, uh, Magical Theory."

"Is that so?" Grimthorpe's eyebrows rose. "Any unusual demonstrations of power? Unexpected talents?"

The question was loaded with implications.

Eld's palms began to sweat, but he resisted the urge to wipe them on his robes.

"N-no, sir." he stammered. "Nothing out of the ordinary."

Grimthorpe's lips curled into a smile that didn't quite reach his eyes. "Come now, Mr. Blackwood. Surely there must be something special about her that's caught your attention. Young love doesn't bloom over mere academic prowess, after all."

Eld felt his face flush with embarrassment.

The headmaster's questions were becoming more and more invasive. There was an undercurrent to his words, a barely concealed hunger for information. Despite his calm demeanor, Grimthorpe was as hungry as a pack of rabid wolves in a forest.

"She's just kind, sir," Eld said. "And funny. We enjoy each other's company."

Grimthorpe sat back, his fingers curled beneath his chin. "I see," he murmured, in a way that suggested he didn't believe a word of it. "Well, it's always wonderful to see students forming such close *bonds*."

The conversation continued in this same way, with Grimthorpe probing for details about Lea's habits, her friends, and even her sleeping patterns.

Despite his best efforts, Eld had paused at that. That particular question had screamed that Grimthorpe knew far more than he was letting on.

Eld felt increasingly like a mouse being toyed with by a particularly sadistic cat. The friendly demeanor of earlier had given way to something far more predatory—a feeling that told Eld Grimthorpe wasn't on his side at all.

Finally, unable to take it anymore, Eld blurted out, "Sir, I don't mean to be rude, but why are you so interested in Lea?"

Grimthorpe paused, studying Eld intently.

Then, he let out a hearty laugh. "My apologies, Mr. Blackwood. I didn't mean to make you uncomfortable. Purely academic interest, I assure you. You see, I have a theory about your friend."

Eld raised an eyebrow, curiosity overriding his unease. "A theory?"

Grimthorpe nodded, leaning in conspiratorially. "I believe she may be an undead spirit inhabiting a human vessel. It's quite rare here, but perhaps more common where she's from."

Eld paused.

Was Grimthorpe trying to throw him off his trail now?

Did he truly believe Lea was some sort of special undead?

Or was it a ruse to get Eld's guard down?

"Of course," Grimthorpe continued. "It's just a theory. Fascinating to consider, though, isn't it? I mean, Lea is unlike any other student at Bathurst."

Eld just nodded, not trusting himself to speak.

Grimthorpe abruptly straightened up, his manner becoming more formal. "Well, I've taken up enough of your time, Mr. Blackwood. Thank you for indulging an old man's curiosity."

Eld stood, grateful for the dismissal.

As he made his way to the door, his gaze fell on a partially open door behind Grimthorpe's desk. Through the gap, he caught a glimpse of shelves lined with ancient-looking tomes. Several of the books bore strange black markings, similar to the Black Sun symbols he had seen before.

Eld's eyes widened.

The missing tomes from the Splintered Dimension!

Grimthorpe followed Eld's gaze.

With a casual wave of his hand, the door swung shut. "Ah, just my private collection. Nothing of interest to a young student, I'm sure. Mostly books for old fogeys like me."

But Eld's mind was already whirling.

Could those tomes hold the key to understanding the Black Sun?

As Eld left Grimthorpe's office, his thoughts were a frightened jumble.

On one hand, the headmaster had been friendly, even complimentary, but there was an undercurrent to their conversation that left Eld feeling very, very unsettled.

He thought of Lea, of her innocence and vulnerability despite her mysterious powers.

If Grimthorpe was involved in whatever was happening with the Black Sun, she could be in danger—no, she would be.

Talbot's warnings echoed in his mind, but as Eld made his way back to his dorm, a plan was already forming. He would need to be careful, to prepare meticulously. But somehow, someway, he had to get into Grimthorpe's private chambers and gain access to those books.

For Lea's sake, and perhaps for the fate of Bathurst itself, Eld knew he had to uncover the truth—no matter the cost.

Chapter 21

Horsing Around

The Spectral Studies classroom buzzed with agitation.

All of the students—Eld included—fidgeted in their seats, eager for the weekend to begin. It was a rather comical sight. The group of nightkin included countless fearsome monsters, ranging from the ordinary like vampires and zombies to the eerily unusual, like staring dolls with blades for hands and stitched monstrosities with four drooling heads.

Yet all of them were just eager to rest for the week and stop working.

Monster or not, the desire for rest was a universal phenomenon, even among the sleepless.

"Class…class…hello…class…" The slow and droning voice echoed through the room. Moments later, Professor Wraith emerged from the ground, a look of consternation on his face. "People…already…aren't…paying…attention…"

Wispy edges lashed out from his body, whipping the students who weren't paying attention.

Eld barely managed to bring up his hand in time to deflect the blow.

Professor Wraith was the absolute worst teacher to have right before the weekend.

Before joining the Bathurst faculty, Wraith had been known as an assassination spirit who was only ever summoned by the desperate.

His modus operandi? Lulling his victims to sleep before killing them.

His naturally droning voice meant that nobody was able to enjoy his fascinating backstory. Nobody had ever made Espionage and Infiltration sound more boring.

Eld sat near the back, his quill scratching furiously across two separate pieces of parchment.

On one, he diligently took notes on the professor's lecture, doing his best to fight off the hypnotic effects of Wraith's voice. On the other, a more intricately detailed list was forming—components and ingredients for a plan weeks in the making.

As he jotted down another item, Eld's mind wandered to Grimthorpe's dragon and hydra. The massive reanimated creatures had been impressive in their size, but Eld had noticed flaws in its construction.

Sloppy stitching, uneven distribution of necromantic energy—signs of a rushed job prioritizing raw power over finesse.

"Craftsmanship," Eld muttered to himself, underlining an item on his list. "That's what really matters."

He glanced up, Lea was directly ahead of him.

Behind Lea was Lilith…a sight that filled Eld with trepidation. But despite Talbot's claims that she was on a warpath, Lilith had treated Eld with almost unusual politeness when he walked into class.

Of course, Eld wasn't sure what that meant, but he was too concerned about his upcoming plan to worry too much.

Lea's head was drooping and her eyes were fluttering as she fought against sleep—though considering the circumstances, Eld had no idea of the source.

Regardless, he reached forward, gently tapping her shoulder. As he did, his heart abruptly surged alive in his chest. No matter how many times he'd felt that feeling, he'd never gotten used to it.

Lea jolted awake, shooting him a grateful smile that made his heart skip a beat.

Eld wanted nothing more than to lean forward and whisper his plans to her, to share the excitement bubbling within him. But the risk of being overheard was too great. He settled for a reassuring nod, silently promising himself to fill her in later.

Just the thought of her excitement brought a smile to his face.

Suddenly, Lilith's voice cut through the classroom's monotony. The banshee's loud shriek cut right through Wraith's slowly droning voice.

"Hey Lea, remember that time King Zo'hyar threw that massive festival to celebrate the alignment of the seven devils?"

Eld stared at her.

What?

He'd never heard of such an event before. His brow wrinkled with guilt. Had he accidentally driven Lilith mad by telling Mortimer about her and Erik?

But it seemed like Lea of all people knew what Lilith was talking about.

Lea's brow furrowed before her face lit up with recognition. "Oh yes! The sky was so beautiful that night, all those colorful lanterns floating up to join the—"

"Gotcha!" Lilith exclaimed triumphantly.

The sound echoed through the room, deafening all the student's ears. The banshee spun in her seat to face Lea, pointing at her with a crooked accusing finger.

"I knew it! You're way older than you're letting on. The Kingdom of Zo'hyar fell over ten thousand years ago!" She leaned in close and whispered. "Eld told me everything."

A hush fell over the classroom as all eyes turned to Lea. She shrank in her seat, clearly uncomfortable with the sudden attention.

"What are you doing?" Eld whispered harshly.

"This is for telling everyone about me and Erik!" Lilith sneered, anger written across her face.

Professor Wraith materialized fully, his ghostly features contorted in annoyance. "Miss Nightshade! This is a classroom, not a gossip circle. Need I remind you that a good portion of us are undead here? Age is hardly a novelty."

Lilith, usually reserved, seemed unable to contain herself. "Professor, you don't understand! Lea's not just old, she's ancient. Even by our standards! The Kingdom of Zo'hyar is so old that most historical records don't even mention it. It's from a time before the Old Ones bombed themselves into oblivion. And a few weeks back Eld—"

The professor cocked his ghostly hips and eyed Lilith. "That's quite enough, Miss Nightshade. One more outburst and I'll throw you in the dungeons until I remember to take you out. And at my old age…my memory isn't very good."

Just as Lilith started to argue further, an unexpected voice chimed in.

"Oh, come off it, Lilith," Talbot drawled.

Eld jerked his head in surprise. He wasn't even aware that Talbot had arrived at class today, but his friend soon emerged from within an ornate harp he'd been lounging in.

A discordant twang rang out as Talbot's fingers flicked skilllessly across the strings. "We all know you're just showing off that you actually paid attention in Ancient History class."

A ripple of laughter spread through the room and Lilith's face flushed. The laughter was more amused than cruel— Mortimer and his gang had gotten kicked out of class by Wraith far earlier in the semester.

Nonetheless, Lilith wasn't happy.

Eld could see the wheels turning in her mind and he knew that she wouldn't let this go easily. It was one of the things he both admired and hated about her—her tenacity. But the last thing they needed was more attention on Lea's mysterious past, so he was glad for Talbot's intervention.

The class devolved into chatter and Professor Wraith's attempts to regain control grew increasingly desperate. Tendrils burst from his body, lashing the students repeatedly, though not drawing blood. According to Talbot, Grimthorpe had given Wraith a strict warning last year after he'd furiously filled up the reanimation wing last year after a particularly soporific lecture.

"Silence, you miscreants!" he hissed, passing through a student's raised hand as he tried to gesture for order. "This is a place of learning, not a tavern!"

Eld's eyes met Talbot's across the room. His lower half was still submerged in the harp.

The tension between them seemed to dissipate a bit.

Talbot floated closer, leaning in to whisper, "Quite the show, eh? Almost makes me glad I tricked someone into dragging me to class today."

Eld smirked. "Oh? And here I thought you came for the riveting lecture on spectral camouflage."

Their shared chuckle was cut short as Professor Wraith swooped past, still trying in vain to restore order.

"What's with the harp?" Eld asked.

"It's extra credit. McGrath promised to bump my grade up if I helped him with a weeklong study in mechanical possession, and I need all the help I can get."

Eld cleared his throat and straightened "Listen, Talbot, about everything that's happened—"

Talbot held up a hand, cutting him off. "Save it, Blackwood. We've both been idiots." He paused and smirked. "Though you've definitely been the bigger idiot."

Eld opened his mouth to speak, but Talbot waved his hand, asking to finish.

"But I suppose that's what friends are for. Keeping each other in check, yeah?" Talbot said.

Eld nodded, pushing his fingers through his hair. "Yeah, I guess so."

The bell rang, signaling the end of class and drowning out Professor Wraith's furious screeching.

Normally, Eld would have laughed, but the sight instead filled him with caution.

Despite Wraith's once intimidating past, he was totally unwilling to go against Grimthorpe's orders…which suggested that deadly darkness lurked behind the lich's scholarly façade.

Talbot gave Eld a nudge. "Now, let's get out of here before we're roped into cleaning up this mess. I've got a reputation for laziness to maintain, after all."

Eld nodded towards Lea, who looked very confused after Lilith's words. "I was going to wait for her. I wanted to make sure she's alright."

He half-feared another outburst from Talbot, but the poltergeist just nodded and smiled.

"Of course," Talbot said. "I'll wait with you."

Eld's shoulders sagged with relief, just as all the other students burst from their seats, jostling for the door.

"Hold it!" Professor Wraith boomed. "Next class, you'll all line up alphabetically and march out like a freshly reanimated army! Maybe then you'll learn some discipline!"

His words fell on deaf ears as the last students disappeared into the hallway.

As Lea, Eld, and Talbot left the classroom together, Eld turned to Lea, whispering under his breath.

"You okay?" he asked quietly.

Lea nodded, but her smile didn't quite reach her eyes. "Yeah. I was just thinking about what Lilith said. It's strange, Eld. I didn't realize that the things I remember were from just so long ago. But I guess I was sleeping under that oak tree for a really long time."

Eld wanted nothing more than to wrap her in his arms and promise that everything would be alright. Instead, he settled for a gentle squeeze of her hand.

"We'll figure it out," he assured her, his heart thumping.

But Eld wasn't nearly as confident as his words suggested.

When though? He asked himself. *How many times have you told her that? You're no closer to answers than you were when you found her!*

He grit his teeth and shook off his doubts, hoping that *this* new plan would work.

Bart and Franky were a little bit more directly effective. They crawled out of Eld's coat, snuggling up next to Lea. She beamed, scratching them in their favorite spots.

That was one of the things Eld liked best about her. Even many nightkin were creeped out by reanimated animals, yet Lea loved them more than anything else.

"Any plans for tonight?" Lea asked, her eyes twinkling.

"I was thinking of going to Necropolis again," Eld said.

"That sounds fantastic," Lea said.

"Going into town for another date?" Talbot asked, flicking his fingers across the harp strings.

"I need to pick up a few supplies in town." Eld shrugged his backpack up further onto his shoulders. "Just some odds and ends. What about you? Did you and Wysper, uh—"

Lea elbowed him and gave him a knowing look, shaking her head.

Talbot slumped in the air, a harsh off key chord ringing out from the harp. "It's complicated. Let's just say that matters of the heart are even more frustrating when you don't technically have one anymore."

Eld raised an eyebrow. "Oh?"

Talbot nodded glumly. "We had a bit of a falling out. Turns out, being lazy and sarcastic isn't as charming as I thought it was."

Lea patted Talbot's incorporeal shoulder sympathetically. "I'm sorry, Talbot. Is there anything we can do?"

The ghost shrugged. "Unless you can turn back time or make me less of a spectral disaster, probably not. But thanks. It's nice to know you guys care."

As they left the school, Eld quickly sketched a spherical ball in the air, his fingers dancing with magic. Once completed, he threw the ball into the sky. It orbited there for a brief moment, occasionally emitting a high-pitched whistling noise.

Moments later, Shuck bounded towards them, a big grin on his patchwork face.

"Thought you'd enjoy the trip off campus too," Eld said, grinning. Since he was quite a bit bigger than his other pets, Shuck didn't always get to travel with Eld, so it was nice to include him when possible.

As the group walked towards the docks, their eyes widened at the sight before them. Massive pumpkin-shaped carriages stood ready, their carved jack-o-lantern-like faces gleaming ominously in front of the murky black water.

"Um… are those new?" Eld asked.

"Almost certainly," Talbot replied. "How do they plan on using a carriage to get across water?"

"Look at this…" Lea muttered, pointing at the side of the carriage.

Eld recognized the now-familiar sigil of the Black Sun.

"It's almost like they want to make that the new school logo," Eld muttered.

"Huh…" Talbot cut in. "I think you're right. Come to think of it, that black sun has almost wiped out the shield and bat…"

Eld blinked in surprise. Since he and Talbot hadn't been talking, he'd forgotten about using the poltergeist's extensive knowledge of the school as a resource in his investigation.

"Have the paintings changed too?" Eld asked.

"Definitely," Talbot replied. "Almost all the paintings have a black sun these days. Some of them even look like they were modified over summer term."

Eld nodded grimly.

Back at the Blackwood family manor, black sun art had been everywhere, ever since he was a child. But if this was a recent change at Bathurst, that only deepened Eld's suspicions that his father was involved.

But despite the eerie décor, what pulled the carriages was even stranger.

Reanimated horses with patchwork bodies of flesh and mechanical parts stamped impatiently at the ground. Steam hissed from vents in their necks, and their eyes glowed with an unnatural blue crackling light.

Professor McGrath stood nearby, bouncing with excitement on his mechanical legs.

"Feast on your eyes or feast your eyes, whatever the saying is! The latest in necrotic transportation technology is here!

These beauties have more corpse-power than a herd of zombie elephants!"

One of his spidery legs withdrew a steaming beaker filled with a thick glowing liquid. "And that's not all! This little concoction here gives them an extra boost."

He grinned merrily and poured the contents of the beaker into a vent on the horse's back.

The horse promptly reared up, letting out a bellowing shout of ecstasy and power.

"It's like coffee, but for the undead!" McGrath crowed. "I'm going to have to place a copyright curse on this formula. It's so strong my beloved horses will be able to gallop straight across the lagoon!"

Judging by the elated grin on the horse's face, Eld had a feeling that the solution was a good deal stronger than mere *coffee.*

Lea and Talbot exchanged a glance, unsure about the safety.

But Eld hurried them forwards.

"It'll be fine," he said.

He had more than enough experience empowering animals, and despite the horses' bizarre and frightening mechanical appearance, he could tell that they were eager to test their newfound power.

Eld entered the carriage first, closely followed by Lea and Talbot.

"Oh, now this is nice," Talbot said, grinning at one of the plush velvet seats. He placed his harp in the chair, then promptly vanished into it.

As more and more students started to file in, curiosity won out over caution.

They set off towards Necropolis and the mists of the lake blurred past as the horses sprinted across the water with the absurd speed that McGrath promised. Soon, the familiar outline of Necropolis was visible in the distance.

Even Talbot was impressed.

"This is amazing! I'd love to get these for the Wilting family estate…I just have the sinking suspicion that it'll take a lot of work to afford them."

It was only at the *very* end that a mishap occurred.

Professor McGrath's voice proudly crowed through the line of pumpkins.

"Jet mode! Now, my beauties!"

Wings burst from the back of the mechanized horses with an echoing metal clank, and Eld's stomach swooped as the whole line of carriages took to the skies.

"What *is* this?" Lea asked.

"Old One technology," Eld replied. He remembered reading about them in the Old One brochures that he and Talbot had researched while trying to find out more about the Black Sun ritual. "Apparently, jets were great metal birds that could fly through the—"

He never got a chance to finish his sentence.

There was a hideous deafening clank, intermingled with pulpy splattering, and the whole line of carriages slammed hard onto the shore.

Eld found himself with an immediate view of the dark night sky. His pumpkin carriage had crumbled to pieces.

Talbot's harp hit the ceiling before falling back down to the ground again.

To Eld's surprise, the harp itself wasn't damaged.

A battered and beaten Talbot emerged from the harp, coughing and cursing.

"I…what just…"

As Shuck shrugged off a loose piece of shattered wood with an irritable bark, Eld stared out the ruined carriage, where the mechanized horses were faintly stirring, black oil-like blood leaking out of their veins.

McGrath picked himself up, cursing and shaking his head—his own mechanized legs were snapped and battered, so the leprechaun was now back at his typical height of three feet.

He marched among the horses, examining their wounds with care that surprised even Eld.

"Unfortunately, I'm going to have to ask Grimthorpe for some necromantic help…" McGrath said. "Hopefully, you lot all have a good time in town. It might be a while before you can return."

"Can't we take the ferries?" a groggy voice shouted from among the other students.

"Ah…well, they are rather upset that I was planning to replace them," McGrath admitted. "They are striking over breach of contract."

The student's groaning and mumbling rapidly built into a furious crescendo. All of the goodwill from the fast trip had dissipated.

McGrath threw up his hands irritably. "Look. If you think *you* brats have it bad, the ferryman's contracts had a far more onerous punishment for breaches. Professor Hemlock is still trying to get blood back in the school bursar's body!"

Grumbling furiously, McGrath attempted to stomp off dramatically, but with his horses injured, he had nowhere to go, so he just wound up stomping right back with equal furor.

As the students slowly dissipated, Eld pulled out his supply list, double-checking the items he needed.

Talbot peered over Eld's shoulder as he scanned the list.

"Chimera scales? Ghostweed essence? Articulated legs?" Talbot whistled. "That's quite the shopping list. So, planning on making a new pet, are we?"

Eld hesitated, then shook his head.

He needed to let Talbot in on his plan. His friend had chosen to accept Eld for who he was—risks and all—it was the leas Eld could do to trust him.

"Not exactly," Eld replied, his voice low. "I'm gathering supplies to rebuild and upgrade Franky. Because I'm planning to break into Grimthorpe's office."

Talbot fluttered violently, his jaw dropping in shock. "You're what? Have you lost your mind?"

Eld quickly explained his suspicions about Grimthorpe's personal collection of tomes and his adventure into the library with Lilith. As he spoke, Talbot's expression shifted from disbelief to concern, and finally to reluctant understanding.

"Well, that explains why Lilith is so angry with you. And why you're so genuinely concerned. You really think Grimthorpe is in on all this, don't you…"

Franky poked out of Eld's coat, the weakened centipede wiggling his legs with determination.

"Even he knows the risks, Talbot," Eld grimly replied. "But after everything that's happened, all the secrets and mysteries I have to do something."

Lea leaned in, her cosmic eyes intense with excitement as she stared from Eld to Talbot. It was clear that getting to the bottom of this mystery was nearly irresistible for her, but she stayed quiet, respecting Talbot's decision.

The poltergeist was quiet, contemplating.

Then, with a dramatic sigh, he said, "Well, I suppose someone has to keep you two out of trouble. Count me in—but if we get caught, I'm claiming ghostly possession made me do it."

"Thanks, Talbot. And look…I think whatever the conspiracy is, it'll extend to the rest of the student body too. Think about it. Dark rituals rarely have a single target. It's not going to stop with Lea."

Talbot laughed. "Well, I better help you then. Friendship and loyalty aren't on the Wilting family crest…but good old-fashioned self-interest is."

Eld chuckled. "Glad to have you. Now, let me walk you through the plan in more detail."

Eld pulled out his list again, running a finger down the written items. "Two main things. First, components for warding spells to protect Franky from detection. And second, various creature parts to hybridize him."

Eld's gaze drifted to Talbot, who had already stopped listening and was absently strumming the spectral strings of his harp.

As bizarre as it seemed, a new idea began to form. "Actually, I might have just thought of a third component we need," Eld said.

A lazy grin spread across Talbot's face.

"Sounds like we've got some shopping to do. But don't expect me to carry anything. These ghostly arms aren't made for heavy lifting, you know."

Eld rolled his eyes. "Wouldn't dream of it, Talbot. I suppose you'll want me to carry your harp case too?"

"Now you're getting it!" Talbot exclaimed, clapping his hands together and starting to fade into the harp. "Consider it payment for putting up with you."

Sighing, Eld wedged the harp between his back and the backpack, adjusting to the extra weight. "Remind me why we're friends again?"

"For my charm and wit, obviously," Talbot's muffled voice from inside the instrument chuckled.

As they made their way through the crowded streets, Eld couldn't help but notice the appreciative glances thrown his way. A group of vampire girls giggled as they passed, one of them calling out, "Nice harp! You play?"

Eld felt his face flush. "Oh, uh, thanks. I'm still learning."

Talbot's voice whispered from the case, "Tell them you're a musical prodigy. Maybe we can get some free drinks out of this—the brilliant musician *and* his brilliant talking instruments. You know, I hear that vamps are great with their fangs. They do this thing where they—"

Lea, who had been quiet until now, slapped the top of Talbot's harp, shushing him, and linking her arm through Eld's.

She jerked him in holding him close. "The harp's okay, but trust me, ladies—it's his centipede you should be impressed by."

Suddenly, she winked and a faint purple glint appeared in her ethereal eyes. Eld felt the air shift. He didn't recognize where it came from, but then he thought back to the book on disenchants and the void magic he'd used.

The vampire girls suddenly stiffened and turned, marching away in jerky awkward motions as if being controlled by a puppet master.

"What did you do?" Eld asked.

Lea blinked in confusion. "Um…I don't know actually. I was kind of just hoping they'd give me some privacy."

Talbot glanced at her, then shrugged. "I've never seen jealousy be so powerful."

Lea blushed and stammered. Part of Eld was flattered, but he was mostly concerned for Lea. Despite her incredible magical abilities, she couldn't control them. If Grimthorpe or Eldritch Sr. attacked, there was a chance she could drive them away, but more likely than not, she'd be utterly helpless.

"You know," Lea mused as they walked, "Back in my day, musicians were quite popular too. Though usually it was always the actual musician getting the attention, not someone pretending to be an instrument."

Eld gave her a furtive glance, still a little confused at what had happened with the vampires. "Your day? Are you remembering more about your past? Whatever happened ten thousand years ago?"

"I'm not sure. The words just…came out. But now that I think about it, I can't quite place when or where."

Suddenly, she cried out, covering her eyes.

"Lea!" Eld exclaimed, steadying her. "What's wrong?"

"The sun," she mumbled. "It hurt my eyes."

Talbot popped his head out from the harp. "Is she okay?"

A chill ran down Eld's spine as he glanced up at the perpetually dim sky. There was no sun visible, just the usual ethereal glow that lit Necropolis.

"Your visions again?" he asked.

She nodded shakily.

"Come on." He guided Lea towards a less crowded side street. "Let's take a break."

They found a small alcove between two buildings, out of the main flow of foot traffic.

Talbot emerged completely from the instrument.

"You alright there, Starry Eyes?" he asked Lea.

She nodded, though she still looked shaken. "I'm fine. It's just frustrating. Every time I think I'm close to remembering something, it slips away. It just gets blanketed by…the darkness of the sun."

Eld squeezed her hand reassuringly. "For now let's focus on getting what we need for Franky. That might lead us to some answers."

Talbot cleared his spectral throat. "Not to be a downer, but shouldn't we get moving? The longer we dawdle, the more likely we are to run into unwanted company."

Eld raised an eyebrow. "Since when are you so concerned about time management?"

"Trust me, you do not want to get caught in the wrong crowd here," Talbot insisted. "These back alleys are dangerous.

Body snatchers and chop shops are always looking for fleshies to snatch up."

As they moved out onto the main street, they had barely taken a few steps when Eld spotted two familiar figures across the street. Mortimer Vex and Erik the Drowned were sauntering down the cobblestones, their eyes scanning the crowd with disdain.

"Keep your heads down," Eld muttered, stepping closer to Lea.

But it was too late.

Mortimer's gaze locked onto them, his lips curling into a sneer. He nudged Erik, who turned to look, water dribbling from his perpetually damp chin. As they passed each other, Mortimer sneered. "If it isn't the pet doctor and his little freak show." His gaze lingered on Lea.

Erik gurgled a laugh, the sound bubbling wetly in his waterlogged throat. "Better watch your back. Accidents happen all the time in Necropolis."

Eld felt Lea tense beside him, her cosmic eyes flashing with an otherworldly light again. This time, the glow was far more powerful than whatever happened to the vamps. But as the light's intensity increased, so did Lea's strain.

She was trembling in place next to him, not even seeing the two men in front of them.

Eld placed his body protectively in front of hers, trying to calm her down before she did something she couldn't control.

Suddenly, Talbot's voice piped up from the harp case. "Hey, soggy bottom! Why don't you go take a dip in the sewers? Might improve your smell. And make sure you keep sitting there glowering by the way. You look so scenic in the witchlight."

Mortimer's face twisted with anger, but before he could respond, a whole parade of ghastly women in tattered jerseys suddenly charged through the streets, excitedly waving a gold and black flag.

"We did it!"

"We captured the Championship Chalice!"

"The Necropolis Night Hags are World Pumpkinball Champions!"

Before Mortimer and Erik could recover, Eld quickly steered their group down a side street, leaving the fuming bullies behind.

"Nice one, Talbot," Eld whispered. He glanced at Lea, who was just coming too.

"What happened?" she asked.

"Don't worry about it," Eld said.

But then he nodded at Talbot. "Let's try and avoid them."

"Of course. Avoid and forget. That's on the Wilting family crest too." Due to the possession, Talbot's words were mixed with the sound of plucking harp strings. "Now, can we please get on with our totally-not-suspicious shopping trip?"

Chapter 22

An Ounce of Warding
is Worth a Pound of Reanimation

Though Eld had been to Necropolis several times before already, the towering gothic structures always dazzled him. He'd grown up in the isolated Blackwood Family Manor, and after that, he'd spent his time Topside with humanity.

Necropolis was a true nightkin community, lined with shops catering to every afterlife and underworld need imaginable. Talbot partially materialized from the harp, placing his hands on Eld's shoulders and scanning the streets.

"Hah! Look at that! Gremlins! Don't see them every single day."

The furry creatures scurried past the group, their arms laden with school supplies. Eld smiled and chuckled to himself as the two groups crossed paths.

Due to their short stature and hyperactive movements, most students, Eld included, tended to automatically assume that any gremlin was a first year. But judging by their brightly glowing alchemical beakers, these were experienced students, probably upperclassmen.

Eld bit his tongue and kept on walking. Gremlins could get awfully vindictive when taunted about their height—a phenomenon known to the nightkin as "gremlin complex."

As Eld and his friends kept walking, they encountered a black cat with glowing eyes reciting potion ingredients to a bewildered zombie.

"Three pieces of bark from a speaking tree, freely granted, then two pounds of ground up moonstone, gathered during the full moon. After that, add two dashes of Evanescent Oil, taken from the Burrowtree Swamp—and only the Burrowtree Swamp, mind you. The stuff from the Permanent Bog won't do you any good. Then add a shot of whisky. Just because there's nothing better than a little alcohol to get the conversation flowing."

"Um…you…how…you can talk?" the zombie stammered.

The cat blinked irritably. "Of course I can talk."

"How?"

"What do you mean how? I just told you the ingredients for a Potion of Animal Speech!"

The zombie just shambled off, shaking his head in disbelief, but Eld mentally noted the potion's ingredients as he continued on.

"It's like the whole town exists just to serve the school," Lea observed.

"Pretty much," Talbot confirmed. "Necropolis lives and dies by Bathurst's whims. Much like the human's college towns."

The glowing poltergeist glanced back and forth, making sure they weren't being followed, then lowered his voice. "Speaking of which, we should hit the underground market first. That's where you'll find the good stuff, Eld."

Eld raised an eyebrow.

Unlike Talbot's meandering boasts to Wysper, here, it sounded like he actually knew what he was talking about.

"You have some experience?" Eld asked.

"Oh yeah, they're great for cheating. They've just got a bunch of old tests stashed in there. Some people say they've even got imps spying on the professors and teaching assistants. Stopped going after my fourth year though. The prices literally went up to an arm and a leg."

The trio made their way through winding streets, passing a neat little bookstore built out of ominous black wood named Quills & Curses. Right next to it was a candlelit café filled with burbling mugs named Bewitching Brews.

But as Eld continued following Talbot, the names of the store became increasingly dubious.

As they walked past a tightly boarded up store named Legitimate Organs, Eld couldn't shake the feeling of being watched. He glanced over his shoulder to see a group of strange, tentacled beings huddled in an alleyway, their eyes fixed on them. It was the Great Old Ones.

Eld frowned, recognizing one of them. "Is that the ferryman? From before? Do you think he's mad about that contract stuff?"

Talbot let out a long groan. "I've heard nasty stories about messing with the old-timers before…hopefully, they know we don't make decisions at the school."

As he continued eyeing the tentacled creatures, Talbot grew increasingly jittery.

"They've never liked us students. They've been here since before Bathurst was built, after all. They're all prophecy and doomsaying and all that jazz." He paused and nervously tutted. "They're not great at parties."

As if hearing Talbot's jab, more of the tentacled beings emerged from the shadows. Their bodies were a mass of writing appendages and their faces were a jumble of mismatched features.

"Um, I think they are coming for us…" Eld muttered.

He raised his hands defensively, preparing to cast some kind of spell. Behind him, Shuck barked angrily, revealing a maw full of snarling teeth.

But the tentacled beings seemingly didn't notice either of them. The largest one, its head resembling a sea anemone, shuffled forward.

"Behold!" it gurgled, its voice shockingly jubilant. "The signs are all around us! The stars grow dim, the seas boil with ancient malice, and the very fabric of reality frays at the edges!"

Its companions joined in, their voices a harmony of ecstatic doom and gloom.

"The Great Old Ones awaken once more and consume all that you see!" croaked one with too many eyes.

"They hunger!" wailed another, inky tears streaming from its numerous orifices.

Whatever was going on, Eld didn't like it. But before he could act, the sea anemone creature's gaze fell on Lea, and its demeanor changed instantly.

"By the void," it said, its tentacles quivering with anxious excitement. "It can't be...My lady, is that truly you?"

The change was so abrupt, it was almost comical. The creature had lost its ominous tone, becoming almost supplicant and respectful.

"Well, I'll be a gibbering moon-beast's uncle!" it exclaimed, now sounding like a friendly neighbor. "Folks, look who it is! It's the lady herself!"

The other creatures crowded around, their apocalyptic warnings forgotten.

"My stars, it really is her!"

"You haven't aged a day, my lady!"

"Remember that time with the seven-headed hydra and the bucket of fish paste? What a hoot!"

Lea shifted uncomfortably and moved closer to Eld. "I'm sorry, do I know you?"

The sea anemone creature chuckled, a sound like bubbles popping. "Oh, of course you wouldn't remember old Squiggles and the gang. I don't blame you. It's been eons, after all! Say, you wouldn't happen to have any of that divine ambrosia on you, would you? For old times' sake?"

"Squiggles?" Lea asked.

"Yep, that's me," the sea anemone creature said, happily pointing at its face. "It was you who gave me that nickname, my lady. I've kept it as a badge of honor ever sense."

Behind him, the other twisted creatures eagerly nodded.

"Yes…"

"An honor…"

"It is Lady Azalea…"

Eld froze.

How did they…

He turned to Lea, who just looked even more disturbed.

"Well, it's nice to see you. But, uh, I, erm, have to get going. Places to be, um, you know what I mean," she stammered.

"Oh, sure, sure," Squiggles said, waving a tentacle dismissively. "Don't let us keep you. But my lady, if you ever want to reminisce about the good old days before time was time, you know where to find us!"

As they hurried away, Eld noticed the inky substance seeping from the creatures' pores. Instead of dissolving behind him, it seemed to meld into his shadow, creating a darkness eerily similar to one in Lea's own shadow.

Eld gulped and turned to Lea. "Did you recognize them at all?"

Lea's features knitted, confusion written across her face. "No, but they seemed familiar somehow. Like I knew them when they were younger? But…"

She glanced down at herself, frowning. "I mean. I *feel* pretty young now?"

Then she shook her head, letting out a long sigh. "Just how long was I sleeping behind that oak tree?"

Eld frowned to himself, hoping to hide the unease on his face.

But just what kind of past did Lea have that she was on familiar terms with eldritch horrors? And why did they switch from harbingers of doom to jovial old friends at the sight of her?

Before Eld could even begin to ponder the implications, Talbot interjected. "Look alive, kids. We're here."

A dimly lit shop called Maxine's Magical Miscellany stood in front of them.

The shop occupied a crooked, three-story building that leaned precariously to one side, seemingly always on the verge of toppling over.

Windows of different shapes and sizes dotted the front, some round like portholes, others triangular or star-shaped. The building itself was a juxtaposition of mismatched materials—weathered wood, tarnished copper, and what appeared to be large reptilian scales of some kind in various shades of green and purple.

Talbot nodded at the scales knowingly.

"The school admin comes poking by sometimes, so the store occasionally needs to make a quick escape."

The shop's sign hung above the door, the letters constantly rearranging themselves to spell out *Maxine's Magical Miscellany* in a variety of languages and scripts. Sometimes the letters would even dance off the sign entirely, floating in the air before slowly and seemingly reluctantly returning to their places.

Surrounding the shop was a small, overgrown garden filled with plants that definitely didn't belong in this plane of existence. Mushrooms that glowed, flowers that whispered to each other and vines that reached out to gently caress or possibly strangle, anyone who came too close.

As the trio stepped inside, the air inside was thick with the scent of herbs and preserving fluids. Jars of pickled creature parts lined the shelves and bundles of dried plants hung from the ceiling.

"Alright." Eld took the list from his pocket, going over the ingredients one more time. "We need essence of ghostweed and chimera scales, first"

As he gathered the items, Lea browsed the shelves. Talbot wiggled partway out of the harp and was now floating near a display of spectral enhancement potions.

"Hey Eld, think any of these would help with my, uh, Wysper situation?" Talbot called over his shoulder.

Eld glanced over, raising an eyebrow at the bottle Talbot was eyeing.

It was a bottle of cologne with a list of disclaimers longer than Eld's leg—the contract to purchase it drifted all the way to the floor, ending with the ominous line "your descendants may not sue Maxine in your place."

"I don't think that's going to help your issue," Eld said. "Unless your goal is to become even more intangible, I'd steer clear of that."

Talbot sighed dramatically. "Worth a shot."

After Eld finished gathering the items, he turned to Talbot, who just nodded at the counter.

"She'll show up."

As Eld put the items on the counter a gnarled hand shot out from behind a beaded curtain, grasping his wrist. He yelped in surprise, nearly dropping his basket of supplies.

"You seek to bend the rules of life and death, young necromancer," a raspy voice said. An ancient crone emerged from the back room, her milky eyes fixed on Eld with unnerving accuracy.

"I mean, he is a necromancer." Talbot pushed out his chin and shook his head slightly. "It kind of comes with the territory, you know? Bending the rules of life and death?"

The old woman ignored the poltergeist. "Beware. The path you walk is treacherous, and the price of failure is steep."

Eld swallowed hard, his heart racing. "I don't know what you mean."

The crone cackled, releasing his wrist. "Of course you do, child. Why else would you need chimera scales and ghostweed? But fear not. I have something that may aid you on your quest."

She disappeared behind the curtain once more, returning moments later with a small carved box. "This contains the essence of a dream eater. Use it wisely, and it may reveal truths hidden even from yourself."

She slid the box forward, caressing it gently. "It can be yours for only thirteen easy payments of six silver and sixty-six copper!"

Eld reached for his purse, but Talbot rolled his eyes. "Eld…you can find essence of dream eater anywhere, for much cheaper. That's an actual legal substance, you idiot. Get what you came for and lets go."

The crone glared at Talbot and then took the box back. She quickly counted the supplies Eld had on the counter and with a dismissive wave said, "twelve coppers."

Their next stop was a shop specializing in biomechanical enhancements—just what he needed to upgrade Franky's mobility and sensory capabilities.

This building was much shabbier than Maxine's. It was a simple gunmetal grey dome that whirled mechanically, twitching and spinning in place. Every so often, a few spindly spider legs would poke out before abruptly retracting back into the metal half-sphere.

Like Talbot said, it seemed like the stores in the Black Market occasionally had to make a quick getaway.

As soon as Eld walked in, he found himself facing a very surly looking gnome with an angry expression and a pitch-black beard. When he saw Eld, Lea, and Talbot, he muttered something under his breath about upstart leprechauns before sauntering off to the back of the store.

"He used to teach at Bathurst, but got replaced by McGrath," Talbot murmured. "I should have told you before, but, uh, don't mention it."

Eld just nodded.

Looking through the store, the goods on supply were very similar to McGrath's, albeit with a good deal more sparking and smoking. Eld would probably have to use the lessons he'd learned in biomechanics to upgrade them for stealth purposes…which, Eld supposed, was exactly why this gnome had been fired.

Examining a particularly intricate set of articulated legs, Eld's mind went back to a thought he had back in the carriage.

He pulled Franky out of his coat.

The slowly healing centipede chittered eagerly as he stared at the parts at the store.

Eld lowered his breath, quickly asking for permission to carry out his improved plan.

The centipede glanced at Talbot, then back at Eld. His response was a many-legged shrug, followed by a nod.

"You sure?"

The centipede nodded again with more certainty this time. Eld nodded back.

The plan was risky, but after his last mishap, Franky was eager for some backup.

"Talbot." Eld removed the harp from his back and held it out in front of him. "How would you feel about merging with Franky? Not permanently, of course, but as a sort of possession?"

"What are you doing?" Talbot's voice came from behind Eld.

Eld swiveled around.

The poltergeist had floated over to a glowing bronze gauntlet that crackled with electricity. Shaking his head, Eld quickly shoved the instrument back behind his back. "Oh. I thought you were still in the harp. What I was asking is what do you think about possessing Franky for this little excursion into Grimthorpe's office."

Talbot's features contorted. "Me? Possess your zombie centipede? Are you out of your mind?"

Lea leaned in. "Actually, that's not a bad idea. Talbot, you could provide additional control and intelligence, maybe even help Franky navigate Grimthorpe's defenses."

Eld nodded. "I was going to use an oculus spell and try to guide him from outside the office with some mechanical add-ons, but if you were possessing him, I think things would go a lot smoother."

Talbot floated in circles, clearly agitated. "Oh sure, let's just stuff the ghost into the bug. What could possibly go wrong?"

"I know it's asking a lot and if you don't want to, I understand," Eld soothingly replied. "But think about it, you could refine your possession skills, if you get caught you can just phase out and go invisible and it might be a good distraction from, you know, the Wysper situation."

At the mention of Wysper, Talbot deflated. "Fine, but if I end up stuck in that creepy-crawly forever, I'm haunting you for eternity."

Eld grinned. "So nothing would really change?"

Talbot rolled his eyes, but Eld could tell that he was in.

Grinning, the necromancer added a few more items to their cart—spectral binding agents and ectoplasmic lubricants that would help facilitate the ghost-insect fusion.

Their final stop was *The Necronomic Nook*, a dusty bookshop tucked away behind a pitch-black alley.

The bookstore seemed to expand out of the darkness as Eld walked forwards, stretching into existence. The inside could not have been more different from the dingy entrance.

"This is the place I told you about," Talbot muttered. "The one that sells old tests…crime really does pay."

Plush carpets muffled their footsteps, and ornate bookshelves lined the walls. Perched atop a gilded desk was a raven, its feathers an impossibly deep black. It wore a tiny hood, giving it an air of mystery.

The raven tilted its head back and forth, inspecting them with one eye at a time. "Welcome. Seeking knowledge, are we? Or perhaps something more?"

Eld stepped forward, lowering his voice. "I heard you have some specialized texts available. Advanced reanimation techniques. Maybe even stuff on dimensional manipulation."

The raven's eyes glinted.

It hopped down, revealing a hidden compartment beneath its perch. With a flick of its wing, it produced a stack of hastily scrawled pages. "Freshly transcribed," it whispered. "My own feathers, you know. Keeps me grounded, quite literally."

As he handed the pages over, Eld opened up his purse.

"How much?" he asked.

The raven stared at Eld, its eyes glinting as its head turned to inspecting.

"I have more than enough coins," the raven said. "Just look at my glorious estate."

Eld gulped. Talbot's words flashed through his mind—that the copied tests were worth a literal arm and a leg.

But at the end, the raven just poked its beak at Lea's finger.

"I'd like that, if you'd please."

"My finger?" Lea asked.

"What? No!" the raven squawked. "The ring! It seems very rare."

"Oh, this?" Lea asked. She pointed at an aged silver ring on her finger. It had been there when Eld found her under the oak tree.

"Yes!" the raven replied, its eyes dancing with glee.

"Um, okay," Lea said, sliding it off.

Eld held his breath, expecting some kind of arcane magic to occur, but the silver ring was just a beaten-up silver ring.

"Here you go," Lea said.

"Excellent," the raven replied, flapping its wings happily.

As they completed their transaction, Eld couldn't help but notice the raven's nest. It was a chaotic collection of shiny objects—coins, jewelry, even a small tiara.

The bird followed his gaze, puffing up proudly. "One must have hobbies, yes?"

"Of course," Eld replied, nodding and collecting the pages.

After they left the shop, Eld turned to her.

"I can get you a new one if you want," he said, blushing a little at the implication.

"No need," Lea replied. But then she caught herself. "Um, well, I mean, if you want to, you can…"

Talbot grumbled as they left.

"What gives? Just a ring for you guys. But an arm and a leg for an honest specter like me trying to copy some tests?"

Eld glanced back at the shop, his eyes lingering on the legs.

"Maybe the raven was found out," he said. "Turned into a secret agent. It's probably an easy way for the school to identify cheaters. It's hard to miss someone missing an arm and a leg."

"Well, I'm glad I dodged that particular sting operation," Talbot laughed as he led them deeper into Necropolis's underbelly, where a grinning goblin with shaggy black hair and lime green skin stood guard over a trapdoor.

The goblin cackled. "Welcome to the Don't Ask, Don't Tell Market! Where the merchandise is fresh, and the questions are stale!"

Descending into the underground bazaar, Eld's senses were assaulted by a jumble of sights and smells. Stalls lined the twisting tunnels, offering everything from pickled eyeballs to still-beating hearts.

"Remember, we're looking for specific components," Talbot cautioned. "Try not to get distracted by the local color."

That was easier said than done.

As they navigated the market, Eld found himself constantly amazed, slightly horrified and somewhat disgusted by some of the wares on display. A group of night hags argued over the price of a jar of toenail clippings, while a skeleton dressed in a surprisingly dapper suit hawked *gently used* pelvises. They reached a secluded corner where a group of mole-like creatures huddled around a makeshift counter. Their eyes lit up as Eld approached.

"Well would you looky here!" The largest mole exclaimed. "If it ain't Eldritch B Blackwood, the pet doctor 'imself, in the flesh!"

Eld blinked in surprise. "You know me?"

The mole grinned, revealing rows of sharp teeth. "Know you? Why, you're practically our patron saint! Ever since you started reanimating pets, business has been booming. Folks always need spare parts for their zombie poodles and skeletal parakeets."

"How do people from Topside get down here?" Eld asked.

"Why, same as you. There are many hidden ways into the underworld without dying. And you know how particular those humans can be about their precious pets," another one of the moles answered.

As someone who was very particular about his own precious pets, Eld felt no small amount of pride, but the moles were looking at him *very* hungrily. He couldn't help but hope they were merely hungry for a good deal. "Well, I'm glad to have helped. I'm actually here for some components myself."

The largest of the mole's eyes narrowed and he ushered Eld closer. "Of course, of course. But tell me, what would you say to a little *arrangement*?"

"How about this?" The lead mole raised a claw. "We'll give you the finest turtle shells this side of the Styx, in exchange for…oh, let's say, the sound of your firstborn's laughter?"

Eld shook his head. "I don't even have children!"

The mole waved a clawed hand dismissively. "Details, details. We can wait."

Over the next few minutes, Eld found himself engaged in a strange negotiation that felt more like a game of multidimensional chess. The mole people, it turned out, were fickle and bizarre. They seemed to delight in offering outlandish trades and impossible favors, all with a gleeful disregard for anything resembling logic.

Eld had no idea what their objectives were. Sometimes, it seemed like they just liked to hear themselves talk.

Finally, after what felt like an eternity of bargaining, Eld managed to secure the components, including many he didn't know he needed until the moles convinced him otherwise. There were turtle shells for protection, chameleon scales for temporary invisibility, and a collection of alchemical ingredients for his warding potion.

And the price was a favor to be called in at a later date, the nature of which the moles refused to specify.

It was dubious, but considering the circumstances, Eld was afraid that if he didn't act, there wouldn't be a later date—a fact he tried to warn the mole people of, but to absolutely no avail. If anything, the moles had seemed excited by the prospect of the world ending, claiming it was a

With everything on Eld's list found, the trio made their way back to the main streets of Necropolis. The perpetual twilight of the university town seemed even dimmer now, as what passed as night in the underworld began to set in.

"Should be enough time for the carriages to be improved," Talbot noted.

"Yeah, I think I hear that infernal neighing," Eld replied.

Indeed, McGrath and his horses had returned, waiting at a hastily erected station by the lake.

As they approached the carriage station, a small voice called out from the shadows. "Eld? Eld B? The Greatest Pet Doctor in History?"

Chapter 23

The Dog Days Are Beginning Again

A figure pushed through the crowd of nightkin, moving towards Eld.

As they drew closer, Eld realized it was a young human boy, no more than fourteen or fifteen. His clothes were tattered and travel-worn, but there was a fierce fire in his eyes.

"Eld?" Lea asked, turning towards him.

Eld felt a lump grow in his throat.

He'd seen this kind of thing before.

The boy had a small bundle strapped on his back. Even from a distance, Eld knew there was only reason why someone would work so hard to find him.

The boy's eyes lit up as he spotted Eld and he rushed forward.

As he drew closer, Eld saw that his suspicions were correct. The strapped up bundle was the body of a dog, carefully wrapped in bandages, but still showing signs of decay and damage.

Behind Eld, Shuck let out a low sad whine, padding back and forth in distress.

"By the gods above and below! It's you! It's really you!" he exclaimed, his voice cracking. "Eld B., the greatest pet doctor in history. I've been searching for you for so long!"

Ignoring Talbot and Lea's surprise, Eld stepped towards the boy, his voice gentle. "You have come a long way, haven't you? What's your name?"

"Ellis," the boy replied. He carefully lowered his cargo to the ground. "And this is…was…Max. He was my best friend. Please, can you bring him back?"

Eld examined the dog's remains. As the boy said, he'd been searching for Eld for a long time.

The dog's front paws were missing, and through long experience, Eld could tell that some of the interior organs had already started decaying. Some of the dog's flesh had been cut away—likely an amateurish attempt to remove mold.

Eld felt a familiar tug at his heart.

This was why he had become a necromancer in the first place—to ease the pain of loss, to bring joy back into people's lives.

"I'll do my best, Ellis," Eld began, but before he could continue, a booming voice interrupted.

"Absolutely not!"

The crowds moving back and forth parted as one of the Great Old Ones from earlier lumbered forward. This one had a pink elongated squid-like head that poked right through its black cultist-like robes. "This is an outrage! A powerless mortal, here in our sacred haven? The ferrymen are supposed to prevent such intrusions!"

Talbot snickered. "You know there are other ways to get to the underworld now, right? This isn't Year Zero, buddy. There's the Ethereal Elevator, the Nightmare Steed, the Underbelly Sewers…hells, didn't you see those flying horses earlier?"

The tentacled monster wasn't convinced.

"This is an outrage! I've been living in Necropolis for thousands of years!"

Every single one of the tentacles pointed at the boy, the undulating appendages quivering with unholy indignation.

"And each year, you *students* make it worse. I was already furious when we let in necromancers and warlocks! Those are barely more than upjumped humans if you ask me. But this…this is just too much! If we let the top siders in, who knows what will happen next?"

Eld stepped protectively in front of Ellis, who quivered in fear.

The boy had braved much to be here, but a screeching eldritch abomination was enough to unnerve even seasoned fighters.

But then Lea stepped forward. Eld could tell that she was stared, but her eyes darted from the bundle on the boy's back towards the Great Old One.

With each step, she seemed to grow larger, more confident and commanding. Her shadow seemed to swell and darken behind her until it'd grown into a massive yawning void. "Surely, exceptions can be made? This boy has shown great bravery and resourcefulness to come this far."

The Great Old One's many eyes swiveled towards Lea, a flicker of recognition and fear passing through them.

It started to bow, and Eld thought their worries were over.

But then the squid-head caught itself, standing its ground.

"No exceptions!" it thundered. "Too many of our traditions have already been eroded. This one, at least, must stand. The boy must leave immediately or die!"

Based on the leering hatred in its eyes, Eld knew better than to test it. As impressive was Lea looked, she couldn't actually control her magic.

He waved his hands, quieting Talbot before the poltergeist could escalate the situation further.

Ellis crumpled next to Max's remains, tears welling in his eyes. "But you don't understand! I've come so far, worked so hard!" His words tumbled out in a frantic rush. "I snuck past a three-headed dog, descended through all of the abyssal pits, made deals with angels and daemons alike, and covered myself in rot to disguise my living scent. I've protected Max's body for weeks, fighting off scavengers and worse!"

"*You* need to leave," Eld said. "But Max doesn't. I promise—I'll take care of Max. Once he's healed and reanimated, I'll find a way to return him to you."

The boy sniffled, looking up at Eld. "You promise?"

"I promise." Eld nodded and extended his hand. "Now, can you tell me exactly when Max died, and what injuries he sustained?"

Ellis started to recount Max's final days, Eld knelt beside the boy, his hand gently resting on the tattered bundle containing Max's remains.

"And then on the third day of fever, Max just didn't wake up." Ellis motioned to the remains.

Eld nodded solemnly. "I'm sorry, Ellis. Can you tell me more about the fever? Any unusual symptoms?"

Considering the time since the dog's death, it was important to separate the decay process from the actual cause of death.

While Ellis described Max's illness, Lea watched Eld intently. "You're really good with kids."

Eld glanced up, catching her eye and smiling. "It's part of the job. You know, consoling clients and all that."

"I think it's more than that. You truly care," Lea replied.

Talbot's voice drifted from the harp. "Oh, for the love of all that's unholy. Are we going to stand around all day, or are we going to help this kid? I'm getting hungry and the refectory is serving goat hearts and bull eyes."

The Great Old One, who had been hovering nearby, suddenly fixed its gaze on Eld and Lea. Its tentacles writhed. "Most unusual. A being of such power, *interested* in a mortal necromancer with such little power? Inconceivable!"

Lea turned to the creature. Despite her blush, her lips curled with irritation. "Do you have something to say?"

The Great Old One recoiled. "N-no, great one. I...I must be mistaken. Carry on with your...mortal interactions."

"Then begone!"

As she spoke, Lea's voice seemed to emanate from everywhere. Her eyes turned bright purple and she hovered slightly off the ground.

Though they were in the middle of a crowded market, the entire place fell quiet. The squid-head bowed hastily before slinking away, muttering to itself.

"What was that about?" Eld asked. He could hardly tell if that was a command or a spell.

Lea landed on the ground. As she blinked, the eyes faded from her eyes and she shrugged. "I...I don't know."

She shook her head. "Let's just get Ellis to one of the exits, then help him."

Eld nodded. "Yeah."

They walked through Necropolis, Ellis turned to Eld, nervously biting his lip. "So, Mr. Eld, how many pets have you brought back?"

"Just Eld is fine, and I've lost count, honestly. It's got to be over a thousand."

"Wow..." Ellis breathed. "So you'll be able to bring Max back too?"

"There's no guarantees," Eld said. "But I promise that I'll do my best."

Ellis gulped nervously, then nodded. As they continued walking, he continued bombarding Eld with questions, undoubtedly to get his mind off of Max.

"What's the biggest animal you've reanimated?"

"Maybe a dragon, though I did fix up a manticore recently."

"Can zombie pets learn new tricks?"

Shuck answered that one for Eld, letting out a happy bark and wagging his tail affirmatively.

Leaving Necropolis behind, they continued till they made it a large cavernous wall and stopped at the base of a tall switchback that climbed the entire height, disappearing into the clouds above.

"This is an exit," Talbot said. "Probably one of the safest ones. It takes a long time, but you'll get out."

"We'll go part of the way with you," Eld said. "But you'll have to be on your own after. We have school."

"Speaking of which, why don't you entertain us with the tale about how you got down here, kid," Talbot said from the harp.

"It all started when Max got sick," Ellis began. "The local chirurgeon couldn't do anything, and then Max didn't make it. I'd heard stories about you, Eld, the miracle worker who could bring pets back from the dead."

Eld raised an eyebrow. "How did you even know where to start?"

Ellis grinned. "Well, I went to a fortune teller and she told me you were in the underworld. So then I had to sneak onto a ship because the only entrance I'd ever heard of was at Mount Hekla. I knew it was just a rumor, but I had to try. I hid in a crate of fish for weeks."

He shuddered, clutching his nose with both hands. "Ugh, I can still smell it sometimes."

Talbot floated by, shaking his head and placing his solidified palm on the boy's shoulder. "Kid, trust me, that's nothing compared to the stench of the undead. You get used to it eventually."

Lea laughed at Talbot's almost satirically feigned worldliness. "I'm supposedly older than you, Talbot, and I'm still not used to it. Go on, Ellis. What happened next?"

"After the ship, I had to cross these huge mountains." Ellis gestured wildly, throwing out his arms. "There was snow everywhere, and the wind howled like a banshee." He caught himself, turning through the streets of Necropolis. "No offense if there are any banshees around. I suppose I have to be careful here."

"Oh, *some people* have to be very careful around banshees," Talbot snickered.

"How did you manage to keep Max preserved during all this?" Eld asked, hurriedly changing the subject.

Ellis raised his hand to scratch at a fresh scar across his cheek. "That was the hardest part. I had to fight off all sorts of creatures that wanted to…"

He stared at Max's body and shuddered. The words were too painful for him to even say them.

"Well, you know. There was this pack of ghouls that almost got him."

"Ghouls?" Lea asked. "How did you escape them?"

"I tricked them!" Ellis beamed. "Told them I knew where a much better feast was. Led them right into a cave full of really angry goatmen!"

Talbot snorted. "Kid, you've got some serious guts. Or a serious death wish. Maybe both."

"The trickiest part was fooling one of the ferrymen. I covered myself in mud and rotting plants, and practiced my best zombie impression."

Lea dipped her chin and her jaw dropped. "You managed to trick a boatman? That shouldn't be possible."

"Yeah, he was an old guy. With tentacles. It seemed like he didn't see or smell too good."

Eld just shook his head. "I don't even know where to start!" he exclaimed.

Talbot was right.

This kid had both serious guts and a serious death wish. It must have been the same Great Old One ferryman who'd brought them to Necropolis last time, and if the squid-head was anything to go by, that stunt wouldn't have ended very well, if Ellis had been discovered.

Ellis gulped. "I don't know. I just really needed to get here. For Max."

Talbot spoke up. "Well, kid, I've got to hand it to you. That's one heck of a story. You'd make a pretty good poltergeist if you weren't, you know, alive."

Eld placed a hand on Ellis's shoulder. "It was incredibly brave, what you did. But also incredibly dangerous. Promise me you won't take risks like that again. Once you get out of here, I need you to *stay* out of here."

As Eld spoke, he felt a brief chill and glanced behind them.

Nobody was there...

Nobody but Lea and Talbot, that was.

Eld had thought the chill had come from some of the Great Old Ones following him, but as he thought about it more, he realized it might have come from Lea herself.

He shook his head, resolving to deal with that later.

"Look," Eld said. "I promise I'll help Max. Just make sure you stay safe."

Ellis gulped and nodded, but Eld could tell that he needed more assurance.

"I gave you my word," Eld solemnly intoned. "And I intend to keep it. When he's restored, I'll bring him to you."

They reached a cave halfway up the stairs and paused, Eld knelt once more. "I promise I'll take good care of Max. Now what you need to do to get out of here is—"

Lea stepped forward. "I'll guide him back myself."

"Lea?" Eld asked.

She stared up into the darkness, an odd certainty in her voice. "I remember the way, somehow."

"It's a two week trip," Talbot said. "It might be best to…"

"No, I need to do this," Lea said. "I just…I think walking this path will help me regain my memories."

Eld raised an eyebrow but nodded, he wasn't about to question her. Lea's past was a mystery he didn't understand. It was best to let her act freely. And in a way, this might be all for the best. With Grimthorpe looking for her, she couldn't take the ferry, but she would be safer Topside, at least for now. "Alright then. May the moon light your path."

He watched as Lea and Ellis disappeared into the mists of the caverns. When she turned to wave goodbye, a gentle warmth spread through Eld's chest. They weren't touching hands, but for a brief moment, Eld could have sworn he heard his heart beating.

Talbot and Eld descended the stairs back into town and towards the carriages.

Eld's attention was on the task ahead. Not only did he have to reanimate and repair Max, but he also needed to upgrade Franky to break into Grimthorpe's office.

Fortunately, the repaired horses were even faster than before, and even McGrath wasn't hubristic enough to try the jet mode again.

As soon as they got back to their room, Eld jerked his head at the door.

"I'm going to need some privacy for this," he said.

Talbot poked his head out of the harp and groaned, but Eld raised an eyebrow.

"You are going to be possessing Franky for a bit, so I'm pretty sure you want me to do a good job."

Talbot let out a dramatic sigh.

"Fair enough, I suppose we do need some quality control."

He waved his hand at Shuck.

"Come along Shuck…maybe I can find a nice unclaimed bone for you to gnaw on."

Shuck shook his head, his eyes locked on Max's small body.

"You want to stick with them?" Talbot protested.

"Well, unlike you, Shuck knows how to stay quiet," Eld joked.

With an exaggerated wail of protest, Talbot vanished through the floor.

Eld stepped inside, took a deep breath, then closed the door behind him.

This was what he lived for—the delicate work of bringing life back to the lifeless. It wasn't just about the magic. It was about the craftsmanship, the attention to detail that made each reanimation unique.

He began by carefully examining Max's remains, noting every injury and sign of decay.

While the fever was what had killed the dog, the sheer amount of time that had elapsed—plus the damage during the trip—was the real barrier here. Even if Eld brought Max back to life, he wouldn't be able to move comfortably. The thought of Max not getting to play with Ellis broke Eld's heart, and he made sure to evaluate everything extra carefully.

When he was confident in his assessment, he set to work, his knife flying as he whittled new wooden legs to replace the missing ones. Eld had always had a knack for woodworking—it required the same steady hand and eye for detail as his necromancy.

Hours passed as Eld worked tirelessly, putting everything he knew and everything he had learned at Bathurst to use. He murmured incantations over Max's body, channeling necromantic energy into the dog's body. Slowly but surely, fur began to regrow, damaged tissue knit itself back together, and the wooden legs he had crafted began to meld seamlessly with what remained of Max's limbs.

It was well past midnight when Eld finally sat back, exhausted but satisfied.

Max lay on the workbench, his chest rising and falling with un-life. The dog's eyes flickered open, glowing with a soft, ethereal light.

"Welcome back, boy." Eld scratched behind Max's ears.

The zombie dog's tail thumped against the table, and Eld could see it looking around for its owner. Shuck bounded forward, eager to temporarily take the young dog under his wing.

There was no time to rest, though.

Reanimating Max was important, but Eld also owed a serious debt to an old friend.

After a brief break to stretch out his tired limbs and steady his hands, Eld turned his attention to Franky, carefully attaching the new components he had purchased. The centipede would need to be faster, stealthier, and more resilient if it was going to infiltrate Grimthorpe's office.

With the final turtle shell piece in place, Eld stepped back to admire his handiwork. Franky was now part centipede, part chameleon, part turtle, and all undead.

The hybrid creature skittered across the workbench, testing out its new body.

"You know, Franky, most people would say a giant bug like you shouldn't be possible." Eld carefully attached the new legs. "But we're not most people, are we? With my special formula and your undead strength, we're rewriting the rules."

Franky's antennae eagerly twitched in response.

"Just be careful and take your time getting used to everything," Eld said. "And make sure that you're still, well, you."

Eld knew from experience that incorporating parts from different creatures could lead to changes in personality and behavior. It was always a bit of a gamble, but considering Franky's damaged body, he didn't have much of a choice.

After a few minutes of experimentation, Franky turned to Eld and gave what could only be described as a nod. No words were exchanged, but after decades of living together, Eld understood perfectly. Franky was ready.

"Alright, old friend. Let's see what you can do. We're going to need a lot of practice until you're ready to infiltrate Grimthorpe's office. I really don't want a repeat of next time."

In response, Franky's body began to shimmer.

The chimera centipede cycled through a kaleidoscope of colors and patterns, trying to find the perfect camouflage. At the end, Franky had vanished—almost.

Eld could still hear him moving as his new mechanized legs clattered against the ground, and every so often, the air would shimmer and he'd reappear again.

Still, it was very good for a first try.

Eld let out a whistle. Despite their unsavory nature, the mole men's advice had been perfect. "Impressive, Franky. Very impressive."

"We're still going to have to work on it though. It'll take a bit before we're ready."

Franky chittered in agreement and continued practicing.

Meanwhile, a soft whine drew Eld's attention.

Shuck and Max, the newly reanimated dog, were playing in the corner of the room. He walked over and knelt between the two undead canines, scratching them behind their ears. "You two are getting along well, aren't you? Max, you're looking better already. I think we'll be able to get you back to Ellis soon."

As if on cue, Bart poked his head out of Eld's pocket, and Spinderella, his newest eight-legged friend, climbed onto his shoulder. Surrounded by his companions, Eld felt a sense of calm settle over him.

This was what he was meant to do, what he was good at.

"Alright, gang." Eld stretched and stood up. "I think it's time we—"

His words were cut short by a frantic chittering sound.

Franky had reappeared on the workbench. But something was different. The centipede was making strange movements with its mandibles.

"F-Frr…" Franky chittered, the sound unlike anything Eld had heard before. "Frie…Friend…"

Eld's jaw dropped. "Franky? Are you talking?"

The centipede cleared its throat—or whatever passed for a throat in his bizarre fused anatomy. "Hello," he finally managed.

Despite the insectoid clicks, his voice sounded almost human.

Eld stumbled backward, nearly tripping over Shuck.

His mind raced.

Had Talbot already possessed Franky?

No, the poltergeist was nowhere near here.

"This is impossible." Eld sank into his chair. "Franky, how are you doing this?"

Before the centipede could respond, a sharp knock at the door made Eld jump.

"Eld? You in there?" Wolfgang's gruff voice called out.

Still reeling from Franky's unexpected vocalization, Eld stumbled to the door and opened it.

Wolfgang stood there with Orlando peering judgmentally out from behind him.

"You missed practice," Wolfgang said bluntly.

Eld closed his eyes and sucked air through his teeth as if in pain. He ran a hand through his hair, suddenly remembering his commitment to the Combat Club. "I'm so sorry, Wolfgang. I got caught up in a project and lost track of time."

Orlando stepped forward, his aristocratic features twisted in a sneer. "Allow me to say what Wolfgang won't. You've been slacking. The tournament is in two weeks. If you can't be bothered to show up for practice, perhaps we should find a replacement."

Eld felt a pang of guilt. He had been so focused on his personal mission that he had neglected his other responsibilities. "You're right. Both of you. I'll be down for practice in a minute, I promise."

As Wolfgang and Orlando nodded and turned to leave, Eld glanced back at his workbench.

Franky had disappeared again, leaving Eld to wonder if he had imagined the whole thing.

"This just keeps getting stranger and stranger," he muttered, grabbing his combat gear. "Well, I guess a fight is a way to clear my mind. Plus, I do owe my team."

With one last look at his menagerie of undead companions, Eld left for his practice session.

Chapter 24

Theological Questions for Etymologists

Over the next week, the hubbub of the Tournament of Shadows completely took over the school, and as one of the main competitors, Eld had absolutely no chance of sneaking around.

The entire school had their eyes on him.

Professor McGrath, of all people, had taken a particular interest in the Grave Robbers. Judging by the fervor of his questions, Eld couldn't help but feel like the leprechaun mad scientist had placed a large bet he couldn't afford to lose.

Of course, nobody was more fastidious than Wolfgang. The werewolf was doggedly determined to keep Eld from missing another practice, and he kept popping up out of nowhere to force Eld into surprise sparring sessions that *really* just felt like getting assaulted in the halls.

To make matters worse, Lea was still on her trip, guiding Ellis out of the underworld.

The days leading up to the tournament blurred together in a whirlwind of classes and a stack of homework as Eld found himself juggling more responsibilities than he had ever imagined possible.

Between covering for Lea's absence in classes, completing her homework alongside his own, and maintaining his rigorous training schedule with the Combat Club, he barely had time to breathe.

But as tired as he was, Eld's most important task was still preparing Franky for his upcoming mission. He did not want a repeat of last time. His friend was back and he wanted to keep it that way.

Night after night—even the night before the tournament, long after the students of Bathurst had drifted off to sleep, Eld worked tirelessly with the reanimated centipede, if Franky could even be called a centipede anymore.

Centipedes usually didn't have turtle shells, chameleon scales, and mechanical limbs. And, of course, centipedes couldn't talk. At first, Eld had thought that he'd just been hearing things. Over the last few nights, Franky had corrected that misconception.

"Alright, Franky." Eld stifled a yawn. "Let's try that invisibility again. Remember, focus on blending with your surroundings."

Franky's legs skittered across the desk as the centipede concentrated. Slowly, his body began to shimmer, once again completely fading from view.

"Excellent!" Eld perked up, scooting to the edge of his seat. "Now, let's work on maintaining it while moving. And make sure you stay quiet too."

Franky took a few hesitant steps that gradually turned quieter and quieter. Soon, he was silent as a whisper.

As for his invisibility, there were only a few faint shimmers in the air, mostly when he shifted from one environment to another.

"You're getting there Franky," Eld said. "Just a bit more practice and I think we'll be ready."

"Franky do good?" the centipede asked.

His voice was still a bizarrely human insectoid chitter.

Eld grinned leaned forward, petting Franky on the head. "Very good, Franky. You're making incredible progress—both at sneaking around and, well, just at talking."

"Okay. I keep going."

Franky went back to practicing and Talbot materialized beside Eld. "You know I'm starting to feel a bit obsolete here. Wasn't I supposed to be the one possessing our little spy?"

Turning to his friend, Eld offered him a sheepish grin. "About that Talbot, I don't think we'll need you to possess Franky after all. He's made incredible progress on his own."

Talbot raised an ethereal eyebrow. "I suspected as much. But how exactly did our multilegged friend suddenly develop the ability to talk and think for himself? Last I checked, centipedes weren't known for their sparkling conversation."

"That's just it. I'm not entirely sure. It's like Franky's evolving on his own somehow." Eld shook his head and clicked his tongue. "I'm not surprised though. I've had Franky since I was a little kid and he's always been sharp."

That simplistic explanation wasn't nearly enough for Talbot. This was one of the rare situations where Talbot was actually interested—though to be fair to him, a talking centipede was one of a kind, even in Eld's experience.

The poltergeist drifted closer, peering at Franky with newfound interest. "Evolving, you say? Care to elaborate on that, pet doctor?"

"Well, I have a few theories." Eld ran a hand through his disheveled hair, gathering his thoughts. "It could be that the fusion of different creature parts has created a sort of magical synergy. Or perhaps the repeated exposure to necromantic energy has awakened something within Franky's reanimated carapace. I've had to revive him a number of times now. Father and Cloudehill were never the biggest fans of pets—or pests, as they'd call them."

"Or," Talbot interjected, "You might not be talking to Franky at all. You've somehow managed to bind a fragment of a soul to our insectoid friend here."

The words hung in the air, heavy with implication.

Eld's brow furrowed as he considered, then dismissed the possibility.

"That doesn't make sense Talbot...I mean, Franky is still Franky."

Across the room, the chimeric centipede was still working on his invisibility. The centipede was just as hardworking, intelligent, and loyal as he'd been since Eld's childhood. In fact,

"Watch this," Eld said. "Hey Franky!"

"Yes?" the centipede asked, shimmering back into visibility.

"When was the first time I revived you?"

"Hm. Many years ago! Long time!" the centipede replied. "Hm...you found Cloudehill. Big bad Cloudehill. He was pulling off my legs. You scared him off. Or, well, Shuck scared him off. And you try to fix me up! But I was too damaged. So you revive me with book from spell. Or, well, I mean, spell from book."

Eld raised an eyebrow.

Franky was right, of course. That was exactly how they'd met.

But Eld wasn't surprised that Franky remembered. He was surprised by the centipede's increasingly human-like speech. Franky had spoken only single words before moving onto childlike grammatically incorrect sentences. But by the end there...

"I don't know about this," Talbot said. "Sure, he might remember. But that doesn't mean there isn't a piece of a soul involved."

"What do you mean?" Eld frowned.

"A soul doesn't always take over the body. Sometimes…well," Talbot joined his hands together into a fist. "What if Franky's soul and this other soul merged to create a new being?"

Eld started to speak, then paused.

He'd wanted to say that things didn't work that way—but just looking at Franky's body told Eld that he shouldn't be so sure. If Franky's body was a merged amalgam, why couldn't the same be true for his soul?

In fact, Eld had seen firsthand behavior changes from melding on new parts. A soul was another level entirely, but theoretically, it should be possible.

Talbot sensed Eld's uncertainty.

"You see what I'm saying, don't you?"

Eld sighed. "I don't know, Talbot. That's not something I've ever intentionally attempted. Placing a soul in another vessel…that takes a *lot* of magical power. Of course, I've heard about it—the professors are always going on about their more creative punishments. But that takes a lot of juice and usually only liches have that ability. Besides, where would I have even found the soul *from?*"

Talbot eyed Eld, then glanced over at Franky.

"You feel guilty," the poltergeist said. "You're *worried* you've bound a soul into him."

"Well, I mean, the ethical considerations alone…"

Talbot cut him off with a scoff. "Ethics? You're a necromancer, Eld. You routinely blur the line between life and death. Why draw the line at soul manipulation?"

Eld shook his head. "There's a difference between reanimating a body and meddling with the very essence of a being. If I've somehow bound a soul fragment to Franky, even unintentionally, I'm not sure how I feel about that."

"Well I'm not sure *he* minds," Talbot motioned towards Franky who seemed to be listening to their conversation, his antenna twitching.

Franky scuttled over to Eld and gently tapped his hand with his mandibles.

"Do I have a soul?" the centipede asked.

Eld turned to Franky. Despite his worries, the centipede's innocent question made him chuckle.

"That's a question for a philosopher Franky, not some pet doctor. If you made me guess, you have a soul, but it's the same one you had before. Who said that a centipede can't have a soul?"

He extended his arm, letting Franky climb up onto him. With his new mechanical parts and defensive upgrades, he was quite a bit heavier than before, but thanks to his Nocturnal Combat Club training, Eld had also gotten quite a bit stronger.

"I think I'm me," Franky said. "If I was someone else, I'd be a lot more worried about being stuck in a mechanized centipede."

Eld laughed. "You know what buddy? You're right. Whatever's happening, you're still you. That's what matters."

As the first rays of dawn began to peek through the window, Eld reluctantly called an end to their training session. With the tournament looming just hours away, he needed at least a few hours of sleep.

"Alright Franky. Time for bed. But get over here. There's just one last thing I need to do, just in case we face off against Mortimer tomorrow."

As Eld began modifying Franky's mechanical legs, the centipede chittered and giggled.

"He won't expect this."

"He certainly won't," Eld replied, finishing his work with a sigh. A true modification would have taken a much longer time, but as a one-time surprise, this was perfect.

Collapsing onto his bed, Eld's last thoughts before drifting off were of Lea.

He hoped she was safe, wherever she was, and he couldn't help but feel a pang of disappointment that she wouldn't be there to see him compete.

"Eld, you going to sleep now?" Franky chittered from the desk. "I'll keep watch. Make sure you keep safe. Don't want Wolfgang dragging you to one last practice."

Eld chuckled out a thank you before finally succumbing to exhaustion. At this point, Franky would be speaking better than Eld in a few days.

The next day, Eld awoke to the sound of raucous cheering. The tournament!

He jerked out of bed, quickly blinking the grogginess from his eyes.

Across the room, Talbot was still snoring casually, without a single care in the world.

"Well, that's not too bad," Eld muttered. "It means I'm not *that* late."

"You're not late at all Eld," Franky said, letting out a chittering robotic yawn. "There's forty minutes until the tournament begins, and you're not even the first match."

Eld pushed himself out of bed, waving his hand to call his pets to him.

"Shuck, Franky, Bart, Spinderella, it's showtime!"

The three smaller pets hopped into his cloak, sneaking into their usual positions as Shuck bounded eagerly behind him.

Before long, Eld was back in the utterly packed main halls.

"Pardon me, pardon me," Eld said, gently pushing his way through the crowd.

It was slow going moving through the entire morass of people, but as more and more people realized who Eld was, they quickly let him go through. Freed of the crowd, Eld hurried to the tournament hall, buoyed by a mixture of cheers and confused remarks.

"*That guy* is in the tournament? He doesn't look too tough. Is he some kind of spellcaster?"

"Man, you *don't* want to mess with his pets. I heard they can grow as big as a cemetery!"

As they finally reached their destination, Shuck let out an excited bark.

The tournament hall buzzed with excitement as students and spectators filed in.

Banners representing the different teams fluttered in the enchanted breeze, and the air crackled with barely contained magical energy.

A shambling stitched zombie with four arms wearing the school robes—with a hastily amended black sun stitched over the bat shield—shambled over to Eld.

"Back here, back here," he said. "I'll take you to the competitor's waiting area."

Wolfgang and Orlando were already there, the typically tough duo looking much more nervous than they would have wanted to admit to themselves. Though it wasn't the time, Eld couldn't help but wonder what they thought about the zombie's robes.

"What do you make of this black sun thing?" Eld asked. "You know, over the bat shield."

"*What?*" Wolfgang replied.

From his response, it was obvious he hadn't been thinking about it at all.

"By the Brood Mother's Vengeful Fangs," Orlando cursed. "If you're worried about that, you really aren't ready to compete. The school changes its logo all the time. It seems like every single new headmaster thinks they've got a split personality as a visionary artist."

Eld nodded, then shook off his concerns.

But just as soon as his worries vanished, he caught sight of his parents in the crowd.

His mother waved enthusiastically, but just like before, Eld's father had skipped the event.

"Let's do this," Eld said. At this point, he had no interest in impressing his father. He'd accepted that it would never happen. His only goal was to do his best, for the new friends and companions he'd met at Bathurst.

Wolfgang's savage smile nearly split his face in two. "This is what we've been training for. You ready to show these posers what *real* combat looks like!"

Orlando sniffed disdainfully, adjusting his immaculate robes. "Speak for yourself, wolf-boy. Some of us don't need to resort to brute force to win."

Eld managed a smile at his teammates' bickering. "We've got some tough competition out there. It'll take all our talents to win."

Just then, Mortimer and his team sauntered past, shooting smug looks in their direction. "Better say your goodbyes to the trophy now," Mortimer sneered. "It'll be the closest you ever get to it."

Before Eld could reply, a hush fell over the arena.

Professor Grimthorpe had taken the center stage, his voice magically amplified to reach every corner of the vast space.

"Welcome, one and all, to Bathurst Academy's Tournament of Shadows!" Grimthorpe's words echoed through the arena, met with thunderous applause. "Today, we witness the culmination of months of training, as our most talented students compete for glory and honor! Unlike the earlier rounds, these will be three-on-three team battles!"

But as Grimthorpe continued his opening speech, Eld caught a faint glimmer of shadow in the crowd. As the portal of darkness widened, his attention was drawn to a familiar figure sitting behind the headmaster.

His father, Eldritch Sr.

The lich promptly engaged himself in an intense conversation with Professor McGrath.

Eld couldn't help but notice the bitter expression on both men's faces. Something wasn't going to plan.

But then Grimthorpe's voice cut through Eld's thoughts like a chainsaw through flesh.

"And now, let the Tournament of Shadows begin!"

Chapter 25

The Tournament of Shadows

For the next few hours, Eld and his team fought their way through increasingly difficult matches, their coordination improving with each round. Wolfgang's raw power, Orlando's precision, and Eld's innovative necromancy proved to be a formidable combination.

Their first big challenge came in the quarterfinals, against the Spectral Speedsters—a team of wraiths. The spectral opponents were swift and elusive, but Eld had watched them battle in the earlier rounds and he'd prepared a perfect counter.

With a series of complex gestures—closely copied from one of Professor Hemlock's punishments—he summoned a swarm of ghostly insects, perfectly suited to combating the wraiths. The wraiths might have been able to avoid physical blows, but against other spectral opponents, they were rapidly overwhelmed, falling back with a series of surprised shrieks and shouts.

"Nicely done, Eld!" Wolfgang shouted.

With their greatest advantage disabled, the wraiths rapidly dissipated, surrendering the match.

As Eld turned towards the cheering crowd, his eyes met Grimthorpe's.

The headmaster had a greedy look in his eyes—one that was far too greedy for a teacher examining a prized student. And to make matters worse, his father leaned over, whispering something in Grimthorpe's ear.

Eld hadn't expected his father to be proud—he knew Eldritch Sr. too well for that. But he wasn't even reacting to Eld's victory at all. The two liches were just muttering together, the glinting fires in their eyes telling Eld that their conversation was clearly conspiratorial.

It reminded Eld of the letter in his pocket—the letter he *still* hadn't figured out how to open. Perhaps he could get Wolfgang or Orlando's help with that, but for now, he had to focus on the tournament.

After their conversation about the new school robes, Eld knew that his teammates were thinking solely of victory.

Quickly averting his gaze, Eld retreated to the competitor's waiting area. But as he waited, he couldn't shake the feeling that the pair of liches was still watching him, not even bothering to keep an eye on the match.

In fact, when the quarterfinals ended, Professor Hemlock had to pointedly tap Grimthorpe on the shoulder. It was only then that the headmaster shrugged off Eldritch Sr., hurrying to the stage.

"For the semi-finals, the matches will grow more difficult," Grimthorpe declared. "Behold!"

The battlefield transformed with a wave of his hand.

A circular platform detached from the ground, floating slowly into the sky. Moments later, swirling mist began billowing from the floor, obscuring everything beneath the platform.

An excited squeaking chitter echoed through the waiting area as Professor Hemlock's familiars—a whole horde of bats and mosquitos—materialized into the waiting area.

Presumably, that was how the competitors would be getting up to the stage.

Grimthorpe's voice boomed across the space, "Remember, combatants, victory is achieved by either forcing your opponents out of the ring or incapacitating them. There are no other rules. And for our first match, the Grave Robbers will be facing off against the Scions!"

The Scions.

That was Mortimer's team.

"Let's get going," Eld said.

He hopped onto the swarm of flying pests, which shifted to accommodate his weight.

"Any chance I could bring Shuck up there too?" Eld asked, nodding at the big dog.

The mosquitos and bats buzzed angrily.

Either they thought Shuck was too big of an advantage, or they just didn't want to carry him.

Wolfgang raised an eyebrow, then shook his head. "I don't know about this one, but if you're confident, I'm sure they can get the job done."

He jerked his head at Orlando. "You coming, rich boy?"

The vampire scoffed. "I don't know about the insects, but my family is just as well-versed with bats as any other noble house."

The swarm brought them up to the stage.

When they disembarked, the trio stood back-to-back, facing off against Mortimer's team—Vlad the vampire, Erik the drowned zombie, and, of course, Mortimer himself.

The air crackled with tension as both sides sized each other up.

"Begin!" Grimthorpe crowed.

Without any warning, Mortimer's hand shot forward, a stream of sickly green energy erupting from his fingertips. "Taste oblivion, pet doctor!"

Eld ducked.

The spell sizzled past his ear, leaving a faint hint of brimstone. This was nothing like his usual flames. The sheer power alone…

If Eld hadn't ducked, his head would have been evaporated on the spot. Where in all the hells had Mortimer found a spell like that?

Before Eld could even process what was happening, Erik charged, letting out a gurgling growl.

"Wolfgang!" Eld cried, falling back.

Wolfgang charged forward, raising his twin short swords. He engaged Erik the Drowned, the clash of metal on metal ringing out as Erik parried with his longsword.

Meanwhile, Orlando was locked in combat with Vlad—vampire versus vampire. Vlad's hands dripped with crimson energy as he wove patterns of blood magic.

"Your arcane tricks are no match for cold steel!" Orlando cried. He swung his claymore through the air as he went on the offensive, cutting through Vlad's crimson defenses.

Eld wanted to help, but he was quickly forced back by Mortimer's searing white-hot flames. The fireballs twisted through the air, and all Eld could do was avoid being burnt to cinders.

"Let's see how you handle this, pet doctor!" Mortimer sneered, his fingers weaving patterns through the air as he manipulated the flaming orbs. Unlike Mortimer's usual attacks, the fireballs remained in existence, chasing Eld across the stage.

In response, Eld reached into his pocket, pulling out Bart before quickly channeling his necromantic energy into his tiny companion.

Bart grew to the size of a large dog, his red eyes fixed on Mortimer.

The rat charged at Mortimer, forcing the night-kin to break off his spell and defend himself instead. With his concentration broken, the flames stopped pursuing Eld and dissipated.

Now it was Eld's turn to draw up a spell.

He rapidly traced ropes and chains, hoping to ensnare Mortimer just like he'd snared Cloudehill back in the family manor, but his spell was interrupted by the battle between two hulking muscular atrocities, who barreled straight between Eld and Mortimer like they weren't there at all.

"Die, you filthy mutt," Erik growled.

He slammed his sword viciously, like it was some kind of club.

Wolfgang's short swords were a blur as he fended off Erik's relentless assault. "You're all washed up, drip!" Wolfgang taunted, scoring a hit that sent a spray of foul water from Erik's shoulder.

Right when Eld prepared a second spell, he was interrupted yet again, this time by the two vampires.

Crimson tendrils lashed out from Vlad's hands, trying to ensnare Orlando's claymore. "Your dark arts will not prevail!" Orlando grunted, his blade glowing with a counter-spell as he fought to break free.

By then, Mortimer had gotten back to his feet.

His hands glowed with the same sickly green light as before, but this time, it was very faint, slowly building with every one of Mortimer's gestures.

The first time Mortimer had used that spell, he must have prepared it ahead of time as a surprise attack.

But Eld knew from his own practice experience that in a fight like this, there was no room for complex spells that required so many gestures.

Swiftly, Eld pulled out his dagger, whispering a spell to infuse the blade with necromantic strength. "Bart, distraction maneuver!"

The oversized zombie rat scampered between Mortimer's legs, throwing him off balance. Eld seized the opportunity, closing the distance and slashing with his empowered dagger.

Mortimer howled in pain and fury as the blade left a smoking gash across his chest. He snarled and his hands glowed with fiery energy, but Eld had another pet at his disposal—and he'd prepared for this moment just last night.

Franky burst from Eld's cloak, his mechanical legs whirling.

Before Mortimer could react, the cyborg centipede sprayed icy cold water from the nozzle Eld had installed in one of its legs, dousing out Mortimer's attack. With his hands covered in water, he couldn't conjure any more flames.

The pyromancer nervously glanced around for backup, but none was coming.

Across the platform, Wolfgang had gained the upper hand against Erik. With a series of strikes, he disarmed the waterlogged zombie and kicked him hard, sending Erik stumbling over the edge.

Orlando finally broke through Vlad's defenses. His claymore swept in a high arc, catching the vampire off guard and sending him staggering backwards into the misty pit below.

Mortimer found himself alone, backed against the edge of the platform.

Eld advanced with his dagger, Bart at his heels. Wolfgang flanked from one side, his short swords at the ready, while Orlando approached from the other, claymore ready to strike.

"It's over, Mortimer." Eld jabbed his dagger towards Mortimer. "Yield or take a dive. Your choice."

It looked like Mortimer might continue fighting.

But then his shoulders slumped in defeat. "I yield."

A horn blared, signaling the end of the match. Grimthorpe's voice echoed once more, "Victory goes to the Grave Robbers! They will advance to the finals!"

As the adrenaline of battle faded, Eld felt a wave of exhaustion wash over him.

He dismissed Bart's enlargement with a wave, the rat shrinking back to its normal size and scurrying into his pocket.

Wolfgang clapped Eld on the back hard enough to make him stagger. "Awesome work out there!"

Orlando allowed himself a small smile. "I suppose your unorthodox methods have their uses, Blackwood."

Eld caught sight of Mortimer, as he made his way off the platform before helping Erik up from the side of the pit. The look of disbelief and frustration on Mortimer's face gave Eld some small satisfaction, piercing through his worries about his father and Grimthorpe.

"This isn't over," Mortimer hissed as he stormed past. His glowing eyes blazed with flames as he shot Eld an angry glare. "You got lucky, that's all."

The other semifinal bout was between Lilith's Banshee Bunch and the Mutant Menagerie.

Lilith fought like a woman possessed, ending the fight in moments. A sonic scream sent a man with crab pincers falling straight off the platform and into the burbling mist.

"This isn't good," Eld sighed. "She's going right for me when we start the fight."

"Maybe we can use that to our advantage," Wolfgang observed. "She's their best fighter--

"I doubt it," Orlando said. "Remember? They switched back to individual matches for the finals."

"Right, right," Wolfgang said, blinking and scratching his head. "I took a tough blow to the head in the last fight, if you remember…that whole thing is a blur to me."

The arena fell silent as Grimthorpe's voice boomed across the space. "Ladies and gentlemen, we've reached the final match of the Tournament of Shadows! Facing off today are the Banshee Bunch versus the Grave Robbers!"

Cheers erupted from the crowd as the swarms of flying familiars brought both teams back to the opposite sides of the floating slab suspended over the misty pit.

Grimthorpe continued, "The rules for the final are as follows, Each team will compete in three one-on-one matches. Victory in each match is achieved only through incapacitation or ring-out. The team with the most individual victories will be crowned our champions. Fighters, prepare yourselves!"

Eld gulped. So they were back to one-on-one. And not only that, he noticed Lilith muttering to her team, pointing specifically at him.

"I, um…" Eld started.

"What?" Wolfgang asked.

"Good luck out there," Eld said, smiling.

He'd wanted to ask his teammates to switch with him, but he'd realized there was no need. As strong as Lilith was, Eld was confident in his preparation.

Wolfgang stepped forward first, cracking his knuckles as he faced off against his opponent from the Banshee Bunch, a green-skinned woman wearing the same midnight blue and silver robe as Lilith.

In addition to her screeches, the woman also carried a pulsating white staff. Just looking at the weapon made Eld's mind spin—it seemed to be stuffed to the brim with contracted spirits.

The match was intense, with Wolfgang's dual short swords clashing against his opponent's spectral attacks. In the end, Wolfgang's raw strength and agility won out, as he managed to force his opponent over the edge of the platform.

"Victory to the Grave Robbers!" Grimthorpe announced, as the crowd roared its approval.

Next up was Orlando, his claymore resting on his shoulder ready to swing. His match was a closer affair, with both fighters showcasing impressive skill.

Despite Orlando's best efforts, his opponent's swift movements and sonic attacks proved too much. As the battle teetered on the brink, a well-timed banshee wail sent Orlando stumbling backwards, right over the platform's edge and into the mists.

"The Banshee Bunch evens the score!" Grimthorpe's voice rang out. "It all comes down to this final match."

As Eld stepped onto the platform, his heart pounding, he locked eyes with Lilith across the arena.

Her rapier was at the ready, a determined glint in her eye.

"Ready to lose, backstabbing betrayer?" Lilith called out. Her voice trembled with anger.

"I said I was sorry, Lilith! I didn't have a choice!" Eld gripped his dagger tightly and channeled necromantic energy into the blade. "Mortimer and your zombie boy toy were going to kill me!"

Lilith's only response was clutching her rapier tighter as if she was imagining the handle was Eld's neck.

"The final duel will now commence. Remember, victory is achieved only through incapacitation or ring-out. Begin!" Grimthorpe shouted.

Lilith wasted no time, lunging forward with lightning speed. Her rapier whistled through the air as Eld barely managed to parry with his dagger. The clash of metal on metal rang out, sparks flying as necromantic energy met Lilith's strikes.

Eld was at a disadvantage in terms of reach.

He needed to close the gap.

Feinting left, he suddenly dove right, rolling under Lilith's guard and coming up behind her. His dagger slashed out, but Lilith twirled away, her silver hair whipping around her face.

"Nice try," she snarled.

She breathed in deep and unleashed a piercing wail that sent Eld staggering back, his ears ringing. He needed to neutralize Lilith's sonic attacks—thankfully, his previous escapades had already taught him what to do.

Eld weaved a pattern in the air with his free hand, and sent a wave of nullifying energy towards Lilith, creating a silencing bubble around her.

The spell hit its mark.

Lilith's next attempt at a banshee wail came out as nothing more than a whisper.

Her eyes widened in shock.

Seizing the moment, Eld reached into his pocket and pulled out Bart. With a surge of necromantic magic, the zombie rat grew larger. "Go, Bart!" Eld commanded.

Bart scampered towards Lilith, forcing her to divide her attention.

For the briefest of moments, it seemed Eld might gain the upper hand. But just like how Eld had seen Lilith fight—Lilith had seen Eld fight before too, and even without her sonic abilities, Lilith was a formidable fighter. Her rapier came faster and faster till her strikes were only flashes of silver, keeping both Eld and Bart at bay.

She parried Eld's dagger strikes while simultaneously avoiding Bart's snapping jaws and swiping claws. Not only that, she carefully kept out of range, making sure that Eld couldn't surprise her with Franky or Spinderella.

Slowly but surely, Lilith began to maneuver Eld towards the edge of the platform. Eld was focused on his assault and didn't realize how close he was to the boundary until he took one last step back and teetered precariously on the edge.

Lilith lunged at him, a triumphant grin on her face.

Eld barely ducked to the side, but he still had nowhere to run.

In a last-ditch effort, Eld commanded Bart to lunge at Lilith's legs. As she jumped to avoid the zombie rat, Eld saw an opening. He lurched forward, dagger aimed at Lilith's midsection.

But Lilith had anticipated the move.

Using Eld's momentum against him, she sidestepped at the last second. Her foot hooked behind Eld's ankle, and with a surprisingly gentle guiding hand, she sent him tumbling over the edge of the platform.

Eld's hand shot out, barely managing to grasp the edge of the arena.

He hung there, the misty pit yawning beneath him, as Lilith stood over him, rapier pointed at his face.

"It's over, Eld," she said. Her voice was barely audible due to the lingering effects of his silencing spell. "Let go."

She was right.

Eld let out a sigh of resignation and released his grip, plummeting into the mist below.

A horn blared, signaling the end of the match and Lilith's victory.

As Eld was magically transported back to the arena floor, he heard Grimthorpe announce, "Victory goes to Lilith Nightshade! The Banshee Bunch are this year's champion of the Tournament of Shadows!"

The crowd cheered as Lilith's teammates rushed to embrace her. Eld felt momentary disappointment, but he couldn't deny that Lilith had got the better of him.

As he approached to congratulate her, Lilith turned to face him.

"That was an okay fight," she said, her voice slowly returning. "That silencing spell was a clever move."

"Thanks, I got the idea from a certain husk mage," Eld said, lowering his voice as he extended his hand. "You were amazing out there. You earned this victory."

Lilith looked at his hand, an eyebrow quirked, before taking it.

Her grip was firm as she shook it. "Okay. I forgive you now."

Eld nodded. "I really am sorry about that. It really was a matter of life or death."

"Uh huh." She smirked and winked. "Sure or *maybe* it was just jealousy."

As the closing ceremony started and awards were distributed, Eld searched the crowd for his parents. To his mild surprise, his father had returned to his previous seat. His mother beamed with pride, while his father's expression remained unreadable.

Grimthorpe approached with a look on his face that Eld couldn't quite decipher. "Impressive performance, Mr. Blackwood. Your necromantic skills have improved significantly."

"Thank you, sir," Eld replied, wiping the sweat from his face.

Grimthorpe leaned in, dropping to a near whisper. "I look forward to seeing how you continue to develop your talents. *Interesting* that your friend didn't show up, isn't it?"

Before Eld could even reply, the headmaster had moved on, leaving Eld with a growing sense of unease.

Was this some kind of hidden message?

Had something happened to Lea?

"Not bad, Blackwood," Wolfgang growled. "Next year…next year we'll be back in the mix."

"It was my fault," Orlando angrily replied. "I should have been able to handle my foe."

"We'll be back," Eld said, smiling at his teammates. "But for now…I've got somewhere I need to be."

At first, Wolfgang looked like he wanted to force march Eld to a post-match party, but he must have seen something in Eld's eyes.

"Take care," he said.

Grimthorpe's words echoed in Eld's mind and he hastily returned to his dorm room.

Despite his exhaustion and soreness, he felt utterly invigorated.

The tournament might be over, but the real challenge was just beginning. Grimthorpe's odd behavior, his father's secretive conversations, the mystery surrounding Lea's absence…it all pointed to something big on the horizon.

"Franky, I think you're ready and it's time we started planning our next move. Tomorrow, we get into Grimthorpe's office."

"Yes," Franky whispered. "I'm ready. We will find the truth together and help Lea."

Eld reached off the bed without looking, patting Franky between his antenna. "That's right, buddy. We'll get to the bottom of this, whatever it takes."

As sleep began to claim him, Eld's last conscious thought was of Lea.

Chapter 26

The Problem with
Nominative Determinism

A massive black sun loomed high in the sky, its infinite void-like corona lashing out with countless tendrils of darkness.

The longer Eld stared into the darkness, the more he felt like he was going to go blind. Staring into the normal sun burned his eyes. Staring into the black sun withered them.

Suddenly, in the middle of the pure darkness, a being with cosmic eyes emerged, calling out to Eld from across the voice.

Lea's voice echoed, both distant and impossibly close. "Remember the oath."

"The…oath?" Eld asked.

His voice was weak and feeble, his throat parched and dry.

Lea didn't say anything in response.

And then Eld awoke with a start.

The dream was already fading but its urgency still lingered.

Franky scuttled over to him. "Eld, my friend, master, and companion. Are you alright?"

Taking a deep breath, Eld tried to center himself. "Yeah, Franky. I'm okay. Just a dream. A really bad dream."

"You know, dreams are often nothing more than a random chemical reaction in your brain," Franky chittered. "I read about it in one of the Old One's books."

Eld blinked.

So Franky was reading now too…

"This is getting weird," he said.

"I am simply enjoying speech!" Franky protested. "An entirely new world has opened up to my compound eyes."

Eld snorted. "Fine. Just make sure you're reading Grimthorpe's notes when you sneak into his office.

"Of course," Franky said.

His legs many legs twitched with excitement as he began to eagerly dash back and forth. "Today is the day, is it not?"

Eld nodded.

He'd already decided last night after seeing his father and Grimthorpe, but that dream only made things all the more urgent.

"Let's go," Eld said.

"I understand," Franky said. "I will be the epitome of stealth and deception."

Eld cast the oculus spell, connecting his vision to Franky's eyes. The world shifted dizzyingly as he suddenly saw through the centipede's perspective. He blinked rapidly, adjusting to the strange, multifaceted view.

Next, Eld added on a new spell he'd learned from Professor Hemlock. The vampiric professor was the premier authority on familiars, and Eld had taken full advantage of her classes.

Eld cast the psychic link spell, then closed his eyes and concentrated.

"Can you hear me, Franky?"

"Loud and clear, boss," came the reply in his mind. The reply was followed by a chittering cackle. "Oh, this is exciting. I sound just like a secret agent!"

"Technically, I suppose that's what you are," Eld replied.

On the way out the door, he gathered a few additional reagents and shoved them into his pockets, just in case the spell ran out.

Franky scuttled out of the room, squeezing under the space in the door.

Through their mental link, Eld guided him through the twisting corridors of Bathurst. Even with Franky's invisibility, Eld pushed the centipede to always stay in the shadows, slowly and steadily retracing the path to Grimthorpe's office. Despite the centipede's constant practice, Eld wanted to keep his friend extra safe.

As they approached the headmaster's domain, Eld had Franky pause just outside the door. "Remember, Franky, be extra careful. You won't be the only reanimated creature in there."

"Of course. A dragon and a hydra. Have no fear. I have conducted additional research into their sensory abilities."

Despite Franky's confidence, he heeded Eld's advice. Using his new chameleon-like abilities to blend with the surroundings, the centipede slowly slithered into the office.

After ducking through a crack in the hidden cabinet door, he emerged into Grimthorpe's inner sanctum.

The office was quiet, the dim light from the witchlight lanterns casting writhing shadows across ancient tomes and arcane artifacts. Franky moved slowly and as quietly as he could, his many eyes scanning for any sign of movement.

A low growl rumbled through the room.

Eld recognized the sound, Grimthorpe's reanimated creatures, his hydra and dragon.

"Franky, freeze!" Eld commanded mentally.

The centipede froze, its carapace undulating with shimmering magic as it blended with the stone-tiled floor.

The hydra's silhouette uncoiled from the shadows, its scale-covered flesh sloughing off in wet, rotten chunks as it moved. Each of its seven heads weaved through the air on long serpentine necks. Its jaws opened to reveal rows of yellowed, dagger-like teeth. A noxious green vapor seeped from between its fangs.

The dragon stretched, smoke curling from its nostrils as it creaked to life. Its bones ground against one another as it stood to join the hydra. Empty eye sockets blazed with an unholy, green fire.

Eld grit his teeth so hard that pain spiked through his mouth. He dared not even think too loudly, terrified that these abominations might somehow sense his presence through Franky.

The hydra's nearest head snaked down, so close that Franky's antennae recoiled in the current of its breath. Its forked tongue flicked out, tasting the air mere millimeters from the centipede's hiding spot. A globule of acidic saliva dripped from its maw, sizzling as it hit the stone floor just beside Franky.

Time stretched on slowly.

The seconds were suffocating.

Eld had no idea if the creatures could actually sense Franky or if they'd been disturbed by something else. The hydra's milky white eyes swept back and forth, back and forth. The dragon hissed and snarled, licking its lips.

Just when Eld thought his nerves might snap from the tension, the dragon let out a bone-chilling roar that shook the dust from the ceiling and sent icy fingers of fear crawling up his spine.

Both monstrosities turned their attention elsewhere and lumbered away deeper into Grimthorpe's sanctum.

Eld gasped, gulping in air as if he had been drowning.

Then, just when Eld thought they were in the clear, everything went black. The oculus spell had been canceled.

But why?

This wasn't like last time. The creatures were nowhere near Franky.

"Franky? Franky, can you hear me?" Eld called out mentally.

Silence was the only answer.

Eld frowned. What was happening?

He tried reaching out again, but all he felt through the psychic link was a pitch-black void. Gritting his teeth, Eld broke the connection, gasping as his consciousness fully returned to his own body.

Without thinking, he bolted from his room, racing towards Grimthorpe's office. His thoughts were filled with terrible possibilities.

Had Franky been caught?

Had he been completely destroyed this time?

What if Grimthorpe discovered their plan?

He was halfway there when reason finally caught up with him.

Eld skidded to a halt, bile in his throat. He did not want to lose his friend. He'd do anything to save him. But bursting into Grimthorpe's office would only expose them further. As it was, he could at least pretend there was some kind of mistake.

Feeling sick with worry, Eld trudged back to his room.

He paced anxiously, unable to shake the image of Franky being crushed in the hydra's jaws or incinerated by the dragon's necrotic breath.

But just as he was considering attempting another psychic connection, a familiar skittering sound reached his ears. Eld spun around to see Franky materialize on his desk.

"Franky!" Eld's legs gave out and he crumpled onto his bed, relief washing over him. "What happened? Are you alright?"

The centipede waved its antennae.

"Sorry about that, Eld. I had to go fully invisible. Even shut down my thoughts. Those monsters…it was like they could smell my mind."

"Smell your mind?" Eld asked.

He'd never heard of such a thing before.

"Yes," Franky replied. "They had strange magic. A spell of some kind. I'm sure of it."

Eld nodded, making a mental note for later.

He'd observed several flaws in the necrotic beast's construction, but he hadn't anticipated anything like that. If worst came to worst, he knew he'd have to fight Grimthorpe's pets, and he didn't want himself—or his prospective allies—to be caught off guard.

Eld sagged into his mattress, letting the tension drain from his body. "It's okay, buddy. I'm just glad you're safe. Did you find anything about Lea?"

Franky's legs tapped on the desk. "There were no books about Lea, at least not that I saw. But many of the books were moved or missing. When we went there previously, the shelves were full. Not anymore."

Eld frowned, processing this information.

"That's strange. But maybe…maybe he gave them to my father. They were certainly discussing something."

When Eld brought up his father, Franky suddenly stood up a little straighter. "Yes! About your father! I found something on the desk…maybe…maybe Grimthorpe *traded* those books to your father."

"Traded?" Eld asked. "What do you mean?"

"The Blackwood Familial Tome was on Grimthorpe's desk."

Eld's eyes went wide. "The Familial Tome? Here? But how?"

"There was a note from your father. It said that the tome was on loan and that he'd kill Grimthorpe if he revealed its contents."

Eld let out a long sigh. So that confirmed it then. Grimthorpe was in on this too.

"Alright. Well, it's a shame we didn't find anything…but we have a lot of work ahead of us."

"Wait," Franky said. "I read the contents."

Eld froze, so shocked that he was hardly able to get out his next few words. "How? How did you…"

"I learned to read, remember?"

"But how did you open it? It shouldn't be possible!"

Franky's antennae twitched and he reared up, rubbing some of his legs together. "Oh, now that's a very interesting story. You will be utterly shocked!"

"Franky." Eld groaned. "Now is not the time for dramatics. What did it say?"

"Bah," Franky protested. "You put up with everything the lazy ghost boy does…but once Franky wants to get dramatic, you rush him?"

"Just go on," Eld pleaded.

"Well. The pages I read concerned the Blackwood Family History. And it also explained why the book would automatically open up to me—because I'm a familiar empowered by the Blackwood family line's magic."

Eld blinked. "Wait. What do you mean? Familiar? Blackwood family line? But father said that the Blackwoods didn't use familiars!"

But then his breath caught in his throat as he thought of Hieronymus's defaced tome.

"Oh yes," Franky said, chittering eagerly. "The story is *very* different from what your father said. The Blackwoods weren't like your father at all. They weren't warriors—they were death druids. They were experts at making blood oaths and other pacts. They cooperated with animals and other nightkin, gently reanimating those who fell."

It took a while for Eld to comprehend what Franky was saying.

Death Druids.

Magical beings who balanced life and death...

Eld considered this, realization slowly growing on his features. It sounded so much like his own approach to necromancy, so different from his father's harsh, militaristic view and the necessity of becoming a lich.

It explained...

Well, everything.

Why the Blackwoods lived at the boundary of Topside and the Underworld.

Why the Blackwoods continued giving birth to human children.

Why there were so many ancient Blackwoods with their familiars buried alongside them.

Why Eld's father had barred him from seeing the Blackwood Familial Tome, ever since Eld had seen that incomplete Perfect Familiar Reanimation spell.

And most of all, it explained how he felt when he and Lea touched. It even explained that vision he'd seen. The manic Lea hadn't been trying to hurt anybody—no, she'd been creating a blood oath with a Blackwood family member.

"An old blood pact...that has to be it," Eld murmured. "Did you see anything else?"

"Not much. Much of the early book had been destroyed. Grimthorpe was using his magic to restore it, but it was *very* incomplete. I learned that the Blackwoods got their name from living in a dark forest long ago. They lived in peace with zombies and rotting animals."

Franky gestured at Eld with his many legs, mechanical and biological. "You are the heir to the Blackwoods. Not your father. And the Blackwood family oaths…they are bound to you now."

"What do you mean?" Eld asked.

"Due to their knowledge of both life and unlife, the Blackwoods are some of the only undead who can still bear children," Franky explained. "Each time a firstborn child is born the oath is passed down. But only first born. Like you, the first born of the first born of the first born of the first born of the first born of the—"

"Okay I get it," Eld interrupted, frowning. "So…well, what happened? We don't live in a forest anymore. We live in a manor. And, well…this sounds like it was time before the Old Ones."

"Yes, it was," Franky said. "A long time ago…before even the beginning of time…before the humans took over Topside and made Playstations and owned Carls Jr.'s, before their mistakes brought them back to the Medieval era…the living were very weak. The nightkin ruled beneath their black sun. Only the Blackwoods supported living in peace."

"My father…" Eld muttered. "He's always going on about the superiority of the undead. I thought it was just him being, well, him. But there's more to it, isn't there?"

Franky nodded sagely. "Eld's father very old. Maybe only few generations from ancient times. So maybe he remembers what happened. He wants to bring back the old days."

"Wait. How old are we talking about here?" Eld interjected.

"The book wasn't very clear," Franky replied. "And unlife can last a long time. I mean, both you and I are far past the normal lifespans for our species…" The centipede hybrid chittered thoughtfully. "I think the person who made the original pact—the pact with Lea…I think it may have only been three or four generations before you. And based on what the book said, he may have been one of the very first Blackwoods."

"Only three or four…" Eld muttered.

His mind reeled as he thought back to the Family Crypt.

He hadn't noticed it at the time, but it had only gone back a few generations…

His father, already ancient by most standards, was even older than he had realized. And this pact, whatever it was, stretched back to the very foundations of his family line.

"So my father sees our ancestor's actions as a disgrace…?" Eld thought out loud. "A mistake he's trying to rectify."

"Seem so." Franky nodded. "The notes in the tome suggested that Eld's father very angry about family history. Want to change it. Even your names suggest it."

"Our names…" Eld muttered.

Franky was right.

Eld B. and Eldritch P.

Blast versus Pact.

Eldritch Sr.'s father had probably hoped that he'd turn out like…well, like how Eld himself had turned out.

Eld stood up, pacing the room as he tried to make sense of it all.

As if in response to his thoughts, Eld felt a strange pulsing in his veins.

It was as if his very blood was confirming his suspicions, urging him forward on this path. "If I could undo this pact magic somehow maybe I could help Lea. Stop her from suffering these memory problems and power surges. The blood pact might even be causing all this."

But even as hope blossomed in his chest, a small voice of doubt nagged at him.

Lea had made the pact for a reason. Would she want to undo it? What if she'd just forgotten the reason she'd made the pact in the first place?

Eld shook his head, pushing the doubts aside.

Whatever happened, he would just let Lea make the decision. For now, he just had to tell her what they'd learned.

Eld conjured up a leash and collar, which he gently put around Max. The reanimated dog wagged its tail excitedly.

"Come on, boy," Eld grinned. "Let's go find Lea and Ellis. It's time you went home, and we've got a lot to talk about."

Chapter 27

University Research Shows that Conspiracies are Innately Prone to Discovery

Eld's footsteps echoed in the corridors of Bathurst Academy as he made his way towards the main hall, Max trotting beside him. His mind spun wildly with every step he took.

The revelations in Grimthorpe's office…

The truth of the Familial Tome, no, the truth of the Blackwood *Family* in general.

He shook his head and turned to Max.

Seeing the tiny dog trotting behind him brought a smile to his face, a smile that other Blackwoods must have shared as well. Whatever his father may have lied about, at least some good would come out of all this chaos—a brave young boy reunited with his beloved pet.

As they rounded a corner, the air in front of them shifted, adopting a strange mirage-like pattern Eld had seen many times before while traveling through the desert.

Trickery was afoot.

Eld's hand went to the hilt of his dagger. But before he could draw the weapon fully, a familiar face materialized out of thin air.

"Lilith?" Eld relaxed, sheathing his dagger. "How did you—"

"Invisibility spell," Lilith cut him off. "Crafted it myself. Turns out that paying attention to Professor Wraith's lectures has its perks."

"Wait. You created your own invisibility spell? That's incredible!"

Normally, invisibility was a complex process, requiring either body modifications like Franky's or a long list of reagents. While Lilith's spell hadn't been perfect, she'd done it with gestures and speech alone.

Lilith smiled proudly, but it quickly faded. "We need to talk, Eld. About Lea."

Eld groaned. "Lilith, we've been over this. I already told you about her and—"

"This isn't about before," Lilith waved her hand dismissively. "This is about what Lea really is. She's a danger to all of us."

Lilith's lips were pursed and her face was even more pale than usual. She was clearly worried—just worried enough that it triggered Eld's suspicions too, even though he didn't want to admit it.

Max nudged Eld's leg, glancing at Lilith with a curious look on his face. The dog wasn't sure what to make of this—but he definitely wanted to be reunited with Ellis.

"Alright, let's hear it. But can we walk and talk? I promised someone I'd bring their dog back as soon as possible."

Lilith cast a furtive glance around the main hall and then nodded curtly, falling into step beside Eld. The only sounds were the click of Max's claws on the stone floor and the distant, ethereal sounds of Bathurst.

Finally, Lilith spoke, brushing her silver hair from her face. "I've been doing research, Eld. A lot of research. In fact, I may have *borrowed* some more books from the Splintered Dimension."

Eld stumbled briefly, thinking back to their harrowing trip and the spectral librarian.

"You…what? You went back? Lilith, do you have any idea how dangerous that is?" Eld asked.

She waved off his concern. "Well, my invisibility spell works wonders on specters—there's certain shades of light they can't see. But that's not the point. The point is, I've discovered something about Lea. Something big."

Eld's insides twisted with dread at the frightened tone in her voice. "Go on."

"Lea isn't just some undead with amnesia. She's a Great Old One. Do you have any idea what that means? She might be a nice girl…for what it's worth, I like talking to her…but her true nature…she's an eldritch horror! One of the most powerful to ever exist!"

Eld blinked rapidly, momentarily taken aback. "Eldritch horror? You mean like…me?" he thumbed at himself, confused.

Lilith let out a groan. "Not you, you idiot. Lea! Eldritch. As in…well, the word. Not the name."

"Right, right," Eld said, shaking his head. It wasn't exactly the first time he'd heard that word, but in the Blackwood home, people didn't use "eldritch" as an adjective often, for obvious reasons. "But wait…you said Great Old Ones…like the old fogeys in Necropolis? I mean, they knew Lea…"

Lilith's face went pale. "Well. That's just more evidence. Back in the peak of their powers—before the rise and fall of the Old Ones—the Great Old Ones were ancient beings of unimaginable power. They used to rule this world and countless others, but their influence has faded over time. Most have receded into other dimensions or other realities. And the ones who stayed have only the barest glimpse of their power. And Lea…well, if my research is right, she might be one of the most powerful of them all. An eldritch god."

Eld's thoughts went back to the way the ancient creatures in Necropolis had reacted to Lea and her inexplicable bursts of power. Combined with the many gaps in her memory and the frightening visions he'd seen from her…

It was all starting to fit together in a terrifying new context.

He thought back to the blood oath he thought his family might have had with her. Just moments ago, he'd been thinking about finally breaking it, but just what would happen if he did?

Lea clearly wasn't an ordinary person. The sheer amount of magic she possessed proved that. So what would undoing the pact even do?

"But Lea…" he trailed off, hesitating. "She's not…she doesn't seem…"

"Monstrous?" Lilith finished his sentence for him. "That's probably because she's lost her memory, Eld. The power is still there. It's lurking beneath the surface. You've seen it yourself, haven't you? The way she can do things no ordinary student should be capable of? The way she sways nightkin with only a mere glance?"

Eld was at a loss for words.

"She's dangerous, Eld," Lilith insisted. The banshee poked his chest hard with her finger, trying to make her point stick. "Not just to you, but to everyone at Bathurst. Maybe to the whole world. This isn't…it's not just…this isn't a woman you can just take on a date!"

Eld gulped. "Well, I mean, you know…"

He had been thinking of asking her to the Necropromicon, perhaps after saving Max.

But Lilith's words really brought things back to context. This whole time, he'd been acting like these were two separate things—there was a dark conspiracy and then there was his relationship with Lea.

But the truth was that it was a dark conspiracy centered *around* Lea.

Eld's steps slowed.

He thought back to the moments when Lea's power had manifested—the way reality itself seemed to bend around her, the glimpses of something vast and incomprehensible behind her cosmic purple eyes.

"She's not evil." Eld held up his hands waving them in front of himself. "She's kind, and gentle, and—"

"Eld," Lilith said. "I'm not saying Lea is evil. I'm saying that her power is beyond *anything* we can handle, beyond anything even Grimthorpe can handle. She could kill us all just on accident. Just think about what she's done in class…powerful magic effortlessly completed, and I'm sure you've seen displays of far greater power. And sure, she can't control that power now…but what if she could? Could anyone be trusted with that power?"

Eld had, but he still shook his head.

"It just doesn't make sense. Power is one thing, but she—"

"You're thinking with your dick," Lilith snapped, her patience finally breaking.

"I'm…I'm…" Eld stammered. "Well, I mean, you know…

Lilith sighed contemptuously. "You know, Talbot said that you were thinking of taking her to the Necropromicon."

When Eld just kept on stammering, Lilith cursed. "By the Brood Mother's Cursed Womb, Eld…the winter solstice is approaching—the night when the power of all nightkin is at its peak. That's the night of the Necropromicon, if Lea's true nature emerges then, it could be catastrophic. What if she loses control? Students could be hurt! And what if Lea is part of what Grimthorpe is planning? What then?"

Part of Eld wanted to deny everything Lilith was saying, to defend Lea at all costs.

Another part, a part that had been growing increasingly uneasy with each new revelation, couldn't ignore the logic in Lilith's words.

"I need to think about this," Eld said, sighing and rubbing his temples.

Lilith's expression softened slightly and she reached out to grip his shoulder. "I know it's hard to hear, Eld. But please, promise me you'll be careful. Let me help. I care about you and I don't want to see you get hurt."

The sincerity caught Eld off guard.

He looked at Lilith—really looked at her. He saw, well, her.

She wasn't just the brilliant, competitive classmate he had known, nor was she the girl he'd had a few awkward run-ins with. Lilith was a friend who was genuinely concerned for his well-being.

Eld gently shrugged off Lilith's grip, then nodded at Max.

"Lea is waiting with the boy's owner. You can come with me, but…well, please don't push anything on either of us. I just need time to process all this…I need to think about what's actually happening."

To his surprise, Lilith nodded immediately. "Look, Eld. This isn't about Lea. It's not personal. I'll do whatever I can to help her too, so long as it keeps everyone safe…I just don't know if it'll be a result that you or her will be happy with."

Eld shook his head, his whirling thoughts nowhere near settling. "Let's deal with it later," he said. "Come with me to the ferries."

With Ellis, he had to sneak out of the underworld the slow and old fashioned way. For Eld and Lilith, they could just take a boat and meet them outside. After all, the two were legitimate nightkin.

Lilith and Eld soon left campus, but as they approached the docks a commotion just outside the structure caught their attention.

"Wait." Lilith grabbed Eld's arm. "Someone's coming."

She cast her invisibility spell over them both. The sensation was odd—like being submerged in cool water, but still able to breathe.

Eld frowned. "Did this really make us invisible? I—oh."

When he turned to Lilith, he saw that they were indeed invisible. In fact, he couldn't even see his hands when he looked down on them. He took an awkward step forward, then almost stumbled.

"Shh…" Lilith hissed. "Don't move! I'll guide you! Just stay slow."

Lilith had much more experience than Eld with moving when she couldn't see her limbs.

The two pressed themselves against a rocky wall just as two figures rounded the corner, Headmaster Grimthorpe and Professor McGrath. The two men were deep in heated conversation, their voices rising with each exchange.

"I know what you're doing now, Grimthorpe." McGrath stomped his mechanical legs in agitation. "Do you really think I'm so blind that I can't piece together what those components you ordered were for?"

Grimthorpe's face remained neutral. "I don't know what you mean. My research into the Black Sun is purely academic."

McGrath let out a bitter laugh. "Academic? Is that what you call conspiring to plunge the world into eternal darkness? To bring back an age when *monsters* ruled over humanity? Ruled over so called lesser nightkin like me and my family?"

Grimthorpe's voice remained unflinchingly innocent. "Eternal darkness? What could you possibly mean?"

As McGrath grew increasingly agitated, his mechanical legs began sparking angrily. "The Neverending Night! That's what I mean! You want to bring the Black Sun back in the sky and bring back the Neverending Night!"

Lilith stiffened beside him.

Though he couldn't see her, he was sure that her face was locked in shock and terror.

The Neverending Night…

To most, it was just a curse. Something people said to express surprise. But to Grimthorpe, it was an actual objective.

"The Neverending Night was dangerous for us too, you fool," McGrath continued. "Have you forgotten the darker predators that lurked in those endless shadows? My method— using technology to augment our powers—is far safer."

Grimthorpe was silent for a long time.

But then his laughter cut through the night—a cold, hollow sound.

The façade fell.

Gone was the gentle mentor Eld had known. In his place stood a being of terrifying power and ruthless ambition.

"*Safety*. Is that what we've been reduced to? Cowering in the shadows, pretending to be less than we are?"

A third person glided into view—Professor Hemlock, the vampiric Hemomancy instructor. As soon as Eld saw her, he knew that something was wrong. She hung back, her face seemed vacant and her movements were strange.

Her usual menagerie of bloodsucking familiars was nowhere to be seen, and she stood with her arms wide, as if trying to block McGrath's path.

"I've seen how you look at that girl," McGrath said, jabbing a mechanical leg at Grimthorpe. "I see the hunger, I see the ambition. I know why you really canceled the Midnight Exhumation. Ever since Headmaster Vilethorn stepped down, you've been obsessed with finding some way to bring back the old days. You want to free her from her blood oath!"

Eld's confusion deepened.

Headmaster Vilethorn?

He'd been told that the tradition of preserving the heads of former headmasters went back to the founding of Bathurst, but when he was in Grimthorpe's office he didn't remember seeing a Headmaster Vilethorn.

Grimthorpe sneered "Girl? That *thing* is no mere girl. She is the key to bringing back the Neverending Night. Her misguided mercy is why we're in this mess to begin with. And I have no intention of freeing her—I will enslave her, use her as a power source to blanket the entire world in glorious darkness."

Belatedly, Eld realized that they were talking about Lea.

McGrath took a step back, recoiling and cocking his head to one side. "You're insane, Grimthorpe. I won't be part of this madness. I'm going to the school board. Hades, Pluto, and Anubis will hear about this! They'll end this nonsense."

"Oh, my dear McGrath, you never had a chance," Grimthorpe sighed.

Grimthorpe's hand shot out, crackling with sickly green energy. McGrath barely had time to scream before the disintegration spell hit him in full force. In a matter of seconds, McGrath was reduced to nothing more than a charred head and a few scattered mechanical parts.

Eld bit down on his fist to keep from crying out. Beside him, he felt Lilith trembling, her breath coming in short gasps.

Grimthorpe surveyed the remains of his former colleague and chuckled.

"The school board…You fool. Contacting the school board requires a two-month-long ritual, and then they take another three months to act. By the time the infernal bureaucracy finally realizes what's going on, I will have achieved godhood."

Then Grimthorpe knelt, grasping McGrath's head by his hair and lifting it to his eye level.

"A real shame," Grimthorpe went on. "You really were a promising student. If it wasn't for the fact that you were such a damn sticker for the rules. Well, I guess that's just what they say about engineers…"

Grimthorpe sighed and dropped the head onto the ground.

Then he turned to Professor Hemlock, who was staring at McGrath's remains in horror. Her face twisted and turned, a small but fierce fanged snarl appearing on her lips.

Eld's eyes widened as everything clicked into place.

She was being controlled!

"Now then, Hemlock," Grimthorpe said. "We can't have *that*. Things were a lot more fun when you were nice and obedient. Missing your colleagues just won't do."

With nothing more than a gesture, Grimthorpe forced her to walk towards him. Every single one of her steps was a struggle. The real Hemlock was there, battling for freedom, but her resistance was futile.

Grimthorpe materialized a stake in his outstretched hand.

"You understand, don't you?" Grimthorpe's voice was almost gentle as he guided the stake to Hemlock's heart. "The old ways must return. The strong must rule. Those who stand in the way…well. They must stand no longer."

With a sickening wet sound, the stake plunged home. Professor Hemlock's shocked scream was cut brutally short as she crumbled to dust.

Eld's vision swam, bile rising in his throat. This couldn't be real. It had to be some terrible nightmare. It was only Lilith's trembling beside him and the acrid smell of death in the air forced him to accept that it was in fact very real.

The dust that had once been Professor Hemlock settled on the floor.

Grimthorpe turned, his gaze sweeping across the corridor. His eyes fell directly on where Eld and Lilith stood.

Eld thought that Grimthorpe was going to step over to them, but Lilith's invisibility spell held true. Whatever spectrum of light that specters struggled to see, it seemed like liches struggled to see them as well.

It wasn't until the sound of his footsteps had completely faded that Eld dared to breathe again.

"Oh gods," Lilith whimpered. Her face was ashen, more so than normal. "Oh gods, oh gods, oh gods."

The distress finally got to her and her invisibility spell flickered and died.

Eld couldn't find words as his body abruptly materialized back into visibility.

Grimthorpe, the man he had looked up to and respected was a cold-blooded murderer. He wanted to enslave Lea and bring forth a real Neverending Night.

"We have to do something," Eld finally managed to speak. "We have to stop him."

Chapter 28

Promposals are Getting
Way Out of Hand These Days

But despite Eld's bold words, the two friends walked in silence, staring at the ground before their feet until they arrived at the Bathurst docks.

The stench of decay and the whispers of the damned hung heavy in the air. Cloaked ferrymen guided boats back and forth through the mists. Eld kept his eyes peeled for the Great Old One he'd seen traveling the first time to Necropolis with Lea, but the tentacles were nowhere to be found.

Max let out a loud whimper.

"Hey! Hey!" Eld soothed him, carefully gripping the leash. "Calm down there boy."

"Can't blame him for being spooked," Lilith muttered.

Eld nodded, clenching his teeth. The horror of what they had witnessed still clawed at the edges of his consciousness, threatening to completely overwhelm him.

"The Necropromicon!" Lilith suddenly exclaimed.

"Hm?" Eld asked.

As she spoke, Lilith stared straight ahead. She seemed to be piecing things together as a way to compartmentalize what had just happened. "Earlier. I was warning you that Lea would be most dangerous at Necropromicon...but that must be when

Grimthorpe will make his move! It's when the winter solstice is at its deepest when the veil between dimensions is thinnest."

Eld slapped his head, his fingers gripping into his hair as his eyes widened. "And with so many students gathered in one place…"

She gulped and nodded. "It's the perfect opportunity for a mass sacrifice."

Eld thought of his friends. Talbot, Wolfgang, even Orlando…

He thought of his classmates, people who he knew mostly just by sight but always waved to in the hallways.

Hells, even Mortimer, Erik, and Vlad…

Everyone would unknowingly be walking into a trap.

And worst of all, Lea was in incredible danger.

Grimthorpe's words echoed in Eld's mind, like a message from a haunted Old One recording. "I will enslave her, use her as a power source to blanket the entire world in glorious darkness."

Eld shuddered again, shaking his head. "We have to stop this, we don't have a choice. It's worse than anything I could have imagined."

Lilith let out a hysterical laugh. "Stop him? Eld, did you see what he did to McGrath? To Hemlock? He'd obliterate us without breaking a sweat."

"So we just let him destroy the world?" Eld demanded, his fists clenched at his side. "We let him sacrifice all of our friends?"

"No, but…but do you even have a plan?" Lilith asked. "I don't…I don't even know where we could start!"

Eld stared off into the gloomy docks.

"We need to protect Lea," Eld said. "She's the key to all this. We…we can just run. Make sure Lea is safe, and then, well, without her, there will be no event."

At first, Lilith looked hopeful, but then her eyes narrowed. "Do you think it will be that simple? We just saw how brutal Grimthorpe is. Who's to say that he won't sacrifice everyone anyway?"

Eld didn't know what to say to that.

"Excuse me…" a skeletal ferryman asked. Its empty eye sockets fixed on Eld with an unsettling intensity. "Are you just here to argue by the sea? Or do you have someplace to be?"

"Passage for three," Eld hurriedly replied. "To the gates of the mortal realm."

There was a long moment of quiet, broken only by the lapping of dark waters against the dock. Then, with a sound like dry leaves rustling, the ferryman laughed. "Very well, boy, but beware. The path between worlds is treacherous. We are not meant to travel between the Underworld and Topside."

Depending on one's taste in tentacles, the journey to the underworld was either a strange but wonderful dream or an absolute nightmare. The spectral tentacles faded in and out of Eld's vision, somehow gossamer light and all-encompassing at the same time.

The boat glided through caverns where stalactites dripped acid and stalagmites writhed like flickering shadows. They passed shores where the damned screamed in eternal torment, their withered bodies desperately reaching out towards the boat.

"It wasn't like this on the way down," Eld muttered.

The ferryman only chuckled in response. Lilith huddled close to Eld, her usual bravado melted away by the horrors surrounding them. Max whined, pressing tightly against Eld's leg.

Eld gave the dog a friendly scratch on the head. "You don't need to worry, boy. You're undead now. They won't hurt you…I hope."

As they neared the barrier between worlds, reality itself seemed to fray at the edges. Colors bled into one another, solid objects became translucent, and whispers filled the air.

"Hold on tight to the ship. The crossing can be disorienting," the ferryman called from the bow.

Eld obeyed, grabbing onto the boat. A strange cold strength seemed to flow into his fingers from the wood, temporarily soothing him.

And then their world exploded into chaos.

Eld felt as if he were being turned inside out, his very atoms screaming in protest as they were wrenched between dimensions. Just when he thought he could bear no more, everything snapped into focus.

They found themselves on a mist-shrouded shore, the gnarled trees of a forest looming before them. In the distance, Eld could make out the faint lights of a small town.

"We're here," the skeletal ferryman said, his jaw clacking. "Not just a port town, The Port Town."

"Thank you," Eld said to the ferryman, leaning over the side of the boat.

The skeletal being inclined its head. "May the darkness have mercy on you, young necromancer. You'll need it in the days to come."

His voice sounded strangely somber as he said it.

But before Eld could ask if the skeletal ferryman possibly knew anything about Grimthorpe's plans, the boat and the ferryman faded into the mist, leaving Eld, Lilith, and Max alone on the shore.

Max's tail suddenly perked up and then he began pulling on his leash.

"Wait. They are here?" Eld asked.

The dog began tugging faster and faster, his excitement growing with every step.

Lilith glanced at Eld, raising an eyebrow. "Did they know you'd take the ferry?"

"I…I don't think I arranged it," Eld said.

As they neared the outskirts, a familiar voice called out.

"Mr. Eld!" Ellis came barreling towards him, his face filled with joy. "You're back! I…Ms. Lea said you'd come to this town! She said she knew you'd want to go by ferry. And you brought Max back too!"

The reunion between boy and dog was incredibly sweet…or would have been if Eld didn't know what was in the future.

Max's tail wagged so hard it threatened to fall off again, while Ellis buried his face in the zombie canine's fur, oblivious to the danger looming on the horizon. He gave them a few more minutes to enjoy their reunion, and then cut in.

"Do you know where Lea is?"

"Um, she…she stepped away for a moment. Or…well, *teleported* away."

"Teleported?" Eld asked.

"Yeah…she started doing that a few days after we got here. The air would just shimmer and then…*boom*!"

Eld and Lilith glanced at each other.

With the winter solstice approaching, Lea's powers were dramatically increasing. Teleportation was a skill that it'd taken Eldritch Sr. decades to master. Perhaps, if worst came to worst, she could use it to run away.

Eld knelt, placing a hand on Ellis's shoulder. "Listen, buddy. I need you to do something very important for me. You need to take Max and get as far away from here as you can. Go somewhere safe, somewhere no one will find you, and stay away from *that*."

Eld pointed back to the opening of the small cavern they had entered the mortal world from.

"You can't go to the Underworld again," Lilith added.

Ellis looked up, confusion and fear warring in his eyes. "But why? What's happening?"

Eld struggled to find the right words. How could he possibly explain to a child that the world was possibly ending? By the Thrice-Called Brood Mother, even staying away from the underworld probably wouldn't do any good if Grimthorpe's plan succeeded.

He shook his head and gulped, deciding to try and keep things as simple as possible. "Something bad is coming. Something dangerous. I need to know that you and Max are safe, okay?"

The boy hesitated then nodded. "Okay, Mr. Eld. We'll go. Will I ever see you again?"

Since Max had been reanimated with Eld's magic, Eld could track the dog down. It'd be nice to see how the brave boy and his dog again...

But that required Eld to be alive.

"I hope so, Ellis. I really do," Eld grimly replied. "But just trust me and stay away from here, alright?"

"Okay," Ellis replied, nodding.

As they watched Ellis and Max walk off into the distance, Max's tail still wagging like a rotor, Lilith turned to Eld. "What now?"

A shimmer in the air caught Eld's attention. The world seemed to ripple, and suddenly Lea was standing before them, her eyes swirling with enough speckled light for an entire galaxy.

She let out a delighted laugh. "Hah! That was pretty good! I've been getting better and better at that. Teleportation accuracy and all—"

She suddenly broke off, inspecting their haggard and worried appearances.

"Eld? Lilith? What's going on?"

Eld and Lilith recounted everything that had happened—Grimthorpe's betrayal, the murders of McGrath and Hemlock, and the plot to bring about the Neverending Night. With each revelation, Lea's expression grew darker, and the stars in her eyes seemed to flare.

"So what are you going to do about it?" Lea asked.

When Eld told Lea his plan, silence fell over the group. Eld expected Lea to agree that they needed to run, to hide, to gather their strength before facing such a formidable enemy.

Instead, Lea said, "We're going back."

Eld blinked in disbelief. "What? Lea, did you hear what we just said? Grimthorpe is planning to enslave you, to use you as some kind of cosmic battery!"

Her hair writhed like living tendrils. "Let him try," she replied.

For a moment, she looked almighty. All-powerful. Eld dared to dream of victory.

Lilith cut that moment short immediately.

"You can't control your powers, can you? At least, not when you're tense."

"Um, well, I mean…" Lea stammered. Her hair drooped and the sparks stopped dancing around her.

"Lea…" Eld started.

"Listen to me," Lea said, shaking her head. Her voice was iron and with every word, her cosmic gaze intensified. Magical powers or not, Eld realized he was standing before a very determined woman. "Running isn't the answer. A life on the run is not what I woke up for. And even if we escape, what about everyone else? What about the next time when Grimthorpe finds some other poor soul to use for his schemes?"

Eld didn't want to live a life on the run either.

He could hardly believe the words he spoke next. But the longer he talked, the more confident he grew. He wasn't confident that he was going to win—but he was certain that he was doing the right thing.

"Okay," Eld said. "So we'll fight. We have a month until the Necropromicon. We use that time to prepare, to gather allies. There must be other professors, other students who will stand with us when they learn the truth."

To his surprise, Lilith nodded. "Agreed."

Lea smiled. "Thank you, Eld. For everything. I know…well, I know that none of this could be easy for you. You're a good man. A peaceful man."

Eld met Lea's gaze and he felt something shift within him. The fear was still there, but it was overshadowed by a growing determination.

Whatever Lea truly was—eldritch horror, cosmic entity, or something beyond his comprehension—she was also his friend and the woman he cared for most. And he would stand by her, no matter what awaited them.

"Alright." Eld squared his shoulders and straightened his jacket. "Let's go save the world."

"I guess we should make this official then." Lea reached out and grabbed Eld's hand. "Will you go to the Necropromicon with me?"

Chapter 29

Only One Thing Can Defeat an Unholy Alliance...an Even More Unholy Alliance

The catacombs beneath Bathurst Academy had never felt more oppressive to Eld as he paced the length of the Combat Club chamber they'd claimed as their war room. Shadows danced on the walls, cast by guttering candles that seemed to flicker in time with his racing thoughts.

Grimthorpe's words—an announcement magical broadcast through the school just moments ago—echoed through his mind. "Professor McGrath will be returning home to visit his ailing mother. Meanwhile, Professor Hemlock is suffering from a bout of scarlet fever. Both hope to return after the Necropromicon."

It wasn't just the lie that bothered Eld...it was the timing. Grimthorpe thought that nobody would even be around after the Necropromicon to discover his deception.

Lea and Lilith huddled over a makeshift table, their heads bent close as they pored over hastily scrawled plans and arcane diagrams. Every so often, skittering and mechanical clanking echoed through the room as Bart, Spinderella, and Franky cavorted around the room.

"We can't just wait for the Necropromicon. We need to strike before it," Eld said, announcing the thought that'd been tumbling through his mind. "The element of surprise is our greatest advantage."

As Eld spoke, he glanced at Lea. As ridiculous as it sounded, he would be sorely disappointed if he couldn't go to Necropromicon with her, lives on the line or not. She caught his eye and winked, mouthing something that he hoped went along the lines of "rain check."

Lilith looked up from the diagram she was drawing, her silver hair catching the candlelight like spun moonbeams. "I don't disagree, Eld, but we can't just charge in willy-nilly. Grimthorpe has centuries of experience and who knows what kind of power at his disposal. Not to mention his undead pets. Our first step needs to be recruiting allies. And to make matters worse, Grimthorpe is loved by almost all of the faculty and students. If we start spouting off about eldritch gods and mass sacrifices, we'll be laughed out of Bathurst, and that's if we're lucky."

Eld turned to Lea. "Any chance you could just…you know?" he asked, waving his hand.

"Just what?" Lea asked.

"You know, like what you did with the vampires. And the Great Old Ones. Just mind control them."

"Mind control them?" Lilith asked, her eyes widening with keen interest. "That would solve our problems right away, wouldn't it?"

"Oh, you mean that…" Lea said. Her voice trailed off, and the swirling constellations in her eyes temporarily dimmed. "I don't…I don't know how that works…sometimes, when I speak, my voice thrums with power, and then people listen, but I…"

Her voice trailed off, dwindling to nothing.

Like her other magics, Lea couldn't control it.

"Don't worry about it," Eld said, smiling. "We can handle this ourselves…but we can't just get anybody. We need to be selective, strategic."

"And I know just who we're going to ask first," Lilith said. Her eyes lit up with an idea that seemed to simultaneously excite and horrify her.

"Who?" Eld asked, genuinely surprised.

"Talbot," Lilith replied.

Eld and Lea exchanged looks.

"Talbot?" Eld eyebrows shot up towards his hairline. "As in, Talbot Wilting? The ghost who considers getting out of bed an extreme sport? I love him as much as anyone else. He's my best friend here, but he's not exactly the greatest at combat. He's already let me down once before."

Franky chittered with amusement.

"Hah! Good idea! Lazy ghost…big help. Much wow!"

Eld chuckled. "Just the mere thought of asking Talbot for help turned Franky stupid again."

Franky chittered irritably, launching into a long tirade about freedom of expression and creative speech patterns that Eld gently tuned out.

Lea tried to soften her skepticism, but it came out all the same. "Are we thinking of the same Talbot? The one who once asked if he could summon a proxy to attend classes for him?"

Lilith held up her hands defensively. "I know. Hear me out though. Talbot's a poltergeist, right? He can possess objects. I've been working on a magical suit of armor recently—one that's too heavy for any normal person to lift. But in the right noncorporeal hands, it could be a huge asset."

Eld stroked his chin thoughtfully. "Well, that's not a *completely* horrible idea. Talbot does know the layout of Bathurst better than almost anyone, considering how many times he's repeated his first year. But the last time I asked him for help, well, that suit of armor shut down faster than a vampire nightclub at daybreak."

"Come on, it's worth at least asking him. Maybe becoming friends with you has changed Talbot. Helped him grow up a bit," Lilith insisted. "Besides, who would ever suspect Talbot of being involved in a rebellion? It's the perfect cover."

With a collective shrug that seemed to say "*What do we have to lose?*" the group set off to find their potential first recruit.

Predictably, they found Talbot in his bed.

The poltergeist was sprawled out in a dramatic pose of relaxation that would have made a fainting Victorian lady proud. As they entered the room, Talbot cracked open one spectral eyelid.

"Whatever it is, the answer's no." He twirled one hand in the air. "Unless it involves more sleep or less effort. In which case, maybe."

Eld took a deep breath, steeling himself for what was sure to be an uphill battle. "Talbot, we need your help. The whole world is in danger."

Eld gave Talbot the rundown of everything that had happened—Grimthorpe's betrayal, the murders of McGrath and Hemlock, and the plot to bring about the Neverending Night.

With each revelation, Talbot's expression gradually shifted, going from bored disinterest to mild concern to something approaching actual alarm.

"So let me get this straight," Talbot said when they had finished. "You want me—*me*—to help you take on the most powerful necromancer in Bathurst, possibly the world, in a fight that will almost certainly get us all killed or worse?"

"Yeah, that sums it up," Eld admitted.

A slow grin spread across Talbot's translucent face. "Well, why didn't you say so in the first place? I would have still said no, but it would have saved everyone the time."

Eld groaned. "Talbot, come on. We need—"

"I'm kidding." Talbot straightened and floated off the bed. "Of course I'll help."

Lilith's brow furrowed and she put her hands on her hips. "Just like that? No arguments? No complaints about how much effort it'll take?"

Talbot shrugged. "Look, I've been stuck in this first-year rut for longer than I care to admit. Maybe it's time for a change. Besides, if Grimthorpe succeeds, there won't be any more school to slack off in, will there?"

As they left the room, their alliance had become one member stronger. It was a small victory, but Eld couldn't help but grin from ear to ear.

With Talbot's possession skills by their side, the next stop was the student workshop. Now that Professor McGrath was gone, the student's projects were left unsupervised, meaning that the amount of work being done was rapidly approaching zero.

Most students were happy for the break, but most students weren't preparing for war, and none of them had Lilith's brilliance.

As they entered, Eld's eyes widened at the sight before him.

What had once been a cluttered storage room was now a mad scientist's dream, filled with bubbling beakers, crackling electrical components, and half-assembled mechanical parts.

It was the exact sort of scene that would have made McGrath proud if it weren't for the tragic fact that he'd left this mortal coil.

"What do you think, Talbot?" Lilith asked. "Not a bad perk for joining up, don't you think?"

In the center of it all stood her crowning achievement, a suit of armor unlike anything Eld had ever seen. It was much larger than a normal man, its proportions more akin to those of a small giant. Plates of enchanted metal gleamed in the workshop's harsh light, interspersed with crackling panels of pure energy.

"That's for Talbot?" Eld asked, his voice a mix of awe and trepidation.

Lilith nodded, a manic look in her eyes. "I've been working on it non-stop...or should I say, *we've* been working on it non-stop. After a few dead ends, I started asking Lea for help."

Lea stepped forward, beaming proudly. "We've incorporated elements from every branch of magic we could think of. Necromancy for durability, golemancy for movement, even a bit of blood magic for power regulation."

Talbot drifted closer to the suit. "And I'm supposed to possess this?"

"And whatever else is around," Lilith said. "We also included an experimental possession projection system, to let you take control of other objects in the area too. I don't know how long this will last against Grimthorpe, but with your ability to control objects and this suit's capabilities, you'll be a one-ghost army."

Talbot began to experimentally possess the armor.

The suit stood stock still, but seconds later, Talbot let out a whoop as its limbs twitched and servos whirred to life.

"Aw yeah!" Talbot cried. "This is almost enough to get me excited!"

He swung the suit's arm…

And immediately punched an awkward hole in the lab's wall.

Seconds later, he floated out, a sheepish grin on his face.

"Huh. This is great…but I think I need more work."

Chuckling, Eld turned his attention to their next potential allies.

He pulled out a small scroll and a quill before jotting out a quick message, explaining the situation in the vaguest terms possible while still conveying the urgency of their need.

"Franky, I need you to take a message to our friends in the burrows in Necropolis. Can you do that for me?"

The centipede saluted with one of his legs. "Your missive shall be delivered with utmost promptness."

As Franky scuttled off into the shadows, Eld turned back to the group.

"Now we wait and hope that the mole people are in a helpful mood," he said.

"The mole people?" Lilith asked.

Eld nodded.

"Why…why would you think they'd help you?" Lilith asked.

"Well. They like me—they said that pet reanimation is good for their business."

"Their organ stealing business?" Lilith asked, raising a thin eyebrow.

"There's no need to be so blunt about our prospective allies," Eld replied. "And besides…I owe them a favor."

"*You* owe *them* a favor," Lilith asked.

"Yeah. And, well, I need to be alive for them to cash in that favor…so I'm hoping they'll help us."

Lilith stared at Eld, quirking a brow, then just shook her head. "The consecutive logical leaps here…it boggles the mind."

"Be careful about deals with the mole people…" Lea suddenly chimed in. "You never know what they will ask for in return."

Her voice trailed off ominously—so ominously that Eld wished she'd told him that before he'd made a deal with the mole people.

With that anxious thought on Eld's mind, the hours passed like molasses. The tension in the workshop grew with each tick of the clock.

"So…what *do* you think the mole people will ask for?" Lilith asked.

"Maybe we shouldn't have even asked them to help," Talbot replied, nervously glancing around. "Come to think of it, in all my time at Bathurst, I can't think of a single person making a deal with them at all."

"Maybe we better prepare this armor," Lea said, the constellations in her eyes swirling anxiously.

"Yeah, let me get back to it," Talbot said.

His body fizzled, vanishing before appearing inside again.

After a significant amount of trial and error—mostly error—Talbot managed to fully merge with the armor, stomping around the room with all the grace of a drunken elephant.

Beside him, Lilith and Lea made last-minute adjustments, muttering to each other in a shorthand of magical jargon that Eld could barely follow.

A few moments later, a scratching sound at the door made them all freeze.

Franky's voice came from the other side. "I have returned Eld—with our prospective allies in tow!"

Eld hurried to open the door, revealing Franky and a nervous-looking mole creature. The mole's eyes darted around the room, widening at the sight of Talbot in his massive armor.

"Mr. Eld!" the mole squeaked, wringing its paws. "Your message was very cryptic. Very worrying. What is the big trouble?"

Eld knelt, trying to appear as non-threatening as possible. "Thank you for coming. We need your help. Something dangerous is coming."

The mole's whiskers twitched anxiously. "Dangerous? What kind of dangerous? If too dangerous, well, then no more debt! Could be good for business! But if only medium dangerous, then, well, maybe some tough customers."

"Well, this will be *very* bad for business. If Grimthorpe succeeds in his plan, there won't be any customers left for your unique goods. Except for the Great Old Ones… but I doubt they'll buy from you."

The mole's eyes bulged even further. "Grimthorpe? The Headmaster involved? Oh no, oh no. Very bad. Very scary. And the Great Old Ones…terrible for business. Always talking about how they used to be able to take stuff for free!"

Eld pressed on, sensing an opportunity. "If you help us stop this, think of the business opportunities. You'd be heroes. People would be lining up to buy from the moles who saved the world."

"Moles who saved the world…"

The mole person seemed to like the sound of that.

He paced in tight circles, muttering to himself. His eyes spun in different directions as if trying to look at every possible angle of the situation simultaneously.

Finally, it came to an abrupt stop.

"We decide!" the mole declared, quivering with nervous energy. "As favor to Eld, we choose to not join fight! Stay home instead!"

Eld blinked, confusion painted across his face. "Wait, what? I wasn't asking for a favor. I was just telling you what was happening. And doing me a favor would mean *joining* the fight."

But the mole was already scampering towards the exit, moving with surprising speed for such a small creature. "Deal made! You owe us nothing now!" it called over its shoulder. "We no help fight Grimthorpe! Good luck!"

And with that, the mole disappeared into the shadows, leaving behind only the faint scent of damp earth and a profound sense of bewilderment.

Eld stood there trying to figure out what had just happened. "What just happened? Did we just lose an ally we never had in the first place?"

Lilith pinched the bridge of her nose, exhaling slowly. "I think we did. And somehow, we're supposed to count that as a win?"

"I think he said you don't owe them a favor anymore," Lea said. "In exchange for them not fighting."

Eld shook his head, still struggling to wrap his mind around the mole's logic. In a way, Lea was right. When making the deal, he never could have imagined what the mole people would ask for.

Just trying to parse what the mole people's logic felt like reading Urquruan hieroglyphics, so Eld decided to just move on before his brain twisted itself into a knot.

"Well, let's move on," Eld said. "Next up is Wolfgang. He's loyal, he's strong, and he has influence with a lot of the other students."

Lilith nodded. "Good thinking. Let's go find our furry friend."

They found Wolfgang out in the cemetery working out with a pair of broken headstones, grunting loudly as he lifted them over his head.

"Wow…" Lilith murmured. "He works out with the fervor of a man hoping he can one day punch right through his personal daemons."

Eld knew she was right, but now wasn't the time to psychoanalyze his friend.

When Wolfgang saw Eld and the others approaching, he paused, wiping sweat from his brow.

"Eld!" Wolfgang exclaimed. "Just the man I wanted to see. I've been hearing some strange rumors."

The werewolf trailed off as he saw the group's expressions. "Ah. So they're not just rumors, are they?"

Eld shook his head, grimacing. "I'm afraid not. We need your help. Grimthorpe is planning something terrible, and we're the only ones who can stop him."

"*Grimthorpe?*" Wolfgang asked. "I thought it had to be some kind of prank by Mortimer…this *is* much more serious than I thought."

Wolfgang listened intently as Eld laid out the situation, his face growing more serious with each passing moment. When Eld finished, the werewolf was silent for a long moment, his amber eyes distant.

"You know, Eld…my old man always went on and on about just keeping my head down and looking out for myself. The lone wolf is strongest…that's what he used to say."

Wolfgang snorted. "A load of rubbish, if you ask me. I'm done living by his rules. I'm with you, Eld. All the way. Whatever it takes."

Eld felt a wave of relief wash over him. "Thank you, Wolfgang. You have no idea how much that means."

Wolfgang grinned. "Besides, someone's got to keep you scrawny necromancers from getting yourselves killed. Might as well be me."

Wolfgang raised an unexpected point. "Have you considered reaching out to Mortimer and Erik? Vlad has a bunch of millions too. Could be useful."

Eld recoiled at the suggestion. "Mortimer? Erik the Drowned? They're assholes, Wolfgang. They can't be trusted."

Wolfgang held up his hands placatingly. "I'm not saying I like them, but think about it. They're followers, not leaders. If Grimthorpe's plan comes to light, they might just side with whoever they think is going to win. It might just be worth getting them on our side."

He had a point there.

But Lilith shook her head.

"I don't know about that," she said. "From my personal experience, Erik just goes with the flow. And Mortimer, well, he acts primarily on spite and secondarily on self-interest. There's no use trying to recruit them."

Well, if Lilith didn't want to recruit Erik, that just convinced him further.

But before Eld could say anything else, a commotion at the entrance to the cemetery caught their attention. Orlando von Ravenscroft glided in, his vampiric grace at odds with the thunderous expression on his face.

"Blackwood!" Orlando called out. "A word, if you please."

Eld exchanged worried glances with his friends before stepping forward to meet Orlando. "Is something wrong?"

Orlando's features twisted in anger. "*Is something wrong?* You tell me, Blackwood. I couldn't help but notice you've been gathering allies. Planning some sort of rebellion, perhaps?"

Eld's heart sank.

Had their plans been discovered so soon?

"Oh, don't worry," Orlando said, waving his hand. "The school hasn't discovered you. But my thralls—or, rather, I mean *fans*, well, they tell me everything."

But before Eld could formulate a response, Orlando continued. "Back to your conspiracy. Why didn't you think to include me? After all we've been through? I thought we had bonded, Blackwood. Two noble sons, rising above expectations."

Eld blinked, momentarily stunned by the unexpected direction of Orlando's tirade. "I…what?"

Orlando rolled his eyes dramatically. "Oh, don't play coy. I overheard you talking to Wolfgang about your *dick father*. You were referring to *our* shared burden of familial expectations, weren't you? Seeing as we're two scions of prominent nightkin houses?"

Eld was about to correct Orlando's misunderstanding, then closed it again as a new possibility dawned on him.

Technically, Orlando was right. They *did* have stuff in common—they'd just never talked about it before. And there was no better time than the present to make common cause.

"You're right. I should have come to you first. We could use someone of your talents."

"Well…of course you could," Orlando replied, looking slightly mollified. "But what exactly are we talking about here? What's this rebellion all about?"

Taking a deep breath, Eld launched into a very abbreviated version of their predicament. As he spoke, he watched Orlando's expression carefully, looking for any sign of betrayal or deceit.

To his surprise, the vampire's face showed only growing interest.

When Eld finished, Orlando was quiet for a moment, tapping one perfectly manicured finger against his chin. "The Neverending Night, you say? Hmm. Intriguing. But ultimately unnecessary."

"Unnecessary?" Eld repeated, confused.

Orlando waved a hand dismissively. "Of course. I have my own plans for vampiric dominance. But not this crude, world-ending nonsense. No, when I achieve my destiny as the Ultimate

Being, I'll have no need for eternal darkness. In fact, the sun will be quite useful in keeping the lesser vampires in line."

Eld struggled to keep up with Orlando's grandiose declarations, so he decided to just cut to the point. "So…you'll help us then?"

"But of course!" Orlando declared, as if it were the most obvious thing in the world. "After all, what's the point of becoming the Ultimate Being if there's no world left to rule?"

As Orlando swept away, Eld turned back to his friends, his head spinning. "I'm so confused. Did that just happen?"

Lea placed a comforting hand on his shoulder. "As strange as that was, I think we just got ourselves a powerful ally."

Lilith nodded in agreement. "Narcissistic and slightly unhinged as he may be, Orlando's support could tip the scales in our favor."

In the distance, Orlando's ears twitched.

"I heard that, banshee…but I'll ignore your harsh words for now. I'm off to find my enthralled fans. They'll be delighted to know that I'm taking *every* single one of them to the Necropromicon."

Chapter 30

Before Embarking on a Journey of Revenge, Dig Up Two Thousand Graves

The dark forest outside of Necropolis was a tangled mass of gnarled trees.

Shadows writhed between the trunks as if the very darkness had taken on a life of its own. Eld stood at the forest's edge, his breath misting in the chill air.

Lilith was tinkering more in the workshop, Wolfgang had redoubled his training, and Orlando…well, he seemed to just be enjoying the company of his fans, but Eld was sure he'd show up when it mattered.

It was just him, Talbot, and Lea, just like old times.

Lea stood to his right, her cosmic eyes swirling with infinite galaxies. The starlight that seemed to emanate from her skin cast endlessly shifting on the mist-shrouded ground. Tendrils of purple haze leeched up from the black earth to coil around her.

At this point, it was almost impossible to hide her true nature. The pulsating magic surrounding her screamed that she was no ordinary person. Eld couldn't help but wonder what would happen by the time the winter solstice rolled around.

To his left, Talbot hovered lazily. "Ready to go make some new friends? Get it? *Make new friends*? Because you're a necromancer?"

Eld didn't reply. He stared straight forward. The last time he'd been here, he'd fled through the forest with Lea's sleeping body after digging her up from the graveyard.

He'd been frightened, worried, terrified.

This time…

Well, he still felt those things.

But he felt confident too. Now that he knew the true history of the Blackwood family, he knew that centuries of necromantic knowledge stood behind him. It was the perfect opportunity to strike back.

"Yeah. You get it." Talbot snickered.

"I do." Eld took in a deep breath.

This was their last chance to find more allies.

Lea had gone back to Necropolis, hoping to recruit the Great Old Ones, but they had mysteriously vanished, seemingly overnight. Due to spending so much time investigating this conspiracy, Eld hadn't paid much attention in Doomsaying class, but that certainly didn't seem like a good sign.

He shook his head. "You know what? Let's just get this done."

He patted the side of his leg, calling Shuck to his side. The big black dog sniffed the ground before them, his tail slowly wagging.

Together, they ventured deeper into the woods, fallen leaves crunching beneath their feet.

The canopy above grew denser with each step until even the meager light of Bathurst's eternal dusk was reduced to slight, shifting patterns on the forest floor.

Eld's menagerie of reanimated companions fanned out around them—Franky and Spinderella skittering over rotting logs, Bart scuttled along at the bases of twisted trees, and Shuck walked faithfully next to Eld.

Surrounded by the decay and darkness of the old woods, Eld felt a strange sense of belonging, the feeling slowly overtaking his fear and anxiety. This was his element, the domain of a death druid, and for once, he didn't feel like an outsider.

"Hey, Shuck, what do you think about all this?" Eld asked, running his fingers through the fur along the reanimated dogs back. "Think we can find some new friends?"

The zombie dog turned its head, mismatched eyes glowing faintly in the gloom. Its tail wagged with such vigor that it almost fell off again.

"Considering what happened last time, I'll take that as a yes," Eld said, glancing over at Lea.

As they pressed on, Eld found his gaze continually drawn to Lea.

Here in the surprisingly peaceful and quiet forest, her radiance seemed even brighter than before. The corona of void magic surrounding her pulsated like the light of an angler fish as she anxiously glanced back and forth, occasionally gnawing her lip.

The juxtaposition of her cosmic power and her current vulnerability struck him with a bittersweet ache in his chest.

Lea caught him looking. "You know despite all the danger, I'm happy to be here with you, Eld. I missed you when I went top side."

"I, um." He palmed the back of his neck. "You too."

Her words sent a warmth spreading through him, and he felt his undead heart beat a single time.

But his warm feelings were tempered by protectiveness.

Lea might have once been an eldritch being of unfathomable power, but in terms of her actual fighting ability, she was just another first-year student at Bathurst.

She was a quick study, but she still had little experience. And despite the awe-inspiring things that happened around her, she had no way of consciously controlling her power.

"We need to be stronger," Eld muttered, more to himself than anyone else. "All of us."

As if on cue, the idea of lichdom whispered in the back of his mind, promising power and immortality.

In that single moment, Eld's peaceful mindset vanished. His thoughts of the ancestral Blackwood death druids vanished.

In fact, Eld couldn't help but wish that he'd only he'd listened to his father.

If he had, that would have put him in the perfect position to *oppose* his father. If he was a lich, he could go toe to toe with Grimthorpe with magic alone, he wouldn't need to endanger his friends and companions. He wouldn't have to rely on such a desperate gambit as dredging the forest for last-second allies.

Franky scuttled up to Eld's shoulder, chittering inquisitively. "Boss. My servo-sensors are detecting swirling emotions. Is everything alright?"

"Servo-sensors?" Eld asked.

"Lilith helped me add them," Franky explained. "Back in the workshop. They amplify my centipede abilities to detect pheromones so that I can detect the emotions of other species. All the better to help you in our quest."

Eld chuckled. "I'm fine, Franky. I'm just not sure this is going to work. I know it's the best plan we have though."

"An army of big scary monsters will send even Grimthorpe screeching for the hills," Franky replied.

"Well, that's the plan, Franky," Eld replied, smiling weakly. "Though I'm not sure how big or scary we can make them with what we've got to work with."

By then, Shuck had stopped walking, his tail wagging and growing ever more furious. Clearly, this was the place.

Eld surveyed the forest floor, littered with the detritus of countless small lives lived and lost. It was a far cry from the manticore he had reanimated, and Eld had no idea where he'd even find such a powerful corpse to begin with.

But as his eyes fell on Franky, a new spark of inspiration struck. Franky, who was getting smarter and smarter with every passing moment.

"Maybe we don't need big and scary," Eld mused aloud. "Maybe what we need is clever and unexpected. Maybe we need numbers."

Eld consulted his tome of spells—now significantly updated thanks to his studies at Bathurst—and set to work.

His hands wove patterns in the air, channeling necromantic energy into the scattered remains around him. Lea and Talbot watched as creatures began to take shape—but not the lumbering monstrosities one might expect from a necromancer's army.

Instead, Eld took a page out of the late Professor Hemlock's book—crafting a wide assortment of smaller creatures. Last time, he'd solely channeled spirits during the Tournament of Shadows, but this time, he bound those spirits back to old flesh.

As Eld worked, he consulted his small, leather-bound tome filled with hastily scrawled notes and diagrams, the very best of the spells and combinations he'd learned in his classes.

Every so often, he stepped forward with stitches and needles to make some finer modifications.

To Eld's surprise, he felt a pang in his heart as he emulated Professor McGrath's Weave and Bind method. The leprechaun artificer was probably one of the most unsettling teachers at Bathurst, but he'd deserved a far better fate than what he'd gotten.

McGrath and Hemlock were at the top of Eld's mind as he worked. In a way, by applying their lessons to battle Grimthorpe, he was avenging them too.

The thought caused Eld to redouble his efforts and before long, an army of deadly whimsy rose from the earth.

Eld went beyond simply reanimating corpses. He crafted tools, weapons, and distractions that could turn the tide of battle in unexpected ways.

First came a squadron of reanimated frogs with unnaturally elongated tongues, perfect for snatching weapons from unsuspecting hands. An entire force of undead spiders chittered from inside tiny stitched-together ragdolls, ready to be released at a moment's notice. And most impressive of all, a fur coat stitched together from various undead animal pelts, imbued with a life of its own.

"A coat?" Talbot asked.

"The perfect attire for a fancy battle," Eld replied.

"I think it looks quite dashing," Lea chimed in.

As Eld continued working, he stitched together a living fur hat, complete with a wiggling tail.

Lea giggled. "Eld, this is brilliant! Unconventional, but brilliant!"

Talbot, who had been watching with an air of lazy amusement, yawned loudly as he surveyed the rising forces.

"It's exhausting just watching you…" the poltergeist groaned.

But Eld wasn't done working yet.

Still thinking of Professor Hemlock, he concentrated and imbued his new fur coat with vampire-like qualities, allowing it to detach and fly around, latching onto foes and draining their energy.

"You might be onto something here. Based on what I know of him, Grimthorpe and his followers will be expecting brute force. They won't know how to handle this," Talbot said.

"That's the idea. We may not have the raw power to match them, but we can outthink them," Eld replied. "Overwhelm them with the unexpected. And I'm not done yet."

He glanced at the reanimated fur hat, wondering just what he could do to make it special. Maybe he could consult Lilith for ideas when he got back.

As the forest grew darker, the eternal twilight of Bathurst deepening into true night. Off in the distance, Eld saw will-o-wisps bobbing back and forth.

"Stop," Eld murmured, raising his hand.

The reanimated army promptly ceased their scuttling.

He jerked his head towards the will-o-wisps.

"I think we're being summoned," he muttered. "Probably some announcement by Grimthorpe, if the will o' wisps have come this far."

Lea and Talbot stood up behind him, hastily shushing the troops.

"Let's head back," Eld said. "Don't want them to think anything is wrong."

He opened up his usual black coat, gathering as many of his new allies as he could. Then he put the rest in the fur coat and hat, tying them onto Shuck.

"Shuck, can you lead them back to our room?"

Shuck wagged his tail and Eld grinned.

"Alright. Good boy—I know I can always trust you."

As they walked back to Bathurst's main campus, they saw that the grounds were swarmed with spectral will-o-wisps.

The lights bobbed insistently around them.

A slow whisper emanated from the glowing lights.

"The headmaster awaits you in the main hall…all students are being summoned for an important announcement."

Eld, Lea, and Talbot nodded at each other, their faces pale but determined.

They made their way back to Bathurst and as they entered the great hall, Eld saw Grimthorpe standing at the front of the room, in front of the assembled students.

"My dear students," Grimthorpe began, his eyes sweeping across the crowd, "I have an exciting announcement. This year, attendance at the Necropromicon will be mandatory for all students."

A murmur of surprise rippled through the crowd.

Eld exchanged worried glances with Lea and Lilith. This confirmed their worst fears—Grimthorpe was indeed planning something big, and he needed all the students present to pull it off.

As Grimthorpe continued his speech, peppering it with jokes about antisocial behavior and the importance of academic engagement, everything started adding up—Lilith's theories, the pieces of information they had gathered.

Eld glanced through the crowd, hoping to find Wolfgang, Orlando, *someone.*

With everyone assembled here, this was their chance to stop Grimthorpe before he could enact his terrible plan.

But as Eld met eyes with Wolfgang, the werewolf shook his head a single time before glancing through the crowd.

They couldn't possibly attack Grimthorpe now.

Their alliance still wasn't strong enough.

And as for the other students, Eld still had no real proof of what Grimthorpe was doing. It would be far too dangerous to act now—for all he knew, everyone might just take the headmaster's side instead of his.

Their current level of preparation still wasn't enough.

They needed additional variables in their favor…

But how?

As the assembly dispersed, and they made their way back to Eld's room, Eld felt a strange presence lingering at the edges of his perception.

Reaching out with his necromantic senses, he was shocked to recognize the ethereal signature of Professor Hemlock.

"Professor?" Eld whispered, his voice barely audible.

There was no response.

But she was there. He knew it.

It was just the faintest whisper.

"Lea…" Eld whispered. "Can you feel that?"

"Yes…" she whispered. "But…"

On instinct, Eld reached out and grasped Lea's hand, intertwining their fingers.

For some reason, it felt like the right thing to do.

The moment their skin touched, a jolt of energy passed between them. Lea gasped, and her cosmic eyes flared.

"Eld, what's happening?" Lea asked, her grip on his hand tightening.

"I think…I think you're helping me…" he said.

As Eld extended his awareness, trying to make contact with Hemlock's ghostly essence, Lea's power surged uncontrollably. The air around them warped and twisted, reality bending under the weight of their combined energies.

A pulse of power erupted from their joined hands, yanking Professor Hemlock's spirit towards them.

In that moment of chaos, Eld's necromantic abilities flared. There was a blinding flash of light, followed by silence.

"Oh dear," came a voice that was partly arachnid clicks and cultured academic tones. "This is unexpected."

Still holding Lea's hand, Eld looked down to see Spinderella, the spider on his shoulder, now slightly larger and emanating an aura of intelligence that hadn't been there before. Her personality had been strangely split somehow.

At times, Eld felt the shy but loyal spider from before.

But at others…

"Professor Hemlock?" Eld asked.

The spider-professor hybrid wriggled its legs in what might have been a shrug. "It appears so, Mr. Blackwood. Though I must say, this is not how I envisioned my afterlife."

Lea's eyes were wide with shock, her hand still clasped tightly in Eld's. "Did we just…?"

"Accidentally merge Professor Hemlock's soul with a spider?" Eld nodded. "Yeah, I think we did."

In a weird way, this was a relief.

Back then, Talbot had accused Eld of trapping another person's soul inside Franky.

Well, now he got to see what it actually looked like. It was the strange case of Professor Hemlock and Ms. Spinderella…

Spinderella-Hemlock cleared her throat—or whatever passed for a throat in her new form. "While this is certainly not ideal, perhaps we can use this unique situation to our advantage. I believe I can be of assistance."

"Assistance?" Eld asked.

"Yes, with our little headmaster problem. There are other professors who would stand against Grimthorpe, if only they knew the truth."

Acutely aware of their need for more experienced allies, Eld nodded slowly. "Alright, Professor. What do you suggest?"

Spinderella-Hemlock outlined a plan to gather sympathetic faculty members.

But as she spoke, Eld couldn't shake the feeling that they were balancing on a knife's edge. One wrong move could send their entire plan crashing down around them. After all, what if the professors were more loyal to Grimthorpe than to Hemlock?

But as he looked at Lea, Eld knew he had to take this chance, no matter the risks. He hated to admit it, but his alliance wasn't powerful enough yet—especially if Grimthorpe sought backup from Eld's father.

Eld squared his shoulders. "Okay, team. Let's do this."

As they set off to put Spinderella-Hemlock's plan into motion, Eld's hand brushed against something in his pocket. He pulled out a crumpled envelope, his eyes widening in recognition.

"Oh! The letter!" he exclaimed.

With everything that had happened—and Grimthorpe's plan unveiled in other ways—he'd completely forgotten about it.

"That seal," Lea muttered.

"Does it look familiar?" Eld asked.

"Um…no? I was just wondering why you haven't opened it yet."

"What?" Eld asked. "I couldn't. It—"

Lea reached out, her fingers brushing against the sealed envelope.

To Eld's surprise, the seal crumbled at her touch, the letter falling open effortlessly thanks to Lea's void magic. Eld unfolded the parchment slowly, and with trembling hands, Eld began to read.

The note was startlingly simple.

Grimthorpe.

For our plan to succeed, you must break the blood oath created by my cursed ancestor.

Thankfully, my no account eldest son—Eldritch B. Blackwood—is the perfect sacrificial lamb.

End his life and the great beast Azalea's power will be ours.

Eld knew his father.

But he still had to read the note three times before comprehending it.

"What is it?" Lea asked. "Your face is very pale."

Eld clenched his teeth. "I knew my father didn't like me, but I didn't know he sent me here to be a sacrifice!"

Eld stood up and paced across the floor of his room, crumpling his father's letter to Grimthorpe.

Lea reached out trying to comfort him. "Maybe you read it wrong."

Eld handed the note over.

As she read, her face twisted in horror—then anger. "Great beast? How dare he!"

"You have my condolences Mr. Blackwood," Spinderella-Hemlock said. "If it's any consolation I've always hated your father, but this doesn't change anything. We have faculty to recruit."

Eld glanced down at the letter and then up at Lea.

Channeling a spell into his hand he incinerated the parchment into ash and let it fall to the floor. "Alright. Who's first?"

Chapter 31

The Tragic Difference Between Work Friends and Real Friends

Eld, Lea, Lilith, and Talbot crept through the halls.

The bizarre fusion of spider and deceased professor, Spinderella-Hemlock, perched on Eld's shoulder, her eyes darting about nervously. Every so often, Eld felt the two personalities inside the body shifting control, but it made little difference—both were extremely nervous.

"I still can't believe we're doing this," Lea whispered. "Recruiting professors for our rebellion? It feels wrong somehow."

"Well, I mean, it can't be worse than *that*," Lilith whispered, pointing at Spinderella-Hemlock.

Spinderella-Hemlock's fangs clicked. "This body wasn't my first choice either," she said, her voice defensive. "I—"

Before she could finish her sentence, her complaint dissolved into a bunch of mishmashed chittering.

Lea and Lilith stared at Spinderella-Hemlock in alarm, but Eld just laughed.

"What's so funny?" Lea asked.

"Spinderella is saying that Professor Hemlock isn't exactly the bodymate she would have preferred," Eld chuckled.

Lea's eyes swirled with stars and she frowned before gently interjecting. "Um, Professor? Not to be rude…but were you well-liked by your colleagues?"

The spider-professor hybrid chittered her mandibles indignantly. "Of course I was! We were all the best of friends. They'll be furious when they learn of my untimely demise."

Eld gulped.

Considering Spinderella's irritation, he wasn't so sure about that.

Hemlock had been a wonderful teacher, but he could definitely see how her finicky ways might rub her colleagues the wrong way. Not to mention the fact that she kept an exorbitant number of pests with her at all times. Eld had a feeling that the other professors all slept under malaria nets.

Eld hesitated before saying, "Perhaps they'll want to avenge both you and Headmaster Vilethorn. That might be a strong motivator."

Spinderella-Hemlock waved a spindly leg dismissively. "Oh, please. The old headmaster was just some guy. They'll be far more concerned about me, I assure you. And not only did Grimthorpe *kill* me, he took over my mind, too. I'm sure my dear friends would find this an unacceptable violation!"

When the Hemlock side finished speaking, Spinderella began chittering angrily again.

Eld snorted. Spinderella was wondering how Grimthorpe had taken over Hemlock's mind, so she could do it too.

As they approached the first professor's office on Spinderella-Hemlock's list, tension hung heavy in the air.

Talbot, floating lazily behind the group, cleared his throat. The poltergeist tugged at his ghostly collar. "I'm thinking maybe I shouldn't be part of this recruitment drive."

Lilith turned, raising a brow. "Why's that?"

Shrugging, Talbot faded in and out. "Let's face it, I'm not exactly the poster child for academic excellence. My presence might, um, discourage the professors from joining our little rebellion."

"That's actually not a bad point, Talbot," Eld said.

"Kicking you out is a great idea—you're a horrible student." Lilith nodded enthusiastically. "Considering how many times you've failed your first year, the professors would probably be afraid of our rebellion failing."

"Couldn't agree more," Talbot said. "Time to skip this presentation—and take a nice long nap."

As Talbot began to drift away, looking all too pleased with himself, Spinderella-Hemlock suddenly shot out a strand of webbing, ensnaring his harp.

"Not so fast, Mr. Wilting." The spider-professor reeled him in. "If you're not coming with us, you're going to practice with that suit of armor. No slacking off!"

"Ugh, did that string come from your butt?"

"On my abdomen, my spinnerets to be exact," Hemlock corrected. "Now come along."

Talbot's protests faded as Spinderella-Hemlock dragged him away, leaving Eld, Lea, and Lilith standing before the first professor's door.

"Did she just leave too?" Lilith asked.

"Um, Professor?" Lea called down the hall.

Aside from Talbot's groaning, there was no response.

Eld sighed. "You know, she was like this in class too…once she got focused on correcting a particular mistake, she just forgot everything else."

Lea gulped. "I mean. I guess we'll have to go alone then."

Eld sighed. "Cross your fingers and pray to whatever deities you believe in that this works."

With exaggerated care, they crept into the office of the Professor Mammon, Director of Human Studies.

The room was filled with mundane human artifacts and magical paraphernalia. A toaster sat next to a crystal ball, while a stack of fashion magazines teetered precariously beside a tome of eldritch lore. The one on the top advertised a swirling red gala dress.

Professor Mammon himself was a ghost, a portly and mustachioed translucent man hovering behind a desk. He looked up in surprise as they entered. "I'm sorry? Are you students? I don't believe you've taken my classes before."

"Professor Mammon," Eld began. "There's not too much time to introduce ourselves, but we're all first years and we need your help. Bathurst is in danger, and—"

He was cut off as Spinderella-Hemlock scuttled into the classroom, waving one of her legs. "Reginald! Old friend! It's me, Hemlock!"

The ghost professor's mouth when slack with shock. "Hemlock? But how? Why are you a spider?"

As Spinderella-Hemlock launched into an explanation, Eld noticed the ghostly professor's expression growing increasingly annoyed.

"...and so, we need your help to stop Grimthorpe and save the school!" Spinderella-Hemlock finished, placing four of her eight legs on her abdomen.

The ghost professor was silent for a long moment before speaking. "Hemlock, do you remember how you used to burn the coffee in the staff room?"

Spinderella-Hemlock clicked her mandibles in confusion. "Well, yes, but I don't see what my love for piping hot coffee has to do with—"

"I'm a ghost, Hemlock. I can't even drink coffee. But every morning, I'd float into that staff room and be assaulted by the stench of your burnt offerings."

Eld, Lea, and Lilith exchanged uncomfortable, furtive glances as the professor continued his tirade.

"And let's not forget the time you tried to steal my wife!"

Eld couldn't help but ask. "Steal her?"

Hemlock shrugged. "Well she was quite beautiful and you were quite dead, Reginald. At the time vampires were very popular so I took advantage of the situation."

The professor nodded vigorously. "Yes! Hemlock here thought it would be a grand idea to swear a blood oath with my wife! Does that sound appropriate to you?"

Eld fought back a snicker. Lea elbowed him gently, but he could see the corners of her mouth twitching as well.

The professor's expression softened. "But if what you're saying about Grimthorpe is true, then the fate of the school—and perhaps the world—is at stake. Annoying as you may be, Hemlock, I can't stand by and let that happen."

Buoyed by their first success, they moved on to their next target, the Daemonology professor. They approached his office and the air grew thick with the scent of brimstone and exotic incense.

Eld turned to Lilith, muttering under his breath. "So…was Hemlock friends with *him?* Or with one of the daemons who possessed him?"

"I heard that, Mr. Blackwood," Spinderella-Hemlock replied. "And I was friends with the original Professor Albright. I never got along well with the current daemon possessing him, though in the past, there were a few daemons whose company I…rather enjoyed."

She tittered far too suggestively for Eld's comfort. After reanimating Professor Hemlock, he was really learning a bit too much information about her.

Eld's knuckles grazed the door and it swung open with an ominous creak.

Professor Albright stood at the threshold.

"Took you long enough," Albright growled. Within moments, Eld knew that something was wrong—the scholarly professor's voice had a menacing growl lurking beneath the surface. "Get in here before someone sees you."

He ushered the group into the office.

"So, about—"

Albright started to speak but stopped, his body convulsing.

His head snapped back, mouth agape as inky black smoke poured forth. The smoke manifested into a vaguely humanoid shape beside him, its eyes were like embers in a face of living shadow.

"So these are the little rebels," the daemon purred. "How quaint." A smoky finger gestured at Eld. "You know…you *were* one of the most entertaining students I've ever had…"

Eld swallowed hard. Lea's hand found his, grounding him.

Now fully himself again, Albright cleared his throat. "Yes, well. Hemlock's death wasn't some unfortunate accident, was it?"

Spinderella-Hemlock puffed up, her legs twitching indignantly. "Of course n—"

"Murdered," Albright and the daemon said in unison. "We suspected as much. Neither you or McGrath have taken a vacation in at least a hundred years. Though I'll admit, if not for this whole conspiracy business, I might've been tempted to do the deed myself."

The spider-professor deflated. "But why?"

Albright pinched the bridge of his nose while the daemon cackled. "Your blasted blood magic, Hemlock. You would bathe in a storm of blood every morning, but your rooms are above mine…do you have any idea how difficult it is to maintain a summoning circle when the floor's vibrating like a ship in a storm?"

The daemon nodded. "Most undignified, being yanked back and forth between realms. Gave me a frightful headache."

As Spinderella-Hemlock sputtered indignantly, Eld stepped forward. "Professor, we need your help—both of you. Grimthorpe's planning something catastrophic."

Albright and the daemon exchanged a look. "We've had our suspicions. He's been far too interested in certain forbidden texts lately."

"Nasty business, those books," the daemon added. "Even I have standards."

Eld began outlining their plan, but Albright held up a hand, stopping him mid-sentence. "Hold up. You're planning to strike before the Necropromicon? Absolutely not. You'll fail."

Lilith's brow furrowed. "But we thought surprise was our best advantage."

"We have no need for surprise," Albright stated.

"What?" Eld asked, his eyes narrowing with suspicion.

He half thought that Albright was some kind of double agent at this point.

Clearly, Lilith thought the same way. "If we wait until Necropromicon, we'll be playing right into Grimthorpe's hands!" she exclaimed. "What are you playing at?"

A grin spread across Albright's face, mirrored by the daemon's smoldering visage.

"Playing? On the contrary, Miss Nightshade…an event as big as the Necropromicon requires security. And we've contracted a Daemon Bouncer Service for the event."

The daemon preened. "My cousins, actually. Dreadful brutes, but very professional."

"Wait until the Necropromicon, and we'll have an army of infernal security at our disposal," Albright said.

Eld's jaw dropped. "Daemon Bouncers? That's an actual thing?"

"Indeed." Albright chuckled, leaning back in his chair as the daemon performed an eerily graceful pirouette. "All the rage for high-end supernatural soirees. Utterly incorruptible once contracted."

"We take our work very seriously," the daemon added. "Any troublemakers will find themselves ejected from this plane of existence entirely."

With Albright, his daemon, and an entire squad of infernal bouncers on their side, their chances had improved dramatically.

Eld squared his shoulders. "Alright, we'll wait for the Necropromicon. But what do we do until then?"

Albright's eyes narrowed. "Why, prepare for the party of the century, of course. And perhaps a little lesson in advanced summoning wouldn't go amiss."

Albright began pulling out tomes and the daemon started drawing complex sigils in the air. Eld realized their rebellion had just gained some very powerful—and very dangerous—allies.

As they left the Daemonology professor's office, their spirits were high.

Two powerful allies gained, and a plan that seemed more feasible by the minute.

"Just one more to go," Eld said, consulting Spinderella-Hemlock's list. His face fell as he read the names. "Huh? What is this? Some kind of joke?"

Lea peered over his shoulder. "Professor Grimthorpe himself? Professor Hemlock, this can't be right."

The spider-professor clicked her mandibles in confusion, peering over. "Oh. My mistake…I just handed over my list of friends…I forgot to update it."

She chittered out something, then gestured emphatically with a leg.

Nothing happened

"Oh, bullocks," she sighed. "It seems like my magic has vanished in this form…just tear his name off, if you don't mind."

Chapter 32

Dancing on Their Graves, Our Graves...Really Just Everyone's Graves

The grand hall thumped with loud rattling music as spectral musicians shook maracas filled with loose rattling bones.

"Oh, to have my vampire body..." Spinderella-Hemlock moaned. "The Thankful Dead were always one of my favorite bands..."

Eld barely heard her.

The room before him was a spectacle of supernatural extravagance, decorated with floating witchlights and shimmering black tapestries made of woven moonlight and shadow.

Every single one of the paintings depicted the Black Sun. Since Grimthorpe had picked out the paintings, Eld knew this wasn't just a random omen. Perhaps the tapestries were part of the ritual.

Eld's heart raced, threatening to burst from his chest like some kind of eldritch parasite.

Ever since he'd woken up Lea, it had felt like his heart was coming back to life. Now, it felt like he was feeling all the nervous physical reactions he'd eschewed over the last few decades.

Bart the zombie rat perched on Eld's shoulder, wearing a diminutive wizard's robe complete with a pointed hat. His red eyes glowed as he surveyed the room, whiskers twitching as he carefully watched for threats.

Shuck lumbered at Eld's side. The reanimated dog's mismatched parts had been re-stitched with new, golden thread that sparkled with each step he took. A ruffled collar adorned its neck, giving the zombie canine an air of aristocratic undeath.

Franky the centipede skittered at the back of the group. The reanimated arthropod sported a tiny top hat between his antennae and a miniature bowtie screwed onto a metal plate, allowing it to stay in place despite its numerous legs. His chitinous body glistened with a fresh black polish.

"I even got an oil change for this event," Franky chittered. His mechanical arms whirled with new power.

Spinderella-Hemlock had taken up residence on the top of Eld's hat. She wore a tiny graduation cap and glasses, maintaining her professorial dignity even in her arachnid form. Every so often, Spinderella's original personality came back to the surface, but it seemed like she enjoyed the finery too. The spider's eight eyes blinked in asynchronous patterns as she took in the grand hall.

Eld's outfit drew curious glances from the other attendees.

His newly stitched fur coat—oversized to accommodate all the pelts he'd reanimated—swished dramatically with each step, the mishmash of pelts creating a quilt of textures. Atop his head perched a raccoon tail hat, its bushy appendage wagging happily with each movement. His rattlesnake hide boots clicked against the polished floor. At his hip hung a ceremonial sword, its jeweled hilt catching the light and throwing miniature rainbows across the room.

As Eld made his way further into the hall, his attention was drawn to the imposing daemons flanking the entrance.

The daemon bouncers were ten-foot-tall guards with bodies made of living flames. Their red skin glistened beneath the endlessly lit fire surrounding them, and their muscles ripped beneath elaborate armor forged out of a metal so dark it looked like the void of space.

Every one of them carried a different weapon, which seemed like the only way to tell them apart.

The daemon right in front of Eld held a wickedly curved scimitar, and the one behind him carried a halberd. Off in the distance, a daemon with a whip gestured crudely to direct people into different lines. A strange aura surrounded each of their weapons, a razor-sharp light that cut into Eld's mind whenever he glimpsed at it.

Spinderella-Hemlock chittered from inside Eld's hat. "Those weapons...they won't just cut the body. But the soul as well."

"My sensors detect a danger level of twenty," Franky said, his voice awestruck.

Eld didn't know what scale Franky was using, but the tone of voice was enough.

He swallowed hard, his throat suddenly dry as the deserts of a hell dimension.

Technically, he knew these were his allies, but he'd read enough legends to know about the dangers of daemonic contracts. He couldn't help but wonder if these infernal guardians would truly be on their side when the time came.

A bead of sweat trickled down the back of his neck as he debated whether to acknowledge them.

Due to Albright's possession, Eld hadn't actually learned very much about daemonology this school year. His inexperience left him unsure of the proper etiquette when dealing with beings who could probably tear him limb from limb without a second thought.

Before he could decide, one of the daemons leaned down, its hot breath tickling Eld's ear and carrying the faint scent of sulfur. There was a slowly revving chainsaw strapped to this particular daemon's back. "We have additional backup coming," he whispered, his voice like gravel being crushed. "Rest assured."

Then, as quickly as it had broken protocol, the daemon straightened as if nothing had happened.

Eld did his best to maintain his composure, but his nerves were screaming like a horde of reanimated hounds.

He took a deep breath and reminded himself that he had faced far stranger things than potentially treacherous daemon bouncers. After all, he had once had to wrangle a reanimated singing squid that had decided it wanted to be a land creature back into the seas. Surely this couldn't be more daunting than eight suckered tentacles with delusions of pedestrianism.

"Eld! There you are!" Lea's voice cut through his thoughts like a ray of starlight piercing a dark void.

She abruptly appeared at his side, looking resplendent in a gown that seemed to be woven from the very fabric of the cosmos. Nebulae swirled across the bodice, stars twinkled in the folds of the skirt, and the long silken train behind her left a faint trail of stardust in her wake.

Eld felt his cheeks warm as he took in everything about her, momentarily forgetting why they were there. His favorite thing was how warmly she smiled at his pets as they eagerly greeted her.

"Lea, you look…" Eld fumbled for words.

"Beautiful, I know," she said, smiling mischievously. "And thank you. And you look like you raided a *very* fashionable taxidermist's shop. Did you leave any animals for the rest of the forest?"

Eld chuckled, some of the tension relaxing from his shoulders. "Well, one must dress for the occasion, especially when said occasion might involve saving the world."

Moving onto the dance floor, Eld's eyes darted around, cataloging the positions of friends and foes alike.

Lilith stood near one of the refreshment tables, engaged in a conversation with Orlando.

The banshee's silver hair seemed to move of its own accord, reflecting her agitation, while the vampire's usual air of aristocratic boredom was betrayed by the tightness around his eyes and the way his fingers drummed restlessly against his leg, clearly itching to wrap around the hilt of a sword.

Wolfgang caught Eld's eye from across the room and offered him a reassuring nod.

The werewolf was wearing a simple black suit and tie with a white shirt, an imitation of Old One fashions Eld had seen in one of Professor Mammon's magazines. His eyes shone with a feral light, and his muscles seemed to ripple beneath his elegant formal wear, as if he was only a heartbeat away from transforming.

Eld's brow furrowed as he realized someone was missing from their motley crew. "Where's Talbot?" he asked, scanning the room for any sign of their ghostly companion.

"I haven't seen him. You don't think he forgot, do you? Or worse, decided that saving the world was too much effort?" Lea said.

Spinderella-Hemlock scuttled down his hat and perched on his shoulder next to Bart. "If you're looking for that layabout Wilting. I left him snoring in his bed. The nerve of that boy, sleeping through such an important event! In my day, students would have given their fangs for the chance to attend a Necropromicon, let alone participate in a world-saving rebellion!"

Eld, electing not to mention that Professor Hemlock's "day" was just a few days ago, let out an exasperated sigh. "Professor, we need everyone here. Talbot's part of the plan!"

Hemlock's eyes blinked in unison. "Well, perhaps if he had shown more initiative during his many, many years as my student, I would have been more inclined to drag his spectral behind out of bed. Do you know how many times he failed Intermediate Haunting? The boy couldn't even rattle a chain convincingly! And he's supposed to be a poltergeist!"

A commotion near the entrance made Eld turn. Mortimer Vex and his gang had arrived, their raucous laughter cutting through the ambient noise of the party like a scythe through cemetery grass. Erik the Drowned flexed his waterlogged muscles, sending droplets flying as he guffawed at something Mortimer had said, the water leaving small trails of algae growth wherever it landed.

The whole bunch of them were acting like a bunch of hooligans, and they stank of enough liquor to, well, intoxicate a zombie.

"Honestly, you'd think being several centuries old would lend one some maturity. They're acting like they're at their first Deathday party," Eld muttered.

Eld glanced at Lilith to see if she was paying any attention to Erik, but her attention was focused entirely on Orlando.

Lea squeezed his hand, her touch sending a jolt of energy through him that made his hair stand on end. "Some people never grow up, no matter how long they live. But we have bigger concerns right now. Like the fact that Grimthorpe is staring at us as if we're the main course at a ghoul's banquet."

She was right, of course.

Eld's turned to the raised dais in the center of the banquet hall where the professors sat.

They chatted and laughed, the picture of academic camaraderie, but Eld could see the strain in their smiles, the tension in their shoulders. It was like watching a group of rabbits trying to convince themselves that the fox in their midst was just another long-eared, carrot-munching friend.

But still, Eld felt optimistic. It wasn't just the two professors they'd recruited—those professors had told their friends as well. Everyone at the table was plotting against Grimthorpe.

To his surprise, Hemlock huffed indignantly, her mandibles clicking in extreme disapproval. "Look at them, carrying on as if nothing has happened! Not a stitch of mourning attire among them. Have they no respect for the dead? Why, in my day, we would have worn black for at least a century after the passing of a colleague!"

"I think they're just trying to keep up appearances," Eld said softly. "After all, they are supposed to believe that you're on a trip. But if you pay close attention, they look about as relaxed as a ghoul at a vegetarian buffet. See how Professor Cadaver's stitches are straining? And I swear I just saw one of Professor Mammon's ghostly hands pass right through his goblet."

The spider-professor scoffed in disagreement. "Nonsense! They're clearly enjoying themselves far too much. Why, in my day—"

Whatever reminiscence Spinderella-Hemlock had been about to launch into was cut short as the lights dimmed and the music swelled.

A spectral orchestra emerged from the walls, playing a tune that seemed to bypass the ears entirely and resonate directly in the soul, a melody that spoke of ancient rites and eldritch powers.

At that precise moment, Grimthorpe's voice filled the hall.

"Welcome, students and faculty, to this year's Necropromicon!" The headmaster's gaze swept across the room. "Let the festivities begin!"

With those words, couples paired off, swirling across the dance floor in a dizzying array of colorful robes and glittering jewelry.

Eld watched as Professor Albright led a dainty gorgon he didn't recognize in a waltz that seemed to defy the laws of physics, their feet barely touching the ground as they moved through steps that occasionally appeared to take them in directions not entirely aligned with this reality.

"May I have this dance?" Eld asked.

He turned to Lea with an exaggerated bow that sent Spinderella-Hemlock scrambling to hold onto his shoulder.

Lea laughed, the sound like tinkling starlight, galaxies being born in the space between seconds. "I thought you'd never ask. Just try not to step on my toes—I'd hate to have to explain to Grimthorpe why there's a localized black hole on the dance floor."

"Wait." Eld's brow knitted. "Is that something that you can do?"

"No idea," Lea smiled and jerked him onto the dance floor.

They joined the throng of dancers.

Here they were, on the brink of a potentially world-ending confrontation, and they were dancing as if at a normal school function. Well, as normal as a function could be when half the attendees were various flavors of undead and the other half were nightkin practicing dark arts that would make most people's hair turn white from sheer terror.

"You know under different circumstances, this might actually be fun." Lea twirled as Eld spun her, her dress leaving a trail of cosmic dust that hung in the air like a miniature nebula. "It's not every day you get to dance with a dashing necromancer at a party that could end with either the world being saved or completely destroyed."

Eld dipped Lea low enough that her hair nearly brushed the floor. "Who says we can't enjoy ourselves a little before saving the world? After all, if these are our last moments, I'd rather spend them dancing with you than fretting about impending doom."

But with that said, even as they continued to dance, Eld's eyes never stopped moving.

Orlando led Lilith in a stiff, formal dance, both of them far more focused on scanning the crowd than on their footwork. The vampire's movements were almost too perfect, while Lilith occasionally forgot to touch the ground entirely, her banshee nature causing her to float for moments at a time.

Even Hemlock eventually found a partner, skittering off of Eld's hat and performing an awkward eight-legged shuffle with a very confused-looking chipmunk familiar.

The sight of the spider-professor attempting to lead while her arachnid body moved in eight different directions at once was almost enough to make Eld forget the danger they were in.

Almost.

As midnight approached, the tension in the room grew.

"It has to be midnight," Lea murmured. "According to Lilith's research, everything has to happen during the winter solstice."

"And reading Grimthorpe's notes, I'm sure he doesn't want to wait a second longer," Eld replied.

Eld could feel the building tension thrumming through the soles of his feet, a faint vibration that seemed to emanate from the very stones of the school. It was as if the entire structure was holding its breath, waiting for the moment when everything would change. He exchanged a glance with Lea, seeing galaxies swirling with apprehension.

Grimthorpe's voice suddenly cut through the music. "Attention, everyone! It's time to announce this year's Necropromicon King and Queen!"

"Were we supposed to vote or something?" Lea whispered.

"I have no idea." Eld glanced around.

Everyone else seemed just as confused.

The music screeched to a halt, all eyes turning toward the headmaster. Eld felt his stomach drop as Grimthorpe's gaze settled on him and Lea, a predatory look in those ancient eyes.

It was only then that Eld realized what was about to happen.

"Will Eldritch Blackwood and Lea please join me on stage?"

Lilith caught Eld's eye from across the room, her expression screaming "trap!" louder than her banshee wail ever could.

Eld hesitated, his mind racing through possible scenarios, each more disastrous than the last.

Was this the moment Grimthorpe would spring his trap?

Or were they walking into something even worse than they had anticipated?

Eld glanced through the room, wondering if he should call for his team to strike right away.

"I'm waiting..." Grimthorpe said.

Eld and Lea glanced at each other.

Maybe their best bet was to get close to Grimthorpe...

But what would happen if they got there?

The fur coat around Eld's body shifted elegantly, reminding him that he had hidden backup.

As Eld continued staring at Grimthorpe, he could hear Erik's indignant sputtering. "I didn't know there was going to be a king. I should be king!" the waterlogged bully protested, sending a spray of brackish water across nearby students. "I even have a wave for something like this! Look!"

He demonstrated, his arm moving in a jerky motion that looked less regal and more like he was trying to shake off a particularly stubborn leech.

"Um, maybe Erik should go," Eld said. "I could abdicate for him!"

"No, I want you..." Grimthorpe said.

The headmaster's smile was wide and welcoming, something that Eld didn't particularly enjoy. No offense to Spinderella-Hemlock intended, but it was the look of a spider inviting a fly to tea, with the unspoken understanding that the fly would be the main course.

Time seemed to slow as all eyes turned to Eld and Lea.

Eld tensed, ready to spring into action.

He could feel Lea beside him, her power crackling just beneath the surface like lightning waiting to strike. Though considering her unpredictability, Eld just hoped that it would be directed at the proper source.

This was it, the moment everything would go down.

Then an explosion rocked the hall.

The floor at the center of the hall burst in a shower of stone and dust, sending students scrambling for cover and professors diving under tables. From the newly formed crater emerged a massive figure, metal gleaming in the magic and steam hissing from joints.

Eld's jaw dropped as he recognized the towering thing. "Talbot?"

Encased in a suit of magical armor that stood at least fifteen feet tall, Talbot looked around. His face was visible through the helmet's visor, wearing an embarrassed expression. "Don't get your ectoplasmic panties in a bunch ladies, I'm here!" Talbot's voice boomed from within the construct, echoing off the walls and causing several of the more fragile decorations to shatter. "Sorry I'm late! I overslept!"

The entire hall froze in stunned silence.

Then Talbot shrugged his massive metal shoulders, the movement causing several nearby students to stumble back in fear. "Oh. Wow. I came early for once. Nothing's happened yet! Okay, I'll just attack then!"

He raised the construct's hand and a bolt of crackling energy shot from the palm, striking Grimthorpe square in the chest.

The headmaster flew backward, crashing through the back of the stage in a shower of splinters and smoke, his dignified demeanor quite literally going up in flames.

Chaos erupted.

Chapter 33

Ghostbusters, Zombiebusters, Lichbusters, Et ceterabusters...

Before the Necropromicon, the main hall had been converted into a ballroom. In the blink of an eye, Talbot's clumsy intervention had converted it again into a battlefield.

Dozens of mindless husks filed out from behind the stage. Others clambered into the ballroom, bursting from the walls. Still more fell from the ceiling, and students began screaming as the husk's drool fell upon them like rain.

"Blackwood!" a furious voice cackled.

Eld turned, then groaned.

Utterly oblivious to the larger conspiracy unfolding around them, Mortimer saw Grimthorpe's attack as the perfect opportunity to settle his grudge against Eld. He lunged forward, brandishing a silver-tipped cane like a club, the end twinkling with blood-red fire.

Sidestepping, Eld narrowly avoided a swipe aimed at his head. "Mortimer, this isn't the time!" he shouted. "You don't know what's happening!"

But Eld's attempts at reason were drowned out by the clash of steel, the crackle of magic, and the cacophony of battle.

"This is the perfect time!" Mortimer laughed. "Have you and your idiot friends lost your minds? Attacking the Headmaster? Who knows what I'll get if I bring you down?"

Falling back, Eld conjured spell after spell, parrying Mortimer's assault as best he could.

Unlike during his previous battles, Eld was careful to keep his range. With the awareness he'd gained from the Nocturnal Combat Club, he slowly and steadily backpedaled, avoiding additional foes while elegantly tracing his fingers through the air.

Chains flew towards Mortimer, but the pyromancer fired off a flame spell and then swung his cane to shatter the burnt metal.

Mortimer lunged forward, making a particularly reckless stab to try and close the gap. His cane whistled through the air, only barely missing Eld.

Seizing a brief opening, Eld traced a shimmering claw in the air, then clapped his hands together. Skeletal appendages ripped from the floor to grasp at Mortimer's ankles. For a brief moment, Eld dared to hope that he'd won as Mortimer let out a cry of shock.

But with a sneer, the ghastly pyromancer smashed the bony hands with a single swing of his flaming cane. "I've been waiting for this moment for so long, Blackwood. Always going around helping people, acting like you're better than everybody else."

Mortimer darted forward, flames briefly sparking at his feet, almost like the Old One's engines. With no other choice, Eld drew his ceremonial sword, barely deflecting the blow in time.

The impact reverberated up Eld's arm, and he staggered back. The sword was, after all, purely ceremonial.

"You need to stop and get out of my way!" Eld groaned. "You're *clueless* about what's happening here!"

Mortimer's only response was to conjure a disc of whirling flames. As he ducked under Mortimer's reckless attack, Eld briefly considered using one of the ragdolls he'd created, but he needed those for Grimthorpe.

Instead, he turned to a new spell he'd theorized—one that'd been inspired by Talbot and Wysper's conversation on pranks. With deft fingers, Eld traced out a hive and clapped his hands together, concentrating his necromantic energy.

A horde of glowing green stinkbugs burst into existence, surrounding Mortimer and unleashing a massive toxic cloud. The bugs might have been spiritual, but the stink—magically broadcast straight into Mortimer's soul—certainly wasn't.

As Mortimer staggered back, Eld broke away, sprinting through the melee towards Grimthorpe.

The ballroom had descended into utter pandemonium, magical combat illuminating the frenzied faces of allies and adversaries alike. Adrenaline rushed through him, and as he thought of Lea, his pulse reignited, even though they weren't touching each other. The thumping drummed in his ears as he watched his friends holding their ground, slowly pushing back against Grimthorpe's forces.

"Eld! Behind you!" Lea's voice cut through the noise.

Eld pivoted just in time to see a husk waiter lunging at him, decaying hands outstretched.

Shuck intercepted the undead servant just in the nick of time. The reanimated canine's jaws clamped down on the zombie's throat and Shuck shook it till its head came loose, rendering it inert in seconds.

"Good boy, Shuck!" Eld called out.

But without granting any reprieve, more undead waitstaff converged on him and Lea, their murky yet ravenous eyes fixed on their targets.

Lea raised her hands.

Void magic burst from her body and Eld thought that this would all end in a single moment.

But then her magic dissipated. Lea was struggling to cast even the simplest spell, her face was pale and her hands were trembling badly. The constellations in her eyes flickered and dimmed.

"Stay close!" Eld yelled, reaching out to her.

"This isn't a job for students, Mr. Blackwood," a chirpy voice cried.

Spinderella-Hemlock scuttled from Eld's hat and onto the ground.

The blunderbuss concealed within Eld's raccoon hat—a special design created by Lilith—unfolded itself. Hemlock caught it with three arms, aimed, and fired, the blast tearing through the ranks of the undead.

Hemlock's eyes beamed with a manic glee as she aimed again. "Take that, you mindless flesh-bags!" she cackled. The blunderbuss roared to life once more, sending another group of zombies flying. "Oh, how I've missed this!" Hemlock exclaimed, her mandibles clicking excitedly. "It's been far too long since I've had a proper academic debate!"

Another blast sent her tiny little body recoiling and another wave of undead was sent sprawling.

Hemlock scrambled to her feet, her laughter grew more unhinged with each shot. "This is for every student who ever fell asleep in my class!"

She fired, taking out a husk's midsection. "And this is for that time someone put whoopee cushions on all the chairs in the faculty lounge!"

She turned to Eld, all eight eyes sparkling with joy. "Mr. Blackwood, I do believe I've found my new favorite teaching method! No more dungeons, no more bats or mosquitoes, just cold, hard firepower!" she declared before unleashing another barrage of blasts. She was cackling so maniacally that Eld was worried he'd somehow stuffed McGrath into Spinderella's body too.

All around the, the fight surged like a tempestuous sea.

Shuck leaped at another zombie, clamping down on its leg and dragging it to the ground with primal ferocity. Bart, amplified by Eld's magic, darted through the fray, his newly massive teeth and claws causing havoc wherever they went. Franky reared up on his dozens of hind legs, his mechanized limbs gleaming.

"Franky Blast!"

Lightning sizzled from his limbs, cutting a hole in the literally shocked husks.

Unfortunately, Eld's heart sank as he spotted Erik the Drowned rapidly approaching through that hole, his face contorted with rage.

Erik's waterlogged flesh glistening in the magical light, looked particularly incensed. "You think you can steal my crown?" he snarled, water dribbling from his lips. "I was destined to be Necropromicon King! I'm destined to be all kings!"

Eld could hardly believe what he was hearing.

"Erik, you're missing the bigger picture," Eld began, attempting to explain the dire situation. "This goes beyond some dance—"

But Erik was beyond reason. "I was sacrificed! My dream of becoming Necropromicon King was stolen from me!"

"You didn't even know there was a Necropromicon King until a few minutes ago!"

"It doesn't matter! It was my destiny!"

The waterlogged thug moved with unnatural quickness. Before long, he was right in Eld's face, his breath stinking of rotten fish. He grabbed onto Eld, and his cold fingers sent shivers down Eld's spine, disrupting his focus and making spellcasting impossible.

Eld tried shoving him off, but Erik's cold and clammy skin made it nearly impossible for Eld to gain a solid grip.

He swung a meaty fist at Eld, connecting with his shoulder and sending him staggering backward across the floor.

Lea's scream pierced the air. "Eld!"

Struggling to his feet sent pain radiating through Eld's body, but then the drowned zombie was onto him again. Eld fell back, desperately swinging his ceremonial sword to try and ward him off. Erik's athleticism had turned the fight into a desperate scramble for survival.

As Erik closed in for what seemed like the killing blow, a thunderous roar echoed through the ballroom.

Fully transformed into a werewolf, Wolfgang barreled into Erik with the force of a freight train. The two powerhouses clashed in a whirlwind of teeth and claws.

Eld staggered upright, gulping in air as he frantically scanned the room.

"Eld!" Lea cried. "You're alright!"

"Hopefully Wolfgang is too," Eld muttered.

But it seemed like the werewolf was holding his own. The furious brawl between Wolfgang and Erik was far more vicious than the battle at the Tournament of Shadows. Their furious fight left craters all throughout the ballroom, sending torn-off chunks of fur and gushes of black blood mixed with briny saltwater flying haphazardly through the ballroom.

Suddenly, echoing toll bells blared, sending an otherworld shiver through Eld's very being. The sound wrapped itself in his mind, ruthless as an anaconda strangling its prey.

A fiery voice bellowed.

"Uphold the contract!" before charging into the fray.

The tide of battle shifted as daemonic reinforcements arrived—massive beings that towered over the crowd, wearing absurdly massive white dress shirts and sports coats that made them look like a parody of private security.

"We're winning…" Eld breathed.

The daemonic bouncers clashed with reanimated corpses, and more and more students were joining their side, their faces twisted in fury at the thought of the administration interrupting Necropromicon.

Talbot was the biggest rabble-rouser of them all. He fired electricity from his armored hands shouting "Lightning Bolt! Lightning Bolt! Lightning Bolt!"

Skittering and squealing echoed through the chamber as swarms of mosquitos and colonies of bats burst into the chamber. The whole mass of pests began sweeping Grimthorpe's troops right off their feet.

"My millions of pets!" Spinderella-Hemlock cackled. "It's so good to be reunited with you!"

But then, Eld felt a faint tingle in the air.

Large black portals twisted, tearing a hole in the very fabric of reality, and Eld recognized the distinct magical signature of his father and brother.

Moments later, a horde of reanimated troops teleported in.

The sight of Graves, his father's butler, snarling at the front of the reinforcements confirmed Eld's worst fears.

"Graves!" Eld shouted, hoping to appeal to the butler's long-standing loyalty. "I order you to stand down!"

The butler turned, his eyes narrowing and he bared his teeth. "You are no longer the heir, Eldritch. Your name has been struck from the Familial Tome. Cloudehill has claimed his rightful place. I serve him now."

The betrayal stung, but there was no time to dwell on emotional wounds.

"Seems like anyone worth anything is getting struck from the Familial Tome these days," Eld quipped. As he spoke, he twisted his fingers behind his back, creating a simple flare spell to gather Talbot's attention. "You know Graves…I learned my father's secret. He—"

"Don't you dare!" Graves shouted.

With a brusque wave of his arm, he directed his soldiers to fan out. Their target was clear—Eld.

But then Graves frowned.

"Wait. What is that light?"

The wall of the ballroom exploded behind him.

"Oh crap, I missed!" Talbot cried.

The poltergeist—and more importantly at this specific moment, his possessed mech suit—stomped towards Eld, his weapons bristling and armor shining. "Lightning bolt!" Talbot shouted, sending chain lightning arcing through Grave's soldiers. "Hey, Eld! Looks like you could use a hand!"

Relief washed over Eld like a tidal wave as his friend shielded him. "Talbot, you magnificent specter!"

Talbot's grin widened, though now that Eld was right next to him, he realized that the poltergeist looked slightly overwhelmed by the mech's controls. "Uh oh, Eld. It says I'm out of lightning bolts! Do you think I should recharge? This machine might be like me. Needs to sleep a little."

"What? Are you kidding?" Eld asked. "No! Keep fighting!"

"Hey, come on man. Don't get your robes in a knot."

As Talbot spoke, the zombies hammered his mech suit, but with little effect. Their limbs snapped and the stitches fell apart as they struck.

Eld rolled his eyes. Classic Cloudehill stitching.

"Okay then," Talbot said. "Um…let's see what this fancy button does, shall we?"

One of the arm panels opened, glowing with bright mint blue light. Then a vacuum roared to life, sucking up nearby zombies with incredible force and tearing them limb from limb.

"I think this is for ghosts…" Talbot said. "But it's so strong it's sucking these guys up too!"

Eld dodged away from the suction, reaching over to scoop up Franky and Spinderella-Hemlock on his way out. "Hey! Watch where you're aiming that thing!"

With his father's forces scattered, Eld thought he had a moment to catch his breath, but Graves proved relentless.

Even as the other husks were drawn towards Talbot, the butler sneered, advancing on Eld with murderous intent. "Your father has given me the honor of killing you. Your affinity for filthy animals never had a place in the family's noble legacy. Once you're dead Cloudehill will be the oath bearer and the Blackwood name will go down in history for restoring the Black Sun!"

Graves raised a crossbow and fired.

Franky jumped into the bolt's path and squeaked in pain as a bolt pierced its side. "No!" Eld cried out, rushing to his pet's aid. To his relief his upgrades worked, Franky jerked the bolt out with his mandibles and continued fighting.

Unfortunately, Graves lurched forward while Eld was distracted, his fist connecting with Eld's jaw. Eld staggered back, tasting blood. He tried to retaliate with a quick jab, but Graves deflected it effortlessly.

"Is that all you've got, young master?" Graves taunted.

Eld gritted his teeth and kicked Graves back, using a push kick that Wolfgang had taught him.

Then he summoned a burst of necromantic magic with a swift twitch of his fingers. He hurled the green ball of flame at Graves, but the butler dodged, closing the distance between them again in an instant.

Graves' knee drove into Eld's stomach, forcing the air from his lungs. Eld doubled over and Graves brought his elbow down on the back of his neck. Eld crumpled to the floor, his vision blurring.

"Pathetic," Graves sneered, looming over him. "Your father was right to choose Cloudehill. You should have been a lich decades ago, you failure."

Those words ignited a fire in Eld's chest. He swept Graves' legs out from under him, then scrambled to his feet. Unfortunately, Graves recovered quickly, lashing out with a series of precise strikes.

Eld conjured a magic shield, but each impact weakened the magic, shrinking the shield each time. He was being overwhelmed, driven back step by step. Just as Graves seemed poised for victory, Shuck lunged from the side, sinking his teeth into the butler's leg.

Graves howled in pain. "You twice-damned mutt!"

Eld feinted for his ceremonial sword.

"I didn't know you studied the blade," Graves mocked, throwing off Shuck.

"Yeah, not really," Eld replied. Instead of drawing the weapon, Eld tore off his fur coat and hurled it at his opponent. Mid-air, the coat transformed, sprouting fangs and claws as it enveloped Graves.

Graves stumbled back, momentarily disoriented by the bizarre assault. Eld kicked off his rattlesnake skin boots, which came to life and slithered towards Graves, sinking their fangs into his flesh.

"What manner of sorcery is this?" Graves screamed, his body convulsing as paralyzing venom coursed through his veins.

His eyes blazed with fury as he tore the animated coat from his face. "You'll have to do better than that, boy!"

Eld raised his hands and cast yet another spell, combining both the lessons he'd learned at Bathurst with his affinity for the natural world.

A horde of ravenous locusts streaked toward Graves, tearing apart the butler's rotting flesh. Yet Graves still advanced, slower now, but terrifyingly determined. Just as he reached for Eld's throat, Bart scurried up Graves' leg and sank its teeth into his neck, tearing open the butler's throat first.

Graves' eyes rolled back, and he collapsed to the ground, finally defeated.

Panting heavily, Eld stood over his fallen opponent. "I may not have your experience, Graves, but I have something you'll never understand—the determination to stand as my own man."

Even on the ground, Graves' severed head continued its taunts. "You didn't win properly. Just tricks and—"

"That's enough from you." Eld picked up Graves' head and drop-kicked it across the room. Perhaps it was just his imagination, but even in the din of battle, he thought he heard a very satisfying splat.

Eld's pets returned to his side, injured but alive.

Bart limped back, a fork comically stuck in its head and he collapsed at Eld's feet. Eld couldn't help but roll his eyes. "Oh, get up, you melodramatic rat. You're already dead. There's no way a tiny little fork would hurt you"

Eld healed Bart with a quick spell, the rat shaking off his injuries and chittering in gratitude.

Eld's enchanted coat reattached itself, though his sentient rattlesnake skin boots were too preoccupied with biting zombies to return just yet.

Surveying the chaos, Eld spotted Vlad locked in combat with Orlando, their respective vampire armies clashing in a blur of fangs and superhuman speed. Wolfgang continued to tear into Erik, the bully and his cronies backing away in terror.

Mortimer was nowhere to be found. Perhaps he'd fled to wash off the stench of the stink bugs.

Grimthorpe and Professor Albright were engaged in a cataclysmic duel, their spells lighting up the ballroom like a supernatural fireworks display. Grimthorpe's calm facade had shattered, revealing the battle-hardened maniac beneath.

Eld knew he had to intervene.

Reaching into his robes, Eld's hand closed around a series of writhing and twitching hastily tied together sacks.

As Eld ran the epicenter of the magical duel, Grimthorpe unleashed a devastating blast that sent the daemonology professor flying. Professor Albright hit the ground with a sickening crunch, bones shattering on impact.

Grimthorpe turned his attention to Lea and Eld.

Before Eld could get to Grimthorpe, Grimthorpe boomed, "Noitatnacni cinomed!" In a flash, Lea vanished from Eld's side, reappearing next to the lich on the raised stage. Magical bindings snaked around her, wrapping her in place.

Eld froze.

What?

How…

Sparks trailed around Lea's body. He could see her trying to run, trying to teleport, but it was no use. The spell had anchored her to Grimthorpe's side.

Grimthorpe's lips curled into a sneer. "Come and claim her if you dare, boy. Your pitiful skills are no match for true power!"

"Eld, run!" Lea shouted, her voice strained. "It's too dangerous!"

But Eld wouldn't run. He wouldn't abandon her, not now, not ever.

"Lea!" Eld shouted. "I'm going to save you!"

As he ran to the stage, a faint smile—shocked but happy—crossed her lips.

With every step he took towards her, Lea's magic began to build, a palpable force that made the air around her shimmer and warp. Her eyes, once filled with starlight, began to darken, the cosmos within them collapsing into twin voids. Her hair writhed like tentacles, each strand seeming to reach out hungrily towards Grimthorpe.

Even the headmaster looked worried, his confident smirk faltering.

But then, as suddenly as it had begun, Lea's power fizzled out.

Her eyes rolled back, and she slumped forward, unconscious. With a slightly shaky wave of his hand, Grimthorpe reinforced the necromantic bindings holding her in place.

That mysterious magic…

He recognized it.

It was Grimthorpe's time magic.

Previously, it could only be used to restore lost documents, but now, it was far more powerful than it'd ever been before. It was holding Lea in place, slowing her movements down to virtually nothing. That was what allowed Grimthorpe to restrain her, though the magic took its toll on the headmaster. Eld could have sworn he saw a faint tremor in that seemingly regal visage.

Grimthorpe raised his hand again.

Eld braced himself, expecting some kind of an attack, but all Grimthorpe did was curl his body fingers, taunting Eld.

"Come," the headmaster chuckled, teeth clacking.

It was clearly a trap…

But for what?

Chapter 34

Love, Death, and
Other Awkward Spells

As Eld slowly stepped forward, Grimthorpe remained motionless, waiting, making no move to cast a spell or launch an attack. The lack of action was more terrifying than any overt threat.

Around him, the battle raged on. His friends were locked in combat with Grimthorpe's forces, the chaos only intensifying with each passing moment. Spells flashed, weapons clashed, and the air was thick with the acrid smell of dark magic.

But most importantly, no one seemed available to help him or Lea.

Eld was alone—but he already knew what he had to do. He steeled himself and charged towards the stage, his feet pounding against the floor.

As Eld ran, Grimthorpe's smile grew wider, more crazed. The headmaster's lips moved rapidly, chanting words in a language so ancient that the cracked syllables made Eld's ears ache to hear them.

Strange energy crackled in the air, making Eld's skin prickle and his hair stand on end. The floor beneath Eld's feet began glowing, runes appearing in a spiraling pattern that spread outwards from the stage.

Screams erupted from all corners of the room as people collapsed, their souls visibly tearing from their bodies and flowing towards Grimthorpe, feeding his dark ritual. Even the strongest fighters in the room were brought to their knees, their life force being siphoned away.

Eld's loyal pets fell beside him, their reanimated bodies going still as the necromantic energy powering them was drawn away.

Shuck hit the ground with a dull thump, Franky clattered, then remained still, Bart squeaked his last. Even Spinderella-Hemlock was helpless before the curse. For a brief moment, the vampire professor's shocked face was visible as it seeped out of the spider's body, then it joined the ectoplasmic swill surrounding Grimthorpe.

But Eld kept running.

He knew it wasn't just Lea counting on him anymore—it was everyone.

His blood burned in his veins, every cell in his body screaming in agony, yet for some reason, despite the physical pain, his spirit remained unaffected by the soul-draining spell. He could feel the power of his Blackwood bloodline, the ancient magic that ran through his family, and his bond with Lea, protecting him from Grimthorpe's ritual.

As Eld reached the stage, he pulled out the twitching ragdolls he'd prepared.

But before he could throw them, Grimthorpe's cackled loudly.

"Perfect! Perfect!"

The headmaster raised his arms, and suddenly, buckets appeared above the stage, tipping over and drenching Eld and Lea in blood. The crimson liquid began to glow, clinging to their skin like a living thing.

Grimthorpe doused himself as well, his laughter growing more maniacal by the second.

"What in the Brood Mother's Boundless Stomach is this?" Eld shouted, trying to wipe the blood from his eyes.

Grimthorpe's eyes glittered with triumph. "This, my boy, is the culmination of centuries of planning. The blood oath that binds your family, started by the first Blackwood, flows through you—the first son of a first son of a first son. But now, I will transfer that oath to myself!"

Horror dawned on Eld as he realized the full scope of Grimthorpe's plan. The headmaster intended to steal the very magic that defined the Blackwood lineage, to gain control over Lea's slumbering power.

The blood seemed to wrap itself around Eld as the spell took hold, necromantic energy binding Grimthorpe, Lea, and Eld together in an unholy trinity.

Eld felt their minds clash, a psychic battle more intense than any physical confrontation he had ever experienced. Grimthorpe's will pressed down on him like a mountain, suffocating him, the liches centuries of power and experience threatening to shatter Eld's mind like a discarded beaker.

Rallying his thoughts, Eld fought back with everything he had.

He thought of his simple and happy days with his pets, of exploring Necropolis with Talbot, and of Lea—Lea most of all. And as he thought of Lea, he felt her consciousness stirring beside his own. Together, they pushed against Grimthorpe's presence, struggling to maintain their individuality against the onslaught of the headmaster's iron will and countless centuries of magical experience.

Grimthorpe's voice echoed in Eld's mind, taunting him. "Your father sacrificed you, boy. He was disappointed in you, saw you as weak. He chose your brother over you without a second thought."

The words were meant to hurt, to distract, but Eld found them oddly ineffective. "Yeah, my dad's an asshole. Tell me something I don't know."

The thought of the false legacy he had been fighting against his whole life ignited a new fire in Eld's chest.

In the spectral miasma surrounding Grimthorpe, he felt the spirit of his pets. Grimthorpe's flaming eyes flickered as something temporarily distracted him. With renewed determination, Eld withdrew the twitching ragdolls from his cloak.

"Dolls?" Grimthorpe sneered, confused. "Your father was right. You are just a child playing at—"

Eld threw the dolls.

Grimthorpe didn't get to finish his sentence, as the dolls burst open in mid-air. Hundreds of tiny yet ravenous spiders poured out, swarming over the headmaster's body. Grimthorpe screamed as the arachnids burrowed into his body, seeking out the marrow in his bones.

Blue spirals emanated from his body, wrapping themselves around the zombified insects. Grimthorpe's empowered time magic was able to slow down the assault, but there were just too many bugs.

And with Grimthorpe distracted, Eld struck. He pushed his consciousness forward, feeling the vast strength of the harvested souls flowing into him.

"What…what *is* this…" Eld breathed.

As the magical strength flowed into him, the words dropped out of his mouth, almost of their own accord.

He was in control of the pact now. He hadn't just stolen Grimthorpe's work. Eld's own blood was practically boiling in his body, dancing with magic as he finally fully took control of his ancestor's blood pact with Lea.

The power was intoxicating, offering him strength beyond his wildest dreams. If he accepted it, he could become a lich himself, gaining the respect he had always been denied.

No, people wouldn't just respect him.

They'd *fear* him.

He could do whatever he wanted.

Eld wavered, torn between two options.

If he took this power now, he would become practically a god.

If anything bad happened, he could reanimate anyone. There would be no real difference between them being dead or undead, and he would be in control. He could give his pets the power they truly deserved, the strength to make sure nobody would ever hurt them again.

He could reshape the world as he saw fit.

But then his eyes fell on Lea.

This wasn't about power or respect. It was about doing what was right.

Mentally pushing himself felt like tearing his soul in half, but Eld ended the ritual. The stolen souls rushed back to their owners, leaving Eld feeling hollow and drained.

But he didn't stop there.

It wasn't enough just to end this threat. He had to make sure that nobody else—whether it was Grimthorpe, his father, or even Eld on his darkest day—could try and claim this power for themselves.

With the last of his strength, he reached out and shattered the ancient pact that bound Lea.

"You fool!" Grimthorpe screamed, his voice filled with panic and rage. "No! You don't know what you've done!"

Cracks appeared in Lea's human visage, lines of darkness spreading across her skin like a shattering vase. With a bizarre sound—deafening yet whisper soft at the same time, Lea's mortal shell exploded outward, releasing the power contained within.

Darkness flooded the room, so thick and absolute that it devoured the light and shadows along with it.

Lea's true form was vaguely woman-shaped, but so dark that she just looked like a hole in reality. Tentacles flared out where her hair had been, writhing and twisting in patterns that threatened to drive Eld mad if he stared for too long.

The air grew heavy, pressing down on everyone in the room with an almost physical weight.

Eld felt like he was underwater, every movement requiring immense effort.

The very fabric of reality seemed to warp around Lea, straight lines becoming curves, and solid objects rippling like water.

The ground beneath her feet seemed to fizzle in and out of existence.

An angry rumble filled the air.

It reminded Eld vaguely of the bronze doors surrounding the off-limits Splintered Dimension, only at a far greater level. The sound was broadcast directly into Eld's body—it wasn't so much of an actual noise as a vibration that resonated in Eld's bones.

Even though it was Lea's voice, the sound was so deep and terrible that it threatened to shatter Eld's mind completely.

"I MADE THAT PACT FOR A REASON," the voice boomed, each word accompanied by a ripple of distortion that spread through the room. "THE UNDEAD, LIKE GRIMTHORPE, WERE OVERSTEPPING THEIR

BOUNDS, CONTROLLING THE WEAK. I SOUGHT TO
MAINTAIN BALANCE."

Grimthorpe, his face contorted with fear and desperation,
raised his arms. He'd finally managed to shake off Eld's sacks of
insects.

"I won't lose! I can't!" he screamed, his voice thin and reedy
compared to Lea's cosmic utterance. "Not when I'm so close!"

A beam of sickly green energy erupted from Grimthorpe's
hands, a disintegration ray of such power that it consumed his
entire arm and shoulder in the process, turning it into chunk of
desiccated bone. The spell struck Lea dead-on, but the self-
sacrificial spell might as well have been a gentle breeze for all the
effect it had.

Lea's response was swift and terrible.

A wave of darkness radiated out from her, washing over
Grimthorpe like a tsunami of void. Where it touched him, the
headmaster's body simply ceased to be. He shattered into
countless fragments, each piece smaller than a grain of sand,
scattering across the hall like a dust storm.

Grimthorpe's destruction signaled the battle's abrupt end.

Without their master's necromantic will, the remaining
husks fell to the floor. The zombies sent by Eld's father
promptly fled. Some were captured, but many others escaped to
carry news of the night's events.

In the sudden quiet, Eld turned his attention to his pets.

Their absorbed spirits had returned, but they weren't in
great shape. After all, they'd just fought in a ferocious battle. He
knelt beside them, channeling what little energy he had left into
healing their wounds.

One by one, they stirred, returning to his side on the stage.

Shuck let out a happy bark as Bart danced on his head.
Franky sent celebratory sparks of lightning into the sky.
Spinderella-Hemlock looked set to make a great victory speech,

only for her Spinderella side to conveniently drown it out in a storm of happy chittering.

A cheer went up from the crowd, students and faculty alike applauding Eld and Lea's victory.

"Kiss! Kiss!"

"Let the Necropromicon Queen and King kiss!"

"Yes! Kiss! Kiss!"

The crowd's chanting grew louder and louder.

All Eld could do was stare in bemusement.

The whole thing seemed totally out of place for the battle that had occurred, not to mention the nearly unfathomable being that Lea had become.

But with all that being said…

Eld wanted that kiss.

He stepped forward.

Lea shimmered and twisted, the darkness condensing slightly into a more human-like shape. Flashes of red appeared in the void where her face should be, giving the impression of a blush.

She moved towards Eld, the air around her rippling like heat waves.

"Eld…" she said.

Her voice had grown much softer. Though it still reverberated in Eld's body, she sounded just like who she was before.

Eld's heart raced.

This would be he and Lea's first kiss.

Despite her new appearance, he knew that this was still the girl he had fallen for. But as Lea drew near, Eld felt an invisible force pushing against him.

He felt a faint fearful tingle in the back of his mind, warning him to stay away.

But he ignored it.

Yet the closer she got, the stronger the repulsion became.

It was like there was some kind of invisible barrier between them. The closer Eld got, the farther he seemed to get. His mind felt strange and twisted, and his instincts told him that he was on the other side of the room, even though Lea was right in front of him.

Then, for a brief hopeful moment, it seemed like he'd pushed through.

Suddenly, he was flying backward, launched off the stage as if fired from a cannon.

He crashed into a table, sending cups and plates flying. Franky chittered with laughter from his perch on a nearby chair.

"Everlasting Night," Eld muttered, his whole body aching from the impact. He paused for a moment. The curse felt strange coming from his mouth, now that it'd taken on such a different meaning.

He shook his head, resolving to think about it later. "I think I just felt my unlife flash before my eyes."

Lea resonated in his mind again, softer this time but still carrying an undercurrent of power that made his teeth vibrate. "I'm so sorry, Eld. I…I don't know what happened…"

Eld got back to his feet, groaning, his entire body aching. It felt like he hadn't just gotten hurled into a table—it felt like he'd gotten hurled around the world and back again.

It seemed utterly impossible.

But considering Lea's power, it was probably what had happened.

"I guess we'll have to figure this out somehow," Eld said.

Lea's face was a cosmic black void, but as he stared at her, Eld could have sworn he saw the brief hint of a hopeful smile. "Are you…are you sure?" she asked.

Eld nodded. "Of course."

"Okay then…" she said. "With you…I think we will figure it out somehow."

Eld couldn't help but smile. After all, what was life—or unlife—without a few challenges?

The night had not gone as anyone had expected, but they had survived.

They had won. And now, they faced a future full of uncertainties, but also possibilities.

As he dusted himself off, he realized that this was just the beginning of a whole new adventure. And despite the cosmic horrors, despite the near-death experiences, despite the fact that he couldn't even kiss the girl he liked without being thrown across a room, he wouldn't have it any other way.

"Well," he said, addressing his gathered pets and the stunned crowd, "I guess this is going to take some getting used to. Anyone up for round two of the Necropromicon?"

Epilogue

It's Not Over 'Til It's Over

Cloudehill Blackwood, self-proclaimed master manipulator and lich extraordinaire, lounged on his obsidian throne inside his room in the Blackwood estate, idly twirling a femur between his bony fingers.

The scrying glass before him flickered with the nervous faces of his gravedigger minions. If he could smirk, he would have. Unfortunately, his father's facial modification spell only worked for frowning.

Nonetheless, Cloudehill enjoyed the way they squirmed under his gaze. This, he thought, was what true power looked like.

"Listen up, you slack-jawed sacks of rotted meat," Cloudehill growled. "I need more corpses. The age of the badass lich is upon us, and I am that badass lich! I won't be caught with my phylactery out in the open!"

The lead gravedigger, a sallow-faced man with dirt perpetually caked across his body, cleared his throat. "Begging your pardon, Lord Cloudehill, but we've run into some logistical issues."

Cloudehill's jewels in his eye sockets flickered. "Logistics? Ha! I don't know the meaning of the word!"

The gravediggers chuckled nervously—the precise chuckle of an underling with an unfunny boss.

For a while, the two parties stared at each other in silence.

Eventually, Cloudehill leaned closer to the scrying glass. "No really, what in the name of the thirteen hells is that? Sounds like an excuse for incompetence to me."

"W-well, you see, sir," the gravedigger stammered, "it's about resource management and—"

"Resource management?" Cloudehill interrupted. "The only resource you need to manage is your shovel or-or…you'll be managing my bony fist up your poop chute! Got it! Now, what's the real problem?"

The gravedigger took a deep breath. "We've exhumed—"

"Exhumed?"

"We've *dug up* all the graves in the area, sir. We've shipped every part we could find. There's simply nothing left to dig up."

For a moment, Cloudehill sat in silence.

Then, he burst into laughter, a sound like dry leaves scraping against tombstones. "Nothing left? Impossible! There are always more graves. People are dying all the time!"

"But sir, we can't just dig up fresh graves. There are laws, and the families might notice—"

"Laws?" Cloudehill scoffed. "Maggotmuncher, I *am* the law—or I will be soon, anyways! And as for families, well…" His hand began to glow with silver-blue light, frost forming on his fingertips. "If they wanna complain, I'll give them something to really cry about. One touch of my freezing spell, and they'll be able to mark their loved ones graves forever as ice sculptures!"

The gravediggers exchanged terrified glances.

The leader cleared his throat again. "Lord Cloudehill, perhaps we could consider alternative sources? The only thing left is ancient burial grounds—"

"Ancient burial grounds?" Cloudehill's jewel eyes lit up with an unholy glow. "Now you're thinking with that sponge you call for a brain! Yes, that's perfect. Go find me some cursed tombs, some forbidden necropolises. That's where the real quality corpses are! They don't make them like that anymore."

The gravedigger blinked rapidly, clearly caught off guard by Cloudehill's enthusiasm. "Sir, those places are incredibly dangerous. The curses alone could wipe out our entire workforce."

Cloudehill waved a bony hand dismissively. "Details, details. Just send in the expendable workers first. Use them as curse detectors or something."

"Expendable workers?" the gravedigger repeated. "Sir, we don't have—"

"Oh, for the love of all that's unholy." Cloudehill groaned. "Do I have to think of everything? Fine, here's what you do. Go to the nearest village, tell them you're recruiting for a, uh, *treasure hunting expedition* or some ghoul. Offer them riches beyond their wildest dreams. Then, when they show up, surprise! They're the new curse detectors."

The gravedigger stared at him.

Cloudehill grinned, clearly pleased with himself. "See? Problem solved. This is why I'm in charge, and you're just the guys who play in the dirt."

"Sir that's highly unethical and—"

"Unethical?" Cloudehill's voice dropped. "Maggotmuncher, let me remind you who you're talking to. I'm a lich and a Blackwood. I've committed atrocities that would make your ancestors roll in their graves. Speaking of which, have you dug *them* up yet?"

"N-no, sir," the gravedigger stammered.

"Well, there you go! Start with those. Family graves are always a good source of quality bones. Nice and sturdy, kept strong by generations of guilt and obligation."

The gravediggers looked at each other, clearly at a loss.

Finally, the leader spoke up again. "Sir, even if we do all that, it's not sustainable. You can't just get more ancestors…that's not how they work. We need a long-term solution for corpse acquisition."

Cloudehill leaned back in his throne, stroking his bony chin thoughtfully. "Hmm, long-term solutions. Yes, very important. Very…logistical. Alright, how about this, we start a war."

"A war, sir?"

"Did I stutter? Yes, a war! It's perfect. Lots of death, lots of corpses, and best of all, no one questions why you're digging up bodies in a war zone. It's expected!"

The lead gravedigger took a deep breath. "Lord Cloudehill, starting a war is a complex process. It requires careful planning, political maneuvering, resources—"

"Bah!" Cloudehill waved his hand again. "You're overthinking it, I'll do it myself. Watch and learn."

He turned to another scrying glass and waved his hand, shifting the frequency to contact someone else. Moments later, the image of a neighboring noble house's ruler—a rather confused zombie—appeared.

"Hey, you! Your mother was a gremlin, and your father smelt of bat droppings! Consider this a declaration of war!"

He turned back to the gravediggers. "There. Look how he did it. War declared. Problem solved."

The gravediggers stared at him in stunned silence.

Finally, the leader spoke up. "Sir, I don't think that's how international relations work—"

"Of course it is," Cloudehill insisted. "I've just insulted his parentage. No self-respecting ruler could let that slide. Trust me, the armies will be mobilizing as we speak."

As if on cue, the scrying glass lit up again.

The confused zombie's face reappeared, looking even more confused than normal. "Lord Cloudehill? Is everything alright? Do you need assistance?"

Cloudehill's jaw dropped, quite literally—he had to reattach it. "What? No! I just insulted you! Grievously! Don't you want to go to war over it?"

The ruler blinked. "Didn't you just adapt a Monty Python quote? I'm rather fond of that movie, actually, and one of my servants happens to haunt an Old One television. Perhaps we could arrange a viewing party instead of a war?"

Cloudehill slammed his fist on the arm of his throne. Unfortunately, the sheer force of the blow caused his pinky finger to clatter to the floor. "No! No viewing parties! War! I demand war!"

"I'm sorry, but I must decline," the ruler said politely. "We're rather busy with a public works project at the moment. Perhaps another time? Do take care, Lord Cloudehill. You seem a bit stressed."

The scrying glass went dark.

Cloudehill turned back to the gravediggers, who were suppressing their laughter like their lives depended on it—which it did.

Eventually, the lead gravedigger cleared his throat. "So, about our corpse shortage."

"Enough!" Cloudehill roared. "I don't want to hear any more about your petty problems. No more talking, no more big words, no more ethics! You have your orders. Get me more corpses, or I'll add yours to the collection. Is that clear?"

"Y-yes, Lord Cloudehill," the gravediggers stammered in unison.

"Good. Now get out of my sight before I decide to practice my freezing techniques on you."

"If the only tool you have is a hammer, it is tempting to treat everything as if it were a nail," Cloudehill mused to himself. "And my Blizzard Blast is the finest hammer in all the realms."

His self-congratulatory reverie was interrupted by a commotion outside his chambers.

The doors burst open, and a group of battered zombies stumbled in, pieces of them falling off as they moved.

"Master Cloudehill," one moaned, its jaw hanging by a single tendon. "We were defeated. It was disastrous."

Cloudehill leaped to his feet, frost spreading across the floor where he stood. "Defeated? By whom? Was it that ruler I insulted? I knew he was secretly plotting against me! Those stupid gravediggers were wrong! This war is on!"

"The woman," another zombie gurgled, ichor dripping from its lips. "Stronger than we thought. And young Master Eld…he defeated Graves. And Grimthorpe too!"

Rage burned in Cloudehill's jeweled eyes.

He lunged forward, snarling, plunging his hand into the zombie's skull. He yanked out its brain, eyes, and ears, the undead creature collapsing into a heap of useless flesh.

"That's what you get for bringing me bad news."

The other zombies hastily left the room, setting all new records for shambling speed.

Cloudehill stomped over to an arcane device in the corner of the room, shoving the stolen organs into various receptacles. Like with most machines, Cloudehill didn't understand how it actually worked, but at least he knew what it did.

Moments later, the memory machine whirred to life, projecting images of the battle onto the wall.

As he watched the events unfold, Cloudehill's jaw literally dropped, bouncing to the floor. He hastily picked it back up again, jamming it back on so he could curse in disbelief.

The sheer power radiating from Lea was beyond anything he had ever seen.

As for Eld…

Cloudehill had to admit that his brother's performance was impressive, at least for him. Those ridiculous pets of his were more formidable than Cloudehill had ever given them credit for.

"Well, well, brother," Cloudehill muttered, absently conjuring a ball of frost in his palm. "It seems you're not quite the failure father always said you were. I might have to try and kill you the next time we fight."

Still, he couldn't help but feel a twinge of satisfaction.

Eld might have won this battle, but Cloudehill was still the heir.

He was the one Father had trusted with the family's darkest secrets, and Eld had already been struck from the Familial Tome.

Of course, *as* heir, Cloudehill had to inform his father of what had happened.

With that, Cloudehill made his way down to the lowest level of the Blackwood Family Manor, to a chamber Eld had never even known existed. As he approached the massive iron doors, he could feel the thrum of eldritch energy pulsing from within.

He pushed the doors open, revealing his father hunched over an enormous summoning circle. The design covered the entire floor, glowing runes pulsing with dark power.

"Father," Cloudehill began, but Eldritch Sr. cut him off with a wave of his skeletal hand.

"I know, Cloudehill. Graves's enchantments have already informed me of the debacle at Bathurst." The elder lich didn't even look up from his work. "Preparations are already underway."

Cloudehill's gaze swept across the room, taking in the sheer scale of the summoning circle. This was no mere sacrifice ritual—this was something far grander and more terrifying.

"Father, what exactly are you summoning? Is it something that can help me with my corpse shortage? Because let me tell you, these gravediggers are useless. I tried to start a war to get more bodies, and—"

"Silence," Eldritch Sr. snapped. "Your petty concerns are meaningless in the face of what's to come."

A voice like the grinding of tectonic plates rumbled through the chamber, shaking dust from the ceiling.

"Eldritch Sr., my old friend," the voice boomed. "What is your command?"

Cloudehill felt a chill run down his spine.

Whatever his father had called forth, it was ancient and unimaginably powerful. "Um, hello there," Cloudehill called out. "I don't suppose you know any good gravediggers, do you?"

Eldritch Sr. shot him a withering glare. "Shut up. Immediately."

Cloudehill shut up. He did so immediately. It was a good thing the undead didn't need to breathe.

Turning back to the summoning circle, Eldritch Sr. spoke. "There is an item I've left in Bathurst Academy. It's hidden deep beneath the school, in the Bones of the Founders. Retrieve it for me."

"Is that all?" the voice inquired.

"No," Eldritch Sr. replied. "Before returning, use it to kill my son."

Cloudehill felt a surge of triumph.

Finally, Eld would be out of the way for good. But as he caught his father's eye, he saw no warmth there, no pride in his remaining son. Only cold, calculating purpose.

"Leave us, Cloudehill," Eldritch Sr. commanded.

"Well, that sucked" Cloudehill muttered to himself as he climbed the stairs back to his chambers, "But at least I won't have to deal with those incompetent gravediggers anymore. Maybe being a disposable pawn in a cosmic game of chess isn't so bad after all."